Man
of
Honour

JANE
ASHFORD

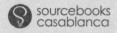
sourcebooks
casablanca

Published by Sourcebooks Casablanca, an imprint of Sourcebooks,
Inc.
P.O. Box 4410, Naperville, Illinois 60567-4410
(630) 961-3900
Fax: (630) 961-2168
www.sourcebooks.com

Originally published in 1981 by Warner Books, Inc., New York

Printed and bound in Canada
WC 10 9 8 7 6 5 4 3 2 1

One

"WHAT DO YOU MEAN YOU HAVE NOTHING AVAILABLE?" demanded Mr. Eliot Crenshaw. The cold anger in his eyes made the small innkeeper quail.

"I swear it's true, sir. My missus has took the gig, being as my youngest daughter is about to be brought to bed in Hemsley, the next village but one, you know. She won't be home for a sennight. There's the old cob left in the stables, but he won't draw a carriage, and with this snow now…" He looked out the window of the taproom at the driving blizzard. "Well I can't see as how any animal could." He paused apologetically, conscious of the gentleman's impatience.

"Damn the snow," said Mr. Crenshaw, but he too looked out the window. It was obvious that the weather was worsening rapidly, and having already endured one accident on the road, he had no wish to risk another. But his situation was awkward. "Your wife is away, you say? Who else is here?"

Mr. Jenkins showed signs of wringing his hands. "There's just me tonight, sir, begging your pardon. Betty, the girl as comes from the village to help out, went home early on account of the storm. And my stable boy broke his fool leg last week, climbing trees he was, the witless chawbacon, at his age! I don't see how I'll serve a proper supper. And the lady!" This last remark ended with something like a groan, and the man shook his head. "This ain't a great establishment, you see, sir, off the main road like we are and keeping no post horses. We ain't used to housing quality, and that's the truth. I don't know what I'm to do."

Mr. Crenshaw eyed the distraught host with some contempt. His mood had been decidedly soured by recent events. In the course of a relatively short daylight drive, his fine traveling carriage had been severely damaged by a reckless youngster in a ridiculous high-perch phaeton. His horses had been brought up lame and their high-spirited tempers roused, and though he knew he was fortunate to have escaped without serious injury, the problems which now faced him as a result of the accident did not make him thankful.

He had been escorting a young visitor of his mother's to the home of her aunts. Only his parent's most earnest entreaties had persuaded him to do so, and he was now cursing himself roundly for giving in, for Miss Lindley's maid had been badly hurt in the accident, forcing them to leave her at a cottage on the scene and walk alone to this inn. Here he found there were no females to chaperone the girl; the blizzard was steadily increasing in intensity, and there was no conveyance of any kind available, even had it been possible to go on. Eliot Crenshaw was not accustomed to finding himself at a stand, but now he passed a hand wearily across his forehead, sat down at a taproom table, and stared fiercely at the swirling snow outside. He clenched a fist on the table top. "Bring me a pint," he said resignedly.

In the little inn's one private parlor, the Right Honorable Miss Laura Lindley, oldest daughter of the late Earl of Stoke-Mannering, sat miserably holding her hands out to the crackling fire. She was chilled to the bone, her bonnet was wrecked, her cloak torn and muddy, and her green cambric traveling dress was as disheveled as her black curls. There was a nasty scratch on her left cheek and a bruise above her eye. But these minor discomforts worried her less than the rising storm and the smashed chaise they had left leaning drunkenly by the roadside. What was she to do? Her aunts had expected her a full three hours ago, and these two elderly ladies, by whom she had been brought up, were notoriously high sticklers. The smallest deviation from the rules of propriety was enough to overset them completely. What then could they feel when they knew that their cherished niece was stranded alone at a country inn with a man she scarcely knew?

Laura caught her breath on a sob. She had only just persuaded aunts to allow her to spend a season in London. Though her twentieth birthday was past, she had never been to the metropolis, and it had required all of her argumentative skills and the help of some of her aunts' old friends, Mrs. Crenshaw among them, to get the necessary permission. She was to have gone to town next month, but now… Laura sighed tremulously. Now, it appeared that she would never have a London season. She had waited two years after her friends' debuts and argued her case with the utmost care, only to see it all come to naught because of this stupid accident. She grimaced. That was always the way of it—the things one wanted most were snatched away just when they seemed certain at last. She took several deep breaths, telling herself sternly to stop this maundering. Perhaps Mr. Crenshaw would find some way out of this dilemma. He seemed a most capable man.

But in the taproom, at that moment finishing his pint of ale, Mr. Crenshaw did not feel particularly capable. He had badly wrenched his shoulder falling from the carriage; his exquisitely cut coat, from the hands of Weston himself, was torn in several places and indisputably ruined, as was much of the rest of his extremely fashionable attire. In fact any member of the *ton* would have been appalled to see this absolute nonesuch in his present state. This was not the top-of-the-trees Corinthian they knew, and though he would not have admitted it, the elegant Mr. Crenshaw was just now at his wit's end.

With a sigh he rose and walked stiffly to a small mirror which hung over the bar. He made some effort to straighten his twisted cravat and brush back his hair. The face in the mirror was rather too austere to be called handsome. Mr. Crenshaw's high cheekbones and aquiline nose gave his dark face a hawk-like look, and this was intensified by black hair and piercing gray eyes. The overall effect was of strength but little warmth; very few men would wish to cross this tall, slender gentleman, and fewer still would succeed in beating him. Pulling at his now disreputable coat and brushing the drying mud from his once immaculate pantaloons and tall Hessian boots, Mr. Crenshaw turned from the mirror with a grimace and walked across the corridor to the private parlor.

Miss Lindley rose at his entrance. "Did you find…?" she began, but the realities of the situation made it seem foolish to ask if he had gotten another carriage, and she fell silent.

Mr. Crenshaw bowed his head courteously. "Please sit down, Miss Lindley. I fear I have bad news." And he explained what the innkeeper had told him.

Laura put a hand to the side of her neck. "Oh dear, how unfortunate that his wife should be away just at this time." She tried to speak lightly, but a sinking feeling grew in her stomach. Her aunts would never forgive her, even though this predicament was certainly not of her own making.

"An understatement," replied Mr. Crenshaw drily, "because I fear we must spend the night at this inn. It will be impossible to go on in the snow, whatever vehicle we may be able to discover." A particularly loud gust of wind howled outside as if to emphasize his point. "I would willingly ride the cob back to the village and try to persuade some woman to return and stay with you," he went on. "But I do not think any would consent to come, and frankly I am not certain I could find the village in this infernal storm."

Laura nodded disconsolately. "Of course you must not go out in such weather." She clenched her hands together and fought back tears once more.

Mr. Crenshaw looked at her. "I say again how sorry I am, Miss Lindley."

"Oh, it is not your fault. I know that. You saved us all from being killed! If only Ruth had not been hurt or if I had stayed with her at the cottage. But when that young man was taken in there as well and the woman was so eager that I should *not* stay… and I was certain we would find another carriage. I did not realize that the snow…" Her disjointed speech trailed off as she watched the storm uneasily.

"Nor did I," replied Mr. Crenshaw. "Weather like this should not come at this time of year. However, it remains that it has. We must make the best of it."

"Yes. I suppose there is no way to send a message to my aunts? No, of course there is not."

He shook his head. "I fear not. But surely they will realize that you have been delayed by the weather. I wager they will be glad you are not traveling today."

Laura smiled weakly. "I see you are not acquainted with my aunts," she said. She looked down at her clasped hands and swallowed nervously. She had suddenly become conscious that she was completely alone with a man and a stranger, a thing her aunts had never permitted in the whole course of her life.

Mr. Crenshaw frowned. "I am not. They are very strict with you, I take it."

She nodded. "They are… older, you see, and…" she faltered.

"I am beginning to," he responded grimly. "What an infernal coil! Why did I allow Mother to bully me into escorting you?"

Laura's eyes widened. "I am sorry," she said miserably. She had a somewhat clearer idea of Mrs. Crenshaw's motives than her son had. That lady had told her that the carriage ride would be a perfect opportunity for Laura to try out her social skills. No one knew better than Mrs. Crenshaw the restrictions her aunts had put on Laura, and no one felt for her more keenly. She had added jokingly that Laura must do her best to captivate her son, for she had been trying to get him safely married these past five years. The girl stole a glance at the tall figure standing beside the sofa. There could be little question of that, she thought to herself. Mr. Crenshaw appeared to take no interest in her whatsoever; indeed she found him very stiff and cold.

But the thoughts running through her companion's mind would have surprised her. He was observing that the Lindley girl was very well to pass, even in her current state of disarray. In other circumstances, at Almack's for example, he might have asked her to dance without any fear that she would disgrace him. A tall, willowy girl, Laura Lindley was a striking brunette, with a thick mass of black curls and eyes so dark as to be almost black as well. Her skin was ivory pale, particularly now after this strenuous adventure. The customary deep rose of her cheeks and lips, an enchanting color Mr. Crenshaw had noted earlier, had drained away and she looked very tired and disheartened.

Resolutely Mr. Crenshaw redirected his thoughts. This was an utterly improper time to be thinking of the girl's looks. He and the lady were in a damnable situation. The lines around his mouth deepened as he reconsidered the problem.

Watching him, Laura shivered a little. He looked so grim and angry.

"Are you cold?" he asked quickly. "Draw nearer to the fire. I have not even asked if you would care for something. Some tea, perhaps?"

Laura allowed that some tea would be most welcome, and Mr. Crenshaw went out to find the landlord.

Two hours later they sat down to dinner in somewhat better frame. Though they had not changed their attire—Laura's luggage remained with the wrecked chaise and Mr. Crenshaw had none—Laura had tidied her hair and dress and washed, as had her companion. The scratch on her face was shown to be minor when the dirt and dried blood were sponged away, and though the bruise had turned a sullen purple, it too was clearly not serious. Both felt much better as they started on the oddly assorted dishes the innkeeper had assembled. There was bread and butter and cheese, a roast chicken, some boiled potatoes, and a large pot of jam. Mr. Crenshaw eyed the repast ruefully and made Laura laugh as he, with a cocked eyebrow, helped her to chicken.

As they ate, he began to talk lightly of London. He had heard from his mother that Laura would be making her come-out, and he told her of the places she would see and the things she might do.

"There is Almack's, of course," he said. "I have no doubt that you will spend many evenings dancing there. And there will be routs, Venetian breakfasts, musical evenings, and the like. You can have no idea how busy your life will become."

At this catalog of delights, Laura could not keep a tremor from her voice when she agreed, and her expression was so woebegone that her companion said, "What is wrong? Have I said something?"

She shook her head. "No, no, it is just that… well I shall not go to London now, I daresay, and I was feeling sorry for myself." She looked wistfully down at her plate.

He was frowning. "What do you mean you will not go?"

"Oh my aunts will never let me leave after this, this… that is…" She stammered to a halt, not wishing to burden him with the certain consequences of their misadventure. There was nothing he could do, after all, and the incident was no more his fault than hers.

"Nonsense," he replied. "Why should they not? You have simply an unfortunate accident on the road."

"Yes I know, but you do not reason as my aunts do, of course. They worry so, and they do not understand modern manners. At least that is what they say. When the curate wished to visit my sister… to pay attentions, you know, they forbade him to enter the house ever again." She smiled slightly at the memory. "It was very awkward, because they are the heads of the relief committee, and the curate was in charge of that. The vicar was nearly driven distracted." Raising her eyes; Laura saw that Mr. Crenshaw had returned her smile, and hers broadened, showing two dimples.

"Was your sister heartbroken?"

"Clarissa?" Laura gave an involuntary gurgle of laughter. "Oh she did not care. She wishes to marry a duke."

He was taken aback. "A duke? Which duke?"

Laura looked mischievous. "It doesn't matter; she is determined to make a grand marriage." Her smile faded. "That will be impossible now, of course. I mean, she will never be married after this. My aunts will keep us so close, I suppose we shall not be allowed even to go to the country assemblies." Her momentary high spirits dissolved in melancholy reflection.

Mr. Crenshaw frowned once more. "You must be mistaken. They cannot be so gothic."

Laura remained unconvinced, but she did not argue further, not wishing to tease him with her problems. Silently the two finished their repast.

After a time Laura rose. "I shall go to bed, I think. I am tired out."

Mr. Crenshaw also stood. "Of course. The landlord has left your candle." He fetched it and lit it at the fire. "There is no one to take you up. Yours is the room at the head of the stairs."

"Thank you." She took the candle and started out of the room. As she was about to enter the hall, he spoke again.

"I shall spend the night in the innkeeper's chamber. It is the best I can do."

Laura's mouth jerked. "Haven't you a sword?"

"I beg your pardon?"

"Like Tristan."

Mr. Crenshaw looked blank. The girl must be on the edge of exhaustion, he thought to himself. He fervently hoped he would not be called upon to deal with an attack of the vapors.

Laura shrugged. "Never mind. I didn't mean anything. My aunts call levity my besetting sin."

The man looked at her.

"Good night," she said.

"Good night," said Eliot, much relieved.

Lying in bed some minutes later, enveloped in one of the landlady's voluminous nightgowns, Laura listened to the howling wind outside and the scratching of the snow on the windowpanes. She could not help shedding a few tears now that she was alone again. It all seemed so unfair, and she felt so helpless. Various schemes for resuming their journey occurred to her and were rejected. They were trapped for as long as the blizzard raged. If only Mr. Crenshaw were not so angry with her. That, on top of everything else, depressed her immeasurably. She was still thinking of him when the fatigue of the day caught up with her, and she slept.

❧

The next day dawned clear and cold. Almost two feet of snow lay on the ground. Looking at it from her window when she woke, Laura thought that in any other circumstances she would have found it beautiful. Such a heavy fall was indeed rare in this part of the country. But today she wished the snow gone to Scotland, for the roads looked quite impassable. No one was out.

When she had put on her rumpled green cambric once again and descended the stairs, she found Mr. Crenshaw wrapping himself in the innkeeper's greatcoat.

"Good morning," he said. "I am going to take the cob into the village and see about hiring a vehicle. My driving coat is ruined, but Mr. Jenkins has kindly lent me his."

The innkeeper, hovering in the background, made an inarticulate noise. The seams of his dun coat were strained to the point of splitting, as Mr. Crenshaw was much the larger man.

"Do you think we shall be able to travel?" asked the girl. "The snow looks so deep."

"We shall see," was the only reply.

Mr. Crenshaw started out, the old horse clearly reluctant to make his way through the snow. Laura watched anxiously through the parlor window as he moved slowly along the nearly invisible road. Then a slight noise behind her made her turn to the landlord in the doorway.

"You'll be wanting some breakfast, miss," he said. "I haven't got no chocolate nor any fancy vittles. I ain't much accustomed to cooking, I have to say. The missus sees to that, would she was here." He looked acutely uncomfortable.

Laura smiled a little. "Some tea will do nicely… and some bread and butter, perhaps. I do not take a large meal in the morning. How far is it to the village?"

Heartened by her friendly tone, the little man came into the room. "It's all of three miles, miss. I only hope that old horse of mine makes it. This weather is a marvel, ain't it? Two feet of snow in March. Why, it's rare we get so much all winter."

Mr. Crenshaw did not return for hours. The morning passed, and midday. Laura ate a light luncheon of cold chicken, sat by the window awhile longer, paced about the room, and finally asked the landlord for something to read. An extensive search unearthed only an ancient Bible and three dog-eared back numbers of *The Spectator*, all of which Laura had already read. With a sigh she returned to the parlor and resigned herself to boredom, but a few moments later Mr. Jenkins triumphantly produced a greasy pack of cards. She set out a game of Patience, thinking it was better than nothing, and managed to become a little interested, though she continued to listen for the sound of a horse outside.

Late in the afternoon, after three games and several cups of tea, the sound came at last. Laura ran to the window eagerly. Mr. Crenshaw was indeed returning, but he rode slowly, head bent, and alone. The only visible change from the morning was the case he carried behind him. He looked wet, cold, and annoyed.

He had found no vehicle for hire in the village. None of the villagers had been willing to brave the snow for any sum of money, and no woman would consent to ride behind him to the inn. His tedious, uncomfortable ride had not improved their circumstances, except that he had been able to pick up Laura's dressing case from the chaise and have the vehicle hauled into a barn out of the weather. When Laura thanked him for this thoughtful action, his expression remained set. His disgust and ill temper were obvious, and though he could not and did not blame Laura, neither was he feeling in charity with her. However fair he endeavored to be, he could not stifle the thought that if it weren't for her, he would not have been placed in such an awkward position.

❧

In the end they spent three days at the inn. The roads remained impassable until warmer weather returned and the unseasonal snow began to melt. At that point Mr. Crenshaw was able to find a farmer willing to hire out his dilapidated gig, and they resumed their journey through mud and streaming rivulets of slush.

Both were silent as they drove. The time at the inn had not been particularly pleasant. Though he was always polite, Mr. Crenshaw had carefully avoided Laura, making two unnecessary trips into the village and leaving her alone much of the rest of the time. The girl had retreated into brooding on her own concerns, and she felt a vast relief when they were on the road again at last.

Only about ten miles of their journey remained, and they covered it quickly, even in the gig. They drew up before Eversly, Laura's home, at midday. Almost before the vehicle had stopped, the front door was flung open and several women hurried out. With a sinking heart Laura saw her two aunts, her younger sister, and their old nurse.

A frantic babble arose around her as she climbed down from the gig. Her Aunt Eleanor gripped her hand hysterically. "Oh my dear, we feared you were killed or set upon by highwaymen or kidnapped! We have been beside ourselves with worry. And this storm, the way it seemed to strike out of nowhere. We couldn't think what to do. We sent two of the footmen out to search for you, but they were forced back by the snow. Are you all right, are you hurt, what happened?"

But Laura could not reply, for on her other side; her Aunt Celia was saying, "Thank God you are home safe. What can Anne Crenshaw have been thinking of, sending you out in this weather? You ought to have waited. When we received your note saying that you were starting, the snow had just begun. Where did you put up?"

Laura's sister, a confident young maiden of eighteen, added her own bit in calmer accents. "You've hurt yourself." Clarissa reached to touch the scratch on Laura's cheek. "Whatever have you been doing, Laura? Have you had a great adventure without me? I shall never forgive you."

Suddenly complete silence fell. Looking up, Laura saw that Mr. Crenshaw had climbed down from the gig and walked around to them. Her aunts were staring at him, openmouthed, and Clarissa was grinning wickedly. Laura flushed. "This is Mr. Eliot Crenshaw," she said, "Mrs. Crenshaw's son. He was kind enough to escort me home." She swallowed nervously.

"How do you do," said Mr. Crenshaw.

"Laura," said her Aunt Celia in an ominous tone, "where is your maid?" She ignored the man completely.

"Ruth was hurt in the accident," replied Laura. "We must send someone to her immediately. I hope..."

"Accident!" shrieked Aunt Eleanor. She leaned heavily on Clarissa. "Oh where are my drops? I feel a spasm coming on."

Mr. Crenshaw's expression was stiffly polite. "We had some trouble on the road. Perhaps we should go into the house where we can sit down, and I shall tell you about it."

Aunt Celia eyed him with suspicious hostility. "Indeed we should," she said, and turning, she led them all up the steps and through the front door.

When they reached the drawing room, Laura was ordered upstairs with her sister. She protested, but Mr. Crenshaw agreed with her aunts, and she gave in. She had no wish to endure the inevitable scene in any case.

Clarissa took Laura's arm as they went up to their bedchamber. "What has been happening?" she asked in thrilled accents. "You must tell me everything."

Laura gave her a quick account of the events of the previous days, and Clarissa sighed ecstatically. "Why am I never so lucky? Nothing exciting ever happens to me. How I envy you, Laura."

The older girl looked at her in amazement. "How can you say so? This is disastrous. Our aunts will never let us out of the house again."

A hint of something like shrewdness glinted in Clarissa's eyes. "Perhaps," she replied. "One never knows."

Laura stared at her "I do not understand you, Clarissa. You know how they feel about scandal of any kind. They will never forgive me."

Clarissa shrugged and turned away toward the window. "All the same, it is very romantic. A storm, a lonely inn. Is Mr. Crenshaw very charming?"

Laura shook her head. "No, he is not," she answered shortly. "He can be polite enough, but I doubt that he likes me. He showed no signs of it. In fact he seemed angry with me the whole time."

"Oh dear."

"What is the matter with you, Clarissa?"

The younger girl's eyes brimmed with mischief for a moment, then she shook her head. "You are too nice, Laura. You have listened too well to our aunts."

Laura put her hands on her hips and frowned.

"What are you up to? Tell me this instant. What have you done?"

Clarissa was the picture of injured innocence. "I? *I* have not been traveling about the countryside with a man."

Her sister was about to give her a sharp setdown when a maid knocked and entered with a summons to the drawing room. Laura's face fell. "Yes, I will be there directly," she said. She looked to Clarissa for sympathy. "It is time for my scold." But Clarissa only grinned mysteriously and raised her eyebrows, and Laura strode out of the room in annoyance.

Once in the corridor, she paused a moment to think and marshal her arguments. Laura had been dealing with her aunts' vagaries for most of her life, and she had become expert at compromise. It seemed to her highly unlikely that she would still be permitted to go to London, but she knew that calm rationality was vital in the coming encounter. The events of the past few days had shaken her customary even temperament, but now she made an effort to regain her composure and capacity for tact.

When Laura entered the drawing room, she was surprised to find only Mr. Crenshaw. "Where are my aunts?" she asked.

"They have left us to discuss a matter of some importance," he answered.

Laura was astonished. Her aunts had never done such a thing before. She looked up at Mr. Crenshaw, wide-eyed.

He smiled. "You have no idea what I am going to say?"

Laura started to shake her head, then stopped as a terrible suspicion crossed her mind. "Oh no, you are not..."

"Yes, Miss Lindley. Will you do me the honor of becoming my wife?" He looked at her quizzically.

"Oh no," said Laura again. She put a hand to her forehead and sank down onto the sofa in front of the fireplace. "You cannot... *they* cannot force you to do this. I had no notion. It did not occur to me that they would be so utterly gothic as to... Oh but this is outrageous."

Mr. Crenshaw laughed. "It is that. But do not waste your pity on me. I began to expect something of this sort when you told me about your aunts. I was fully prepared, and I am not easily overborne, even by the vapors." His lips turned down. "Particularly by the vapors. There is no question of force. I am ready to be married, and I do not doubt but what we shall suit very well when we get to know each other better. So?"

Laura looked at him. "But you cannot wish to marry *me*? You have only just met me. I am not... You do not. Oh this is ridiculous."

Mr. Crenshaw smiled again. "It is certainly unconventional," he agreed, "but your aunts think it necessary. I find it acceptable, as I have no doubt you will too, when you have had time to consider properly."

"But I have not even had a London season," wailed Laura irrationally.

"You may burst upon the *ton* in full glory as a married woman, however," laughed Eliot. "A tremendous advantage, though you do not know it yet. And I fear you were right when you said that your aunts would not allow you to go to London. They are set on this marriage."

"I cannot understand you. How can you be so calm and matter-of-fact?"

He shrugged. "I have never been romantic about marriage. I have seen my friends marry for money, for love, to please their families, and for other less sensible reasons. It is always the love matches that come to grief." He paused as if suddenly struck by a new thought. "Perhaps there is someone you are attached to and wish to marry? That would alter the case completely."

Laura shook her head; she was feeling rather stunned.

"Well then, by birth, fortune, and education, we are well matched. I should do my best to make you happy. What do you say?"

She stared at him blankly. "I… I have to think. I am not certain. Can one marry in such a way?"

Two

WITHIN A WEEK IT WAS SETTLED; ELIOT CRENSHAW had returned to London, and Laura was left shaken and breathless. She was never certain afterward just what had made her agree to the preposterous scheme. Her aunts' unwavering conviction that unless she married she would be irretrievably ruined certainly had some influence. A visit from Mrs. Crenshaw also swayed her. This kind lady, though full of apologies for the scrape she had unwittingly had some hand in, told Laura frankly that she was delighted. Laura was just the daughter-in-law she would have chosen, she said positively, and just the woman to make Eliot happy.

On this point Laura had been most doubtful. But Mrs. Crenshaw's insistence, along with her son's calm assurance that he was well pleased with the match for his part, unsettled her. And the final straw was her sister's attitude. Clarissa was the most vehement of all. She nearly begged Laura to accept. In fact the only surprise Clarissa showed during the whole affair was when she heard that her sister might refuse. This, she thought, was madness.

"If you do not marry now, we are lost," she had told Laura. "They will never let us go to London, or anywhere. We will never meet any eligible gentlemen. We will become spinsters like our aunts, Laura. You will run the household with great fortitude, just as Aunt Celia does, and I shall have to take up the vapors to conquer my boredom." She sighed comically. "I suppose I should get some smelling salts and begin to practice. I do believe I feel a spasm coming on now." She clutched her throat dramatically.

Laura had laughed. "You never could have the vapors, Clarissa; do not be ridiculous."

But Clarissa was not to be fobbed off so easily. She looked squarely into Laura's eyes and said, "*Now* I could not, of course... but after twenty years shut up in this house with you and my aunts? Who can say? You must take this chance to get us free, Laura. I love Aunt Celia and Aunt Eleanor, but they do not understand... oh anything."

After this conversation Laura had thought long and hard. She knew very well what her sister meant; she too had sometimes felt hemmed in and desperate at Eversly and had longed to escape and live a different kind of life. Here, it seemed, was her chance, but what an unnerving chance it was. Could she marry a complete stranger? What did she know of the man, after all?

In the end she gave in. The pressure from her family, the urge to adventure, and the longing to escape all combined to make her throw caution to the wind and accept Eliot's offer. He set off for London to put an announcement in the *Morning Post* and find them a house, and Clarissa and her aunts plunged eagerly into the question of wedding clothes. The event was to take place in the country, at the church near Eversly, in a month's time, and then the couple was to go down to London for the season, accompanied by Clarissa. Some might find this an odd honeymoon plan, but it was one of the things that had reconciled Laura to the scheme in the first place.

✧

The weeks passed rather more quickly than she wished. In her quiet moments Laura often had second thoughts; several times she nearly summoned the courage to change her mind. But each time, she was stopped by the very considerations that had led her to accept the proposition. What lay ahead for her, and for Clarissa, if she did not go through with it?

And so she did. The Right Honorable Miss Laura Lindley, spinster, of St. Andrew's Parish, Lincolnshire, was married to Mr. Eliot Crenshaw of London and Melton Mowbray on a blustery day in April. Her sister stood up with her at the small ceremony, and the three of them set off in a chaise directly after the wedding breakfast. A house had been hired in town, and all was in readiness for the new Mrs. Crenshaw to burst upon the *ton* and make her place in society—all, excepting perhaps the lady herself.

Clarissa, however, was delighted with everything that occurred and all she saw. What might have been an awkward journey in the closed carriage was enlivened by her constant flow of chatter and her intense interest in the landscape and the villages they passed.

She had no doubts of the wisdom of Laura's course, and though this was not much comfort to her older sister, Clarissa's high spirits soon affected them all.

All the talk over dinner at the inn where they stopped for the night and the conversation in the coach the next day concerned what the sisters would do in town and what delights awaited them. By the end of the journey, Laura was feeling almost reconciled to her new state, all the more because her bridegroom had shown himself most solicitous of her comfort. Laura had felt some nervousness when they entered the inn, but Eliot had bespoken a bedchamber for himself and one for Laura and Clarissa without any sign of awkwardness. And when her sister refrained from teasing, Laura began to relax for the first time since she had said, "I will." Perhaps this would not be as difficult as she had feared.

They pulled up at the house in Regent Street about teatime, and the front door was flung open by a smart young footman almost before they could climb down. Eliot offered Laura his arm.

"I hope you will approve," he said. "There was very little time to furnish a house, but I think I have not done so ill. You may change anything that does not take your fancy." With that he escorted her up two steps and into the hall.

Laura found nothing to criticize as they proceeded up to the drawing room, where the tea things had been set out. Though small and narrow, the house was extremely elegant, and the furnishings were in perfect taste. Clarissa exclaimed over everything, calling on Laura to admire the charming little table in the hall, the exquisite blue hangings in the drawing room, and so on and on.

Laura poured tea rather unsteadily; she could not echo her sister's easy admiration, not because she did not admire, but because she was oppressed by the sense that while this was now her home, she felt a total stranger here. What was for Clarissa a novel adventure was for her far more serious. She still could not be certain that she had done the right thing.

After tea the ladies went upstairs to their bedchambers. Laura's was charmingly hung with dark green satin and flowered paper on a straw-colored background. It had the feeling of gardens and springtime, and she was enchanted with it. A dressing room off it held wardrobes, large mirrors, and a hip bath, and when she unbolted a door on the further side, she found that it connected with Eliot's dressing room and his bedchamber beyond. She looked around his rooms with some curiosity. Neither was much decorated, but the furniture and ornaments appeared to be well-worn and familiar objects, and the overall impression was of comfort. Walking back into her own suite, she paused a moment over the bolt on the connecting door. It was obviously newly installed. Laura smiled slightly, considered, then returned it to its original position.

Someone had begun unpacking her valise and had left a can of hot water on the washstand, so she was able to change and make herself tidy. They were to go out to dinner and a play that evening, both to satisfy Clarissa and to spare the staff on their first night, so Laura got out an evening dress. She chose one of her two old ones, a primrose crepe with simple puffed sleeves and one flounce about the hem. Though it was countrified and more suited to a young girl just out than to a married woman, she felt at ease in it and a little less strange to herself. She had put it on and was sitting at the dressing table brushing her hair when there was a hurried knock and a plump young maid rushed in, looking anxious.

"Oh there, ma'am, you're dressed and all already," she said breathlessly. "I just ran down to the yard to see the trunks bein' carried in. I only meant to stay a minute. I am sorry. Here, let me help." She took the brush from Laura and began rather inexpertly to dress her hair.

Laura smiled. The girl was obviously not used to acting as a lady's maid. Sandy-haired and freckled, she looked entirely good-natured but rather heedless. "Who are you?" asked Laura.

The maid started guiltily. "Oh I beg your pardon, ma'am. I'm Mary, Mary Holworth. Mr. Dunham said I was to wait on you, seeing as how your maid is took sick. I'm not too handy with such things as yet, but he said it made no matter because it's just temporary, until your own maid is better."

Laura's smile had broadened. "Mr. Dunham?" she asked.

Mary nodded. "The master's valet, you know. He is quite a gentleman, he is. Why, if he was to become angry with me, I'd, I'd…" Words seemed to fail the girl, and she shrugged. "Well I'm not rightly sure what I'd do, but it would be bone-chilling, I can tell you that. When Mr. Dunham cuts up stiff, he has a rare sharp tongue, ma'am."

"Does he?" replied Laura, much amused. "I must take care not to offend him."

Mary looked shocked. "Oh he wouldn't scold *you*. But he is in charge of the servants, you know, and a stern one he is."

"What of the butler? Does he not object?" Laura wondered if she would find herself managing a rancorous household.

"Well, there ain't, beg pardon, *isn't* a proper butler in the house, ma'am. Mr. Dunham, he oversees everything."

"I see."

Mary returned to the task of brushing out Laura's hair. "How shall I do this, ma'am? Mr. Dunham said I was to be quick and not chatter. My tongue does run away with me sometimes. Mr. Dunham says I'm a regular gabblemonger and must mind it. I do try." She pulled rather hard at a tangle, jerking Laura's head and making her eyes water. "Oh I'm so sorry, ma'am. Did I hurt you? I'm all thumbs this evening, I'm that nervous. I'm just not used to doin' hair." The girl looked as if she might burst into tears.

"It's all right, Mary. Let us just twist it in a knot here." Taking the brush once again, Laura deftly pulled her hair up onto the top of her head and fastened it, leaving several curls hanging above her ears. "There. That will do, I think."

"Oh yes, ma'am," breathed the maid. "It looks beautiful. 'Course it would on you." She gazed admiringly at Laura.

At that moment there was another tap on the door, and Clarissa burst into the room. She was wearing a dress of deep rose pink, with pink ribbons in her hair.

"Are you ready, Laura?" she said. "Come, let us go. I am dying to see the play."

"One moment," answered her sister. She clasped a bracelet on her wrist and draped a gauzy evening wrap over her arms. "There, now I am ready."

The sisters stood together before the full-length mirror. Clarissa, slightly taller than her older sister, was also slender and willowy. Their coloring was the same, and they looked much alike. Clarissa's face had perhaps more vivacity than Laura's, but the older girl possessed the more classic beauty. The vibrant hues of their gowns accentuated their striking looks, and altogether they were a very attractive pair.

Mary breathed a sigh behind them. "Lud, what a picture you two do make," she said. "Begging your pardon, ma'am, but you and your sister are beauties and no mistake."

Clarissa's eyes lit with amusement. "Thank you..."

"Mary," put in Laura.

"Thank you, Mary," continued her sister. "Do you think we shall pass in London?"

Mary's eyes bulged. "Pass, miss? Why, you'll set 'em all on their ears, you will."

Both sisters laughed. "I hope so," added Clarissa, surveying her reflection once again.

There was a sharp knock at the dressing room door, and a harsh voice called, "Mary?"

"It's Mr. Dunham," whispered the maid, looking a bit scared.

Clarissa raised her eyebrows. Laura stepped over to the door and opened it. A spare man of medium height stood without. His hair was iron gray, and deep lines beside his mouth suggested an uncertain temper. But when he saw Laura, he bowed respectfully. "I beg pardon, ma'am," he said. "I came to see whether Mary had come up to you."

"She did," answered Laura, "and I am ready, thanks to her. Is Mr. Crenshaw?" She felt suddenly awkward under this man's noncommittal gaze.

Mr. Dunham bowed again. "He awaits you in the drawing room."

"Thank you. Shall we go down, Clarissa?"

Her sister agreed eagerly.

Eliot was leaning on the drawing room mantel, but he straightened when they came in. He looked austerely magnificent in a black evening coat and pantaloons. His tall slender frame was admirably set off by this dress, and his dark skin stood out against a snowy neckcloth, whose intricate folds were ornamented by a single emerald pin. He nodded approvingly as they stopped before him.

"You look lovely this evening," he said. "Both of you."

Laura found that her heart beat a little faster as her eyes met his cool gray ones and saw admiration there. "Thank you," she said. "I hope we have not kept you waiting long?"

"Not at all. The carriage is ready. Shall we go down?"

Cloaks were fetched, and they set out on the short journey. Soon they were seated in a private room at the eating establishment Eliot had chosen. Clarissa was enchanted. She gazed avidly at the mirrored walls, the branches of candles, the potted palms set in the corners, and the haughty servitors. She was full of questions, and Mr. Crenshaw seemed to gain some amusement from answering her. He ordered a splendid dinner, beginning with soup, beef and oysters, and roasted capons, and continuing through duckling with cherries, a Chantilly cream, and more side dishes than Laura had ever seen at one table. The waiters treated him with marked respect and greeted his choices with admiring nods. Despite being a bit overawed, Laura had to restrain a giggle at their exaggerated obsequiousness.

When the second course was cleared, Eliot turned to her and caught a flash of her amusement. "Are you enjoying yourself?" he asked.

Laura put down her wineglass hastily. "Yes of course," she replied. "This is splendid."

Eliot smiled down at her. "After tonight you will be receiving quite a number of bride visits, I imagine. Our trip to the play is by way of letting people know we have settled in town, you see."

"And your friends will call on me now?" Laura was not sure whether this made her happy or apprehensive.

"Not *my* friends only, or even chiefly. That would not do. But my mother has written to her acquaintances in London, and I daresay your aunts may have done the same."

"Oh yes," put in Clarissa. "We shall have every old tabby in town breathing down our necks."

Eliot smiled. "That is all to the good, though you may not see it. The old tabbies can get you vouchers for Almack's and invitations to all of the fashionable parties. Am I correct in my assumption that you have no older relatives in London?"

Laura nodded. "Our aunts are our only near

relatives. They are our mother's sisters, you know. Mother died when Clarissa was born, and Father was killed in a hunting accident two years later. Our aunts took us then; indeed even I can scarcely remember our parents, and Clarissa has no memories of them at all. Our father had no brothers or sisters. I believe that a second cousin, or something of that sort, took the title. We have never met."

Eliot nodded. "I see. Nor have I met the earl. Well then you will have to rely upon friends of your aunts and my mother."

Laura looked at him quizzically. "I thought that a married woman might dispense with chaperones."

He smiled. "That is true. But as you have not been to town before, I felt you might welcome the advice of more experienced ladies."

"Oh stuff," said Clarissa. "They will only tell us that we may not do *this* and that well brought-up young ladies never do *that* and how can we wish to go to *such* a place or purchase *such* a bonnet?" She frowned darkly. "I thought we had done with all that."

Eliot laughed. "Well I shall not presume to dictate to you, but it is good that there are people to whom you can apply if you get into a scrape."

Laura had been looking at him. "May we not apply to you?" she asked, uncertain whether she was relieved or offended at his delegation of responsibility.

His expression altered immediately. "Of course you may. At any time and for any reason. But I may not be able to guide you in some things." He looked at Laura. "You have made rather a strange bargain, one you understand less than I do, perhaps. I do not wish you to suffer for it."

Before Laura could think of a reply to this unsettling remark, Eliot said, "We must go if we are to arrive before the curtain," and they prepared to leave.

Laura thought over his words during the short ride to the theatre, but she could make nothing of them. What had he meant by saying that he knew more of their bargain than she? Simply that he had more experience of the world? That was certainly true. She sat back in her seat with a sigh. Only time would remedy her inexperience, but perhaps she had better see to it that this happened as soon as possible.

Once settled in their box at the play, they attracted a good deal of attention. A great many people appeared to know Mr. Crenshaw and bowed or waved a hand from their own boxes and the stalls. Quizzing glasses and lorgnettes were raised to survey his companions, and more than once Laura could see the observers exchanging comments about what they saw. The intense scrutiny made her uncomfortable.

"Will your friends stop at our box during the interval?" she asked Eliot. "That is customary, is it not?"

When Eliot replied that it was and they would, Clarissa bounced a little in her chair. "Oh now we shall meet some new people at last."

The curtain rose soon after they arrived. The play was a melodrama, *The False Baron*, and Laura found herself more inclined to laughter than tears. The antics of the villain and the vaporish heroine were ridiculous. She turned to see if her husband found the play as funny as she did and discovered that he was not watching the stage; rather, his gaze rested on her. She could not see his expression in the near darkness, but she hastily turned away again.

At the first interval visitors indeed appeared. Laura met several of her husband's friends—men in their thirties who seemed to an unsophisticated girl very polished and sure of themselves. They were scrupulously attentive to the new Mrs. Crenshaw and flirted obligingly with Clarissa, but Laura did not feel that they really paid her much heed.

One or two younger men also stopped in, sent by their mothers and nervous of claiming acquaintance with the stern Mr. Crenshaw. Eliot was very gracious, however, and all were allowed to deliver the message that their mothers would be calling on the new bride very soon. One of these youngsters, Lord Timothy Farnsworth, seemed struck by Clarissa and remained talking to the sisters for several minutes.

Seeing his wife and her sister thus occupied, Eliot sat back in the rear of the box to chat with one of his closest friends.

"And so you are married, Crenshaw," said Lord Peter Alvanley.

"Yes," answered Eliot. He took out a plain gold snuff box and offered his friend a pinch. "Amusing, is it not?"

Lord Alvanley considered the mixture, took a minute amount, and sniffed it. He raised his eyebrows. "Very good. Well it happens to all of us, soon or late."

Eliot shrugged.

Looking at him, the other added, "Does your bride appreciate the humor of the situation, as you appear to?"

"Women have no humor, my dear Alvanley. They are incapable of it. Emotion, feeling, even passion, yes—but humor? It is a flaw in the entire female sex that they can neither originate nor appreciate real wit. And that is the chief reason we can have no real companionship with women but merely agreeable liaisons."

"You are very severe," replied Lord Alvanley, somewhat taken aback, "and I cannot say I entirely agree."

"Ah, but then you have not made a study of the subject," answered Eliot. "I have. And while I have endured vapors, hysterics, ecstasies, and every other form of excess you can imagine from women, I have found none who could laugh with me. You may take my word."

Lord Alvanley was about to reply when Lord Farnsworth rose to take his leave, and seeing that the curtain was about to go up again, the older man joined him, leaving the Crenshaws and Clarissa alone once more.

"How do you like your first taste of society?" Eliot asked Laura then.

She returned his challenging look. "It is quite stimulating. Or I believe it will be, once I know my way about a bit. I think I shall like it very well."

"Good." He gave an approving nod.

"It's wonderful," put in Clarissa. "And I think I have a beau. Lord Farnsworth asked permission to call on us, Laura. I said he might."

"Farnsworth is a most eligible young man," said Eliot, with a sardonic smile. "Something of a lightweight perhaps, but undeniably eligible."

"Well then he will do for a start," replied Clarissa.

"One can't expect perfection all at once." The others laughed at her as the curtain rose once more.

The second interval was like the first. Laura soon lost track of the names she heard and began to feel tired. They had come to town only this morning, after all, and this had been a long and eventful day. She was not at all sorry when the play ended and they climbed into the carriage to go home.

❧

When they reached the house, they walked up the stairs together. Clarissa went directly to bed, but the newlyweds paused in the corridor outside Laura's room. For a moment she felt nervous again. But then Eliot said, "I wished to tell you that I have no intention of forcing you to do anything you do not like. This must, of course, remain a marriage of form only for some time, until you know me better. I hope we will become good friends, Laura."

"Thank you, Eliot. You are very kind. I hope that, too."

He smiled down at her. "With such good motives we cannot fail. You must always tell me if you think that is not so, and I will endeavor to do better."

"Thank you," Laura said again.

"You need not thank me, Laura… for what is only your due, after all. Good night. Sleep well." And he turned toward the door of his own bedchamber down the hall.

"Good night," echoed Laura. She stood still, alone in the hall, thinking over what her husband had said. She could find no fault with his words, but his tone had bothered her. He spoke to her as one speaks to a child, a child in whom one is not really interested. It was as if... Laura struggled to make her feelings clear. It was as if he had been appointed her guardian suddenly, and he felt responsible for her welfare and happiness but did not really care about her at all. She nodded once. Yes, Eliot was conscientiously doing his duty and nothing more.

As she opened her bedroom door, Laura wondered how she felt about this state of affairs. There were worse things than to be the responsibility of a man of honor. But somehow she felt dissatisfied. She had never wished to be anyone's *duty*. After a time she sighed and went to fetch her nightgown. Perhaps she was being fanciful. It was late, and she was tired. No doubt all would look better in the morning.

Three

THINGS DID INDEED APPEAR MORE CHEERFUL IN THE clear morning light, and Laura dismissed her uneasiness with a shrug. No doubt time would cure any awkwardness in her situation. Mr. Dunham showed her through the house. At first this seemed odd, but since there was no housekeeper and no butler, the task fell to him. And Laura soon found that he was well informed about the details of the establishment and had played a large role in assembling it. She met the cook, a large easygoing woman, and the other servants, and saw the kitchens, the spare bedchambers, and main rooms. The library was still unfinished, but the drawing room and dining room were complete to a shade. She could find no fault.

Mr. Dunham remained rather stiff with her. Did he perhaps disapprove of his master's marriage, Laura wondered? Thus she was a little wary of suggesting changes and was relieved when the tour of the house was over and she could return to the breakfast room for another cup of tea. She found Clarissa there, just beginning her meal.

"Laura, come look at this," cried the younger girl when she saw her sister. "It is the most stylish thing imaginable, don't you think?" She held up a recent number of the *La Belle Assemblée* to show Laura a half dress of bronze green crepe.

Laura smiled. "Very dashing."

"Isn't it? I mean to have one made up. I can wear it with my chip bonnet and my half boots for walking. Can we go to Bond Street this morning?"

"I am not certain, that is…"

Clarissa cocked an eyebrow. "About what? Are you busy with the house? I don't mean to tease you into squiring me about. I should be just as happy with Nancy, I daresay. She is the funniest maid; she seems to know nothing whatsoever of fashion or how to dress hair or anything of that sort. But she would be happy to accompany me shopping; indeed she would consider it a high treat."

"It is not that," said Laura. "It is just that I do not yet know about money, you see."

"Oh." Her sister looked nonplussed. "I did not even consider it. How shatterbrained I am. But you will have an allowance, Laura. It is the customary thing. Our aunts gave me fifty pounds before we left Eversly. Let us begin with that."

Laura shook her head. "I should prefer to be clear on it first. Go on with your breakfast, Clarissa. I will see if Eliot is in."

She found him in the hall, leaving a letter in the tray to be posted. When he saw her on the stairs, he smiled. "Good morning. I trust you slept well?" Laura nodded. "Good. I wanted to talk with you today. I was waiting until you had been over the house. But first, were you looking for me?"

"Yes. Clarissa wishes to go out shopping, and I wondered, that is, I was not certain…" She faltered. It was terribly difficult to ask this near stranger for pocket money.

He held up a hand. "You have hit upon just the matter I wanted to discuss. I thought it best to set up both a household account and a personal account for you. I know you have never managed a house before, and I thought it would be easier. Sums might be deposited quarterly, if that meets with your approval?" And he mentioned an amount that Laura thought immense. "What do you think? Would you prefer to have only one account?"

"No. This sounds best."

"I had thought also that Dunham might be given access to the household account so that he can relieve you of some of the more routine duties. He is part secretary and part valet, you know, and is fully capable of doing accounts. This will be *only* if you like it, of course."

Laura bowed her head. "His help would be welcome," she said, a true enough statement, though she did not relish the thought of spending much time in Mr. Dunham's company.

"Good. I have already placed a rather larger sum in your account, knowing that you would wish to outfit yourself. You may draw on it whenever you please. And you need only make yourself known in the shops, of course."

"Yes. Thank you very much. You are very generous."

He looked down at her. "You needn't thank me,

Laura." When she said nothing, he went on. "I am going to take the team out this morning and see whether they are recovered completely. I shan't be home much before dinner, I imagine. If you wish to go out, there is a barouche in the stables for you. Just tell them to bring it round."

Laura started to thank him again, then merely nodded instead. He wished her a good day and strode out the front door. Then Laura went to the breakfast room, where Clarissa was just finishing.

"It is all settled," she told her sister. "We can go out whenever you are ready."

"Then you are to have an allowance?"

"Yes." Her eyes twinkling, Laura told her sister the figure.

"Good God! Why, that is a fortune." Clarissa looked thoughtful. "Do you suppose, my dear, that Mr. Crenshaw is… very rich? I never considered the matter until this moment. What a ninnyhammer I am; how could I not? He must be very wealthy indeed if he can afford such a magnificent allowance."

"I suppose so," replied Laura. "I had not thought of it either. I left all that to our aunts."

Clarissa shook her head. "We are a sadly impractical pair. A young lady's first thought ought to be whether a man has a proper income, after all. Then she knows how to think of him."

Laura choked. "It is so difficult to remember all the rules of propriety." Clarissa gave a peal of laughter. "But you know, Clarissa, it is all very well to say such things to me, but you mustn't run on in that way before strangers."

Her younger sister dimpled. "Dragon. I know it, of course. I shall be a model of rectitude, have no fear. But I have to say that I am very glad you are rich. It is a comfortable thought. We might have known it, really, if we had bothered to think. Mrs. Crenshaw appears very plump in the pocket. It stands to reason her son is also."

"Plump in the... What does that mean?"

Clarissa grinned. "Rich, of course. Nancy is teaching me all sorts of new words. You never have heard such colorful language, Laura."

"I daresay." Laura made a stern face. "You know quite well that we mustn't use slang. Remember what Aunt Eleanor said." She modulated her voice and managed a very lifelike imitation of their anxious aunt. "Clarissa, my love, whatever can you mean? Such a vulgar phrase. It makes me feel quite faint to hear you speak so. Where are my drops? Have you seen them, dear? I do not mean to complain, but I really do think that I should lie down for a moment or two. And if you would just bring me my shawl, dear."

Clarissa laughed again, and Laura looked guilty. "Oh I should not mock her so. She means well. All the excitement is making me giddy."

Clarissa shrugged. "It's only funning. Come, let us get ready and go out. I long to see the shops on Bond Street at last. We can take a hackney too. I have never ridden in one."

Laura smiled mischievously. "But we have our own barouche. Don't you wish to try it?"

Clarissa had risen and started toward the door, but this stopped her. "A barouche? Do you really, Laura? Oh how splendid! We can drive in the park; that is all the crack, you know. Mr. Crenshaw is certainly doing things in bang-up style. Let us hurry."

&

Their shopping expedition was very lively. For two young ladies who had never been in a town larger than Grantham, the brilliance of Bond Street was irresistible. Each ordered several dresses from an elegant Frenchwoman who presided over a select establishment there, and they purchased bonnets, slippers, and other accessories as well. Laura stopped to put down her name at the circulating library, and Clarissa insisted that they drive past Almack's so that she might at least gaze at the exterior of this hallowed building.

"They call it the Marriage Mart, you know," she told Laura. "I do hope we can get vouchers. It is indispensable."

Laura shook her head. "I begin to worry about you. You are becoming quite a romp now that we are in town."

"Becoming? But I talk so only to you; you know that. Indeed I have always done so. Marriage is making you gothic, sister." She glanced teasingly at Laura.

Laura sighed. "Oh no, but this is not simply a lark for me. I am *married*, Clarissa, and I shall be for the rest of my life."

The younger girl was distinctly taken aback. "You are, aren't you? I hadn't thought of it in just that way." She turned to look closely at her sister. "I have been abominably selfish, treating all this as a glorious adventure when you are *worrying*. I am sorry."

Laura smiled at her stricken expression. "Well it is

not so bad as all that. I am not worrying. But this is not simply a trip to town for me, you see."

"I do see that now," replied Clarissa, looking at Laura. "And so you must help me to adjust to my new state," added Laura lightly. "Now, do you wish to try on that bonnet with the ostrich plumes? Or are you ready to return home?"

Clarissa signified that she had had enough shopping for one day, and they turned toward Regent Street again. The barouche was piled with boxes, though only a fraction of what they had bought, and both footmen had to come out to carry packages into the house.

❧

The girls removed their bonnets and pelisses and went down to eat a light luncheon of cold meat and fruit. They had just finished and moved on to the drawing room when Mr. Dunham announced that they had callers and ushered three elderly ladies into the room.

Laura and Clarissa rose to greet their visitors, who introduced themselves as old friends of their aunts. Mrs. Dillingham, Lady Quale, and Mrs. Boothe were much alike—small, gray-haired, fashionable women in their fifties. Their first interest was Laura's marriage.

"Such a good match, my dear," complimented Lady Quale. "Our young ladies have been setting their caps at Mr. Crenshaw for years with absolutely no effect. We had come near to giving him up altogether. You are a close friend of his mother, I understand?"

Laura agreed that she was.

"Ah. I have not had the pleasure of meeting her myself. She lives chiefly in the country, I take it. Well that probably explains it." She nodded at her companions, who nodded back sagely. "A mother's influence in these matters."

Mrs. Dillingham added, "And you not even out, my dear Laura. What a coup!"

"My aunts were a bit reluctant to send me to London," answered Laura stiffly. She was not enjoying this conversation, but she resolutely kept her composure at the sight of Clarissa's darkening countenance.

"Celia and Eleanor never cared for London," said Mrs. Boothe. "They came out in the same season, you know. A disaster. It is always a mistake to bring out two girls at once. You cannot make a clear impression. Well, well, I suppose they thought you would not care for town life either. Though two such lovely girls!"

"Laura has made a good match without," said Lady Quale, "so it has all worked out for the best."

Seeing that Clarissa was about to explode, Laura said, "You will have some tea, I hope."

Their visitors accepted the offer, and Laura gave the orders. When she returned to the sofa, she found that the conversation had shifted to Clarissa's prospects, and her heart sank.

"You are to make your bow to society this season, my dear?" asked Lady Quale of the younger girl.

"Yes," answered Clarissa shortly, her dark eyes sparkling dangerously.

"Well I should think she will take quite nicely," said Lady Quale to Mrs. Boothe.

"Oh no doubt of it. I shall get you vouchers for Almack's from my friend Lady Jersey. And you must both come to my rout next week."

At the promise of such plums, Clarissa's expression softened markedly, Laura was relieved to see. "You are very kind," she answered. "We should be delighted."

Mrs. Boothe nodded as if this was to be expected. "I shall have a number of eligible gentlemen. I must think who you should meet." She fell silent in concentration.

"What about young Hareford?" asked Mrs. Dillingham. And the three ladies were off on an extended discussion of the current set of bachelors on the town and their relative merits as husbands. Now that their attention was diverted from the sisters, the ladies' talk appeared to amuse Clarissa no end. She glanced at Laura delightedly, just barely repressing outright laughter, and her sister shook her head.

Tea arrived and was served without interrupting the debate. Obviously the girls had unwittingly triggered one of the chief concerns of their callers' lives—the business of marriage. Just as Laura had resigned herself to hearing an exhaustive catalog of every girl the three had seen married since they had come to town and the role each had played in the courtship, Mr. Dunham brought in more visitors. "Mrs. and Miss Rundgate, ma'am," he said.

Laura rose with alacrity as a large, comfortable-looking lady came into the drawing room, followed by a slight pretty blonde girl. "How do you do," said the first. "Anne Crenshaw asked me to call and see how you are getting on in London. May I present my daughter, also an Anne." The girl dropped a small curtsy as Laura expressed her pleasure in meeting a friend of Mrs. Crenshaw's and begged the two to be seated.

Mrs. Rundgate nodded to the three other visitors

and sat down opposite them. Her daughter, after hesitating a moment, went to sit beside Clarissa. "How are you, Mrs. Dillingham?" said the mother. "I haven't seen you this age."

"Quite well, thank you." The four seemed to know each other, so Laura did not attempt introductions.

"And so you are settled in town?" asked Mrs. Rundgate, turning to Laura again. "This is a very elegant house."

"Thank you," Laura replied. "We are nearly settled. There is still some arranging to be done."

Mrs. Rundgate nodded lazily. "What a botheration it is. I always say to my husband, 'Why must we move back and forth from the country year after year? It causes such a vast deal of trouble for me.' But he likes town life, and this year, of course, I am bringing Anne out, so there was no question of our remaining in Devonshire. You must come to the ball I have arranged to present her, in three weeks' time."

Laura nodded a grateful acceptance and turned to smile at Anne Rundgate. "You must be very excited. Is it your first ball?"

"Yes," replied the girl, opening her large blue eyes even further, "I am. It is very exciting." Her voice was very soft and mild.

"I should say so," put in Clarissa. "A ball! I never have attended anything but country assemblies."

The glance that Anne cast at her taller companion was half admiring, half fearful. "Nor have I," she answered, almost inaudibly.

"You will require gowns," said Lady Quale. "Antoinette's on Bond Street is the best place to go."

"Yes indeed; we were there this morning," answered Clarissa blandly. "A charming shop." She ignored her sister's warning look.

Mrs. Rundgate smiled slightly, and Lady Quale raised her eyebrows.

"It is very kind of you to tell us," put in Laura hastily. "We will need advice on such things, I daresay, since this is our first trip to town."

Lady Quale's expression became somewhat less stiff, and she assured Laura that she was completely at her service. "But now we must go," she added, rising. "So many calls to make, you know."

Laura stood also. "Indeed. It was kind of you to come."

The three older ladies were all graciousness as they departed, each promising Laura an invitation to her next entertainment and smiling slightly superciliously when Clarissa bid them good day.

When they were gone and Laura had sat down again, Mrs. Rundgate chuckled. "I know just how you feel, my dear," she said to Clarissa, "but you must not antagonize those ladies. It would do you a great deal of harm, believe me. They have monstrous sharp tongues, and many people find them amusing."

Clarissa looked both rebellious and thoughtful. "It just made me so angry, ma'am, to hear how condescendingly they spoke to Laura. And me."

Mrs. Rundgate nodded. "I daresay. Well I tell you only what is true, my dear. You must decide for yourself." She turned back to Laura, leaving Clarissa to ponder her advice and talk to her daughter. "And so you are bringing your sister out this year? But you are really making your come-out as well, I understand. You have not been to town before?"

Laura nodded.

"Well if there is any way I can help, I would be glad to do it. You have only to say so."

"Thank you. You are very kind."

Mrs. Rundgate shrugged. "I doubt you will need me. Your husband can give you a hint on most things. He is vastly fashionable. But if there is any matter on which you want a woman's opinion, I hope you will come to me. Anne Crenshaw is prodigiously pleased with her new daughter-in-law, and I see that she is right."

Laura flushed a little. "Thank you," she said again.

The older woman made a deprecating gesture.

Laura felt very much at ease with this offhand visitor. She ventured a hesitant question. "You say Mr. Crenshaw, Eliot, is very fashionable?"

"Oh lud, yes. He is one of the Corinthians, my dear. One can tell just by looking at him."

Still more diffidently, Laura said, "I suppose one can, if one knows about such things. But I admit I am not precisely certain what a Corinthian may be, Mrs. Rundgate." With anyone less sympathetic, Laura never would have dared to continue thus.

Mrs. Rundgate seemed at a loss. "Well, la, let me see. A Corinthian is a gentleman who sets the fashion in dress, very scrupulous, you know. All the young men ape him. That is, not *all* of them, not the dandies, of course. They have their own mode. Well, ah, Corinthians are great sportsmen though. They patronize the boxing saloons and that sort of thing. And they have an air about them. That is the chief thing, I suppose. They have a kind of assurance and polish. What a mull I am making of this explanation! I find that though I know perfectly well what a Corinthian is, I cannot seem to define one."

"It is a rather indefinable thing, perhaps," Laura suggested.

Mrs. Rundgate looked relieved. "That's exactly it. One never knows just what it is makes a man striking, but one sees it. Why, you must have noticed Eliot's distinguished manner... and the set he frequents? Top of the trees, my dear, top of the trees."

Laura nodded. "Yes, I see what you mean."

They chatted for ten minutes more about the Rundgates' ball and other events of the coming season. Clarissa and Anne discussed clothes, or rather Anne listened while Clarissa did so. Then Mrs. Rundgate rose and declared that they must go. Their good-byes were much more cordial than those of the first callers, and Clarissa made an engagement to walk in the park with Miss Rundgate very soon.

❧

When they were alone in the drawing room again, Clarissa said, "She is a little ninnyhammer, but quite nice. I shall make a push to rouse her spirit."

"Anne Rundgate?"

Clarissa nodded. "She is a good little mouse. But perhaps it is just shyness. We shall see." She rose. "I believe I will go upstairs. I want to go through the clothes I brought from home and decide what is suitable for London and what is not. I must shop more systematically than I did today, and Anne Rundgate has given me several ideas. She knows what is in fashion just now, I will give her that. Do you care to come with me?"

Laura was about to agree when Mr. Dunham entered the room again. His expression was rather odd. "Pardon me, ma'am," he said, "but there is another caller below. I was not sure, but I thought perhaps you were fatigued and did not care for more visitors. I said I rather expected you were out."

Surprised, Laura said, "Who is it?"

"Ah, it is Mrs. Allenby."

"Allenby? I don't know the name." Laura looked inquiringly at Clarissa, who shrugged.

"How old is this lady?" Clarissa asked, turning to Mr. Dunham with a sudden suspicion. "I cannot endure another old tabby," she explained to Laura.

"As to that miss, she is not old. But ah, well…"

Mr. Dunham seemed at a loss, and Laura was perplexed. She had not thought this self-possessed gentleman could be so awkward. "Is something wrong?" she asked him.

"No ma'am." Mr. Dunham's face was wooden. "I only thought you might be tired."

Clearly this was not the whole truth. But it was also obvious that Mr. Dunham did not mean to tell her what was wrong. "I am not at all tired. Are you, Clarissa?" Her sister shook her head. "Well send the lady up then, Mr. Dunham." The man left the room, rather reluctantly Laura thought, and when he ushered Mrs. Allenby in, he lingered a moment as if he did not wish to leave them.

Looking at Mrs. Allenby, Laura got some idea of the reason for his unease. This caller was quite the most dashing woman she had ever seen. She looked to be about thirty years of age, and she was a gorgeous redhead with flashing green eyes and a beautiful figure. Her gown was enough to make Clarissa speechless with envy, though it was a bit daring for Laura's taste. It was cut very low and made of tissue-thin sea green muslin. Laura had a notion that the lady's petticoat was damped from the way the dress clung to her.

Their visitor had paused a moment in the doorway, surveying the sisters as they did her. Now she came forward and held out her hand. "Hello," she said in a low, musical voice. "You must forgive me for calling without a proper introduction, but our husbands are such friends, you see, and I hoped we might be also."

Laura felt a flash of uneasiness as she replied to this greeting, but she dismissed it immediately. She asked her guest to sit down and introduced her sister. Clarissa eyed Mrs. Allenby with a mixture of envy and challenge in her glance.

"What a charming room," said the latter. "Eliot has found a lovely house for you."

Something patronizing in her tone made Laura's chin go up a bit. "Thank you."

There was a pause. Mrs. Allenby was gazing about the room, taking in all its details and summing up the sisters in short side glances. She did not seem to feel obliged to make conversation.

Finally Clarissa spoke. "Did we meet your husband at the play last night?" she asked. "We met a great many of Mr. Crenshaw's friends. I fear I have forgotten the names."

Mrs. Allenby turned to her, smiling faintly. "Last night? No, we were not at the play last night. We had a dinner engagement."

"Ah," replied Clarissa.

There was another silence.

Finally Laura ventured, "Are you just returned to town also?"

"Oh yes," answered Mrs. Allenby carelessly. "We always go to Melton for the hunting. Do you hunt, Mrs. Crenshaw?" She gave the name a satirical lilt.

"No," said Laura. She did not tell her visitor that her aunts had never permitted it.

"A pity. Eliot has such a lovely place up in Melton. Perhaps you will take it up."

"Perhaps." Laura was beginning to think that she did not like Mrs. Allenby. Was this what the wife of a Corinthian was like, she wondered?

"I should like to hunt," said Clarissa. "You must ask me for a visit, Laura."

Mrs. Allenby smiled slightly again. "I am giving a small card party tomorrow," she said. "That is really why I called. I hope you will come. I believe Eliot means to be there."

For some reason this invitation did not please Laura as the others had. "I am not certain," she replied. "I believe we may be promised for dinner tomorrow evening."

"Ah. Too bad. But you may look in afterward, if you like. We shall start late and keep on forever, I daresay. It is usually so. Come by for a moment, at least."

"I cannot promise," replied Laura.

"But you will try?" asked her guest, with more directness than good manners.

Laura bowed her head, making no promises.

"Well then, it is settled. And now I fear I must go. I do so hope to see you tomorrow." She rose, brushing aside Laura's offer to ring for Mr. Dunham, and left the room.

"Well," said Clarissa when they were alone, "I am not sure I like her, but how dashing!"

"Yes," answered Laura absently.

"Of course, I know I cannot have a dress like that, not now, but someday I shall."

Laura was not really listening.

"I suppose it is all envy. After all, she was polite enough. Did you like her, Laura?"

"What? Oh I suppose so. She stayed only five minutes. I hardly know."

"Well I think we should go to her card party. I daresay we would meet some very interesting people there. Are we engaged for dinner?"

Laura shook her head. "I said so because I was not certain I wished to go. We have so much to do."

Clarissa appeared much struck by this. "Indeed what would I wear to such a party? The gowns I have would make me look a dowd next to Mrs. Allenby. You are right."

Laura smiled. "Well I did not positively refuse. If Eliot is going, he may wish us to come. I will ask him."

Clarissa nodded. "And now I am going upstairs before anyone else arrives. I must look over my things."

Laura rose with her, and the two sisters went out of the room and up the stairs.

Four

DINNER THAT EVENING WAS SOMEWHAT STIFF AT FIRST. Eliot had been out all day and returned only just before the meal. Laura and Clarissa were waiting in the drawing room when he came downstairs. He apologized punctiliously. "I'm afraid my friends are not yet accustomed to the idea that I am married. I could not get away. But it will not happen in the future. I hope I did not keep you waiting long."

This explanation embarrassed Laura. She did not wish to keep him from his usual activities. And so she reassured him hastily and was rather silent during the first part of the meal. Clarissa addressed herself to the excellent ragout of beef at first, then she began to tell Mr. Crenshaw of their day.

A description of their shopping expedition seemed to amuse Eliot. Clarissa told him which establishments they had visited and how they had gotten on. "Madame Antoinette is odiously snobbish, of course. I could see that in a moment. But when we told her that we would need several gowns, each of us, she unbent amazingly." Clarissa dimpled. "It was quite funny. And she seemed impressed when Laura told her her name. Are you known to Madame Antoinette, Mr. Crenshaw?"

He smiled at her. "I do not know the lady personally, but I believe she has a very shrewd sense of London society. She is said to be able to judge one's fortune to a sou. She must be a formidable woman."

"Oh yes," answered Clarissa, "but we found the loveliest ball gown imaginable for Laura. It is pink—not that rubbishy pastel pink that schoolgirls wear, but deep pink, you know, rose pink. She looks ravishingly pretty in it."

"I am sure she does." Eliot looked at her, and Laura felt herself blush.

"Indeed. And I ordered a white gown trimmed with silver ribbon. I shall wear it to Mrs. Rundgate's ball," she told Laura.

Eliot raised one eyebrow. "Has Mrs. Rundgate been here then?"

"Oh yes," continued Clarissa ebulliently. "We had several callers this afternoon. It was very exciting." Her brow darkened. "Except when those three old harpy friends of our aunts' began questioning us so closely. You cannot think, Mr. Crenshaw, how infuriating it was. I wanted to slap them, especially Lady Quale."

Eliot laughed. "An impulse shared by many in London, I understand. Who were the other two harpies?" Clarissa told him, and he nodded. "Well they are considered amusing in some circles, I know. It is too bad that you did not find them so, for they have influence. Do you agree with your sister's opinion, Laura?"

Laura looked down at her plate, frowning. "They

did ask impertinent questions, but they are old friends of my aunts, after all, and perhaps they felt they had the right. I did not mind them overmuch. I can see why people find them amusing."

"Well so they were when they left off catechizing us and turned to other subjects," said Clarissa. She repeated some of their assessments of the *ton*'s young bachelors to Eliot's great enjoyment.

"They described young Farnsworth to the life," he laughed. "What do you think of him now?"

Clarissa shrugged. "I see nothing to fear in someone 'wealthy and wellborn but a complete nodcock.' And in any case he has not called, so the question has not arisen, Mr. Crenshaw."

Still smiling, he replied, "You must leave off calling me Mr. Crenshaw. It makes me feel a stranger in my own house. We are brother and sister now, after all."

Clarissa was taken aback. "What am I to call you then?"

He laughed. "We might begin with Eliot. Later, when you know me better, I daresay you will find other names."

Clarissa laughed. "Very well, Eliot."

He nodded and turned to Laura. "How is Mrs. Rundgate? I have not seen her in years, though she and my mother are bosom friends. Is she as lazy as ever?"

Laura smiled. "She seemed very pleasant and easy-going. I liked her. She is bringing out her daughter Anne this season, you know."

"I did not. In fact I had forgotten she had a daughter. However, it does not surprise me. And now that I think of it, didn't she bring out a daughter already? Two years ago perhaps?"

Laura signified ignorance, but Clarissa said, "Three years ago. Anne is the youngest of her children by several years."

"Ah, I knew I had heard of another."

"You did not meet her?" asked Laura.

"Them," put in her sister before Eliot could answer. "Mrs. Rundgate has four daughters, all married but Anne."

"You don't say," replied the man. "Can I have missed them all?"

Both girls smiled, and Laura said, "You are not in the habit of attending the come-outs, I take it?"

"Exactly. But now that you have brought it to my attention, I must express my admiration for Mrs. Rundgate. Three daughters disposed of and another just fired off. She has more fortitude than I had imagined."

Laura laughed. "Is it such a labor?"

"You have no idea. And if her daughters are the ninnyhammers I suspect them to be, it is even harder."

Clarissa raised her eyebrows. "Why do you suspect that?"

The corner of his mouth curled. "Ella Rundgate has no very strong understanding, and her husband is no better. I would be astonished if they had produced offspring of more than average intelligence; indeed I would be surprised at their being even average."

Clarissa considered this. "Well I admit that Anne seemed to me a rather biddable girl. But she is very sweet."

"A damning sketch. I shall endeavor to avoid this cloying damsel. She sounds like a dead bore."

Clarissa giggled, and Laura could not help smiling. "I see that Lady Quale is not the only Londoner with a sharp tongue," she said.

"Touché," laughed Eliot, seeming much struck. He looked at Laura appreciatively. "And so you have had a busy afternoon. Five visitors."

"Six," corrected Clarissa. "We have not told you about the last. And she was the most interesting."

"Ah. And who was that?"

"A Mrs. Allenby," answered the younger girl, "and what a dasher she is. I have never seen such a dress."

Laura was watching her husband, and she thought she saw an arrested expression in his eyes, though his face remained impassive.

"Mrs. Allenby," he echoed meditatively. "She called here?"

"Yes, and she asked us to a card party tomorrow. Laura does not wish to go, I think, but I am sure it would be very elegant. I should like to see it."

Eliot met Laura's eyes. "No," he said blandly, "once again I believe Laura is right. I doubt you would enjoy it."

"Really? But she said you were going. Don't you wish us to come?" The innocence in Clarissa's voice was a bit too deliberate.

"Did she?" asked Eliot, with no obvious reaction. "She was mistaken. I had no plans to attend."

"Oh," Clarissa said.

Laura almost added, "Had?" But she restrained the impulse. Her husband's tone had not been encouraging.

They had all finished eating some minutes ago, and now Laura signaled her sister that it was time to retire.

They went up to the drawing room together, leaving Eliot over his wine.

When they sat down, Clarissa said, "I do not believe Eliot wishes us to know Mrs. Allenby. It is irritating; we have only exchanged one set of guardians for another. Why should we not go to her card party if we like?"

Laura shrugged. "For my part I have no great desire to go."

Clarissa looked disgusted. "Oh are we never to go out?"

Her sister smiled. "We went out today, our first day in town, and we have been invited to several parties already. Do not exaggerate, Clarissa. You will soon have your fill of society."

But the girl was not mollified. "I shall never have my fill, after eighteen years of none at all. I am going upstairs. Nancy has promised to help me sew up my blue crepe, the one I tore so badly last week." And she strode out of the room.

❧

Thus, when Eliot entered the drawing room some minutes later, he found Laura alone there, reading. He looked around inquiringly, and she said, "Clarissa has gone up to do some sewing."

He nodded and sat down beside her. "That is just as well. I want to talk to you."

"About Mrs. Allenby?"

His face showed faint surprise. "You have guessed that? Well that is all to the good. Mrs. Allenby belongs to a very fast set. She skirts very near the line, in fact.

She would not be a suitable friend for Clarissa by any means, or indeed, even for…" He hesitated.

"Yes?" said Laura. "Or even for me?"

He smiled. "You are very sharp. Yes, that is what I was going to say."

"So you would prefer that I did not make a friend of Mrs. Allenby?"

He looked at her. "I would."

She returned his gaze directly. "She told us that you and her husband are good friends."

"Did she?" he answered a bit ruefully. "I suppose there is some truth in that. We were great friends at one time, but we have, ah, drifted apart recently. I still see Jack Allenby often, but I would not say we are friends any longer."

Laura was silent. She had more questions, for she felt there was more to this situation, but she did not feel able to ask them. She could not rid herself of the notion that it was none of her business. This man might be her husband, but she sensed that he would not permit her to interfere in his life because of it. Too much distance lay between them. In any case she did not wish to do so.

"I did not much like Mrs. Allenby," she said finally, "so it seems very unlikely that any friendship would have developed. But I shall make no effort to see her again."

"Thank you," said Eliot. "I am honored that you take my word in this way."

She looked up at him. "Why should I not? You give me good advice, I hope?"

"I hope I always shall. I try to do so at any rate."

There was a pause, then Eliot said, "Would you care to go out tomorrow night? Perhaps to Vauxhall Gardens? You have not seen them yet."

Laura smiled. "Making sure that I keep my promise, sir?"

He shook his head, smiling. "Not at all. Rather, I'm making sure that Clarissa is amused and does not tease you to death about that card party, and also taking an opportunity to spend an evening with my wife. We should get to know each other better, and I am beginning to think that will be an exceedingly pleasant duty."

Laura flushed a little; his use of the word *duty* turned what might have been a compliment into something else. "I am sure Clarissa would love it," was her only reply.

He raised his eyebrows. "And you?"

"I too, of course."

"Good; then it is settled. I fear I am promised to some friends tonight, and I must leave you. How will you spend the evening?"

"Oh I shall be quite all right. There is no need to worry over me."

"On the contrary," he replied. "You have a book. What is it?" She held up the volume of Scott she had been looking at. "Ah, that should amuse you, if nothing better offers. Do you like Scott?"

"Tolerably well, except when he begins to sermonize."

He laughed. "My feeling exactly. Shall I find you another book? I daresay Dunham can pick out the volumes still in boxes."

"Oh no, this is perfectly all right. I have sewing to do and a thousand other things."

"Ah." He bowed. "I shall take my leave of you then. Good night."

"Good night."

When he was gone, Laura sat quietly for a while, thinking over their conversation. The more she saw of this man with whom she had consented to spend her life, the greater respect she had for him. Clearly he was intelligent, clever, and scrupulously just. An ideal character might exhibit more warmth, she thought, wondering precisely what qualities one ought to prefer in a husband, but she found she could not fault him. She did not feel competent to judge.

After a time Clarissa came in once more. "Are you sitting here alone?" she asked, surprised. "Whatever for? I came back to apologize, Laura. I was horridly childish and petulant just now. I am sorry."

Laura smiled. "It was nothing. And you had no need to worry in any case. Eliot has asked us to accompany him to Vauxhall Gardens tomorrow evening. So, you see, we will go out."

Clarissa clapped her hands. "Vauxhall! How wonderful! I do not deserve such a treat after my tantrum."

Laura laughed. "Well if that is really the way you feel, you may stay home and punish yourself."

"Lawks, no," answered her sister, her eyes sparkling wickedly. "I wouldn't miss it for anything."

Struggling to control her twitching lips, Laura said, "What did you say, Clarissa?"

"I would not miss it for anything?" the younger girl repeated innocently.

"Not that. You know very well what I mean."

Her sister burst out laughing. "Yes. You mean *lawks*. Isn't it a fine word? Nancy uses it whenever anything out of the ordinary occurs."

Her sister joined her laughter. "What can it mean?"

"I haven't the least notion. What shall we wear to Vauxhall? How I wish my new gowns had arrived; perhaps they will come in time." And the ladies became immersed in a discussion of their various toilettes.

Five

THE TWO SISTERS WENT OUT SHOPPING AGAIN ON THE following morning. They visited Hookham's Library as well, and made use of Laura's new subscription to procure the latest of Mrs. Radcliffe's romances. Clarissa bid fair to become addicted to novel reading, which had been forbidden by Aunt Celia.

They did not return until early afternoon, and they found that a number of ladies had left cards during the morning. Clarissa picked them up from the silver tray on the hall table and ruffled through them as she walked up the stairs. She read the names to Laura excitedly. "Lady Darley, the Viscountess Cranleigh, Mrs. Cooper. Oh we have missed a great many people, Laura. How vexing!" They reached the drawing room, and Clarissa tossed her pelisse onto the sofa. "Well perhaps there will be others this afternoon."

Laura shook her head. "For my part I hope not. I am worn out with standing about in the shops and hurrying from place to place. I shall tell Mr. Dunham I am not at home this afternoon."

At this moment Mr. Dunham came in and said,

"There are two gentlemen below, ma'am. They say they wish to pay their respects." Silently he held out two cards, his expression stiff.

Laura read. "Clarissa, it is Lord Timothy Farnsworth. And a Sir Robert Barringfors. A friend of his, I suppose."

"Ha," said Clarissa. "He did come. Please, let us see them."

Laura nodded to Mr. Dunham. "It seems you have an admirer, after all."

"It is about time. I am eighteen years of age and have never had a beau."

Laura's eyes twinkled. "You forget the curate."

Clarissa put a hand to her cheek. "I did. Oh how funny. How could I forget poor Mr. Wigmore? Do you remember his ridiculous little moustache?"

"Yes. And his watery blue eyes and his greatcoat."

Clarissa giggled at the memory of this preposterous garment.

"Poor Mr. Wigmore."

Thus, when the two gentlemen entered the drawing room, they found themselves facing two pairs of twinkling eyes and two merry smiles. Such enhancements on the faces of such lovely ladies more or less sealed their fates. Lord Farnsworth stammered as he said hello and introduced Sir Robert. "B-brought a friend," he said. "Hope you don't mind. H-he didn't wish to intrude, but I said you l-like to meet new people. Strangers in London, that sort of thing. Hope it's all right." Sir Robert bowed rather nervously and said nothing.

"Of course," replied Laura. "Please sit down."

With obvious relief, the gentlemen complied. A silence fell.

"It is interesting to meet new people," said Clarissa. "We have had more visitors already than we would have seen in a month at Eversly. Some friends of our aunts called. Perhaps you know them?" She named the ladies.

Lord Timothy seemed to shudder. "Lady Quale," he echoed. "Friend of m'mother. In fact all four of them are thick as thieves. Terrifying woman. Makes me quake."

His friend nodded in agreement. "Dashed acid tongues they have. Always makes a fella feel he's said something stupid."

Privately thinking that this feeling might not be too far off the mark, Laura nodded sympathetically. "They certainly are formidable."

"And extremely inquisitive," added Clarissa. "I nearly told them to mind their own affairs and leave ours to us."

Lord Farnsworth looked frightened. "Mustn't do that," he said urgently. "They'd put it about town before you could blink. Talk nothing but scandal, you know, and slander. You'd find yourself in the basket before you knew it."

Clarissa smiled. "I shall try to be careful. Perhaps you are fonder of the Rundgates? Mrs. Rundgate and her daughter also called."

"Anne Rundgate?" Sir Robert was heard to murmur. "Taking little thing."

"Do you like her?" replied Clarissa. "I thought her quite nice."

Greatly taken aback, the man stammered, "Oh no. That is, hardly know the girl. Just out, ain't she? Saw her at a party, I believe. Never spoke."

Clarissa appeared a bit exasperated by this disjointed speech, so Laura intervened. "Perhaps you are better acquainted with Mrs. Allenby then? She was our final caller and completes the catalog you have endured so patiently."

But this attempt to put Sir Robert more at his ease failed miserably. In fact both gentlemen now showed signs of agitation, and Sir Robert's eyes bulged alarmingly. "V-vera Allenby," he choked out finally. "She called *here*? But ain't she... That is..." He floundered in confusion, then put a hand to his mouth. "Pardon me, got something in my throat," and he began to cough weakly.

"Fine day today, what?" put in Lord Timothy at this moment. The ladies turned puzzled faces to him, and Sir Robert gazed at his friend with gratitude and awed respect. Lord Farnsworth faltered under this wholesale scrutiny but continued gamely. "Sunshine, you know. Quite warm for April too. I took my team out to Richmond."

Taking pity on them both, Laura said, "Did you? To the park? I have not seen it yet, but I have heard that it is very beautiful."

"Oh yes," responded their visitor. "Flowers, that sort of thing. And it makes a good workout for the horses."

"I should like to see it," said Clarissa. The smile she bestowed on the gentlemen contained an unmistakable message.

"Worth a visit," was Lord Farnsworth's only reply.

His friend nudged him, but he merely looked at him vacantly.

"Be honored to escort you," added Sir Robert then. "Take my curricle out."

Lord Farnsworth started. "Dash it, no. I shall take you, Miss Lindley. Honored. Didn't think of it. That is, meant to ask, that is…"

Clarissa smiled. "I'd be delighted."

Once this was settled, the gentlemen appeared to have exhausted their fund of conversation. Clarissa made several attempts to draw them out, but she met with little success, and both ladies were relieved when their callers rose to depart.

When they were safely gone, Laura said to her sister, "Do you really wish to go?"

"Not particularly. But I must have some beaux, you know—as many as possible in fact."

Laura shook her head. "Those two reedy, dandified *boys*?"

Clarissa giggled. "Oh that is too harsh. They are a little thin perhaps, but it is rather an elegant slenderness, do you not think so? I admit that Sir Robert's waistcoat was a trifle florid, but…"

Laura interrupted her. "Don't try to bamboozle me, Clarissa. And if you call that waistcoat a *trifle* florid, I wonder you would not allow me to purchase the red ribbons this morning. Too arresting, you said, I believe." She gave her sister a quizzical look. "Lawks."

Clarissa burst out laughing. "Very well, I admit you have the right of it. They are not first-rate specimens. *But* they are the only young men I have met, and who am I to dance with if I do not become acquainted with some? It is purely practical. And Lord Farnsworth is a little handsome. I like blond men."

"And bulging blue eyes and a receding chin, no doubt?"

Clarissa laughed again. "Stop, stop. You are too hard."

Her sister joined her laughter. "Perhaps. If they were very clever and witty, one could forgive the rest, but they are such loobies, Clarissa."

The younger girl nodded. "Did you see Sir Robert when you mentioned Mrs. Allenby? He looked just like a fish out of water." Her laughter faded as she recalled something. "That was odd, was it not? Why do you suppose he did so?"

Laura looked down and shrugged. "Who can tell with such a shatterbrain? I wonder if he knew himself?"

Clarissa frowned. "Oh I think he did. He was at great pains to turn the subject. What can it be about?"

"Well I for one am too tired to wonder," answered Laura, rising. "I think I will lie down for a little while. Remember, we go to Vauxhall tonight."

"Yes, I shall be along directly," replied the other absently, but she remained seated, regarding the fire with narrowed eyes.

Laura hesitated, then went upstairs. She really was tired, but as she lay on her bed, her mind was busy. What had Sir Robert been about to say? She had an idea, and it did not please her overmuch. Was Mrs. Allenby in some sense her rival? And exactly what was the contest and her chance in it?

These conjectures did not make it easy to rest, but Laura lay lost in thought for quite some time, staring up at the canopy over her head. She was so engrossed that it was time to change for the evening before she knew it, and she had to hurry.

Nonetheless she was the first down to the drawing room. She surveyed her appearance in the mirror over the mantel, checking yet again the cut of her new gown. It was made of crepe of a clear, pale violet shade and fell in soft folds to the floor. She had refused any complicated trim, and the small puffed sleeves were adorned only with small knots of darker ribbon. Another tied the high waist, and she wore a necklace and earrings of amethyst that her Aunt Eleanor had pressed upon her before the wedding.

"I shall never wear them again, child," her aunt had said sadly. "And they will look so lovely on you. You can wear such things now that you are to be wed, you know."

So she had taken them, and she was glad now. Her black hair was again pulled up in a knot to show the earrings, and she had draped a diaphanous wrap over her elbows. Altogether, she thought as she looked in the mirror, it was an elegant outfit.

"Lovely," said a voice from the door.

Laura turned, wide-eyed, to see Eliot standing there. For a moment she found it difficult to breathe; he looked so very impressive in his evening clothes. His dark, hawk-like face was set off to perfection by the snowy linen, and his tall elegant figure was at its best. He came over to her and raised her hand to his lips. "You will do me great honor tonight," he said.

"Thank you," replied Laura. "It is a pretty dress, is it not?"

He smiled. "Yes… but it is not the dress I meant."

To himself he was thinking that he had been fortunate in his choice. His wife was beautiful and everything he could wish in terms of birth and breeding. He had been right to use rational judgment in this matter and not allow his emotions to sway him. The accident of their union, in which he had acquiesced because it suited him, had been a happy one.

Clarissa hurried into the room. "Am I late?" she said. "I am sorry. That silly Nancy dropped some Denmark Lotion on my dress. We had to sponge it out."

Eliot laughed. "Are you a devotee of facial nostrums? I wouldn't have thought it of you."

Clarissa had the grace to blush. "Nancy bought it for me. But I do not think I shall use it. What a smell!" They both laughed at that, and in good humor started down the stairs to the waiting carriage. Clarissa wore peach-colored crepe this evening, and Eliot remarked on the charming picture the two sisters made as they sat together in the rear seat.

◆

When they arrived at Vauxhall, Clarissa exclaimed at the trees hung with colored lanterns, the tiers of boxes about the stage, and the winding paths through the gardens adorned with statues and pavilions. She had only one complaint about the evening's entertainment. "I think you might have asked one of your most charming friends to accompany us," she told Eliot. "Am I to be without an escort?"

He smiled. "I might say that I hoped to keep two such lovely ladies to myself," he replied, "a compliment which should silence your objections. But in fact

I have arranged that Lord Anthony Trilling meet us at our box." He directed a conspiratorial glance at Laura as he added, "He is a baron, I fear, not a duke. I could not provide a duke on such short notice."

Laura stifled a gurgle of laughter and looked a bit guilty, remembering what she had told him about her sister when they first met.

Clarissa merely looked puzzled. "Why should you want a duke?" she asked. "Most of them are quite old, I understand. What is Lord Anthony Trilling like?"

"That, I shall let you judge for yourself. I see he is before us." And Eliot ushered them toward the box where a man sat alone waiting for them. When he saw them approaching, he rose and bowed. Eliot nodded in response. "Laura, this is my friend, Tony Trilling. My wife, and her sister, Miss Clarissa Lindley."

The gentleman said everything that was proper, and they sat down around the table in the box. Lord Anthony had already procured some of Vauxhall's famous rack punch and the paper-thin slices of ham for which it was famous, and the ladies sampled the latter. As they ate, they looked about them with great interest. The lights, the brilliant crowd, and the music formed an almost hypnotic combination to observers so unused to the gaieties of London. Their escorts watched them with appreciative amusement for a while, until Laura turned back and caught her husband's eye. She blushed a little.

"You must think us quite countrified, gazing about like children," she said.

"On the contrary. Are you enjoying the spectacle?"

"Oh yes. What a beautiful place this is."

"It is splendid," added Clarissa. "This is just how I imagined London would be. I want to go all around the gardens."

Eliot laughed. "Well, if you are finished, we might stroll about a bit."

"Oh yes." Clarissa was on her feet in a moment.

"Would you care for it?" Eliot asked Laura. She nodded, and the four made their way down to the paths.

Clarissa took Lord Trilling's arm and walked on ahead, leaving Laura to stroll beside her husband. It was soon evident that the first couple was embarking on a very spirited light flirtation.

Laura shook her head. "Clarissa is so excited by this trip to town."

"That is only natural, I think. She is very young and has had no taste of the diversions so common to most girls."

Laura agreed. "It is not that I am really concerned, you understand. Clarissa is sensible, and her principles are sound. I am only afraid that her high spirits may cause some misunderstanding or… oh I do not know. I have never acted as a chaperone before." She sighed.

He laughed. "I am sure all will be well. You are an exemplary guide."

Laura made a face. "How dreadfully dull that sounds. I feel much too young to be any such thing."

Eliot looked down at her. "You have, I think, an innate good breeding that outweighs those factors. I have no worries on that score."

This was clearly a compliment, but Laura found it unsatisfying. "Thank you," she answered tonelessly. She watched Clarissa and Lord Anthony ahead of them.

They were talking some nonsense about Mrs. Rundgate's ball, and the gentleman evidently wished to secure her sister's hand for the first dance. Laura felt a pang of envy as she looked on. Clarissa looked so carefree as she tossed her head coquettishly at the slender, dark young man's importunities.

"Tony and your sister seem to be enjoying themselves," said Eliot, following her gaze. "I thought they would." He smiled down at her. "He is extremely eligible."

"Oh I hope Clarissa won't think of marrying for a while," answered Laura. "Indeed I doubt she will."

Eliot merely nodded. The couple ahead had paused, and Laura and Eliot caught up with them as Tony was pointing out the beauties of one of the pavilions. He and Eliot exchanged some banter about his sudden unexpected interest in architecture, while Clarissa giggled and Laura smiled.

During the evening, Clarissa and Tony flirted pleasantly with each other and Laura exchanged commonplaces with her husband. They met several of Eliot's acquaintances, and he introduced her with some pride. But Laura found the outing less enjoyable than she had expected, and after two hours she was very ready to go home. She said nothing in the face of Clarissa's obvious happiness and contrived to remain cheerful and smiling throughout the fireworks display and the dancing.

But later that night, when she entered her bedchamber, she rubbed the back of her neck wearily. The time had seemed long to her, and the event not precisely boring, but unsatisfying. She felt as if something indefinable were missing.

She heard a noise from Eliot's bedroom and stood very still. It was not repeated. She thought again of their evening, of the way Clarissa had laughed and flirted, while she talked so calmly with Eliot. Was she to have only this? She knew nothing of what a marriage should be, having spent her girlhood with two spinsters, but she felt somehow that it should be more than this. She stood for a moment longer, then shrugged and began to undress.

At that moment Mary burst into the room to help her and filled it with excited chatter. It appeared that the laundry had torn Laura's blue cambric. Laura was able to put aside her worry in amusement as the girl went on and on about the vices of laundresses and what she had told the woman or not told her. Mary was not a first-rate lady's maid, but she was a hilarious storyteller. Thus Laura managed to fall asleep immediately, and she did not wake until Mary pulled back the bed curtains the next morning and let the sun fall in across her face.

Six

THE NEXT DAY WAS THE ONE SET FOR CLARISSA'S drive to Richmond Park with Lord Timothy Farnsworth. When Laura went downstairs, she found Clarissa before her in the breakfast room, looking very dashing in primrose-sprigged muslin, and in high spirits. She was full of the previous night's events and prattled on about Vauxhall, the dinner and dancing, Eliot's kindness in taking them, and his friend's manifold charms. After a while she became aware that Laura was hardly attending.

"What is the matter?" she asked her older sister. "Did you not sleep well?"

"Oh no, I slept very well."

"I too, though it is a tribute to my robust constitution. My bed was a shambles."

"What do you mean?" asked Laura.

Clarissa giggled. "Nancy nearly incinerated my sheets. They are all brown and crumbling with scorch marks."

"How?"

"With the warming pan." Clarissa giggled again.

"She was trying so hard to make me comfortable, but she heated it too hot and left it between the sheets far too long. For a moment I thought she had set the house afire. I swear there was smoke."

Laura shook her head. "I shall have to speak to her. These silly maids will bring down the house on our heads one day."

"Oh do not scold her, please. I would not have told you if I thought you would take her to task. It was an accident, and Nancy is terrified of what Mr. Dunham will say when he hears of it."

"But Clarissa, we cannot have the maids burning up the sheets."

Her sister laughed outright. "She will not do so again, I promise you. I have never seen anyone so upset. She has learned her lesson." Her laughter nearly overcame her. "I pointed and said, 'Nancy that looks like smoke,' and she whirled about and screamed, 'Lawks, it's the warming pan. I clean forgot.' And she went running over and dragged it out. You cannot imagine how funny it was."

A smile escaped Laura. "I am beginning to."

"And then she began to apologize. I expected never to hear the end of it. She so wanted to get me some fresh sheets, but she was afraid to go to the linen room lest Mr. Dunham notice and question her. It was the most diverting episode; nothing like it ever happened at home."

Laura's smile became rueful. "No, because Eversly is a well-run household. Until now, I never appreciated Aunt Celia as she deserved." She looked at her sister, now engrossed in her breakfast. "What time do you go?"

Clarissa nearly choked. "Ten," she replied when she caught her breath. "I must hurry."

"Yes, I know how you must be looking forward to this outing," agreed her sister equably.

"Oh I am," laughed Clarissa. "It is my first with a gentleman, after all."

"Indeed. I hope you enjoy yourself."

Clarissa drank the last of her tea and rose. "It doesn't matter if I don't, for I shall have had the satisfaction of knowing that I was at least seen driving to Richmond. That must lead to something."

"You are incorrigible," laughed Laura.

Her sister dropped a quick kiss on her cheek as she left the room. "Of course I am," she said over her shoulder, and she began to take the stairs two at a time.

Laura laughed again, shook her head, and poured out another cup of tea.

Clarissa accordingly went out at ten. Laura sat down to write a long-overdue letter to their aunts, then went down to speak to the cook about dinner. There were no callers, to her relief, and the rest of the morning passed quietly. She did some sewing and looked through two of the cartons of books in the library, finding a novel she had been longing to read. She even put a few volumes on the shelves, though not many, for she feared Mr. Dunham would come in and find her at it. All in all she enjoyed her day immensely, and she began to think that eventually she would make a competent housewife.

❦

Clarissa came sweeping in at teatime, bringing a breath of crisp spring air into the drawing room, and collapsed on the sofa near Laura, pulling off her hat and flinging it away.

"Did you have a good time?" Laura asked.

"Ripping," said Clarissa. "Lord Farnsworth's horses are really splendid, and he let me take the ribbons for a while. We were quite wrong about him, Laura. He has a bang-up team."

"If only I had realized," murmured Laura.

Her sister grinned. "Well I know you aren't as fond of horses as I am, but these were splendid."

"And did you like Richmond Park?"

"Oh, well I didn't actually see it." Clarissa looked sheepish. "When Lord Farnsworth saw how I felt, he took me to Tattersall's instead. We went for a short drive after."

"Tattersall's? Where they auction horses? Oh no."

"It isn't improper, and I adored it. Actually I believe I've bought a horse myself." Clarissa avoided her sister's eye.

But Laura was trying to keep her lips from twitching. "Not a gray?" she managed to ask.

"A gray? No, she's a little brown mare, and…" Suddenly Clarissa's eyes lit. "You mean like the plow horse? At Eversly?"

Laura nodded, and they both dissolved in laughter.

When Mr. Dunham brought in the tea tray, he ignored their merriment stolidly, putting the tea things on a low table in front of the sofa and taking himself off as soon as possible. As he went, Eliot spoke from the doorway. "That was quite a sight. *L'allegro* and *il penseroso*."

Laura turned with a start. "Oh. I didn't hear you come in. Clarissa has been telling me about her drive with Lord Timothy Farnsworth."

Eliot raised one eyebrow. "And you can laugh about it? Your minds must be stronger than I imagined. I should have fallen into a decline and most likely slit my throat after such an ordeal."

Clarissa laughed again. "Oh no, I had the most delightful time. He let me drive his team."

"Then he is also braver than I imagined," said Eliot. "Was it your driving that threw you into such transports?"

"No," giggled Clarissa. "Laura reminded me of the time I purchased the gray plow horse from a farmer near Eversly and brought him home. I so wanted a mount, you see, and our aunts did not like us to ride."

"I do see, and my sympathy for your aunts is wholehearted."

"Well they didn't let me keep him," replied Clarissa, "but they bought me a pony the very next year."

"Exceedingly sensible of them. Why do I suddenly find your Aunt Eleanor's vapors more understandable?"

Laura had been making the tea and pouring it out, and now she choked.

Eliot turned to her. "Yes?" he said blandly.

Her eyes twinkling, Laura shook her head.

They sipped their tea in silence for a moment, Clarissa looking thoughtful. "I can't ride tomorrow," she said to herself. "I promised to go walking with Anne Rundgate." She drank the last of her tea and rose. "I am going upstairs. I shall see you at dinner."

She picked up the bonnet she had flung on the table by the door and disappeared.

A silence fell as Laura and Eliot went on with their tea.

"I am concerned about you," he said after a few minutes.

Laura was surprised. "About me?"

"Yes. I fear you are not liking town life as much as you expected to. You did not care for Vauxhall, did you?"

"But of course I did. I thought it lovely. I don't know what you mean."

"Strange... I got the distinct impression that you were impatient and perhaps bored last night. Do you tell me that you did not wish to come home long before we did?"

Laura started to tell him that she had wished no such thing; then she hesitated and looked up. His gray eyes were very keen, but she saw nothing but kindness in them. She sighed a little. "I was rather tired."

"Were you?" He leaned forward and took her hand. "You must tell me these things." The concern in his voice surprised her. "I want you to be happy, Laura. It is my duty to see that you are."

At the word *duty* Laura stiffened and pulled her hand away. "You are very kind, Eliot. I am quite all right."

He moved a little toward her, and she pulled back.

"I hope so," he said. "You are just the sort of wife I would have chosen, Laura, from among all others. Indeed I did choose, of course. I have no reservations whatsoever."

Laura swallowed. His statement made her feel

acutely embarrassed. Though she knew he meant it well, it reminded her of the circumstances of their marriage and the fact that he had been partly forced into it, and she hardly knew where to look.

"I, I am glad," she stammered finally.

"I am proud of you, Laura. You have beauty, birth, breeding, all the things one desires in a wife. I think we shall deal together splendidly. We made a wise decision."

Some of Laura's confusion dissolved at these rather cold words. He made the marriage sound like a business transaction. It was obvious that, for him, feeling had no place in their marriage. She bowed her head. "I am sure you are right," she replied.

He smiled. "Good. I wish to be as good a husband as you are a wife."

She bowed her head again, but said nothing.

He waited a moment, then rose, putting down his cup. "I must take my leave now. I shall dine at my club this evening, so you needn't wait for me. Good night."

"Good night," answered Laura. Eliot went out, and she was left sitting alone in the drawing room, her teacup halfway to her lips.

Seven

IN THE NEXT FEW WEEKS CLARISSA FURTHERED HER acquaintance with Anne Rundgate, and she spent afternoons and mornings with her and her friends. Though Laura was pleased to see Clarissa so happy at becoming part of an established set, she herself had made no real friends. She was a bit older and more serious than the girls just out... but she was also rather younger, at least in experience, than the young matrons she met. Thus Laura felt a little out of place and spent a good deal of time alone.

Eliot occasionally escorted the sisters to evening parties or to the theatre, but many dinners were served only to Laura and Clarissa while he was engaged with some of his cronies at The Daffy Club or Watier's. Clarissa scarcely noticed, but Laura felt confusion growing in her mind. Was this really the life she wanted, she began to wonder. Though she was not at all certain that she wished to spend more time with her husband—really, she knew too little about him to decide—neither was she convinced that she did not wish to become acquainted with him. Perhaps what annoyed her most, she concluded, was the way the decision was taken out of her hands.

The day set for Mrs. Rundgate's ball was upon them almost before they realized it. Laura's rose pink gown had arrived from Madame Antoinette. It truly was a stunning creation, all of silk and trimmed with exquisite French braid. Clarissa had also received her dress of white brocade shot through with silver threads, and she was vastly pleased with it.

Eliot elected to accompany them, and the three assembled in the drawing room at nine that evening, waiting for the carriage to be brought round. Eliot complimented the ladies on their appearance and, with a graceful bow, presented them with bouquets for the ball. Laura's was pink roses and Clarissa's white, both in intricate silver-filigree holders.

Clarissa fell into raptures and thanked him fervently. "My first bouquet," she exclaimed. "Oh let us go. I cannot wait any longer. What a long day this has been!"

⤮

When their carriage reached Mrs. Rundgate's house, it had to join a line of vehicles waiting to discharge their passengers at the door. The scene was brilliant, with linkboys running here and there waving their torches, chairmen jostling with passersby who had paused to stare at the spectacle, and the brightly lit windows of the house throwing leaping shadows across the pavement as the carriages passed them. Laura's spirits began to rise; the excitement was contagious.

Greeting their guests on the landing, Anne

Rundgate looked very fragile and lovely in pale blue, and her mother was substantial in amber satin. The latter was effusively glad to see them. "Good evening, my dears," she said to the girls. "So glad to see you here. And Eliot... I haven't seen you this age. How is your mother? What a picture the three of you make, to be sure."

Eliot smiled and bowed his head in acknowledgment of the compliment as Laura returned her salutation and Clarissa said to Anne, "Your gown is beautiful. It turned out just as you wished." After that they had to move on to make way for other arrivals on the steps behind them.

In the ballroom Lord Anthony Trilling appeared to remind Clarissa that he had set his heart on the first dance. Laughing, she agreed, and he bore her off toward a group of young people in the corner.

Laura looked about the room. It was impressive indeed. Though not more than half the guests could have arrived as yet, the crowd was exceedingly brilliant. The bright hues of the ladies' gowns and the darker shades of their escorts' evening clothes combined in a tapestry effect and, added to the profusion of flowers, it was nearly overpowering.

Eliot was smiling down at Laura. "Quite a sight, is it not?" he said.

She nodded. "It looks almost like a play. It is hard to believe that such a scene can be real."

He laughed. "I'm not sure it is precisely. There is nothing more artificial than a ball."

Anne Rundgate came into the ballroom then, on the arm of a young gentleman Laura did not recognize. The band prepared to strike up, and Anne took her place at the head of the set.

Laura saw Clarissa join the dancers. She was laughing at something Lord Anthony was saying, and both seemed quite absorbed. Eliot said, "Our hostess has gotten young Redmon to lead off with her silly daughter. Quite a coup. I hope no one tells Clarissa he is son to a duke. She will go off with him from under little Anne's nose before we can blink." He smiled to show that he was teasing her.

Laura studied the young man. "I have not heard of the Duke of Redmon."

"No, Geoffrey is the Marquess Redmon. Courtesy title. He is old Millshire's oldest son. Shall we join the set?"

Laura looked up at him. He was smiling, and he looked supremely confident and at ease. She yielded to an impulse. "But sir, you must know that it is not at all the thing for husbands to dance with their wives. How can you ask me to be so unfashionable?"

His eyes twinkled. "It is perfectly acceptable when they are newly wed," he replied, more than a match for her.

Laura blushed. He held out a hand, and she silently took it and allowed him to lead her into the last set forming near them. To herself she thought that she should know better than to try to rally Eliot. He was up to anything.

They went through the two dances with little conversation. This was Laura's first public trial of her dancing skills, and she was taken up with minding her steps. After a time, feeling that her performance was creditable, she looked about her again. The look of a tapestry was even more marked now as all the figures moved and swayed in careful patterns. The beauty of it pleased her. Clarissa caught her eye from across the room and grinned delightedly, and Laura smiled.

When the set ended, they returned to the chairs along the side wall. Immediately Lady Quale came up to them, smiling at Laura in a predatory way. "Come, my dear," she said sweetly. "I want to introduce you to my friend Lady Jersey. She will give you vouchers for Almack's." And she bore Laura away with her before she could think of any objection.

Lady Jersey was a pleasant woman, who eyed Laura with some curiosity and said, "So you are the young girl from the country who has walked off with one of our greatest matrimonial prizes?" But she promised her vouchers in an easygoing way, and her malice, if that was what it was, seemed wholly good-natured.

After scarcely two minutes Lady Quale whisked her off again, to meet another of her friends, she said. But she merely steered Laura to a vacant sofa along the wall and sat her down.

"There, that is done," she told her. "Now we can have a comfortable coze. How are you, my dear? I have not seen you since Emily Yarbourgh's rout last week." Laura signified that she was well, and Lady Quale nodded. "Your sister seems to be taking well, just as we told you she would. A very vivacious girl."

Laura made no reply, and there was a short pause, a very odd thing in a conversation with Lady Quale.

And when that lady spoke again, there was an uncharacteristic hesitation in her voice. "I particularly wished to speak to you," she went on. "I left my card yesterday, when you were out, you know."

"Oh yes, I am sorry," answered Laura guiltily, for she had not been out at all. She simply had no taste for Lady Quale's acid gossip.

"Well it couldn't be helped, but it was vexing in this case, because I did wish to talk to you." She hesitated, and Laura wondered what she could be leading up to; it was quite unlike her ladyship to beat about the bush. "I don't know quite how to begin," continued Lady Quale, further increasing Laura's curiosity. "It is a delicate matter. I think you know, my dear, that I do not hold with gossip." Laura looked down; this was one of Lady Quale's dearest illusions. "But as a friend of your aunts, I stand in the position of parent to you, and since you have no mother to tell you these things, I felt it my duty to bring it up."

"To bring up what, ma'am?" asked Laura, more and more mystified.

"Well to be blunt, I have been told that that brazen creature Vera Allenby actually called on you."

"Yes. She called after your first visit, on the same day." Laura stirred uneasily in her chair.

"Tch, tch." Lady Quale appeared scandalized. "I can hardly believe it, even of her. She will go too far one day." She looked at Laura, who avoided her eyes. "Well not to wrap it in clean linen, my dear, Mrs. Allenby's name has been linked with your husband's for some time. It is well known that they, ah, that they have some arrangement. It pains me, but I felt you ought to be told. Vera Allenby is not at all a proper person for you to know."

"Ah," replied Laura. She could think of nothing else to say. A cold feeling began in her stomach and gradually spread outward.

Lady Quale looked at her sympathetically. "This is something of a shock to you, I have no doubt, but you must not let it overset you. Such things are frightfully common these days. It is scandalous." She pronounced this opinion with relish. "You cannot conceive how heedless some people are, my dear. And the Allenbys are among the worst."

Laura could not resist. "But her husband? Does he, that is…"

"Oh he is every bit as bad as she. Worse! There is no greater libertine in London. It seems to amuse them."

"And they know about each other's…"

"That is the most scandalous part of it. They have no discretion whatsoever. Why, only think of Vera Allenby's calling on *you*." She lowered her voice. "I have been told by one who should know that it is a game between them. They tell each other everything, but *everything*, my dear."

Laura drew back, disgusted with her companion and with herself for listening to her. "Well I am sure such rumors are much exaggerated," she replied. "If you will excuse me now, ma'am, I must see what Clarissa is doing." She started to rise.

Lady Quale reached out and grasped Laura's arm tightly; her hand felt like a claw. "You will remember what I have said? You mustn't see the Allenbys; very bad *ton*."

Laura moved her head in what might be considered a nod and pulled her arm away. "Pardon me."

She started across the ballroom to where Clarissa was standing. Her head felt light, and she clung to the image of her sister as to a lifeline. But as she walked, she happened to catch sight of Eliot on the other side of the ballroom. With a sinking heart she saw that he was talking to Mrs. Allenby at this very moment. Laura felt totally alone suddenly and terribly exposed traversing the empty center of the room. Everyone here, she thought, knows how things stand with me. It is unbearable.

Just then, Vera Allenby happened to look up and see her. She smiled at Laura with a supercilious mockery that made the girl clench her fists in rage.

But if Laura could have heard what Eliot was saying at that moment, she might have felt differently. "You are becoming quite tiresome, Vera," he told the fuming redhead. "Do leave off and be sensible."

"I don't know what you mean, darling," replied Mrs. Allenby. "I merely asked why I had not seen you this age." Her voice was languid, but there was a hint of steel in it.

Eliot seemed unaffected. "You can't play off your tricks with me, so you may as well stop trying. You know exactly how things stand between us. I told you the day after you called on my wife."

"Your *wife*?" echoed Vera with a sneer. "You cannot tell me that wide-eyed chit is anything to you, Eliot. I know you too well."

"I tell you nothing, and I do not care what you believe." Eliot's eyes hardened. "I made it clear,

I think, that all is over between us, Vera. It was a pleasant affair; we both enjoyed it, and it hurt no one. But now things have changed."

The smile which bared Mrs. Allenby's teeth for a moment was not pretty. It made her piquantly lovely face feral. "No one casts me off," she almost hissed. "It is I who make the rules in this game."

Eliot looked disgusted. "You should have gone on the stage, Vera. If you are going to enact a Cheltenham tragedy, I beg you will excuse me. It is not as if there had been anything but simple liking between us."

His companion's temper overcame her usual skill in manipulating the male sex. "You will be sorry if you keep on this course, Eliot, more sorry than you can imagine."

The corners of his mouth turned down. "Don't be foolish, my dear. You cannot threaten me." And he turned on his heel and walked away from her.

Vera Allenby stood still for a moment, trembling with rage; her green eyes burned. Then, with an effort, she regained control and fixed a smile on her face again. She turned to look about the ballroom, and her eyes fell on Laura, now chatting with their hostess. A glitter came into them. She looked further, found what she sought, and started across the room toward her husband.

Laura was listening blankly to Mrs. Rundgate's amusing description of the trials a ball entailed. "If it's not the maids breaking the best glasses, it's a lost tablecloth or the cook giving notice," she was saying. "And last night I was certain Anne had caught a chill."

At that point Mr. Rundgate joined them. He was

a shy, silent man whom Laura had not met before tonight. He murmured something to his wife that caused her to throw up her hands with an annoyed exclamation. "Excuse us, my dear," she said to Laura. "There is some trouble about the ices. We must get in touch with someone from Gunter's. They *promised* me that all would go smoothly." The couple hurried away, Mrs. Rundgate's laments carrying behind them for some distance.

Laura took a breath and looked about her. Clarissa was dancing, of course. Eliot had drifted toward the card room with some of his friends, and it looked as if they were about to get up a game. She saw Lady Quale in the corner, gossiping with Mrs. Dillingham, and she averted her eyes quickly. She certainly did not wish to join them. In fact, she thought as she scanned the rest of the ballroom, there was no one in the room that she really wished to speak to.

Laura turned and moved toward the long windows at the side of the room. They were somewhat recessed, and though the curtains were drawn, there was a niche between the room and the window. She retreated to one of these and parted the draperies to look out. The view was uninspiring—a small paved yard and the side of the stables.

"Tired of the ball so soon?" asked a pleasant tenor voice behind her. "It is a rather tedious affair, I admit."

Laura turned quickly, letting the curtain drop. A handsome gentleman of middle height stood before her. His hair was dark brown and his eyes a clear, dancing hazel, full of laughter and mockery. He was dressed in the height of fashion, but he wore his evening clothes carelessly, as if they were utterly unimportant to him. His mobile mouth quirked, as he raised an eyebrow and said, "I am committing a social solecism, of course. We have not been properly introduced. I hope you do not mind."

Laura eyed him silently for another moment, then said, "No, I suppose not. I can hardly tell as yet, can I?"

"A wit," he exclaimed, laughing. His eyes lit, little flecks of gold dancing in them, and his smile was beguiling.

Laura could not help returning it.

"Ah, that is better," he said. "You looked so very bored, and such an expression does not become a lovely face as does a smile. Where have you hidden yourself all these years? A ravishing creature like you might have had every bachelor in London at her feet."

Laura was not certain she liked this form of address, but she was not certain she did not either. She raised her eyebrows slightly. "You seem to know me," she said, "but you have not yet told me your name."

"Oh yes, everyone has heard of Eliot's beautiful new wife. And a great many are very eager to meet you. I am shamelessly stealing a march on them. You may be interested to know that you have been set down as a diamond of the first water, Mrs. Crenshaw."

"Really?" replied Laura. She looked at the man inquiringly.

"You are wondering why I do not tell you my name. To be honest, I am afraid to." He smiled mischievously and then, seeing that Laura did not laugh, said, "I am Jack Allenby, you see. Scores of people have told you that I am beneath your notice, I wager."

Laura nearly started when she learned his identity; something cold seemed to move in her stomach again. This was the woman's husband. She looked at him. "Not scores," she answered.

He laughed again. "But some have, is that it? Well I expected nothing less. The tattlemongers do not approve of me at all. I am the terror of mothers with young daughters; they frighten them with threats that I shall jump from behind a curtain and say boo."

Laura was forced to laugh. "Indeed?"

"Well not precisely... but it is true that the old tabbies have no use for me at all. I never bother to speak to them, you see."

"Perhaps you should."

He looked scandalized. "What? When I could be talking with you? I am not a madman, Mrs. Crenshaw, only a little unwise, shall we say, at times."

Laura looked down. "I understand you are a friend of my husband," she said. Mr. Allenby's open admiration made her a bit uncomfortable; she had never received such frank compliments.

The corners of his mouth twitched. "Yes indeed. I have known Eliot since we were in short coats. We were at school together, you know."

"Really?"

He nodded. "Eliot was a year ahead of me, of course, and much my superior in the classroom, but we brushed along more or less amiably because of our mutual interest in horses."

Laura nodded.

"And so, when we came to London, we spent many a convivial evening together, though not often of late. Eliot is becoming quite a settled man, I fear, while I remain shockingly wild. 'Tis a sad thing. But come, let us talk about you. I pushed myself forward to make your acquaintance, after all. How do you like London? You are from the country, I believe?"

"Yes. However, I like London very well. It is an exciting place."

Her companion nodded. "It is that. Everything can be had here, whatever the taste. What is yours?" His eyes danced as he gazed directly into hers.

"Why, I, I enjoy the theatre," stammered Laura. Something in the way he spoke made her feel clumsy and young. "And the parties, of course. I have been in town only a short time."

"Yes. It requires time." He seemed slightly apologetic for making her uncomfortable.

Before Laura could reply, another voice broke into the conversation. "Good evening, Jack." It was Eliot, and Laura felt both relief and something like chagrin. Was she being watched over, like a child?

"Eliot, old man," Mr. Allenby replied. "I was just enjoying a talk with your wife. I congratulate you again."

Eliot bowed his head. "I am sorry to interrupt," he said, "but your sister is looking for you, Laura."

Laura looked up at him. She did not believe this statement, for she had seen Clarissa dancing only a moment ago. She was not certain she was pleased at Eliot's interference. "Is she?" she answered coolly. "I must go to her then."

"Foul, Eliot," said Mr. Allenby gaily. "I cry foul. It is not fair of you."

Eliot ignored this, and after a moment Laura said, "You will excuse me, Mr. Allenby?" and took her leave.

The two men watched her walk away. "Lovely," Mr. Allenby said.

Eliot turned to him again, eyeing him measuringly. "Take care, Jack," he said. "You venture into deep waters."

"Because I talk to your wife, Crenshaw?" he said. "Whatever can you mean? You will make me think she is less the lovely innocent than she appears."

The lines beside Eliot's mouth deepened for a moment, and his eyes narrowed. Then, with a shrug, he moved away.

Mr. Allenby stared after him speculatively. "Discomfited you there," he murmured. "How curious. This could be amusing indeed." Then he too sauntered off.

Eight

LAURA ROSE EARLY THE NEXT DAY DESPITE HER LATE night, and she was finished with breakfast in good time. It was her day to go over the accounts with Mr. Dunham. She went straight to the library and sat down at the desk. The room was now tidy, the books on the shelves at last. As she waited for her husband's stern valet to arrive, she moved in the chair a bit. She dreaded these sessions.

Mr. Dunham entered the library just at the stroke of nine, punctual as ever. He carried the large brown leather household account book and a sheaf of bills. Setting these on the desk, he bowed and wished her good morning. His usual impassivity was accentuated by the serious expression he habitually assumed for these occasions.

He showed her the week's entries in the book and the corresponding bills, carefully explaining the cook's reasons for ordering a larger amount of butter than usual and the various small purchases in other areas. When he came to the question of sheets, Laura nearly giggled. "We have been forced to procure cloth for some new sheets, ma'am," he said stiffly. "One of the maids was careless. If you approve, I mean to set her to sewing the new ones."

Laura nodded. "That is a good idea. Perhaps she will be more careful in the future."

"You knew of this then?"

"Yes. But as she was very sorry, I thought it best to let it pass."

Mr. Dunham bowed his head. He looked, if anything, stiffer than ever. "I see," he replied.

Laura heard a hint of reproof. Perhaps the man thought she should have informed him of the incident? Her mouth tightened a bit. "You know a great deal about household management, Mr. Dunham," she said. "It is quite amazing."

"I have managed for Mr. Crenshaw since he set up on his own," answered Mr. Dunham. There was both pride and resentment in his voice.

Laura realized suddenly that the man was jealous of her. It was not that he resented the tasks put upon him, but rather that he feared to have them usurped. She looked at him more closely. His eyes, held rigidly straight in front of him, were stoney. It seemed unlikely that she would ever win him over. Still she said. "You do a splendid job. I don't know how we would get along without you."

He bowed. "Thank you, ma'am." He began to gather up the loose bills into a neat pile. "If there is nothing else then?"

"No thank you, Mr. Dunham."

He picked up the account book and papers and left the room. Laura sighed a little. Like everything else about her situation, Mr. Dunham was both good and bad. He managed the house superbly—she certainly could not have done half so well without him—but he also made it more difficult for her. She sighed again. Nothing was simple anymore.

She sat for a moment, then rose and went up to the drawing room, finding Clarissa there. "You had a short walk," she said to her, surprised. The younger girl had been out with Anne Rundgate, and she rarely returned from such expeditions before luncheon.

Clarissa looked up, smiling with suspicious vivacity. "I came back early."

"Why?"

Clarissa looked at her speculatively. "Do you promise not to scold me?"

"No," replied Laura. "I dare not promise any such thing. What have you done?"

Clarissa frowned. "I'm not sure I will tell you."

"Clarissa."

"Oh very well. It is nothing really. There is a certain young officer, you see, who is much smitten with Anne. He really is a charming boy, and Anne likes him very well. But her mother thinks he is not sufficiently rich. Did you know, Laura, that Anne will have a large portion when she weds? Mrs. Rundgate fears that Captain Wetmore is more interested in the money than in Anne. But she is quite wrong."

Laura had begun to frown. "What have you done?"

Clarissa pouted. "Nothing, I tell you. Captain Wetmore joined us on our walk in the park, and I simply left them there to talk for a few minutes. It is nothing so scandalous. Anne's maid was with us, and she stayed."

"You arranged a clandestine meeting between Anne Rundgate and a man her mother disapproves of. Clarissa!"

"Oh I knew you would be stuffy. And I did nothing of the kind. You make it sound horrid. We met the captain quite by chance. I did not arrange anything. And Mrs. Rundgate does not precisely disapprove. She just…"

"Yes?"

"Well she is just mistaken. And I am sure she will realize it soon. Anne is in a fair way to falling in love, Laura, and she is too timid to do anything for herself. I had to help her, don't you see?"

"No, I do not. And I forbid you to do anything of the kind again."

Clarissa jumped up. "Forbid me? You are not my guardian, Laura."

"You are in my charge," retorted the other, "and I must see that you do not get into scrapes."

"You must see?" Clarissa's hot temper was rapidly getting the better of her. "You? What do you know of London? I can look after myself as well as you can. Better!"

"I am a married woman," began Laura.

"Married!" exclaimed Clarissa. "Oh yes, and we both know what sort of marriage it was and is." Both girls gasped at this remark, Clarissa at her own temerity and Laura out of shock. She paled, but before she could reply, Clarissa gathered up her skirts and ran out of the room.

It was a moment before Laura could collect herself. Her sister's hasty remark had hurt. She sat down on the sofa and took several deep breaths. When she was calmer, she admitted to herself that Clarissa had been right. Her marriage was no marriage, and she could not claim any greater knowledge of the world than her sister. Her husband spent his time with another woman, and there seemed to be nothing she could do about it. This thought hurt even more, and she had to take another long breath. She shook her head to clear it. She had done a great deal of thinking in the last few weeks, and she felt she had aged more than Clarissa, and learned more. Laura gave a quick nod. That was it. She did feel she could give advice, in spite of her inexperience. A quarter of an hour had already passed, and Laura rose to go after Clarissa.

Upstairs, she tapped on the door of Clarissa's bedroom and opened it slightly, then all the way. There was no one in the room. The dress Clarissa had been wearing was crumpled in a heap by the dressing table, but there was no other sign that she had been in the room since morning. Laura looked about worriedly. Where had her sister gone in her angry mood? She went over to the bell pull and rang for Nancy. After a while she rang again.

Finally Betty, the little kitchen maid, peered fearfully into the room. "Yes ma'am," she said in a scared voice.

Laura raised her eyebrows. "Where is Nancy? Or Mary?"

"Beggin' your pardon, ma'am, but they're out just now."

"Oh. Have they been gone long?"

Betty gave a nervous curtsy. "I'm not certain, ma'am. I've been peelin' the vegetables, I have, and I don't know nothin' about it."

"Very well. Thank you." Laura walked back down to the drawing room meditatively. Her first worry was dissolving with the notion that Clarissa was playing a prank. Her sister had been angry and rebellious, so it seemed likely that she had gone out without a word to show Laura that she was not to be ruled. She sighed and sat down. There was nothing to do but wait until Clarissa chose to come home—there never was when Clarissa did something foolish.

The morning passed slowly. Eliot was out, and no one called. The book she was reading seemed to have lost its hold on her. She was by turns angry with her sister, concerned over her, and sad. They had never quarreled so waspishly before.

⋘⋙

It was nearly two before she heard sounds in the hall below heralding Clarissa's return. And the noise seemed much louder than necessary. Laura rose and went to the stairs. Halfway down, she paused bemusedly to gaze at the spectacle before her.

Mr. Dunham had just admitted several people to the house. Clarissa, Mary, and Nancy were accompanied by a tall young man, standing with his back to Laura. But odder than this was Clarissa's dress. She wore what appeared to be one of Nancy's shabbier gowns, and she had her fashionably cut ringlets tied up in a patchwork scarf. Clogs completed her unusual outfit, Laura saw amazedly, and she had a smudge of dirt on her nose.

At this moment Clarissa looked up and saw Laura. "Hello!" she cried gaily. "You will never guess what has happened."

Laura had to smile a little. "I am afraid to try," she replied. "What have you been up to now?"

Clarissa laughed. "Please do not scold me," she begged. "You have every right to, but I am heartily sorry for my foolishness, I promise you. And this gentleman has very gallantly rescued me, so you see there is no harm done."

The gentleman had turned at Clarissa's first words, and Laura could see that he was a pleasant-faced, well-bred man. "I think you had best come up and tell me about it," she said. And as Nancy and Mary made as if to go to the kitchen, Laura added, "*All* of you."

The group came upstairs and stood rather sheepishly before Laura, who had seated herself on the sofa. "Clarissa?" she said.

Her sister looked down. "Well, I have been foolish, but I am sorry. I was very angry when I left you, you know, though I had no right to be. When I reached my room, Nancy was there, and I suddenly remembered that she had promised to take me to Bartholomew Fair one day. So I said we should go now."

"Clarissa!" exclaimed her sister. "You know that is not a proper place…"

"Yes, yes, I know. And for once it seems the old biddies are right. But I was not thinking. I wanted to do something you would not like."

"Well you certainly did that."

Clarissa looked guilty. "Yes. Well… and so Nancy brought me these clothes. She said I could not wear my own without attracting undue attention. And she fetched Mary, and we sneaked out." Her face changed. "And oh Laura, it was such fun at first. It is in a great field, and there are booths everywhere and so many people. It was very exciting. But then…" She paused and looked down.

"Yes?" prompted Laura sternly.

"Then a very unpleasant man began to speak to us and walk along with us. I told him to go, but he paid no attention. And then he tried to take my arm, and I pushed him away. It was a little frightening." She brightened again. "But Mr. Redmon came along just then and rescued me. You should have seen it, Laura. He knocked the man to the ground with one blow. It was heroic."

Laura turned her full attention to the young man for the first time. "Mr. Redmon," she murmured, trying to recall where she had heard that name before. Then, as she looked at the man more closely, she recognized him as the one who had opened the ball with Anne Rundgate. "But you're…" she began.

"I'm very happy to have been of service," he interrupted quickly. "It's very lucky I happened by." His eyes looked into Laura's intently, as if asking something of her.

"It is indeed, ah, Mr. Redmon. We are very grateful to you."

"My pleasure," he said.

Frowning, Laura surveyed him. Yes, it was definitely the same man, the *Marquess* Redmon. He was tall and stocky, with brown hair and forthright blue eyes. His complexion was ruddy and his hands somewhat calloused. He looked exactly like a country squire rigged up in town dress. There was nothing to show that he was in reality the eldest son of a duke.

"I should leave you now," he continued. "But I hope I may call tomorrow to see that you have fully recovered, Miss Lindley?"

"That would be very kind," answered Clarissa.

He bowed. "Mrs. Crenshaw?"

"What? Oh yes, I should like to talk with you."

"And I with you." He bowed again and took his leave.

Dismissing him for the moment, Laura turned back to the others. "Now," she said.

"Oh isn't he wonderful," exclaimed Clarissa before she could speak. "Like a hero in a novel."

Laura raised her eyebrows a bit at this exaggeration. "He seems quite nice. But I wish to talk about you." Her gaze included the maids. "All of you."

With the departure of the gentleman, Mary and Nancy found their tongues again. A torrent of apologies and justifications for their escapade tumbled out. "Lor, ma'am, we never meant no harm. I never would ha' thought anyone would bother Miss Clarissa. Please, ma'am, don't tell Mr. Dunham." And so on.

Laura held up a hand for quiet. "Enough," she said. The maids fell silent, and she looked at them. "You know you have done wrong, and I shall not scold you anymore, especially since it was as much Clarissa's fault as yours. But see to it that no such thing happens again. Is that clear?"

"Oh yes, ma'am. Thank you, ma'am," said both girls.

"We was only trying to show Miss Clarissa a bit of fun," put in Nancy. "Our sort of fun, you know, ma'am." Laura nodded. "You had better return to your duties now." They curtsied quickly and hurried from the room. Laura turned to Clarissa, whose eyes were far away. "As for you," she said, "I know you were angry with me, and I apologize for speaking hastily to you, but it was very foolish to try to get even with such a silly prank. You might have been hurt, Clarissa."

"What?" replied her sister dreamily.

Laura looked at her sharply. "What is the matter with you?"

"I was just thinking. Isn't he handsome?"

"Who? You mean, ah, Mr. Redmon? Clarissa, you are being silly."

This got the girl's attention. "Silly? Because I think Mr. Redmon is handsome? But he is."

"He is well enough, but that is beside the point. I am trying to bring you to a sense of the foolishness of what you have done."

Clarissa smiled mischievously. "But if I had not done it, I would not have met Mr. Redmon, and I am persuaded that that will be a very important happening in my life." She looked abstracted again. "Yes, I am sure of it," she murmured.

Laura stared at her sister. The sight of Clarissa acting like a mooncalf was a new one. "Well you might have met him somewhere else, I should think. Whatever must he think of you, after such an introduction?"

Clarissa looked up sharply. "He thinks I am unaffected and very adventurous," she retorted. "He told me so."

Laura sighed. "Indeed. Perhaps he was being polite."

"No," insisted her sister. She said it again, more softly. "No. He meant it. I could tell. I think he likes me, Laura."

Clarissa's tone was so happy and ingenuous that Laura had to relent. "I'm sure he does, but will you not listen to me for a moment?"

The younger girl fumed to her. "There is no need. I know what you wish to say, and I agree with you. I was silly and foolish and anything else you like. I shall not do it again, and I sincerely apologize to you for my shocking rudeness this morning. There, is that all right?" She did not wait for an answer but plunged ahead. "Do you think we might invite Mr. Redmon to dinner some night next week, Laura? We could ask him when he calls tomorrow."

"If you like," answered Laura, a little overwhelmed at this flood of docility.

"I can wear my apricot crepe," murmured Clarissa.

"Whom else do you wish to have?"

"What? Why, no one else. There is no one else I wish to see."

Laura shook her head. "We cannot possibly invite a single gentleman to dine alone with us, Clarissa."

"Why not?"

"It isn't done."

Clarissa grimaced, then her face cleared. "Well Eliot can stay home to dinner, can he not? It is only for one night. We must ask him."

"I suppose that would do," replied Laura slowly, "if he is free, of course."

"Well we shall make it when he is. I shall ask him

as soon as he comes in." Clarissa bounced out of her seat. "Oh I am so happy," she cried, as she moved toward the door.

"But Clarissa, you..." began Laura, though it was obvious that her sister did not hear. She watched the younger girl drift out to the stairs and start up to her room. Laura shook her head. What next? she wondered to herself.

Nine

AT TEATIME ELIOT STROLLED INTO THE DRAWING ROOM and accepted the cup Laura poured for him. Clarissa took this opportunity to ask him to dine with a friend of hers the following Friday, and he agreed absently. After a few minutes of desultory chatter, Clarissa excused herself and went upstairs, leaving Laura and Eliot alone.

Laura watched her run up the stairs. "It is the oddest thing," she said to Eliot. "The friend Clarissa was speaking of is the Marquess Redmon. I recognized him as the man you pointed out to me at the ball, but he introduced himself to her as merely Mr. Redmon. And when he brought Clarissa home today, he gave me the unmistakable signal that he did not wish his real name mentioned." After she had spoken, Laura put a hand to her mouth. She had not meant to bring up the subject of Clarissa's scrape.

But Eliot did not appear much interested. "Redmon is a funny chap," was his only reply.

"I suppose so. He seems quite nice, however."

"Umm." Eliot turned toward Laura like a man

coming to a decision. "I wish to talk with you about something important," he said abruptly.

Laura bowed her head, a little resenting this offhand dismissal of her story.

"It concerns a man you met at the ball last evening."

"A man?" asked Laura. "I met so many people." But she began to suspect what was to follow.

"I refer to Mr. Allenby," he answered, a bit stiffly.

"Oh yes, your friend. A very amusing man."

"He is that, certainly. It is one of his talents. But we are not such good friends any longer."

Laura's jaw hardened a little as she thought that it was no wonder, since Mr. Allenby's wife had become Eliot's mistress. But she said nothing.

"I am sorry that you found Jack Allenby so amusing, Laura, for I'm going to ask you expressly not to see him."

She raised her eyebrows, feigning surprise. "Really? Why?" She watched his eyes. "Does he, like his wife, skirt too near the line?" Laura felt greatly daring as she said this. For some reason she wished to force Eliot to tell her the truth, aloud and openly. If he will only say it, she thought, that Mr. Allenby is the husband of his mistress, I will do what he asks. But she trembled with tension awaiting his reply.

"He does," responded her husband shortly. "His reputation is shocking, especially of late. No lady of quality would be seen with him."

Bridling a little at this implied criticism, Laura said, "But he is at all the best parties, I know. Even Mrs. Rundgate asked him. And everyone speaks to him. I don't understand."

For a moment Eliot seemed at a loss. "That is true.

His behavior is perhaps not well known in all circles, and some do not disapprove. But it is one thing to chat with such a man briefly at a party and quite another to receive him at home, or go about with him."

Again Laura raised her eyebrows. She was getting angry at Eliot's hypocrisy. "But I have done no such thing. Did someone tell you I had?"

Eliot made an impatient gesture and rose to stand near the fire. "No, of course not. And I would pay no heed to gossip. But you are pulling this conversation quite off the mark, Laura. What is the matter with you? The last time we had such a talk, you were ready to comply with my wishes." He sounded annoyed. "It comes down to this. I have some reason to believe that Jack Allenby is no longer a friend to me. In fact I begin to think that he would do me an evil turn if the opportunity came his way. There have been some losses at cards and so on. Jack is very vain about his skills and hates to be beaten. And other things. I do not wish you to be involved."

Laura was silent for a moment. She did not put much credence in Eliot's talk of cards, knowing as she did a much more compelling reason why Mr. Allenby might dislike her husband, and she felt both hurt and angry that he would not admit the truth. She resented being expected to obey when she was told nothing, particularly when all London knew.

He is still treating me like a child, she thought. She looked up at Eliot with a touch of defiance. "Oh I think you must be mistaken," she said. "Mr. Allenby seemed to me a very pleasant and polite man. Perhaps you misunderstood something he said, a joke."

Her husband's expression became set. He was beginning to be angry. Laura was his wife, and he felt it was her duty to do as he asked. "I have told you my wishes in this matter," he said stiffly. "I consider the subject closed. You will not receive Jack Allenby."

Laura's eyes blazed. "Indeed? And I am to say no more and ask no more, is that it? I am to do as I am told with no word of complaint and no question? Unfair!" She was thoroughly angry now, and it made no difference to her that the issue was a trivial one. Perhaps she did not care whether she ever saw Mr. Allenby again, but she bitterly resented being ordered about in this way.

The corners of Eliot's mouth turned down. "You are being ridiculous and childish. You know very well that my knowledge of the world is far beyond yours. In effect you refuse to trust me or obey me."

"You are treating me like a child," retorted the girl hotly. "Tell me the truth... so that I may judge for myself. Tell me the reasons for your advice." This last sounded almost pleading.

"I don't know what you mean. I have done so."

"You have not," cried Laura. "You have not!"

Eliot looked at her coldly. It seemed to him that she was being irrational, for no thoughts of Vera Allenby had intruded upon him during this discussion. She did not occupy a position of importance in his mind at any time. And now he was too incensed to think logically.

"You are upset," he said. His jaw was tight, and he looked at her from under half-closed eyelids. Laura's cheeks glowed with her emotion, and anger made her eyes flash gloriously, but he was unaffected. "If you do not choose to heed me," he continued tonelessly, "then I must take other measures." He bowed and turned to leave the room.

"What do you mean, other measures?" asked Laura uncertainly.

He looked back. "Since my opinions are of so little value to you, my course of action can be of no interest."

His tone made Laura shiver, "And that is all?" she cried as he reached the door. "That is all you will say to me?"

"I do not see that there is anything further to say. I asked a small thing of you, and you refused. The subject is closed." He turned away.

Laura jumped up, tears beginning to fill her eyes. She held out both hands and tried to speak. Couldn't Eliot understand that she simply could not bear the thought of Vera Allenby, of his holding her and loving her, as he had never shown a sign of doing with Laura? But she was too choked by tears to speak, and Eliot walked out without realizing she had tried.

Laura heard the front door open and close, and she sank back on the sofa, gradually regaining control. What was the matter with her, she wondered. Two quarrels in one day, first with Clarissa and now with her husband. Even granting that they both had been exasperating, such quick hostility was utterly unlike her. She drew a shaky breath and leaned back.

Until now Laura had always been the most concili-ating of personalities. She and her sister had been oppo-sites in this since they were small children. Clarissa was hot-tempered and hasty and Laura equable and cool. Their aunts had remarked upon it countless times.

Now, she thought as she sat alone in her drawing room, everything seemed changed. She had never in her life lashed out as she had today. Twice today! She frowned and tried to think clearly, but her emotions got in the way. Her earlier anger returned as she remembered the way Eliot had spoken to her. He had no right. He did exactly as he pleased, then expected her to obey his every whim. It wasn't fair.

A small smile lit her features. She could show him she was not a mindless doll, to be ordered here or there. "I shall see Mr. Allenby," she said aloud. "I feel no particular liking for him, but that is all to the good for I shall not be in danger of succumbing to his no doubt exaggerated charms." Allenby admired her, she thought. Perhaps this would make Eliot see her as a woman. Her smile broadened.

Laura found no immediate opportunity to carry out her resolve, but she did not forget it. She was thinking of Mr. Allenby, in fact, when Clarissa's new friend made his call just before teatime the following afternoon. Laura was sitting in the drawing room alone when he was announced. She rose to greet him and told Mr. Dunham that Clarissa should be informed of his arrival.

"In five minutes, please," Mr. Redmon put in. When Laura looked at him with raised eyebrows, he added, "I wish to speak with you first."

Mr. Dunham went out, looking disapproving, and Laura sat down again. "Won't you sit down?"

He smiled nervously. "Not just at first, I think. You must find it rather odd that I introduced myself to your sister as *Mr.* Redmon. You know who I am, it appears?"

Laura nodded.

"Yes. Well it is a bit difficult to explain, but I would like to ask that you do not tell Miss Lindley. It seems that she is unaware of my family connections, and I would very much like to become better acquainted with her before she knows."

Laura looked perplexed. "Why?"

The marquess' ruddy face creased with the effort of explanation. "You see, I don't care much for society. I prefer the country and my land to dancing and that sort of nonsense." He smiled rather sheepishly. "I am my mother's despair. And the thing I dislike most is the society ladies. I can't think what to say to them half the time, and they seem silly and artificial to me. But the thing is, they always pretend that I'm a devil of a fellow." He flushed. "I beg your pardon... I mean, they always act as if I were deucedly witty and clever and, and quite the most amusing chap they have ever come across." The corners of his lips turned down. "It is all because of my position, you see. Most of them wouldn't care if I was a hunchback or an idiot. It makes me so angry, sometimes I want to hit them." He struck his open hand with a doubled fist. "Can you understand what I mean, Mrs. Crenshaw?"

Laura looked at him. "I believe I can."

He smiled gratefully. "And then I met your sister, ma'am. She did not know me, being new in town. I don't go about much, you see, only when I'm forced."

"Yes, I noticed you did not stay at the Rundgates' ball after the first set," said Laura teasing him a little.

He looked down. "No, I slipped out. Rude of me, I suppose, but I only went because my mother promised

Mrs. Rundgate." He met Laura's eyes squarely. "At any rate I liked your sister when we met; and just once I should like to get to know a girl without trading on my title. That is why I did not tell her, and that is why I ask you not to do so. It is up to you, of course."

Laura surveyed him. His face showed only honest anxiety that she agree and a sort of tired hope that she found extremely touching. "All right," she said. "I shall not tell her. But I can hardly see how you will conceal your identity. Someone is bound to mention it."

"I suppose so. But I shall try to avoid those who know me when Miss Lindley is present. I believe I may have given her the impression that I am a little behind with the world just now and of an unknown country family." He watched anxiously for Laura's reaction to this.

She could not resist teasing him a bit more. "You have lied to my sister?" she asked sternly, raising her eyebrows.

"No, no. I never would. But I, well I did not tell her all the truth." He looked so guilty that Laura could not help but laugh.

"Well the truth will come out soon enough, I daresay. But you may count on me. It is ironic. Clarissa always…" She stopped abruptly; she had nearly told him that her sister had always sworn to marry a duke.

"What?"

"Nothing. Shall I tell Clarissa you are here now?"

"Yes, thank you," he faltered, his expression eager. Laughing again, Laura went up to fetch her sister.

She found Clarissa sitting by her bedroom window, and when she told her that Mr. Redmon had arrived, the younger girl sprang up immediately. "Is he here? I was watching, but I did not see him come." Her voice was full of ingenuous happiness.

The two sisters returned to the drawing room together. The look Laura saw the two young people exchange as she and her sister entered said a great deal. They are in a fair way to being in love, she thought, and she felt a pang of joy and sadness mixed.

As they talked, it soon appeared that Clarissa and her admirer had many tastes in common. The sisters asked Mr. Redmon about his home, and he obligingly described the countryside and his horses, making it obvious that these were among his dearest concerns.

"Where do you hunt?" asked Clarissa. "That is something I would like to try."

"You do not hunt?" replied Mr. Redmon eagerly. "I have a young filly nearly grown that should suit you down to the ground, Miss Lindley. How I wish you could try her."

"Yes," agreed Clarissa, "I should like it above all things. Perhaps I can see her sometime. In what county is your home?"

Mr. Redmon looked down. "Millshire," he said, dampening. "Do you ride in town?"

Diverted, the girl shook her head. "At least I have not as yet. But I am getting a mount." She winked at her sister.

Laura smiled. "You may find trotting in the park very slow."

Clarissa nodded.

"Especially after Bartholomew Fair," put in the gentleman mischievously.

Clarissa dimpled and wrinkled her nose at him. "Especially," she agreed. "Did you see…" And they were off on a rousing discussion of the various attractions of this admirable pleasure ground. Laura was highly amused at their descriptions.

"You almost make me wish to visit," she said after they had painted the "nature's marvels" booth in particularly vivid colors. "It sounds quite fabulous."

"What is that, my dear?" said a cool emotionless voice from the doorway. And Eliot strolled languidly into the room.

Laura's heart began to pound. It was the first time she had seen her husband since their quarrel. And now she had revealed Clarissa's scrape to him, and in so doing exposing them all to his displeasure. She clenched a fist in annoyance.

But Mr. Redmon came to her rescue. "I was attempting to amuse the ladies with a description of Bartholomew Fair, sir."

"Ah. So that is where you spend your time, Redmon. You prefer it to the clubs, do you?"

The younger man flushed a little at this thrust, and Laura cringed at her husband's tone. It was the same he had used with her yesterday. But Mr. Redmon was not so easily daunted. "Not at all," he replied. "But I took a fancy to visit the other day. It is an amazing place."

Eliot nodded uninterestedly, and the subject was dropped. The conversation became stilted and difficult. Clarissa seemed embarrassed and awkward, and

Mr. Redmon had little to say under the eye of the older man. Laura, the memory of their disagreement uppermost in her mind, was nearly silent. Only Eliot seemed unaffected. He chatted for a time, then rose again. "I must be off. I came in chiefly to inform you, Laura, that I shall be going out of town for a few days, perhaps a week. Elsmere has invited a group up to his hunting box for some runs."

"Very well," answered Laura. She was angry with him for telling her this so carelessly. He showed no feeling at all, and it must look odd to a stranger that he would speak so.

"I shall see you next week then," he finished, and he left the room.

The mood having been broken, Mr. Redmon took his leave soon after. The dinner invitation was duly delivered and accepted, and he left with the promise to call again soon. When he was gone, Clarissa went into raptures once more. She was far too occupied with her own feelings to notice Laura's preoccupation. Her paean was interrupted only by the necessity of going upstairs to change for dinner, and it continued throughout the meal in one form or another.

Laura listened with half an ear while she thought about her own situation. Eliot was quite clearly reprimanding her by going off in this way. She set her jaw. They would see whether he could cow her. Her expression was so defiant that Clarissa noticed and asked if there was anything the matter. Laura shook her head. "Nothing at all, my dear," she said. "Quite the contrary."

Ten

THE NEXT MORNING LAURA SUGGESTED TO HER SISTER that they take a walk in the park, and, Clarissa being agreeable, they set out about eleven. Laura's anger had cooled only a little and she half hoped they would encounter Mr. Allenby, or even his wife, giving her the opportunity to speak to them and flout her husband's commands. She wished to make Eliot regret that he had spoken so harshly to her, and perhaps to make him apologize. She found, as she considered the matter, that it was somehow very important that he do so and that they settle their quarrel soon.

Thus, as the two sisters strolled about the paths in the park, where the first crocuses and daffodils were just beginning to bloom, both kept a sharp eye on the other morning walkers, Clarissa hoping to see Mr. Redmon. But both were to be disappointed. They saw neither Clarissa's new friend nor the Allenbys, and Laura had just suggested that they turn toward home when they were hailed from behind and discovered Lord Timothy Farnsworth and Sir Robert coming up with them. Laura groaned softly, making her sister giggle.

"Hello," cried Lord Farnsworth cheerfully. "Fancy coming upon you like this. Quite a stroke of luck. Meant to call today, you know."

"No, did you?" replied Clarissa.

"Yes, indeed. Lovely day, what? Sun, air, flowers." He gestured vaguely toward the side of the path.

The two gentlemen were very splendid this morning. The bright colors of their waistcoats and the glitter of the rings and fobs with which they had bedecked themselves were almost too much in the clear sunshine. Sir Robert had daringly replaced his neckcloth with a spotted kerchief knotted carelessly around his throat. He affected a marvelous nonchalance about this innovation, but an uneasy look in his eyes suggested that he was not entirely satisfied with the effect.

In fact one odiously high-nosed old gentleman had already put him quite out of countenance by raising his quizzing glass and saying quite audibly to his companion, "Whatever are the young men coming to these days, March? That fellow is wearing a neckerchief precisely like my groom's."

Thus Sir Robert was not quite himself just now, and after muttering a brief greeting to the ladies, he resumed his jealous scanning of the other strollers for signs that they were critical of his attire.

"We were just about to turn back," said Laura, in hopes of evading the two dandies.

"Famous," replied Lord Farnsworth. "We'll escort you home."

Chagrined, Laura exclaimed, "There is not the least need for that. We do not wish to trouble you."

But they would not allow that it was any trouble, and the group turned onto the path leading toward the gate and Laura's house. Lord Farnsworth kept up a flow of commonplaces, Clarissa occasionally supporting him, and they reached Regent Street soon after.

The gentlemen came in with them despite the hints Laura threw out, Lord Farnsworth continuing a very boring story about the rout he had attended the previous evening, then moving on to the ball they had all danced at not long since. As he said this, he cast a languishing glance at Clarissa, attempting, Laura supposed, to further the absurd fiction that he was smitten with her.

Just then Mr. Dunham entered to announce another caller, and Laura rose with some surprise to greet Mr. Allenby. Somehow she had not imagined that he would call on her so openly.

"Good morning," said Mr. Allenby, taking her hand with a winning smile. "I was passing on my way to the club, and I thought I would just look in to tell you how much I enjoyed our little chat the other night. How are you?"

"Very well, thank you. Please come and sit down."

He looked around the room, his hazel eyes twinkling irresistibly. "Well I don't know that I will, actually, now that I see who is with you. I'm not certain I can stand up under both Lord Farnsworth and Sir Robert so early in the day. Would you think me abominably hen-hearted if I turn tail?"

"I would indeed," replied Laura, laughing, "and odiously unfeeling as well. I have been talking with them for nearly half an hour."

"You are a woman of fortitude. Allow me to compliment you. I perceive there are subtle depths to your character."

Laura shook her head. "How ridiculous you are. Do come in for a moment." They moved across to the sofa and sat down. The three gentlemen greeted one another stiffly. Lord Farnsworth and Sir Robert had gone a trifle glassy-eyed when Mr. Allenby appeared in the doorway. Putting up her chin, Laura ignored the speaking looks they directed at her and turned to talk to her new guest.

This gentleman was smiling at her. "You look the picture of haughtiness," he said. "What has put your back up? I hope it was not I?"

She smiled and shook her head.

"Thank God for that. I should not like to be the target of that look, I tell you frankly."

"Then you must mind your manners, Mr. Allenby," responded Laura teasingly.

"I shall," he promised.

"It was kind of you to call today. Our conversation was cut short at the ball."

"It was indeed. In fact I only dared come here because someone happened to mention that Eliot has gone out of town. I got the oddest notion that he does not wish us to become better acquainted."

Laura drew back slightly. "Very odd," she agreed faintly.

He watched her face. "Isn't it? He is becoming a positive dog in the manger. I hardly know him these days." Still surveying her, he changed the subject abruptly. "And so you are enjoying London?"

Laura looked up. "Everyone asks that. I am, very much."

"Alas, I have been guilty of a cliché. I shall never forgive myself."

She dimpled again. "One must sometimes resort to commonplaces, I suppose, else there would be no conversation."

But he shook his head. "I pride myself upon never doing so. It is my sole distinction, lacking as I do title, fortune, or godlike handsomeness. I have set up as a wit, but already you have punctured my pretensions. You are a dangerous woman, Mrs. Crenshaw."

Laura made a deprecating gesture and was about to reply in kind when Sir Robert broke into their conversation. "Handsome boots, Allenby," he said. "Hoby make them for you?" He was clearly determined to break up the tête-à-tête.

Casting a laughing glance at Laura, Mr. Allenby said, "Yes."

Sir Robert nodded. "Very handsome."

"That is quite a compliment, coming from you," answered the other man. "What do you think of the coat? I had Scott make it up for me with these brass buttons." The quizzing look he flung at her almost made Laura laugh outright.

Sir Robert was torn. He did not care for Mr. Allenby's coat at all; in fact it quite revolted his delicate sensibilities, but he could not say so. He had set himself to protect Laura from the attentions of a man whom she could not recognize, as did he, as a libertine of the worst stripe, and thus he must be conciliating. "Very... ah, very modish," he choked out, "something unusual about it, distinctive." Unable to restrain himself, he added, "But you know, old man, you might try mother-of-pearl. All the crack these days."

"Is it?" inquired Mr. Allenby innocently. "Well perhaps I shall. But I am extremely fond of brass buttons." He examined one of them. "In fact I was thinking just yesterday that I should have a fob made to match."

Sir Robert goggled, sputtered, and finally tottered away, defeated. He could not in conscience continue to talk with a man who would wear a brass fob.

When Sir Robert had returned to his seat beside Clarissa, Laura laughed delightedly. "What a complete hand you are," she told Mr. Allenby.

"Ah. You could do the same. Tell him that you have vowed to wear nothing but brown gloves, or that you prefer tucks to ruffles. The poor fellow cannot endure such brutalities."

Laura laughed again. "I couldn't."

A smile lit Mr. Allenby's eyes, and he rose. "I must go. My victory has exhausted me, and besides, I have a luncheon engagement."

Laura also stood, holding out her hand. "I am sorry."

He bowed over it. "Could I but believe you. Please say everything that is proper to your sister. I have been abominably rude not to talk to her, but tell her I refused to brave her companions. We will not let her know that I infinitely prefer conversing with you."

A little color sprang into Laura's cheeks, and she looked down.

Mr. Allenby watched her. "Tell me," he added as they walked toward the door of the drawing room, "are you so sorry to see me go that you will agree to come driving with me some day soon?" As she hesitated, he added, "Or have the gossips given you such a fear of me that it is impossible? I will not press you, never fear."

Laura raised her eyes; his hazel ones quizzed her. "Of course not," she replied quickly. "I should be delighted to go."

He bowed. "Splendid. Perhaps Tuesday next?"

Laura nodded, and he smiled at her again before leaving the room.

The other gentlemen left soon after, clearly uncomfortable. Then Mr. Dunham came in to announce luncheon. When they had finished, Laura suggested that they write to their aunts, but Clarissa was restless. "I believe I will go out again, to the library," she replied. "I want to exchange my novel. I finished it last night. You needn't come if you're tired. Nancy can accompany me."

Memories of the last time Nancy went out with Clarissa led Laura to say that she would certainly come, and they summoned the barouche to take them to Hookham's.

As they drove, Clarissa scanned the pavements and paid little attention to her sister's remarks. They reached the library and exchanged Clarissa's book without seeing anyone they knew. Clarissa looked disappointed as they prepared to step into the carriage once more.

"Shall we do some shopping as long as we are here?" asked Laura sympathetically.

But Clarissa shook her head. "No. I do not feel like shopping. We may as well go home again."

They were driving along a busy thoroughfare when Clarissa suddenly cried, "Stop," and the coachman pulled up abruptly. The tilbury behind them only just managed to avoid hitting their barouche, and the driver took instant exception to their abrupt move. Another behind him began to shout, and several pedestrians drifted nearer to see what the commotion was about. Laura put a hand to her forehead.

"Oh dear," said Clarissa, but she did not sound particularly sorry. She was waving to a gentleman on the other side of the street.

Laura recognized Mr. Redmon even as she said, "Clarissa, do stop. You are acting like a hoyden."

Eventually their coachman got the barouche pulled over to the side of the street, and the tilbury and hackney passed by, their drivers staring disgustedly at the trio now occupying the carriage. Laura was abashed, but Clarissa did not seem to notice. Mr. Redmon had been uneasy since he first caught sight of them, and now that he had climbed into their coach, he looked even more tense. Laura correctly assumed that fear of recognition occupied him more than embarrassment at having been hailed so abruptly. In this part of town, he might at any moment be greeted as "my lord."

"How funny that we should see you," Clarissa was saying lightly. "Quite a lucky coincidence." Laura smiled, for hadn't they been searching for Mr. Redmon practically the whole day?

"Very," replied the young man, glancing sidewise at the shops nearby. "I hope you will allow me to accompany you home?"

Clarissa agreed happily, and Laura continued to smile

as she watched Mr. Redmon slouch down as far as possible in his seat and pull his curly brimmed beaver down over his eyes a bit more.

"Were you shopping?" asked Clarissa. "We have just come from Hookham's. I am often there nowadays. We had no library in the neighborhood at Eversly, you see, so I am making up for lost time."

"Ah," replied the marquess, his eyes still on the street.

Clarissa began to look puzzled and a bit hurt. "I have become addicted to novels," she added. "I had read none until we came to town."

Mr. Redmon nodded.

Laura intervened. "That is one of the most pleasant advantages of town life," she put in, "the great diversity of entertainments. Having a circulating library nearby seems a luxury to us, but it is the merest commonplace to Londoners."

Neither of the others seemed disposed to reply to this trite statement; in fact they were both silent and uneasy now. So Laura continued, "After a while one begins to wonder how one ever got on without these diversions. It is a lowering reflection. Do you think we shall become utterly dependent on town gaieties?" She looked at her companions. Clarissa said nothing; she was frowning at Mr. Redmon.

The young man started. He had turned quickly to avoid the glance of a man he thought he knew, but as he looked back, he saw that it was someone else entirely. "What?" he said. "Oh yes, just so."

"You do think so?" Laura could not resist teasing him. His furtive demeanor and hunted looks were so ridiculous.

He stared at her. "I... that is, I'm not certain... I fear I did not catch what you said." A disarming smile softened this admission.

"I merely wondered whether the dissipations of town life will spoil us for the country," said Laura.

Mr. Redmon looked surprised, then shook his head decisively. "Couldn't," he said. "Why the country is much more amusing. You can't compare the two." He was relaxing more as they turned from the busy commercial streets onto quieter avenues.

"Well I am not so sure," answered Laura. "I cannot yet decide." They pulled up before her house, and Mr. Redmon jumped out to help the ladies down. Just as Laura was about to invite him in, a voice from the other side of the street interrupted.

"Redmon," cried the man just coming out of a house there, "just the man I want. I haven't seen you this age."

The marquess started and turned quickly. "Hello," he responded. He turned back to the sisters. "Sorry," he gulped, "must go. Very pleasant drive; nice to have seen you. I shall call again soon." And with these hasty words, he practically ran across the street and took the man's arm to guide him away.

"Say, aren't you going to present me?" the man protested, but Mr. Redmon pulled him away, and in a moment they disappeared around the corner of the street.

"Well," said Clarissa. She turned toward the door that Mr. Dunham was holding open. Her expression was compounded of chagrin, puzzlement, and hurt in about equal parts.

"I suppose Mr. Redmon had an engagement and was too polite to tell us so," suggested Laura.

"I would hardly call his behavior 'too polite,'" answered her sister with a sniff. "It was quite the opposite, in fact."

"But..." began Laura.

"Oh let us dispense with Mr. Redmon," snapped Clarissa, and picking up her skirts, she hurried into the house.

Eleven

WITH ELIOT OUT OF TOWN AND CLARISSA INDULGING in something very like a fit of sulks, Laura found the next few days a little flat and began to anticipate her drive with Mr. Allenby with more eagerness than she had expected to feel. Clarissa was going shopping with Anne Rundgate that Tuesday, and she had left the house by the time Mr. Allenby's phaeton pulled up before the door. No one but Mr. Dunham saw Laura go out and be helped into the vehicle or watched Mr. Allenby climb up beside her and take the ribbons.

At first Laura felt slightly uneasy. It was somehow a very different thing to vow independence than actually to carry it through. She was now defying her husband and doing something she herself knew to be imprudent, and she was not even sure she would enjoy it. Seated beside Mr. Allenby and riding through the streets of the West End, she felt the rebellion that had filled her begin to waver.

"Shall we simply tool about the park?" asked Mr. Allenby as they started off. "There will be a crowd there at this time of day."

Laura had a sudden vision of that crowd, all with shocked looks on their faces at the sight of Laura Crenshaw riding beside her husband's rival. "No," she replied quickly, "let us go somewhere else."

Mr. Allenby raised his eyebrows and smiled, but he said only, "Very well. What do you say to a look-in at Kew Gardens? The flowers should be well along now."

Laura nodded. They drove for a while in silence, the girl nervously pleating between her fingers the fringes of her paisley shawl. She had dressed carefully for this outing in a gown of blue muslin with a high neck and long sleeves. The curled plumes on her chip straw bonnet exactly matched it, and a buff parasol with a clear amber handle leaned against her knee. But though she knew she looked well, she could not relax.

"A lovely day," offered Mr. Allenby when he had guided his team through the busier streets near the park and was easing them into a trot.

"Yes," said Laura. She looked about her. The sun was shining, new leaves were coming out on a row of trees along the pavement, and crocuses and daffodils filled the window-boxes of several houses nearby. She took a deep breath of the fresh spring air and shook her head. It was too beautiful a day to waste in useless repinings. She turned toward Mr. Allenby. "I have not yet seen Kew Gardens. Are they very lovely?"

"Oh yes," answered her companion carelessly, "though I fear I am not a devotee of nature and the pastoral scene. I shan't be able to name every weed and bloom for you and tell you its history."

Laura laughed. "Good heavens. Could anyone?"

Mr. Allenby's eyes twinkled. "Indeed. Some of

our young sprigs are positively flower mad. They can recount the lineage and habits of scores of them, tell you the Latin and Greek names, and compose a sonnet on the spot featuring that particular blossom."

She shook her head. "You almost make me wish to hear them."

"Easily arranged. I could find you a round dozen in any drawing room."

Laura laughingly denied any such desire.

"Ah. Too bad. Shall I tell you, then, that you are looking exceedingly lovely today?" He cast a sidewise glance at her profile. "No, perhaps not. Well shall we discuss more serious matters? The progress of the elections, perhaps, or the King's health?"

"How ridiculous you are."

"Ah. No politics," he mused, then said, "Now I have it. I shall tell you tales of your husband as a grubby schoolboy. They say ladies never can resist stories of their spouses when young."

Laura shifted uneasily. The mention of Eliot brought back her doubts, and Mr. Allenby's tone only added to her discomfort. The man had an odd, careless way of talking. A constant undercurrent in his speech seemed to suggest that nothing he said was really important to him, or indeed of any importance whatsoever. He seemed to laugh at everything, especially himself.

"Shall I tell you about the time Eliot was caned for putting jam in the prefect's bed?" continued Mr. Allenby. "Or about our escape to the village one Saturday and the dissipations we enjoyed? We got another whipping for that, but we didn't care a rap, I can tell you."

Laura smiled. "What of your studies?"

"Alas. For my part I learned almost nothing. Eliot was a better scholar, though I doubt that even he could compose a Latin epigram for you now."

"Well I shouldn't understand it if he could. So it doesn't matter."

Mr. Allenby shook his head. "You are a difficult woman to amuse, Mrs. Crenshaw. I cannot seem to hit upon a topic. But here we are." He swung the carriage into the gardens. "Perhaps we will talk of flowers, after all."

Laura looked down, abashed.

Mr. Allenby pointed with his whip. "There, I believe, are hyacinths and daffodils, but I fear my knowledge does not encompass any other of these plants."

"That is a lovely willow," answered Laura. She strove to appear more at ease as they drove about the gardens and talked of the people she had met in London and the things she had seen. Mr. Allenby had very amusing opinions of some of the former. They had turned back and were heading toward town once more when he suddenly said, "You have not mentioned the masquerade. You have been to the play and to Vauxhall, and you will go to Almack's soon, you say, but have you seen one of the London masquerades?"

Laura signified that she had not.

"Ah, but you must."

"What are they?"

"They are great balls where everyone wears fancy dress or dominos and masks. They are vastly amusing. No one is known, you see, though one can often recognize one's friends."

"I have never heard of them."

"Infamous. You must allow me to escort you to the Pantheon then. Next week perhaps? I shall get up a party; we will have a splendid time."

Laura was taken aback. She had gone out with Mr. Allenby once, but had not thought further than that. Now, she was uncertain how to refuse his invitation. "I am not certain, I believe I have engagements for next week."

"Oh no," he cried gaily. "You must cancel them. Stuffy parties cannot compare with the Pantheon Masquerade, I promise you."

This remark made Laura even less inclined to accept. If Mr. Allenby thought the masquerades less stuffy, what must they be like? "I do not think…" she began but he interrupted. "Do not decide now. Think it over. You may tell me anytime this week."

"Well, but I…"

"No, no, I will not accept your answer now."

They were coming into busier streets again, and Mr. Allenby's attention was claimed at that moment by a cart before them. It took some time to maneuver around it with the press of pedestrians in the gap. Laura did not distract him with further objections. She could send a note of refusal, she thought. Indeed it would be easier. So when Mr. Allenby's attention was again turned to her, she allowed him to divert their talk into other channels.

❦

Clarissa returned about teatime, seemingly in a more cheerful frame of mind, and the sisters had tea together in the drawing room. When asked about her shopping expedition, Clarissa obligingly detailed her purchases: two pairs of gloves, some silk stockings, and a branch of artificial flowers she thought would look well with her ball gown. She did not ask Laura what she had been doing, for which the older girl was grateful, but instead added, "And I received a note from Mr. Redmon when I returned. He apologized for his haste the other day. You were right; he did have a pressing engagement."

Laura nodded.

"You know, it is the oddest thing, Laura," continued her sister, "but no one seems to be acquainted with Mr. Redmon. I have asked Anne and several others, but they have not met him. Jane Sandridge thought I meant some marquess; only fancy, there is a Marquess Redmon also. I suppose it must be the name of a town. But the thing is, you do not think... that is, I begin to wonder whether Mr. Redmon..." She looked at Laura helplessly.

Laura raised her eyebrows. "You are beginning to wonder whether he is an eligible party?"

"No! Of course I do not. What an old cattish thing to say." She noted her sister's expression. "Oh. You are roasting me. But I am perfectly serious, I promise you. I have begun to wonder whether Mr. Redmon may not be run off his legs." She grinned. "That means out of money."

"Does it?" replied Laura blandly, refusing to rise to this challenge.

"Yes, and I have been thinking. Perhaps Mr. Redmon cannot afford to join in all the festivities

of the season. I believe it is very expensive to hire
lodgings and so on." She looked down ruefully at her
modish gown. "I never had considered it properly
before. But I believe Mr. Redmon comes from a
country family only moderately well off. Perhaps he
is feeling pinched and… well, embarrassed. He might,
don't you think? And so he would keep to himself and
not mingle with members of the *ton*."

"Perhaps," agreed Laura. "Or there may be some
other explanation. Perhaps he simply doesn't care
for society." Under Clarissa's anxious gaze, she was
finding the deception she had agreed to more difficult
than she had expected.

"Yes," answered her sister slowly. "That is true
too." She considered this for a moment. "It is hard to
know what to think. I have not seen him since that
day we met in the street, you know." She sounded
wistful. "I have looked for him everywhere." She
looked into Laura's eyes. "Tell me, do you like
him, Laura?"

The older girl hesitated. "Yes," she replied
cautiously. "He seems a very estimable man."

Clarissa smiled beatifically. "I think he is
wonderful."

Laura looked at her. She could not quite understand
her lively sister's fascination with such a quiet young
man. "But do you not find him just a little, well, not
solemn precisely, but…"

"Oh I know what you mean," answered Clarissa
quickly. "He does not have the liveliness of some
town beaux… but Laura, he is so kind, and there
is something in his eyes. I cannot explain it to you,

but he makes me feel as if I need never worry about anything again." She flushed a bit. "I sound like a regular ninnyhammer, don't I?"

"No," said Laura. "But you do appear quite bowled over, by a man you scarcely know. You will become better acquainted with him, I hope, before you make a final judgment."

Clarissa made an impatient gesture. "I know the important things already."

Laura frowned. "But Clarissa…"

Her sister rose restlessly. "This is silly. We are talking as if there were something to be decided, and it is no such thing. I am going upstairs to write letters." And before Laura could reply, she was gone.

She was just about to rise and go after her sister when Mr. Dunham entered the room and announced that Lady Quale was below. "She is most wishful to see you, ma'am," he added.

Grimacing, Laura started to tell him that she was not at home to visitors, but she remembered that she had said this the last time Lady Quale called. She could not deny herself every time the woman came. Sighing, she stood. "Ask Lady Quale to come up," she said.

❦

"My dear Laura," said the older woman when she swept into the drawing room. "I'm so pleased to find you alone. I heard a most disturbing story at Mrs. Dillingham's this morning."

Laura's heart sank, but she schooled her face to polite indifference and said, "Really, what was that?"

"They are saying, my dear, that you went out driving

with Jack Allenby this morning. I told Clara Dillingham that it was all nonsense." Lady Quale's eyes gleamed avidly as she waited for the girl's reply.

Laura raised her chin. "As a matter of fact," she answered, with all the dignity she could muster, "it is true. I was out driving with Mr. Allenby this morning. He showed me Kew Gardens. I had not been before, and I enjoyed it very much."

Shock, gratification, and eagerness mingled on Lady Quale's face. "But Laura, how could you?"

Laura pressed her lips together, then said, "I am convinced that the reports about Mr. Allenby are much exaggerated. I assure you he was most gentlemanly."

Her caller shook her head. "Oh my dear, if you have fallen under the spell of his charm, you are lost. I beg you…"

"I have done no such thing," snapped Laura, goaded beyond politeness. "Nor do I see why a simple morning ride should cause such consternation."

"Had it been anyone else, I mean *anyone* else in London, my dear, no one would have remarked it. But Mr. Allenby!" Lady Quale clasped her hands dramatically. "After what I *told* you!"

The memory of this did not improve Laura's temper. She stood. "Thank you for coming," she said, "but I assure you that your *kindness* was completely unnecessary. I am able to look after myself."

The older woman now showed a spark of anger too. "You will ruin yourself if you keep on this way."

Laura's eyes flashed. She looked magnificent as she looked down at her visitor. "I fear you must excuse me. I have pressing duties."

Lady Quale also rose haughtily. "You will regret talking to me in this way, my girl. But not as much as you will regret becoming entangled with Jack Allenby, I fancy. Do you think your husband will stand by complacently? You are out there, I can tell you. And you may be sure your aunts will hear of your conduct."

Laura stiffened, holding her tongue only with an immense effort. "You will do just as you please, of course," she replied at last. And she began to walk toward the drawing room doorway.

Lady Quale followed perforce and was ushered out by Mr. Dunham, who had clearly been attracted by their raised voices. Laura wondered angrily how much he had heard. It seemed the final insult—a hostile eavesdropper in her own house.

Left alone, she clenched her fists. On an impulse she ran to the writing desk in the corner. On a sheet of pressed note paper, she dashed off a note accepting Mr. Allenby's invitation to the masquerade. Let them all say what they please. Let Eliot find out! She was not to be humiliated in this way, not by anyone.

Twelve

NOTHING INTERVENED THAT EVENING TO LESSEN Laura's temper. She went over and over the scene with Lady Quale, becoming angrier with each repetition. The cheek of the woman! Thus she woke the next morning determined to carry through on her impulse, and she set out first thing to buy a domino for the masquerade. She avoided her sister and the servants, for she did not want this outing discussed. As she awkwardly gathered her skirts to climb into a hack near the corner of the street, it suddenly occurred to her that she had never before entered any vehicle without someone's helping hand on her elbow and an escort to see to the details of the journey. Some of her nervousness dissolved in contempt at this realization. What a poor creature she was, after all.

❧

The hack dropped her on Bond Street, and she walked awhile, looking for a small dressmaker's establishment. She did not wish to go to Madame Antoinette with this order. Finally, when she had turned a corner, she found a place that looked to be just what she wanted—a plain, respectable shop without pretensions to fashion. She nodded once and went in.

A stout, rosy woman hurried up as she entered and greeted her cheerfully, but when Laura told her what she was seeking, a frown appeared on her wide pleasant face. "A domino is it, miss?" she replied. "Well now, we don't get many requests for dominoes, and I swear I don't know if we have one made up. Was you wanting a special color? We can do whatever you like in a trice, of course, but if you're set on having it now…" She paused. She was clearly torn between the desire to retain this very promising customer and uncertainty that she could satisfy her.

"Any color will do," answered Laura, "though I should prefer something dark and not too arresting."

"Yes, miss," said the dressmaker vaguely. "Well I shall see what I can find."

A voice came from the back of the room where a group of young girls sat around a large table, sewing. They were only partly screened by a flowered curtain, and clearly they could hear whatever went on in the front. "I believe there are two or three dominoes hanging in the back attic storage room," said one. Laura was surprised at the education evident in the voice. "Shall I go up and fetch them?"

"Why yes, thank you, Marina," said the woman. "You're sharp as ever."

A slender young woman with brown hair and blue eyes rose gracefully from the table and disappeared into the closed staircase at the back of the room.

The proprietress rubbed her hands together happily.

"There you are, miss," she said. "What did I tell you? Won't be a moment, and you can take your choice. That Marina, she's never mistaken. Has the sharpest eyes in the shop. Would you care to sit down while we wait? Perhaps I could get you a cup of tea?"

"No thank you," replied Laura. "I do not require anything."

In a few moments Marina returned. She carried several garments over her arm. As she walked toward them, Laura noticed her graceful carriage and composed expression. The girl looked quite out of place in a dressmaker's shop. And when she spoke again, this impression was intensified. "Here you are ma'am," she said, in accents as cultivated as Laura's own. "There are two dominoes and a hooded cloak I thought might be suitable as well. They were covered with a sheet, so they are not at all dusty."

"Thank you, Marina," said the dressmaker. "You are the one for finding things."

The girl dropped a small curtsy and returned to her place at the table. Laura watched her walk back with some curiosity. What was such a girl doing here? But her attention was quickly claimed by the proprietress, and she forgot Marina as she chose a domino. Of the two offered one was black and the other crimson, and the cloak was of serviceable gray twill. Laura chose the black as being the least likely to attract attention and paid the woman for it. She indicated that she would take it with her, and a bandbox was fetched. It seemed to Laura that if she carried it home herself, no one would notice it.

The bandbox was a bit awkward to carry, but Laura

found another hack almost immediately, and a hasty scan of the street did not reveal any acquaintance who might think it strange to see Mrs. Crenshaw climbing alone into a cab and hauling a parcel after her.

※

Laura reached home without mishap and used her latchkey to get in. Mercifully Mr. Dunham was not on duty in the hall. Laura breathed a sigh of relief and started up the stairs. But as she reached the first floor and passed the door of the drawing room, a voice called to her, "Laura, there you are," and she froze in dismay. Eliot!

He came out of the room as she turned, stunned. "I was concerned," he continued. "None of the servants seemed to know where you had gone."

She gulped. "Oh. Well I just stepped out to pick up a dress that was to be done today." She thrust the bandbox onto a chair on the landing and turned to stand in front of it.

"But one of the footmen could have gone. You should not have to do such errands."

"Oh yes, but you see... that is, there was a final fitting still to be done."

Eliot frowned at her. "But why did you not take your barouche?" He appeared more puzzled than angry.

"It was only a step," she replied more easily. The first lies of her life were both more difficult and easier than she would have expected. "I wanted a breath of air. But you returned a day early, did you not?" She hoped to divert him from the subject of gowns, and she succeeded.

"Yes. I found it somewhat tedious, and besides I was not easy about the way we parted. Come into the drawing room. I wish to talk with you, Laura."

His tone was kind, but Laura was too nervous to pay much heed. "Of course," she said, "as soon as I have taken off my bonnet and tidied my hair. I won't be a moment."

Eliot started to speak, then nodded and walked back into the drawing room.

Sighing in relief, Laura picked up the bandbox and hurried up to her room. She put it on top of the wardrobe, where it was unlikely to be disturbed, then stood a moment with a hand clenched at her breast. She was breathing rather fast, and her face in the mirror was pale. Her plan suddenly appeared to her in a completely different light, and she wished she had never begun it.

After a few moments she removed her bonnet and ran a comb through her curls. Walking back downstairs at a much slower pace than she had come up, she had leisure to wonder what Eliot wished to say to her. Suddenly she froze. Could the rumors of her drive with Mr. Allenby have reached him so soon? She had no doubt that Lady Quale was happily spreading the tale. Calculating quickly, she realized that he must have been on the road most of yesterday. He could not know then.

Eliot sat on the sofa, one leg crossed over the other, when she entered the drawing room. His dark hawk-like face was pensive. He rose as soon as he saw her and ceremoniously ushered her to a seat. Laura sank down and eyed him uneasily. He smiled. "I can hardly blame you for looking apprehensive, though it saddens me. But it is quite my own fault, I know, and I came home expressly to apologize to you for my outrageous behavior last week."

Laura made an inarticulate noise.

"I allowed myself to become angry," he continued, "and to say things I now regret. I have always prided myself on controlling such emotions, and I cannot excuse my failure in this case except by my concern for your welfare. I ask your pardon for my hasty words."

The coolness and composure with which he spoke somewhat lessened Laura's discomfort.

"It is quite all right," she faltered.

"But it is not. I promised you that we would deal extremely well together, and yet at the first strain I gave way to anger. This is not the example I would wish to set."

"Example?" asked Laura. The word rankled, and she spoke coolly.

He nodded. "I, having so much more experience of the world, must necessarily set you an example in our relations. And I have been a poor one. I can say only that I shall try to do better." He smiled, his austere features lighting charmingly, and took her hand. "Come, let us cry friends once more."

Laura's hand trembled in his, and she could think of no answer at first.

Eliot bent closer. "I said that we should become better acquainted, Laura, but somehow I have not found as much time for that as I would have wished. Why is it always the pleasant duties that get neglected?"

Laura drew back a little. Why must he continually

use words like *duty* and *example* with her. Surely he did not speak so to Mrs. Allenby. He did not see her as a blundering, obstinate child, who must be trained and guided. Vera Allenby was all excitement and sparkle, a wicked sparkle. Nothing was changed. Eliot had gotten over his fit of temper; that was all. Laura realized that she was very tired of Eliot's "duty." She had almost come to hate it, as if it were a living creature. She pulled her hand away. "I too have been busy," she said, attempting a light, unconcerned tone.

"The season is hectic," he agreed. "But we can overcome such obstacles, surely. Dine with me tomorrow evening, at the restaurant you liked when we first came to town. We can be alone there." He started to reach for her hand again.

Something deep inside Laura trembled. She hardly knew what she felt. One part of her wished desperately to agree, but another insisted that he often planned such evenings with another woman, whom he no doubt preferred. She drew back involuntarily. "We can't," she almost gasped. "Mr. Redmon is coming to dinner tomorrow."

"Redmon?"

"I told you all about it."

"I'm sure you did. I had forgotten. It is vexing. I have engagements for the following evening, and the next. It must be Monday then."

Monday was the day of the masquerade. Color flooded Laura's cheeks. "I can't."

"Another party?" He smiled. "Could you not change your plans? Cry off?"

Looking into his gray eyes, Laura started to say

that she would, of course, but some stubborn impulse made her ask, "Could you? I am free Saturday."

Eliot shrugged. "Alas. I have promised a friend."

Thinking that she knew quite well who that friend must be, Laura straightened and drew even further away from him. "A pity. I too must keep my promise."

He frowned a little at her tone. "Laura," he began, but before he could go on, Mr. Dunham came in.

At the interruption Laura was suddenly swept by a wave of despair such as she had never felt before in her life. Everything seemed to be going wrong. Would she always be wondering whether Eliot was out with Vera Allenby, while she was left with only the leavings of his time and attention? In that moment she knew that she wanted nothing less than to go to the masquerade, and nothing more than to dine with Eliot. But she had gotten into such a muddle that she must do the thing she hated. Tears were close.

"The Earl of Stoke-Mannering," announced Mr. Dunham impressively.

The Crenshaws stared at the newcomer, Eliot frowning. His appearance was nondescript—pale lashes and eyebrows matching sandy hair and eyes of a washed-out blue. His clothing was that of a prosperous country squire.

Conscious of their amazement, the earl bowed carefully. "Good day. You are surprised to see me, and I can understand your feelings only too well. I took the liberty of calling after I was informed that my cousin had recently married. I can only hope that the familial relationship will excuse my temerity." He bowed again.

Laura blinked, trying to regain control of herself. "Of course. Come in, sit down."

The earl bowed yet again. "I am not mistaken, I hope, in claiming you, madame, as my cousin?"

"No. That is, I think not. I was told I believe that a cousin of my father's had taken the title."

"That is correct. You are right to remind me. We are not cousins, but second cousins."

Laura smiled. "Well it comes to the same thing, I suppose. I am happy to meet you."

"I thank you. And I assure you that your gratifying sentiments are fully reciprocated. It is best to be precise, after all."

"Always," agreed Eliot promptly.

He nodded. "I decided the time had come for me to visit the metropolis. I am confident of my skills in country society, but I lack what I believe they call town bronze." He allowed himself a small smile, as if he had made a joke. "I admit I have never thought such an addition necessary, but at this time another consideration moved me as well. I have come to the conclusion that it is time I married."

"Indeed?" said Laura, repressing a smile.

"Yes. I am two and thirty this year, you know." He smiled complacently. "I was gratified when I found that my second cousins were also in London. I owe you an apology and an explanation, of course, for my lack of notice these past years. It is inexcusable."

"Oh no," began Laura, but he held up a hand.

"I do. I have meant to visit you these five years. When I inherited the title, of course, it was not to be thought of. I was only fourteen years of age, a callow youth. In fact my education and upbringing had not at all prepared me for the position I found myself occupying. No one expected that I should succeed. So for some years I was completely occupied in readying myself for the responsibilities of managing the estate and fulfilling the duties of magistrate and landlord. And later these things in themselves diverted me. Still I know I have been remiss, and I offer you my sincere apologies."

"There is not the least need," replied Laura. The slow precision of her cousin's conversation amused her. "After all, we never communicated with you either." She did not add that it had never occurred to them to do so.

But he was not satisfied. "You are generous. But it was my place to initiate relations."

"Well the omission is righted now," put in Eliot. There was impatience in his tone.

"It is a great relief to me," agreed the earl.

There was a pause. Laura met Eliot's eyes and smiled a little at the combination of amusement and exasperation she saw there. Her husband took out his snuffbox and languidly took a pinch. He offered it to the earl, who waved it away emphatically. "I do not indulge," he said. "The drug tobacco is decidedly injurious to the moist tissues."

Eliot raised his eyebrows but made no retort. Laura thought that he was showing marvelous restraint.

"I understood, madame," continued the earl, "that your younger sister was also in London."

Laura started. "Oh yes, Clarissa is staying with us. I shall call her. She will wish to meet you."

Bowing, the earl signified that he would be pleased, and in a few minutes Clarissa joined them.

"How funny," she said as she sat down, "to meet a cousin one has never seen before."

"Second cousin," corrected Eliot gravely.

Laura made a choking noise.

It was one of the longest half hours she could remember. The earl was not only fairly unintelligent, he was also a prosy bore. And he seemed to feel that his own opinions had a force and rightness denied anyone else's. Several times she feared that Eliot was about to give him a severe setdown, and indeed she hardly could have blamed him.

Their guest devoted himself to Clarissa after she came down. The girl's eyes danced as she responded to his cumbersome gallantries, and often she glanced toward Laura to share the joke. His attentions were so marked that Eliot commented quietly, "Your cousin has clearly come to London to capture Clarissa."

Laura's eyes widened. "Oh no."

Eliot gestured toward the other couple. "Perhaps he has decided that it is his duty to marry a Lindley to compensate you for the loss of the title and the estate."

"Ridiculous," answered the girl, smiling. "He could not."

Eliot merely gestured again.

When the earl rose to take his leave after his rather long visit, there was a general feeling of relief. He bowed to the Crenshaws, then turned to Clarissa and said, "If you care to come down with me, I can show you my team. I drove my curricle here."

Throwing a helpless glance at Laura, Clarissa agreed.

When they were gone, Laura sank back on the sofa. "I thought he would never go," she exclaimed.

Eliot smiled. "He seemed to me an excellent young man, very conscious of his position and duties. I daresay he will make Clarissa an exemplary husband."

Laura gasped. "Oh you are joking." She shook her head. "I nearly laughed aloud when he told you that you should most certainly find the time to visit the British Museum. Your expression was so funny."

"I daresay it was," replied Eliot, smiling in his turn. "But you see, no one has ever suggested such a thing to me before."

Laura gave a peal of laughter. "Did you hear him offer to take Clarissa there to show her the old manuscripts? She was forced to tell him that she is allergic to dust of all sorts."

"No, did she?" asked her husband appreciatively. "Clarissa is a very resourceful girl. I have always thought so, and this confirms it. It was a master stroke."

Laura was overcome by her laughter for a moment, and Eliot watched her with an interested smile. When she could control herself, she gasped, "I beg your pardon, but I have been restraining myself for so long. I cannot help but laugh. He is really a very estimable man, of course."

Eliot nodded. "Very. You know," he added, "I don't believe I ever have seen you laugh so much."

Clarissa came back into the room at that moment, sputtering, "His team! He calls a pair of the most obvious slugs I have ever seen a team. And he has asked me to go out driving with him on Saturday. What am I to do?"

Laura's eyes danced. "Whatever do you mean, Clarissa? I thought him an unexceptionable young man."

"A model of propriety," agreed her husband. "And he seemed quite struck with you, Clarissa. If you can only curb the natural levity of your character, you may have a chance at becoming a countess."

Clarissa was aghast. "You must be joking?" Laura could not restrain a choke of laughter, and her sister whirled. "You are roasting me," she said. "Both of you. And it is too bad. Did I not relieve you of the burden of talking to the earl for quite twenty minutes?"

Eliot appeared much struck. "I had not thought of it in just that way. You are right. Accept my sincere thanks."

This sent both girls off into ringing laughter, and Eliot watched them with a smile and an arrested expression in his eyes.

By the time she recovered her composure, Laura had forgotten the discomforts of their earlier talk, and she went upstairs with Clarissa quite happily, bidding Eliot a cheerful good night.

Thirteen

THE DINNER WITH MR. REDMON WAS LAURA'S FIRST entertainment in her new home. Because of Clarissa's anxiety, the preparations were complicated by too much supervision and, often, conflicting orders. This, on top of Laura's unease about Eliot, which had come rushing back as soon as she was alone, made her tense on Friday evening. At seven, as she stood in her drawing room in a gown of pale cream color trimmed in lace, she almost wished that this dinner were over, or had never been planned.

Since their shared laughter, Laura had been rather ashamed of her petulant defiance of Eliot. In fact she had gone so far as to write a note to Mr. Allenby canceling their engagement for the masquerade, though she had not yet found an opportunity to send it.

Eliot came in before Clarissa. "Good evening," he said. "You are looking beautiful, as ever."

"Thank you."

"I have not asked you who our guests are tonight."

Laura raised her eyebrows. "I did tell you. It is Mr. Redmon."

He looked surprised. "The marquess?"

Laura glanced toward the door apprehensively, but there was as yet no sign of Clarissa. "Yes, but Clarissa knows him as *Mr.* Redmon. I told you of it." He still frowned in puzzlement, so she repeated the story of Mr. Redmon's request.

When she finished, his expression had lightened, but he still looked puzzled. "An absurd scheme. Someone will certainly find him out. I had not thought him such a nodcock." He shrugged. "But if Redmon wishes to play silly games, I suppose he may do so. It is not as if he were pretending to be a marquess when he is not. It must have been amazingly difficult to assemble a party who would not spoil the secret."

"Oh there is no one else. Only Mr. Redmon."

Eliot frowned. "Only Redmon. You mean to say it is just the four of us?"

"Yes."

He stared at her. "But why? This is most unsuitable."

"Unsuitable?" echoed Laura. "But you are here, and they are chaperoned…" She trailed off uncertainly under his stern gaze.

"My dear Laura, one does not invite a young unmarried man to a family dinner, especially in such a small group as ours, unless he is pretty firmly expected to become a member of it very soon. Indeed the very high sticklers would not do so until an engagement is actually announced. It is a clear signal that you want him for Clarissa. You are encouraging her to set her cap at him in the most blatant way. How could you be so heedless?"

"I am not. I did not mean anything of the kind,"

retorted the girl, putting her hands to cheeks that blazed with embarrassment. "I did not think. I see now that it is very particular, but I promise you I did not plan it. Clarissa wished to invite him, and I agreed."

"If you are to allow yourself to be guided by Clarissa, we shall be at point nonplus before we know it."

Laura's hands fell; her eyes began to snap. "Well I do not allow it, as you know very well. This was my mistake. I did not think."

"That is obvious." He glanced at the clock on the mantelpiece. "Well it is too late now to get anyone else. He will be arriving at any moment. But please, in future, Laura, consult me or someone else about these matters. You are not at all up to snuff yet, clearly. You must subdue your pride and your temper and allow wiser heads to advise you. Lady Quale would be delighted to help I am sure. As an old friend of your aunts, she is eminently suited to the task." He looked about the room. "We must simply carry it off as well as we can. Redmon will be surprised, I daresay."

This lecture, with the mention of the interfering Lady Quale, had completed the arousal of Laura's anger. The despair she had been feeling seemed to burn away. She wished desperately to make a cutting rejoinder, to put him in his place and destroy his smug superiority, but she could think of none.

She started to speak, but seeing her expression, Eliot held up a hand. "Let it be," he said. "We shall brush through it, I daresay."

Laura felt this to be the final insult. To be patronized

after all that had happened. A stinging response was on her lips, but at that moment Mr. Dunham announced Mr. Redmon and she was forced to hold her tongue.

It was thus a seething hostess who greeted their guest. She left Eliot to make conversation with the younger man, who did seem rather embarrassed, whether because he found himself the sole guest or because he had difficulty chatting with a man ten years older than himself.

Laura listened silently to several minutes of discussion of a team Mr. Redmon had recently purchased for his curricle. She was surprised to see the marquess, who was, after all, something of an expert on horses, hang on her husband's opinions with a respect bordering on reverence.

She was just about to go in search of Clarissa when the girl came in at last. And Laura had to admit that she had used the extra time to some purpose. Clarissa had chosen a gown of deep gold satin, one of her newest and finest toilettes. The vibrant color, far from overwhelming her complexion, seemed to accentuate it, and her skin glowed softly. Her hair was in curls and her eyes sparkling. Flecks of gold seemed to dance in their black depths, reflected from the dress perhaps.

Altogether she was an entrancing sight, and Mr. Redmon was affected just as she must have hoped he would be. For a moment he seemed rooted to the floor. His jaw dropped slightly, and his eyes widened. But when Laura said, "Good evening, Clarissa. Our guest is before you," in a tone of mild reproof, he started.

"Good evening, Miss Lindley," he blurted, coming forward eagerly. "By Jove, you look lovely."

Clarissa smiled up at him in a way that made Laura want to both laugh and reprimand her for posing. "Thank you," she said softly. "I am sorry I kept you waiting."

As Mr. Redmon stammered out a denial, Laura did smile. Clearly Clarissa was pulling out all the stops tonight. She raised her eyes to share the joke with Eliot, but he was not looking at her. His gaze was on the clock, which now registered fifteen minutes past the dinner hour. Laura's smile faded, and she turned to look for Mr. Dunham. He was standing in the corridor outside, and she gave him the signal. He announced dinner, and the group went in, she on Eliot's arm and Clarissa on Mr. Redmon's.

"You ought to have taken Redmon's arm," said Eliot under his breath as they followed the other couple. "And can you not control your sister? She is being rather obvious."

Laura's temper flared again. She could scarcely control her voice as she replied, "You exaggerate." He would have said more, but she pulled away as they entered the dining room and slipped into her chair unaided.

Laura did not particularly enjoy her dinner. The table and the flowers were perfect, the capons done to a turn, and the roast beef juicy. And if the conversation was not over-lively, her guest at least seemed to find no fault. But whenever she met her husband's eyes down the length of the table, she felt angry and upset again. Why must he treat her so?

The younger couple did most of the talking. Mr. Redmon had begun by apologizing again, and at some length, for hurrying away from their last encounter.

Clarissa accepted his excuses gracefully, then adroitly turned the conversation to horses once more. Soon he was reciting the good points of his new team to her, in a much more animated tone than he had used with Eliot, and she was suitably admiring. It came out that she had always preferred the curricle to all other vehicles and had often wished she could drive such an equipage.

"Really, Miss Lindley?" responded Mr. Redmon on cue. "I should be happy to teach you to drive. With your sister's permission, of course," he added, looking toward Laura.

Clarissa also turned to her, an unmistakable signal in her eyes, and Laura gave her consent. She did not look at Eliot. If he disapproved, she did not wish to know of it.

The remainder of the meal was taken up with the young people's enthusiastic plans for driving lessons. By the time Laura rose to leave the gentlemen, she had developed a severe headache and wished nothing more than to go to her bedchamber and lie down in quiet darkness. Instead she had to accompany Clarissa to the drawing room and endure half an hour of her praises of Mr. Redmon. She stood it as long as she could, but at last her patience was exhausted and she snapped, "Oh, cut line, Clarissa. Must you make such a cake of yourself?"

Her sister's head jerked up, and she stared at Laura. "What do you mean?"

Laura made a sweeping gesture. "The way you are behaving, your dress, everything. Must you be so very obvious? Even Eliot noticed it."

A wave of color washed over the younger girl's cheeks, but she said only, "Noticed what? I do not understand you."

"Do you not?" replied Laura skeptically. "I will make my meaning more plain then. Eliot thinks you are blatantly setting your cap at Mr. Redmon."

Clarissa put her hands to her cheeks, but her eyes flared. "What a horrid thing to say."

Laura raised her eyebrows. "But true?"

"No!" Clarissa's hands fell to be clenched in her lap. "Not at all. I am doing nothing of the kind."

"Then appearances are deceptive," shrugged Laura, "because it certainly did look that way."

"Oh, why are you being so abominable?" cried the younger girl. "Can you not imagine feeling a strong liking for a man and wishing to show it?"

"After talking to him for perhaps two hours in my life?" asked Laura. "No, I fear I cannot. Clarissa, I tell you again that you hardly know this man. You have always been heedless and impetuous, but in this case I beg you to try for a little restraint. Brazen behavior will only give Mr. Redmon a distaste for you."

Clarissa colored again. "That is what you think then?" she answered. "That I am being brazen. Or I should say that is what you *and* Eliot think. He is turning you into just such a cold fish as himself. I will not listen to this talk of restraint and calm judgment. I know my own feelings, and I fancy I can guess at Mr. Redmon's. I despise this hypocrisy of coolness and convention, and if you ever had been in love, so would you too, Laura." With this she turned away and walked over to the fireplace to lean her head against the mantel.

Before Laura could reply, the gentlemen entered the room and she was forced to make light conversation when she felt anything but sociable. Clarissa said little at first, but soon Mr. Redmon had drawn her into another discussion of driving and she regained her spirits. Eliot, after watching them for a moment, came to sit beside Laura on the sofa.

"What is the matter?" he said to her when he had watched her face for a time. "You are upset."

"It is nothing."

He bent his head a little to see her face. "I cannot believe it while you look like that. Did Clarissa upset you?" When she said nothing, he continued. "You tried to reprimand her, I suppose, and she lashed out. She is very hot at hand, your sister."

"She is utterly trustworthy," retorted Laura hotly, quick to defend her sister against anyone else's criticism. "She will not disgrace you."

He raised his eyebrows. "I have no fear of that. You misunderstood me if you think I do. I merely wish to guard her from any hurt or embarrassment that might arise from the too obvious display of her feelings."

"Yes," replied Laura bitterly, "one mustn't display feelings. Not that, at all costs."

Preoccupied, Eliot missed the barb and, evidently thinking the topic exhausted, turned to another question. "You know, Laura," he continued, "I was thinking during dinner that it might be wise for me to invite my mother to stay for the season. You like her, I know. And she is just the person to give you a hint now and then about how to go on. I daresay she could exert better control over Clarissa too. In fact I cannot imagine why I did not think of the scheme ere now. It seems ideal."

Laura's chin had come up, and she was gazing at Eliot angrily. "Oh?" she replied with false sweetness. "Am I to be consulted then?"

He raised his eyebrows at her tone. "Of course."

"Well *I* should prefer that she not visit at this time."

"I thought you were fond of my mother."

"I am," said Laura. She raised her eyes to his. "But I am not in need of a chaperone or of help in controlling, as you put it, my sister."

"I see." He paused for a moment, then went on. "Do you know, I have seen a great many people come to town for their first season, and invariably, when they have been kept on a tight rein by their parents, they spend the first weeks indulging in all manner of escapades. They wish to show the world, you see, that they are free and well able to manage themselves. Most come to grief in one way or another."

Laura merely looked stonily ahead. She refused to give him the satisfaction of seeming to understand what he meant.

"A few," Eliot continued, "ruin themselves utterly, but most simply learn a valuable lesson. I have always thought it a great waste that each crop of youngsters must go through the same follies. But they never listen to wiser heads."

Goaded by his tone, Laura snapped, "As you did, no doubt."

Eliot looked down at her and, surprisingly, smiled. "Oh no. I was as foolish and headstrong as the worst of them. I fell into scrape after scrape, some of them quite unpleasant and mortifying. That is why I wish to offer my advice, I suppose. I really do know how it is."

Somewhat mollified, Laura said, "Perhaps it is the way you offer it. You seem so certain that you are right and others are wrong."

He smiled again. "Ah, but that is so often true." His eyes invited her to smile with him, but she resisted.

"Such a superior attitude can set up people's backs," she answered, trying to make him understand.

But he was disinterested. "I haven't time for dissimulation. There is a right way and a wrong way to go about things, Laura, and I admit that it tries my patience when someone blindly refuses to acknowledge the former."

"Which is your way," added Laura.

"Many times, yes."

"Not always," she answered between her teeth.

He looked at her, perplexed. "It is obvious that you think so, at any rate. Do you not see that that is why I wished to invite my mother? I do not want to be always correcting you, Laura, and acting like a guardian. We can have an easier relationship."

This partial echoing of her own thoughts left Laura speechless for a moment. Did he understand, after all? Before she could speak, however, Mr. Redmon came up to take his leave. Soon after, Clarissa went up to bed, floating on a cloud of elation. Eliot rose and held out a hand. "We may as well follow her. It is late."

Still confused, Laura walked up the stairs beside him. Outside her bedroom door, they stopped. "I hope you will think over what I have said, Laura," murmured Eliot. "I want you to be happy." He bent toward her, and Laura, startled, moved away a little. Eliot smiled and took her chin in his hand. "You must become accustomed to having a husband, my dear," he said, and bending his head, he kissed her full on the lips.

Utterly surprised, Laura did not know how to respond. After all their wrangling, now this. So she merely stood, passive, as he straightened, murmured, "Sleep well," and turned away to his own room.

Laura didn't move for a long moment, then she turned hastily and went into her bedroom, her heart beating wildly. Leaning against the bedpost, she took several deep breaths and tried to calm herself.

A movement across the room caught her eye. It was her own reflection in the mirror over the dressing table. Her cheeks were glowing, her black eyes were very wide, and her uneven breathing was evident. "Whatever is wrong with me?" she said aloud, but the reflection made no answer.

Fourteen

LAURA ROSE IN GOOD TIME THE NEXT MORNING AND washed and dressed quickly. During the night, she had resolved never to see Mr. Allenby again. And she would remind Eliot of his dinner invitation. Surely this would be the beginning of a better understanding between them. She took the note she had written Mr. Allenby and walked down to the front hall to leave it.

But just as she was about to put it down, Eliot looked out of the library across the way and called to her. She started a bit guiltily and stuffed the note into the pocket of her gown. It would not do for Eliot to see the direction. She smiled at him a little shyly, the memory of last night making her flush, and said good morning.

He returned her greeting without smiling. "May I speak to you a moment, Laura?" he asked. "Will you come into the library, please."

His tone was not encouraging, and Laura's smile faded. "Of course," she replied.

In the library he ushered her to a chair, then returned to the desk. He had obviously been looking over some bills and papers. Laura frowned slightly. Was he upset about expenses? But he picked up a letter, written on fine pressed notepaper, and tapped it with his finger, frowning. "I do not like to speak of this," he said finally. "I abhor talebearing, and this is the sort of thing that one should always ignore. But in this case, Laura, I cannot." He tapped the letter again.

Laura stared at it with fascinated apprehension. What did he mean, talebearing? But he was looking at her. "In, indeed?" she stammered.

He nodded. His expression was still set and unsmiling. He seemed a different man from the one who had bid her good night so tenderly. "I imagine you know what it must contain."

Laura merely looked at him, wide-eyed. She shook her head.

"Oh come. Let us not have any silly sparring. The note comes from Lady Quale. She writes to inform me that you have been living in Mr. Allenby's pocket during my absence. A piece of impertinence, of course, but Laura, what do you mean by going against my express wishes in this way? Did I not ask you not to see Allenby?"

The mention of Lady Quale made Laura's eyes spark. "You do not question her tale?" she asked him. "You believe it before I speak?"

"Not if you tell me it is untrue," he answered. "Do you?"

Laura's eyes dropped. She would have liked nothing better at that moment than to tell him so, but she could not lie to him again. She started to speak, but he was before her.

"You cannot. So Jack Allenby first called here, you received him, and then you went out driving with him alone." His voice was like a lash.

Laura raised her eyes again. The look she met in his almost frightened her. There was blazing anger and a bitterness that hurt her to see.

Once more he spoke before she could. "Perhaps I was mistaken in you. You appear to have a taste for company totally out of keeping with your upbringing and birth. But I warn you, I will not allow an entanglement with Allenby. However charming you may find him, and I am told that he can be extraordinarily so, it will not do. Make up your mind to it."

"But I do not find him charming," retorted Laura. "You do not understand." She started to tell him that she had done it only because he had spoken to her so harshly, but he did not let her finish.

"Do not, I beg you, try to fob me off with some faradiddle about Allenby's polite manners, Laura. The point is not whether you like him; you have already told me that you do, you may recall. It is rather that I asked you to do a thing, and you have defied me in the most blatant way. I think we understand each other very well. You knew my wishes, and now I see how you regard them. Very well. Now I shall know how to proceed." He stood. "And be assured that I *can* stop you from doing what I do not like, Laura." His eyes on her were hard. "You have entered a contest you cannot win, my dear."

Laura's desire to explain herself and beg his pardon had faded as he spoke. His contemptuous tone and cutting words hurt her deeply, and his refusal to listen to her explanation angered her. But this time her temper did not get the best of her. The hurt was too sharp, and she felt tears starting in her eyes. Blinking them back, she said, "If only you would let me…"

But Eliot would not pause to listen. He was thoroughly angry and completely taken up with his own inner turmoil. Though he never would have acknowledged it, he was wounded by her defiance. In his view he had done everything in his power to provide for and protect her, and she had thrown it back in his face with contempt. He was in no mood to hear explanations.

"After this," he said, "you will always inform me of your plans to go out and where you are going. I shall judge whether the destination is proper for you. And I have written to my mother; she will be coming to stay with us next week." He picked up a sealed envelope from the desk.

Laura's chin came up. "How dare you speak to me so? I am not a child to be ordered about."

"No? You are certainly acting like one. I have said what I have to say. I think you understand me." And without a backward glance, he strode out of the room.

Laura stood for a moment in enraged astonishment, gasping at his arrogant injustice. If he thought that she would come running to tell him each time she went out, he was much mistaken. Laura reached into her pocket and tugged at the note secreted there. She pulled it out, a bit crumpled, and walked quickly over to throw it in the fire. So she was to be chaperoned by his mother? She would show him. She waited only to see the paper catch fire before hurrying from the room.

Laura and Eliot had no further private conversations before the day of the masquerade. Indeed Laura saw little of the family in the two intervening days. Clarissa began her driving lessons promptly and spent a part of every afternoon with the marquess, tooling his curricle along the little-traveled roads he chose for their sessions. This provided a perfect opportunity for each of them. Clarissa was able to improve her acquaintance with a man she admired, and Mr. Redmon could see her without much risk of being recognized. He had a reasonable excuse for seeking out-of-the-way lanes, telling Clarissa that she must become skilled before trying the busy streets around the park and Bond Street.

Eliot did not again refer to their disagreement, though Laura began to suspect that he had set Mr. Dunham to keep watch over her. She encountered the man much more often than usual, and he seemed to look at her with a combination of narrow watchfulness and vindicated suspicion. This heightened her determination not to be bullied, and she made her preparations for the masquerade with care. She did not wish to be stopped as she went out.

Monday evening, Clarissa was invited to the Rundgates'. She was to take the barouche, and Nancy would accompany her. Laura had cried off, which was not thought at all unusual since the party was composed wholly of youngsters. Thus Clarissa departed blithely just before dinner, wishing her sister enjoyment of the new novel she had gotten that day.

Eliot was not in to dinner, so Laura was spared making excuses when she retired to her room soon after Clarissa's departure. She rang for Mary immediately, pacing the floor until she arrived. When the maid knocked and came in, Laura schooled her features to a bland fatigue and greeted her tiredly. "Hello, Mary," she said, "I find I am quite tired out tonight. I think I will go to bed early. In fact I propose to lie down now and read in bed for a while. I will probably fall asleep quite soon. Would you fetch me a glass of hot milk, please?"

Mary raised her eyebrows. Her mistress had never asked for such a thing before, but she curtsied and said, "Of course, ma'am. I'm sorry you're knocked up. Though it's no wonder, with all the running about you have been doing. Shall I help you into your nightdress?"

"No. I can manage. Just bring the milk, please."

Mary went out, and Laura sank down on the bed and sighed. This was not pleasant. In fact she hated it. She had never tried to deceive anyone in her life, and she did not much like herself at this moment.

Briefly she considered simply forgetting the whole matter. She could truly go to bed now and read her novel, sending a note of apology to Mr. Allenby tomorrow. She was tired and had a slight headache, and the thought of such a lazy evening attracted her much more than the prospect of a noisy masquerade. But even as she almost gave in, she shook her head. She had decided on a course of action, and she would carry it through. The words Eliot had used to her were intolerable; he must be made to understand that she could not be ordered about.

Sighing again, she put on her dressing gown over her dress, pulled down the bedcovers and got into bed. Her evening dress would be a little crumpled, but no one would see it under the domino. She pulled the coverlet up and reached for her nightcap.

Mary returned in a few minutes with a glass of hot milk on a tray. She found Laura propped up on her pillows, reading. "Here you are, ma'am," she said, putting the tray on the table beside the bed. "Nice and hot. Cook made it herself."

"Thank you," said Laura. "That is just what I want tonight. I daresay I shall be asleep in ten minutes. Please do not let anyone disturb me, Mary."

"No ma'am." Mary moved about the room for a few minutes, straightening things and making certain the curtains were pulled tightly shut; then she bid Laura good night and went out.

Laura waited several minutes more before she got up again and took off her dressing gown. She shook the creases from her dress and pulled the covers back up on the bed, laying her nightcap on the pillow above them. Then she pulled the bedcurtains shut, put away her dressing gown, and retrieved the domino from the depths of her wardrobe, where she had thrust it the week before. She snuffed all of the candles but one, setting it on her dressing table so that she could straighten her hair. She found as she did so that her hands were trembling.

At last she was ready. She went to the door and listened. There was no sound in the corridor. Putting out the last candle, she eased the door open and slipped out. There was no one about, and Laura walked quickly to the back stairs at the end of the hall. The servants were safely out of the way in the kitchen by this time of night, and Eliot was not yet home. She ought to be able to get out through the side door unnoticed.

And indeed she did so. Once outside she paused to pull the black domino over her lavender crepe gown; she had chosen subdued colors this evening. She left the hood down at first, for now that she was ready, she paused. In the last few minutes, she had been occupied by getting out of the house unnoticed, but now, she had a minute to think. Did she really wish to do this thing, she asked herself? The anger that had led her to the decision had long since cooled, and she knew the answer was no. She did not wish to. Laura frowned, half turned, and put her hand on the door latch once again. She would not go. She had started to lift the latch when she suddenly heard noises within. She turned quickly and ran across the area to the archway that led to the street. There she waited a moment to see if whoever was approaching would go away again.

A light showed beyond the door; then it opened to show Mr. Dunham carrying a branch of candles. He held it up and peered about the flagged area as Laura shrank back into the shadows. It seemed to Laura that the man looked about for a long time, but finally he retreated. He shut the door, and Laura heard the sharp click of the bolt on the other side being shot home. She clenched her fists. She could not return this way now. Her only entrance was the great front door, and if she used her latchkey at this hour, someone was bound to see her. She twisted her hands together briefly, then pulled up her hood, and stepped into the street.

Laura groped in her reticule and retrieved the

piece of paper containing the address of Mr. Allenby's friends. She had agreed to meet him there, for he could hardly come to fetch her. As she found a hack and climbed in, Laura was once again, and more forcefully, struck by the impropriety of this arrangement. As she rode, she wished miserably that she had never begun it and hoped that no one would see her arrive in this unorthodox manner.

∽

Her wish was not granted. As she paid off the driver in front of the narrow house on Mount Street and turned toward the front door, she saw that at least two other guests had witnessed her arrival. A cloaked couple stood on the steps already, and the door was just opening for them to enter. Laura ducked her head, letting the hood of her domino fall forward, and reluctantly moved to join them. She hardly dared to meet their eyes as they went in together; they were strangers to her and merely murmured greetings. But when she did look up, Laura was surprised to see that they showed no curiosity or shock whatsoever. The woman's languid face showed mild amusement, that was all.

Before they could remove their cloaks, a gay voice called from the head of the stairs, and all three looked up to see a slender woman in pink gauze waving to them. "Do not take off your dominoes," she cried. "We are ready, and you are the last to arrive. Let us go. It is so stupid to sit about here when we might be dancing." With that she disappeared.

The woman next to Laura murmured, "Lila is *aux anges* this evening, I see. That is a relief."

The woman's companion bent to whisper something in her ear, and she laughed ringingly, throwing back her head to reveal carefully dressed brown locks streaked with gray and a visage rather heavily covered by cosmetics.

Neither of the two addressed Laura, and she stood a bit uncomfortably until the rest of the party came strolling down the stairs, chattering and laughing. Some wore dominoes and others carried them negligently over their arms. Their appearance reassured Laura a bit. Though she knew none of them, she was certain she had seen several at parties she had attended.

She saw Mr. Allenby the moment before he joined her. He also wore a black domino, which hung open now over a blue coat and fawn-colored knee breeches. Two masks dangled by their strings in his hand. Laura breathed a sigh of relief. She had noticed that many of the group carried such masks and was wondering with dismay where she would find one.

Mr. Allenby greeted her with a smile and twinkling eyes. "You are here!" he exclaimed. "Do you know, I had a premonition that you would not come. How splendid that I was wrong."

Laura smiled. "I very nearly did not."

"Aha. I knew it. I felt it earlier this evening. We are attuned, you and I. And what made you change your mind?"

Laura started to tell him that a servant had locked her out of the house, but it came to her suddenly that he might not appreciate the joke, so she simply shrugged.

"You needn't tell me," he went on. "It was your spirit, Laura. You have the courage and curiosity to try new things, and so you came to watch the spectacle. Admirable."

At this moment the carriages arrived, three of them, and the party set off for the Opera House. Laura had never visited this building before and so was unprepared and nearly dazzled by the brilliance within. Candles in crystal chandeliers illuminated the painted ceiling and tiers of boxes decorated with crimson, white, and gold. But it was the amazing crowd on the stage that held Laura's eye. Though it was early yet, the ball was already in progress, and the dancers wore every imaginable costume, from dominoes like her own to slashed doublets and hose or motley and bells. Laura watched wide-eyed as this throng revolved about the stage, until Mr. Allenby touched her arm and led her to the box the party had procured for the evening.

Laura found with relief that this was on the second tier, the ideal location it seemed to her. From there one could see the spectacle perfectly but was not subject to the annoyances of ogling bucks and importunate strangers liable to beset those in the first tier, whose boxes opened onto the dance floor.

She sat down, and Mr. Allenby took the chair beside her. The couple who had arrived with her occupied the opposite corner of the box, but the rest of the party began to drift off to the stage. Laura looked at them as they went out, and sensing her concern, Mr. Allenby said, "I would have introduced you to everyone if we had not been hurrying out just as you came. Lila should have spoken to you, of course, but I fear she is a heedless creature. I apologize for her."

Laura shrugged a little and turned to look at him. The sight was slightly forbidding; they had tied on their masks in the carriage, and all she could see was two eye slits in a black-silk ground. She thought she glimpsed a hazel twinkle as she replied, "It is of no consequence. I was late."

"So you were," he agreed equably. "I can introduce you to Sybil and her young friend if you like, but it will be difficult to pry them apart."

Laura turned to look at their companions, then swung quickly back. The woman, Sybil, was behaving with a freedom that quite shocked the inexperienced Laura, and the man had removed his mask and let his hood fall, revealing a thin face that proclaimed his extreme youth.

"Why, he looks scarcely fifteen," she whispered in a scandalized tone before she thought.

Mr. Allenby nodded. "If that. I take it you are not eager to be introduced?"

Laura looked down and shook her head very slightly.

"You show good taste," he said lightly. "I could wish that they had not elected to stay in the box with us. Suppose we go and dance?"

Laura agreed, and they made their way through the crowds and down to the dance floor. But this did not much ease Laura's discomfort, for many couples on the floor were behaving as freely as Sybil, or more so, and though no one offered to accost her, she did not feel at ease.

Mr. Allenby sensed Laura's nervousness. When the music ended, he guided her over to the side of the room and bent to say, "You are not enjoying yourself, are you? I had thought that you might be entertained by the spectacle, but I believe that is not so?"

Laura looked up at him, seeing only black silk, and shook her head slowly. "I am sorry," she replied.

"Nonsense. It is I who should apologize. I would never have brought you here had I known what your reaction would be." He looked away for a moment, then added absently, "Though God knows, I should have foreseen it. I am getting quite out of touch." He sighed. "Would you like to leave?"

Laura hesitated. "I do not wish to take you from your party," she said. "If you could find me a hack perhaps."

"Of course I shall escort you home," he said in a tone that brooked no argument. "What a care-for-nobody you must think me." He looked around. "But I must go back to the box to tell them I am going. I do not see any of our party about."

Accordingly they returned to the box, and Mr. Allenby went over to their hostess. She protested loudly, and he was detained a moment answering her teasing remarks. Laura bent her head in her hood, pretending that she could not hear some of these, for their intent was shocking.

As she looked at the floor, a voice spoke suddenly very close by. "Good evening, Mrs. Crenshaw. How charming to see you again."

Laura froze for an instant, then turned to the woman behind her. There was no mistaking that voice, and the curl of flaming red hair that fell from beneath the hood of a brilliant emerald green domino confirmed that this was indeed Vera Allenby. "Good evening," answered Laura.

"Are you enjoying the masquerade?" she asked. "It is brilliant tonight, is it not?"

"Yes, I suppose it is."

"You do not sound over-pleased with the spectacle."

"I have the headache," said Laura. "I am just going."

"Oh no. How tedious for you. Why not have a glass of champagne. Champagne always cures my headaches."

Her tone was at once so patronizing and so false that Laura could scarcely keep from snapping at her. "I think a good night's sleep will do better," she replied coldly.

"Ah yes, bed. That too is a fine cure." Mr. Allenby joined them then, greeting his wife blandly. "Well I mustn't keep you," continued Vera. "*Au revoir.*" Then she turned to speak to Sybil.

"Shall we go?" said Mr. Allenby when she did not move. He gestured toward the door.

Laura started forward. Her whole body trembled after the encounter with Mrs. Allenby; she was astonished at herself. As soon as the woman had spoken, she had felt a rush of hatred such as she had never before experienced. She was still nearly overcome by the strength of the emotion. Going down the stairs, she wavered and nearly tripped.

"Are you all right?" asked her companion solicitously. "Take my arm."

"No, no, I am fine. I missed the step." Taking several deep breaths, Laura managed to calm herself a bit.

When they reached the entrance hall, it was deserted. Mr. Allenby looked around, hesitated, then led her to a small room just off it, which was also empty. "I must go out a minute to find a cab," he told her. "You should be all right here. I won't be long."

Laura nodded and sank down uneasily on a chair in the corner. She fervently hoped that no one would disturb her, for she had seen how unescorted women were treated here.

Nothing broke the quiet for a short time, and Laura had just begun to relax slightly when she heard running footsteps and a girl burst suddenly in upon her. The newcomer wore a red domino which was now pulled open to show a drab brown gown beneath it. The hood was awry, and the girl's mask had been torn. It dangled by one string down her shoulder. But these things Laura noticed only in passing; the girl's obvious distress and rasping breath held her attention, and a vague familiarity in her features transfixed her.

The intruder had been looking behind her when she came in, but now she turned and started when she saw Laura. The terrified expression on her face roused the other's compassion.

"It is all right," said Laura. "Can I be of assistance?"

Though none of the strain left the girl's features, a spark of hope lit her eyes. "Oh if you would but lend me a small sum for a cab, I should be forever grateful," she said. "I could return it to you tomorrow."

As the girl spoke, Laura suddenly recognized her. "Why, it is Marina, is it not? From the dressmaker's?"

The girl's eyes widened, and she looked, if anything, more desperate. "Yes," she whispered. "Do you come there? Oh please, do not tell madame."

"Of course I will not," responded Laura. "And you must let me take you home."

Marina shook her head. "Oh no. I shall be all right. But if you could lend me a few shillings, I swear I will return it tomorrow."

"Of course. But won't you let me…"

Marina shook her head violently. "I must leave immediately." She pulled her domino straight and tried unsuccessfully to right her mask. Footsteps approached in the hall, and she froze for a moment, her expression wild, but they passed by and she relaxed again.

Laura had meanwhile taken some money and one of her cards from her reticule. "Can I not get someone to find you a cab?"

But Marina shook her head again. "No. I shall be all right now, I promise you. And thank you. I shall return the money tomorrow."

"It is not necessary."

"It is," answered Marina fiercely, and she threw one intense glance over her shoulder as she fled the room at the sound of new footsteps. She brushed past Mr. Allenby, who was returning, and disappeared.

Mr. Allenby looked at Laura with surprise and concern. "Are you all right?" he asked. Laura nodded. "Ah. That's good. It took me confoundedly long to find a cab. Let us hurry before some poacher steals it."

They went out quickly. Laura looked about, but she saw no sign of Marina as she climbed into the hack. She hoped that the girl had found another and wondered briefly why she had been in this place and what had happened to her.

Mr. Allenby was all apologies as they drove. "I never should have taken you there," he said. "Will you forgive me?"

"It doesn't matter," replied Laura. She was tired, and the headache she had claimed was becoming real.

"Ah, but it does. I shall never forgive myself. Will you give me another chance to prove that I am not a hopeless lout? Come to our card party tomorrow. I promise you that it will be nothing like the masquerade. You will enjoy yourself."

"Oh I do not think…" began Laura.

"Wait. Send me a note tomorrow morning, when you are rested and have had time to consider the matter. Please."

They accomplished the rest of the journey in silence and soon approached Laura's house. She was glad to see that there were no lights in the library. She had half feared that Eliot might be sitting there, even though he had gone to his club this evening.

She climbed down quickly and bid Mr. Allenby good night. At her request he did not leave the carriage but watched as she unlocked the front door with her latchkey and slipped inside. There was no one in the hall, and Laura breathed a sigh of relief. She moved quickly to the stairs and almost ran up them. Just before she reached the first landing, she heard the sound of a door shutting downstairs, but she saw no one before she reached her room. Once there, she wasted no time in undressing and falling into bed. It had been an evening that she wished only to forget as quickly as possible.

Fifteen

WHEN LAURA WOKE THE NEXT MORNING, HER HEAD-
ache was still with her. She lay still for some time,
thinking over the events of the previous day and
feeling heavy-eyed and depressed. She wondered what
would be the consequences of her foolishness in going
to the masquerade. She had somehow expected to go
and get it over, and then to forget it. But she saw now
that they had by no means come to the end of the
matter, as she had known since she encountered Mrs.
Allenby in the opera box. That woman, and Laura
felt a flash of dislike as she thought of her, would not
rest until Laura had been humiliated. She had heard
this in Vera Allenby's voice as surely as if she had said
it aloud. Laura shook her head as she remembered
the way Mrs. Allenby had looked at her. If the other
woman knew the true state of the Crenshaw marriage,
she thought, she would not be so bitter. Eliot's mistress
almost certainly saw a more tender side of him than
Laura ever did. The idea made her clench her fist. It
was intolerable that this thoroughly unpleasant woman
should have this advantage over her.

Laura dressed and went down to the breakfast room. It was empty when she entered, though the table showed that one person, probably Eliot, had eaten and gone. Laura rang for fresh tea and sat down to toy with a piece of toast. She was not at all hungry. She drank two cups of strong tea but ate almost nothing, then rose again and paced about the room. What was she to do now?

As she went out into the hall on her way to the drawing room, she was suddenly hit by a wave of sadness. What had happened to her life, she wondered dismally? It had never been so complicated and unhappy before. In fact she had never felt so low. She stood for a moment, struggling to control the tears that had started in her eyes. She put out a hand blindly and grasped the stair rail.

After a time she went into the library with some idea of finding Eliot and thrashing things out with him, but he was not there. He had been working in the room; there was a pile of mail on his desk and several slit envelopes beside it. Indeed he appeared to have departed in a hurry, for one letter lay open on the floor next to his chair, which had been shoved back crookedly.

Sighing, she went over and picked it up. She was about to put it back on top of the pile when the signature caught her eye. In a bold script full of flourishes was written "Vera." Laura struggled with herself for a moment, then tossed her head and began to read. If Eliot left such letters lying about, he must expect that someone would find them. Perhaps he had meant her to.

The note was not long. It began, "Dearest Eliot," and continued with the very information that Laura feared. "Is it not delightful that Jack and your lovely wife have struck up such a friendship? They looked quite charming together at the Pantheon Masquerade last night. Do you remember our first masquerade? I confess I will never forget it. We have a card party tonight, you remember. Do come. Late, as usual. Yours, Vera."

Laura's hand was trembling by the time she reached the end of this missive, and she moved blindly to an armchair and sank down in it. This was the end. Eliot would never forgive her. Why, why had she done it?

All the anger and defiance that Laura had once felt was gone now, leaving only miserable despair and guilt. Would Vera Allenby talk of her escapade to everyone? Even gossips like Lady Quale? Laura's head sank onto her hands. She could not doubt it. The story would run through the *ton* in a day. Completely overcome, Laura gave way to the tears that had been threatening all morning.

She cried for some time and was just getting control of herself again and groping in her pocket for a handkerchief when the door of the library opened suddenly and Mr. Dunham walked into the room. He stopped abruptly when he saw her, taking in her tearstained face and miserable expression. "I beg pardon, ma'am," he said with a slight bow, "I did not realize you were using the library. I often work here in the morning hours."

Laura rose and turned half away from him. "Yes, of course," she replied in a strangled voice. "I was just going."

"Do you require some assistance?" asked Mr. Dunham drily. "Shall I ring for your maid?" He did not sound really interested.

"No, no," said Laura. Bending her head, she hurried from the room.

She nearly ran up the stairs to her bedroom. Providentially it was empty. The maids had finished making up the bed. Laura fell into a chair and cried a little more. Why had it to be Mr. Dunham who found her? He disliked her, she was convinced, and he would no doubt run to Eliot with the story at the first opportunity. Her husband would return from visiting his mistress only to hear that his wife had been weeping over his desk. Laura noticed suddenly that she was still holding Vera Allenby's letter. Eliot would see that it was gone. She nearly groaned aloud. He would despise her, on top of everything else.

Laura struggled to calm herself, and after several minutes she partially succeeded. She looked at the letter again and frowned. The card party mentioned was the one she herself was invited to. Her frown deepened as an idea began to form in her mind.

Then she rose and went to her writing desk, pulling a sheet of paper toward her and dipping a pen into the ink well. She nibbled on the opposite end as she thought. Eliot would be at that card party tonight. Perhaps if she confronted him there, her presence would... Laura paused. Would what? What did she imagine he would do if he saw her at the Allenbys' party?

Various unpleasant answers to this question occurred to her, but she brushed them resolutely aside and began to write. She would face Eliot and his mistress and make him choose between them. There, at Vera Allenby's house, he could not continue to deny his connection with her. And once it was out in the open, perhaps they could come to terms. Anything was better than the cold distance and angry disputes which constituted their lives now.

Laura finished her short note of acceptance and sealed it. As she got up to take it downstairs, she glanced in the mirror. The signs of tears were gone; she saw instead a very resolute face, with a crease between the dark eyes and a set mouth. She smiled a little. It was fitting that this was a card party, for she was taking the biggest gamble of her life.

As she walked back up the stairs, Clarissa came out of the breakfast room and greeted her. "Are you going to the drawing room?" she asked. "I shall come with you."

Thus encouraged, Laura turned toward the drawing room, and soon the sisters were seated side by side on the sofa in front of the window. Clarissa looked down, drumming her fingers on the arm of the divan. Laura stared out the window, lost in thought.

At last Clarissa turned toward her abruptly. "Nancy says you were not feeling well last night. I hope you are better?"

Laura started. "Oh, yes, yes. I am perfectly well now. I was merely tired." Clarissa nodded, and Laura went on. "Was your party amusing? Did Mrs. Rundgate have dancing, after all?"

"Yes," replied her sister without animation, "but it was rather silly, you know, just an impromptu hop. I was bored."

Laura smiled at her expression. "How jaded you are

becoming. I can remember when 'an impromptu hop' was the summit of your ambition."

Clarissa smiled now too. "Not the summit, I hope."

"Indeed. Did you not even say to me once that if you could go to the dance at the squire's, you would never ask for more?"

Clarissa laughed. "But that was ages ago. I was a child still."

"It was not quite a year ago," Laura reminded her.

The younger girl's eyes widened. "It was, wasn't it? It seems like another life, like years and years past. How strange." She gazed off before her.

Laura watched her for a moment, smiling, then said, "How are your driving lessons coming along? You do not find them boring, I fancy?"

Clarissa dimpled and shook her head. "I enjoy them no end. I am becoming quite a first-rate whip, you know."

"I don't doubt it. Mr. Redmon is a good teacher then?"

"Splendid." Clarissa's eyes grew faraway again, and she rose to walk about the room. "I am certain now, you know, Laura, that I love him."

Laura sobered quickly. "Are you?" she answered, trying to speak lightly. "You scarcely have had time to really know him, even now."

Clarissa turned on her. "I do know him," she insisted. "I do."

"Ah. And has he... does he return your regard?"

Her sister's belligerence evaporated, and her face fell. "I do not know that. Sometimes he seems to show a marked preference, but at other times he is very stiff and almost cold. I do not understand it." She gazed at Laura eagerly. "I have thought, you know, that perhaps it is because of his situation. He does not have much money, I think. Perhaps he fears that would stand in his way." She looked scornful. "As if I would consider such a thing."

Laura looked at her hands. It was becoming more and more difficult to keep her promise to Mr. Redmon, and it was beginning to appear unwise as well. Clarissa should be told the truth, whatever the consequences, now that she was becoming involved with him. She determined to have a talk with him at the next opportunity and urge him to tell her. And if he would not, she would.

When she said nothing, Clarissa eyed her. "Do you know anything of his family or his situation?" she asked. "Do you think I am right?" Her answer was obviously important to Clarissa, and Laura hesitated before responding. Clarissa came to sit beside her again and took her hand pleadingly. "Oh Laura, do you know anything? You must help me. I shall never be happy without him."

Laura looked into her younger sister's eyes. She had never seen Clarissa so serious. "I can tell you nothing now," she replied finally, "but I will find out. I will help you."

Clarissa squeezed her hand and smiled unsteadily. "Oh I knew you would. We have always stood by each other, have we not?" She rose again and paced about. "But I think I know what you will find. From several remarks he has made, I am convinced that Mr. Redmon comes from a respectable but not wealthy family. He has no fortune." She leaned on the mantel and continued meditatively. "Though that can be cured, I think."

"What do you mean?" asked Laura.

Her sister looked up sharply. "What? Oh I was merely thinking aloud. It is nothing."

Laura watched her narrowly. Clarissa's cheeks reddened slightly, and finally she laughed. "Oh do not look so. I shall do nothing terrible, I promise you. In fact I doubt I shall do anything at all. You must trust me to be wise."

Laura smiled slightly. "I have little reason to do that, especially after the madcap pranks you have played."

Clarissa grimaced. "But I am older and wiser now."

"Older, yes."

The younger girl laughed again. "Well, you shall see."

Laura was by no means prepared to leave it at that, but Mr. Dunham entered the drawing room just then to announce some morning visitors. "Mrs. Rundgate and her daughter are below, ma'am," he told Laura.

"The Rundgates? Oh send them up. I have not seen Mrs. Rundgate for weeks."

In a moment their callers were upstairs, and the ladies were greeting one another cordially. Laura sat down on the sofa with Mrs. Rundgate, while the two younger girls put their heads together in the corner. Anne's mother watched them indulgently.

"Girls are so flighty," she told Laura. "They form what they imagine to be eternal friendships in a moment. Anne insisted upon coming in as we passed by today, even though she and Clarissa had a long talk yesterday. They always find something new to say.

Well, well, I am pleased she has chosen a sensible girl like Clarissa."

Laura, who had been watching the two as Mrs. Rundgate spoke, frowned slightly. Anne was nearly hidden by Clarissa's back, but the taller girl had moved sharply a moment since, and Laura had caught a glimpse of Anne's face. Her expression was extremely distraught; indeed she seemed near tears. Then Clarissa had taken her arm and moved to shield her from the others' gazes. Turning back to Anne's mother, Laura murmured something noncommittal, but she wondered worriedly whether Clarissa had done something to upset her friend.

"And so, how are you, my dear," continued Mrs. Rundgate. "I have not really talked to you this age."

"I am very well, thank you," said Laura. "I have been busy, as have you, I daresay."

The older lady sighed, her ample bosom rippling. "I have indeed. It is a prodigious task to launch a daughter, and after three others I am quite worn down. Thank heaven Anne is my last. And I tell you in confidence that I believe she will be off my hands very soon now."

"Really?"

"Yes, young Whinthorpe's attentions are becoming quite marked. I think he can be brought to a declaration any day." She smiled complacently toward the corner where her daughter sat. "A very creditable match."

Laura considered. "I don't believe I have met him."

"Well no, you wouldn't have. He is just one of the young sprigs, you know, but a very nice gentlemanly boy. I think he will do very well for Anne. She could not be happy with a nonpareil. Wouldn't do at all."

Laura said nothing, for to agree with this very true assessment might seem impolite.

"And so, I can return to the country after this season with all my work done," continued Mrs. Rundgate, "all my girls provided for."

"I hope I can soon offer my felicitations," said Laura.

"So do I, indeed, though it never does to count on something as chancy as a young man's intentions. I will not be easy until it is settled." She looked at the two younger girls again. "For I don't mind telling you, my dear, that I have not been entirely easy in my mind about Anne recently. She seems out of spirits much of the time. I think perhaps London does not agree with her. Your sister has been a vast help. She can always pull Anne from a fit of the dismals in a trice."

"Can she?" asked Laura weakly. She had suddenly remembered Clarissa's mention of a young soldier in connection with Anne Rundgate, weeks ago.

"Oh yes, it is the most amazing thing. But Clarissa is a high-spirited girl. Just what Anne needs. She tends to mope."

"Ah," replied Laura.

Mrs. Rundgate consulted the clock on the mantelpiece and rose. "Anne, we must go. I promised your aunt to arrive by ten, you know." She turned to Laura. "So good to see you, my dear. I am sorry to hurry off, but I did promise my sister to arrive betimes. We are to visit our old governess together, and she frets if we are late." All of the ladies rose, and the sisters bid their guests good-bye.

When they had gone and Clarissa had sat down again, Laura cocked her head at her sister. "Are you pushing poor Anne Rundgate into something imprudent?" she asked her. "She seemed very upset when you were talking."

Clarissa looked very innocent. "What do you mean?"

"I mean," replied Laura, eyeing her suspiciously, "that you must not drive that poor girl to desperation with your mad schemes. She is not as strong as you, Clarissa. Her mother said that she is often melancholy lately and that you cheer her when you come. Have you embroiled her in something?"

Clarissa got up and turned away. "You do nothing but accuse me of foolishness these days, Laura. Do you truly think that I would harm Anne? Can you think me so unfeeling?"

Laura hesitated, looking at her sister's back. "No, of course not. But perhaps you do not realize that others are not so adventurous as you." She watched Clarissa for a moment, then said, "Mrs. Rundgate tells me that Anne is about to receive a very favorable offer from a Mr. Whinthorpe."

Clarissa whirled. "Whinthorpe!" she exclaimed, in strong accents of disgust. "That spineless palaverer. He is nothing more than a zero, Laura. Anne cannot marry him."

"Her mother believes that she would be happy with him. She told me that Anne needs a gentle, undemanding man."

Clarissa colored slightly. "Perhaps that is true, but not Whinthorpe. She needs someone who truly loves her and whom she loves."

"Perhaps Mr. Whinthorpe loves her. How can you tell?"

"Well she does not love him. In fact she holds him in the greatest aversion. He is a toad, Laura, all bowing and silly compliments."

"This is Anne's opinion?" asked Laura.

"Yes. She does not like him, I tell you."

"Because you tell her not to?"

"No! I have nothing to do with the case. Anne fell in love with Captain Wetmore before I even came to London."

Laura frowned. "Oh Clarissa, I wish…"

"You wish me to allow my friend to be forced into an unhappy marriage. I will not. I am not such a beast. Have I not seen how a match based on something other than love can be?" When she had said this, Clarissa looked surprised. The two girls stared at each other wide-eyed for a moment; then Clarissa clapped a hand to her mouth and ran out of the room.

Laura sank back on the sofa and continued to stare. Clarissa had meant her marriage, of course. She remembered tonight's card party again and shivered slightly. If it could not be mended after that, it might be broken forever. She thought bleakly of thirty, perhaps forty, years spent in disputes and cold politeness. What would become of her then?

Sixteen

When she stood before her mirror later that evening, Laura nodded. She looked striking. If Eliot could ignore her in this gown, all was indeed lost. Her dress was red, not rose or dusty red, but crimson. It was made of an embossed brocade, which gave it a rich texture, and was cut with the utmost simplicity. Small puffed sleeves covered her shoulders, and the skirt fell in straight folds to the floor. The bodice was low, but not so low as to make her uncomfortable, and she had tied a slender red velvet ribbon around her white throat, a small white cameo in its center. The bright colors made her skin look particularly creamy, and her unadorned black locks gleamed. Her dark eyes sparkled as she took a last look, then turned to pick up her wrap.

Mary was in ecstasies. "Oh ma'am, you do look that beautiful. What a gown that is, to be sure. I've never seen its like. You will be the prettiest lady at the party."

"Thank you, Mary," answered Laura. Her maid thought that she was going to one of the numerous *ton* parties scheduled for that evening. Indeed invitations to three lay in the pile on her writing desk. "Will you ask them to bring the carriage around?"

Mary went out, and Laura followed more slowly. As she passed Clarissa's door, she paused a moment, then went on. Her sister thought herself in disgrace after their words this morning. She had credited Laura's unusual exclusion of her from the outing to their disagreement, and Laura had allowed her to do so, grateful for this excuse. She would let Clarissa brood until tomorrow.

The carriage was ready when Laura came down, and she went straight through the hall and out the door. But as she climbed up, she noticed that Mr. Dunham was standing at the back of the hall, watching her. Her eyes widened briefly, then she looked away from him. The footman put up the steps and sprang up behind, and they were off. Mr. Dunham shut the door behind them slowly, his eyes on the carriage.

For a moment Laura felt as though she were choking; then she shook her head. I cannot be silly, she thought—not tonight.

During the short ride, Laura thought over her plan. She would arrive at the card party after it was well under way; she had seen to that. When she got there she meant to go straight to Eliot and take his arm, remaining with him for the evening. Her message would be unmistakable, for he must understand that she wanted to separate him from Vera Allenby and become more of a wife herself. And there would be nothing that woman could do. Laura was, after all, Eliot's wife.

An almost grim expression crossed Laura's face. Eliot had not come in all day, even for dinner, so she had not seen him since she found Mrs. Allenby's letter. Perhaps he had forgotten that he dropped it when he ran to her. In any case he would certainly not be expecting to see his wife at this party. For a moment Laura's heart almost failed her, and she came near to telling the coachman to turn back. But then her chin came up once more, and she sat back. It was best to get it over.

The Allenbys' narrow townhouse was brightly lit, and the door was open when Laura arrived, light streaming out into the street. She climbed down, instructing her coachman to return at midnight, and walked up the steps to the hall. A footman in blue livery took her cloak. She looked about her with some curiosity, but there was nothing to criticize in the marble-floored hall and the gracefully curving staircase. A vase of exotic pink-and-purple flowers, whose type Laura did not recognize, sat on the hall table.

She started up the stairs resolutely, and the noise mounted. A buzz of chatter and the clink of glasses came from the large salon on the first floor. Laura stood for a moment on the threshold, scanning the crowd for Eliot, but she did not see him. The air was rather smoky from the many candles in great silver holders scattered throughout the room. The mass of people seemed very closely packed, and the glitter of jewels and fobs was dazzling.

At first Laura thought that there was no one she knew present; then she saw the woman Sybil sitting in the corner. Beside her was another very young man, not the one from the ball, but one who was gypsy dark and rather nervous looking. She also recognized Lila, her hostess that night, and some others, but there was no one she knew well. A little taken aback, she started to move out of the doorway. Suddenly Jack Allenby was at her elbow.

"My dear madam," he said, bending close to her. "You arrive at last. I had nearly given you up. How cruel you are. I was overjoyed when I received your kind note, but then you toy with me in this way. The party has been in full swing for two hours."

Laura moved away a little, saying, "I am sorry. I could not get away." She was still surveying the crowd for Eliot.

Mr. Allenby cocked an eyebrow. "Ah. The jealous husband, perhaps? So fatiguing."

Laura ignored this remark and made as if to move into the room. Mr. Allenby took her arm. "Some champagne?" he asked. "It is the very best, I assure you. We provide only the finest at these little gatherings. People expect it when they are losing money."

Laura allowed herself to be guided to the side of the room and given a glass of champagne. She had sampled it only a few times in her life and frankly preferred less strong beverages, but she did not say so tonight. The pleasant warmth it spread through her limbs was welcome. It dissolved the cold fear that lay in the pit of her stomach.

She continued to watch the people around them. There was still no sign of Eliot, but she did not dare ask for him. "Your party is a great success," she said to Mr. Allenby. "What a crush."

"Oh Vera's card parties are legendary," he replied lightly.

Laura looked around. "But why do you call them card parties?" she inquired. "No one is playing."

Her companion laughed delightedly. "Ah, here speaks the gamester. No one is playing here, my dear Mrs. Crenshaw. The cardrooms are behind us." He gestured, and when Laura turned, she could indeed see into a smaller room at the back of the salon where card tables had been set up. It was much less crowded and appeared quieter.

That is where Eliot will be, she thought to herself. "May I watch the game?" she asked Mr. Allenby.

He laughed again, rather recklessly. Laura wondered how long he had been drinking champagne. "Of course," he exclaimed. "I shall find you a seat. What is your game?"

She did not answer him but moved instead toward the cardroom. He followed quickly, his hand under her elbow. Several people greeted him as they made their way through the mass of guests, and Laura thought one man leered at her offensively. She was glad to reach the other room, where no one even looked up.

"So," said Jack Allenby in her ear, "what shall it be? Whist? No, too slow and old fashioned. Piquet? No. I daresay you are not quite so practiced as some of our players. Ah, I have it. The newfangled game, *vingt et un*. You will like that." As Laura tried to examine the players at the various tables, he led her to one in the far corner and tapped a gentleman there on the shoulder. When this man looked back inquiringly, Mr. Allenby gave an unobtrusive signal, and suddenly the chair was vacant. He pulled it further out and seated Laura, who was still scanning the room. "There you are, my dear," he said smoothly. "You are set up for the evening."

Recalling herself, and swallowing her disappointment at not finding Eliot among the gamblers, Laura turned and looked at the strange faces around the table with dismay. She started to rise. "Oh but I do not know how to play. I do not wish…"

"No need to worry," Mr. Allenby said and pushed her down again. "I shall help you, at first. There can be no objection to that, I think?" He looked around the table, and though one young man across from Laura smirked, there was no protest. "You will get the hang of it in no time," finished the host.

Laura turned to him, her face flushing, and murmured, "But I have not brought any money. I have only about three pounds in my reticule. I did not mean to play. I do not wish to…"

"But of course you must," cried Mr. Allenby, embarrassing Laura. "It is perfectly easy." He signaled a servant, who brought pen and paper, and he showed her how to write out a vowel. "Your credit is good with us, my dear," he said. "Everyone plays so."

Looking about her, Laura saw that indeed many of the players had piles of paper before them rather than money. She hesitated one more moment, thinking miserably that she did not wish to play this unknown French game and that she certainly did not want to sign away her allowance for such a purpose. But everyone was looking at her expectantly. Mr. Allenby had put her in an impossible position. She bent and rapidly wrote out the note. She made it for fifty pounds, thinking that she would thus avoid the necessity of doing this distasteful thing more than once. She would play for a short time, until this sum was gone, and then go to find Eliot.

Mr. Allenby explained the game to her, in what he seemed to think were very clear terms, but Laura did not really grasp the rules. She let her host manage her funds, as his interest in the game far surpassed hers, and let her eyes wander about the room. She never had seen such a solemn party in her life. The people at the tables, chiefly men but with a liberal sprinkling of women as well, were intent and deadly serious for the most part. Only here and there did one smile, and in many cases these smiles held only the feverish gaiety of the winner.

Mr. Allenby turned up the corners of her cards and made a bet. The stakes seemed very high to Laura; her fifty pounds would not last long at this rate. He pulled up a chair next to hers and was becoming engrossed in the cards. He again tried to interest Laura in the progress of the game, but she could not care about the odds.

They lost that hand, and the next, and Laura's money was gone. She started to rise, but Mr. Allenby pulled her back. "You must not abandon the game now," he exclaimed, "just when your luck is about to turn. It must, you know." He signaled for more champagne and persuaded her to write just one more vowel. "Another fifty pounds," he insisted. "You will double that in no time and soon be ahead, you will see."

Reluctantly she did as he asked, taking the pen and the glass he handed her. She would give in this time but would insist upon leaving the table when this sum was gone. But she did not do so. Each time her champagne glass was empty, Mr. Allenby quietly saw that it was filled, and soon she had no clear idea of what was happening. She signed several chits, each she thought for another fifty pounds, but she was not certain of how many. The cards began to blur before her eyes, and she blinked. Mr. Allenby still managed her hand; indeed he had become almost oblivious to anything but her cards and her glass. Laura shook her head fuzzily. There was something she must do here, but she had forgotten what it was. She put down her glass and stared at it accusingly.

Several hands later Laura felt someone behind her and turned to see Vera Allenby standing there, smiling. She started to rise, but the other woman put a hand on her shoulder. "No, no, I would not think of interrupting your play. I am merely acting the hostess for a moment between hands." Her smile seemed hateful to Laura.

Mr. Allenby had looked up at the sound of his wife's voice. "I am managing Mrs. Crenshaw's cards for her," he put in.

"Ah," replied Vera. A signal seemed to pass between them. "Well then, *bon chance* to you both." She started to turn away, then looked down again. "But you have no champagne, Laura. What are you thinking of, Jack?" She summoned the servant, who filled Laura's glass again.

Laura thought of protesting, but she was too tired, and the glitter in Mrs. Allenby's eyes seemed to suggest that she hoped Laura would make some outcry. She allowed the other woman to turn away without speaking, but as she watched her make her way around the tables, stopping here and there to chat for a moment with her friends, she suddenly remembered Eliot. She had come here to find Eliot, in the house of his mistress.

Laura pushed back her chair and got to her feet. The effort was more than she had imagined it would be, and she stood swaying for a moment. Mr. Allenby turned quickly and said, "Where are you going? A new hand is just starting. This one will bring you luck, I am sure."

But Laura shook her head. This, at least, she knew—she did not wish to sit here and watch cards spin dizzily before her any longer. She turned carefully and headed toward the salon. The room was less crowded now, and as she leaned against the doorjamb, she could see everyone there. Several people looked amused at the sight of her, but there was no sign of Eliot or of anyone she knew. She turned back to the cardroom once more, but he was not among the players either. She had made a terrible mistake. Eliot had not come here, or if he had, he had left without speaking to her. The small comfort that he had not obeyed Mrs. Allenby's instructions was lost in her overwhelming regret for having been a fool.

In despair she started unsteadily across the room. When she passed the fireplace, she glanced at the mantel clock. A quarter past twelve! Her carriage would be waiting. What had she been thinking of to stay so late? She tried to hurry and brushed against a man standing nearby. He turned with a frown, but this faded to a smile when he saw her.

"Well, well, what have we here?" he said. "Hello my fine ladybird. How may I serve you?" He grasped her arm, and the number of teeth showing in his smile made Laura feel faint.

How ridiculous, she thought. Whatever is the matter with me. She tried to pull away, but her weak efforts only made the gentleman smile more broadly.

"Do you wish to lead me somewhere, darling?" he asked. "I will follow anywhere."

Providentially another voice broke in. "She's run off her legs, Carstairs. I'll take her." It was Jack Allenby, and Laura looked up at him with real gratitude.

The other man did not release her and looked at her now with even more interest. "Is this the little Crenshaw then?" he asked his host. "They say you have her constantly in tow these days. A pretty piece. But you mustn't be a dog in the manger, Jack. If she wants other company, you must efface yourself."

"She doesn't," answered Jack shortly. He pulled Laura away from Carstairs and led her toward the door. Behind them Laura heard the man make a remark, and the two gentlemen with him laughed. She flushed.

"Thank you," she said faintly. "I was going to my carriage."

Mr. Allenby made no answer, but merely led her along the hallway. Laura shut her eyes for a moment and swallowed. She did not feel particularly well, and she never had wanted anything so much as she wanted to go home now.

They stopped walking, and Laura opened her eyes, expecting to see the front door and a footman holding her cloak. But instead they stood alone in a small, darkened parlor. She could not tell in what part of the house it was. She looked at Mr. Allenby. "What is this room?" she asked. "What are we doing here?"

"I wished to speak to you privately," he answered. "The breakfast room seemed the best choice."

Laura stepped away from him and strove to gather her fuzzy wits. "I want to go to my carriage now, please," she said as firmly as she could. "I am tired. We can talk some other time."

Her companion laughed. "Tired? You are foxed, my dear, quite prettily foxed. It adds a wild color to your cheeks. In fact a touch of champagne makes you utterly entrancing." He started toward her, and Laura backed away.

"What did you wish to speak to me about?" she asked quickly.

Mr. Allenby laughed and continued to approach her. "Why, I only wished to tell you that you have lost more than two thousand pounds tonight, my adorable Laura. I thought perhaps you had forgotten to tally your chits."

Laura stopped dead, and the color drained from her cheeks. "Two thousand pounds!" she cried. "It can't be!"

The man was watching her with amusement. "No? Ah, but perhaps you have forgotten that the last two vowels you signed were rather larger than the others. You made no objection, as all present can testify." His eyes, usually twinkling with merriment, now held an excitement Laura found obscene.

"You know very well I did not see the figures," she snapped, "and so I shall say."

"Repudiate debts of honor?" inquired Mr. Allenby. "Oh no, I do not think so. You will see it differently when you are more clearheaded. Your scrupulously honorable husband would never allow it." He saw her cheeks whiten further and laughed. "I shall not tell him, never fear." He moved toward her again. "Or shall we say, I shall not tell him if you and I remain friends." He was close to her now and slipped an arm about her waist. "*Dear* friends, perhaps?" Suddenly he pulled her against him and forced her lips to his, crushing them in a passionate kiss.

For a moment Laura felt frozen. All the embarrassments and unpleasantness of the evening combined to render her unable to move. Then she came to herself and fought desperately. Jack Allenby was amazingly strong for such a slight man. She could not get free, and his hold on her increased as he pushed her toward a corner of the room where Laura suddenly remembered seeing a divan. She twisted with all her strength and managed to bring them up short against a table in the middle of the room. It was only for a moment; then he forced her away, but that moment was enough for her to grasp a vase which sat there. Before she could think, she had raised it and brought it down with all her strength on Jack Allenby's head.

The man's grip slackened, and he fell heavily to the floor. Without waiting to see whether he would rise, Laura dropped the vase on the carpet beside him and fled. In the corridor, she was confused at first, but soon came to the staircase and saw into the hall. There was no one there but a footman. She glanced quickly in the mirror hanging above a small table across the corridor, straightened her hair and bodice, then walked carefully down the stairs. The footman saw her coming and went to fetch her cloak. In a moment he was bowing her out the door, and she was flooded with relief to see her carriage waiting on the opposite side of the pavement.

When Laura climbed in, the coachman said, "We was just about to knock, ma'am. Thought you might have forgotten the time." Laura said nothing, but nearly fell into the coach in her eagerness to be away. When the vehicle started up, she huddled in the seat and thrust all thoughts from her mind.

❧

When they reached her house, she stumbled on the top step, causing both servants to rush to help her. "I am all right," she insisted. "Only rather tired." But she swayed again even as she reassured them and had to cling to the banister going up the stairs.

Her mind was still fuzzy, and as she paused in the corridor outside her room, supporting herself with one hand against the wall, all her despair came flooding back. She had so wanted to talk to Eliot, to get everything clear between them. And what had she accomplished? Nothing. Trying to straighten, she looked at the door to his room. Perhaps it was not too late; perhaps she could still do so, before he had the chance to hear of her foolishness from someone else.

Trembling, she walked to the door, swallowed, then reached for the knob and turned it. The door swung open.

Warm light from the bedchamber illuminated her

in the doorway. Eliot was standing before the fire-place, wearing only his shirt and breeches. He looked up, startled.

"Why, Laura."

She looked at him beseechingly. With the wild color in her cheeks echoed by the dress she wore, she was incredibly beautiful. She held out a hand. "Eliot, I... I am so sorry."

Before she could go on, he was across the room. He pushed the door shut and took her in his arms. "It doesn't matter," he said, unable to take his eyes off her. "We can make it all right." And bending his head, he kissed her.

All that Laura could think about was how different this was from Jack Allenby's hateful kiss. The things she had wished to say fled from her mind, and her arms automatically went round his neck. Without another word Eliot picked her up and carried her to the bed.

Seventeen

LAURA WOKE ALONE, WITH THE SUNLIGHT STREAMING through a gap in the bedcurtains. She sat up quickly, then sank back, putting a hand to her head. It ached abominably. She pushed aside the curtain and put her feet over the edge of the bed. It was late morning; no one had called her, and Eliot was up long since. She stood, then clung dizzily to the bedpost for a moment, her stomach churning. Too much champagne had left her feeling terrible. But in spite of this her lips curved upward as she walked carefully through the dressing rooms to her own bedchamber.

When Mary had brought tea, and Laura had washed and dressed, she felt somewhat better. But the lessening of her physical ills merely brought mental ones into sharper focus. What was she to do? She had lost two thousand pounds, Mr. Allenby had said. She shuddered a little as she thought of him. Where was she to get such a sum? And if Eliot should find out about her losses, after last night. Laura shuddered again. All would be ruined. He had forgiven so much already.

She went downstairs. She wanted no breakfast, but

she ate a slice of toast to quiet her stomach. Clarissa was in the drawing room when she walked in and greeted her, but to Laura's surprise she said nothing further. The older girl was grateful for the silence at first; then she recalled that Clarissa thought her angry, and she made an effort to speak. "Clarissa, I am sorry for our quarrel yesterday. Let us forget it, shall we?"

Her sister started and turned from the window. "What? Oh yes, of course. I am heartily sorry for the things I said, Laura."

"Let us say no more about it."

Clarissa nodded and turned back to the window absently. Laura frowned and was about to ask her what was wrong when Mr. Dunham came in. "There is a young woman to see you, ma'am," he told Laura. "She says you are expecting her."

Laura turned her frown on Mr. Dunham. "*Expecting* her?" She considered, then shrugged. "Send her up."

Shortly thereafter Mr. Dunham returned, followed by a slender young woman neatly dressed in dove gray. He announced, "Miss Marston," rather stiffly, and left the room.

"Marina," said Laura. "How do you do?" She was not unhappy to see the girl, but she reminded her of the masquerade, and this only suggested her other follies as well.

Marina dropped a small curtsy. "I am sorry I was not here yesterday," she said. "I could not get away."

"Yesterday?"

"To return the money as I said I would. Here it is."

This dialogue had aroused Clarissa's curiosity, and her interested examination of the coins passing between them made Laura uneasy. "You needn't have taken the trouble over such a tiny sum," she said to the girl.

"It was not tiny to me," replied Marina. "Indeed it was a godsend."

"Do sit down," said Clarissa. "We have been very dull this morning." She was clearly intrigued by Marina. Looking at both girls, Laura judged that they were about the same age. And though Clarissa's dark beauty overshadowed the other girl's brown-haired prettiness, Marina had an air of distinction, and her clear blue eyes, which looked upon the world calmly and with an air of expecting nothing, lit her rather thin face.

"Thank you, but I cannot stay. I have only a few minutes away from the shop."

"What shop?" asked Clarissa. Then she looked to Laura to see if she had made an error.

"I am employed in a dressmaker's shop," replied Marina without embarrassment.

Something in her straightforward manner attracted Laura. Here was an obviously educated girl who was forced to work, yet she seemed neither unhappy nor bitter. Laura suddenly wanted to know her better. "Do stay," she said. "Couldn't you say that you met me in the street and that I asked you in to discuss a dress I wish to have made? I will order one."

Marina hesitated. She did seem a bit embarrassed now. "You needn't… I do not wish to be the cause… I am not…"

Laura held out a hand. "Please."

Marina's calm detachment faltered. She looked

distressed, gazed about the room, and finally bowed her head. "I do not know if I can bear it," she murmured, "to be in such a house again." But she did not resist when Laura took her hand and led her to a chair.

"Where do you come from?" asked Clarissa impulsively. "Pardon me, but surely you have not always been a dressmaker?"

Marina raised her head. Laura was shocked to see that there were tears in her eyes. "No, I have worked for two years. Before that I lived on King Street. Then my father, Colonel Henry Marston, was killed in the Peninsula, and we found that he left nothing. I was forced to find some means of supporting myself." All this had come out in a rush, and now she finished. "There, now you know it all."

"How terrible," exclaimed Clarissa. "You poor thing." She looked to Laura for support.

Laura was watching Marina with compassion and a shamefaced respect. Marina met her eyes directly; there was no self-pity or anger in her gaze. "Come to stay with us," said Laura impulsively. "Let us help you."

Marina was astonished. "I beg your pardon," she stammered.

"Yes," cried Clarissa. "What a splendid idea. Do come."

"But I… You cannot mean this, you cannot have thought. You do not know me. You know nothing about me. Everything I have said might be sheer fabrication."

Clarissa began excited protests, but Laura looked directly at Marina once again and said quietly, "No, it is not."

Marina looked back at her, puzzled and confused.

"It is the truth… but I still do not think you are being rational. I must refuse your offer."

"Think about it first. And please believe that I mean it sincerely."

"But your husband, your friends… they will object. No, no, it is ridiculous." Marina rose as if to go just as Mr. Dunham entered the room again.

"The Earl of Stoke-Mannering," he announced and then ushered the gentleman into the room.

The stocky, sandy-haired earl looked very pleased with himself. He had on a new coat and had inserted some whip points in its buttonhole. Bowing ceremoniously, he greeted his cousins and acknowledged an introduction to Marina with marked affability. As he lowered himself to the sofa beside Laura, he smirked a little. "The three graces," he said.

Marina made as if to depart, but Laura restrained her.

It soon appeared that the earl's jovial mood was due to a transaction he had completed that morning, which he described in great detail. He had managed to purchase a much coveted painting almost from under the nose of a rival collector.

"You are interested in painting?" asked Laura politely.

"Painting, sculpture, literature, all the arts, ma'am. You must come down to Stoke this summer. My collection is one of the finest in the land, I believe." He crossed his legs with complacent pride. "This painting today… it is a Giotto. Very small, it is true, but unmistakably a Giotto, whatever Cummings may say now that he has lost out. A truly charming Madonna."

"The blue one?" exclaimed Marina, "with those floating draperies and the cherubs over her shoulder?"

Then she put her hand to her mouth as if shocked at her own temerity.

The earl turned to her eagerly. "You know Giotto? How unusual. No, it is not that one. Unfortunately that has never been for sale; I doubt it ever will be. This is another. Smaller and without the fine detail, but unmistakably Giotto, as I said." He was very insistent on this point. "Are you a collector, perhaps?" he asked Marina.

She flushed. "Oh no, of course not. But I love paintings. My mother used to take me… That is, I am only an amateur."

This stumbling reply seemed to gratify rather than annoy the earl. "Indeed. My cousins must bring you along to Stoke. I believe you would find my collection interesting. I have several Giottos and some Michelangelo drawings."

Marina looked down, too embarrassed to say more.

"It is extraordinary to meet a young lady interested in art," the earl went on. "I have never before done so. I wish I could show you my copy of Sidney's works; it is a first edition and exquisitely illuminated. I purchased it from a bookseller here in London some years ago for a mere pittance."

"It must be wonderful to read from such a book," replied Marina.

He looked shocked. "Read from it! My dear young lady, this is an extremely valuable manuscript. It is kept locked up and is never touched. My entire collection is housed in a strong room I had built especially for that purpose."

"But do you never see it then?" exclaimed Laura involuntarily.

He raised his eyebrows. "Of course. I often spend entire mornings there, looking over my things. It is one of my chief pleasures."

Laura was silenced, and Marina said no more. The conversation was left to Clarissa, who was looking very bored. "How dreary," she said rudely.

The earl turned to her. "You cannot picture it properly," he said. "If you could just once see the collection, you would understand."

At this moment Marina rose very purposefully, insisting that she must go. Laura followed her to the landing. "You will remember what we talked about?" Laura said as the girl started down the stairs.

Marina paused, gazing up at her. "It is a madcap scheme. You will think better of it, and I will think of it no more."

"I meant it," insisted Laura. "Would you feel better if I checked with my husband?" As she said this, Laura wondered suddenly whether Eliot might object, but she thrust this thought away.

Again Marina hesitated. "It is not possible," she replied finally. And she went out.

When Laura came back into the drawing room, the earl was saying, "A charming girl, very intelligent. Who is she?"

"She is the daughter of Colonel Henry Marston," said Clarissa before Laura could speak. The older girl frowned, but Clarissa merely grinned at her.

"Marston," cried the man, surprising both his companions, "not Marston of the Eighth Foot, the hero of Marengo?"

Laura and Clarissa looked blankly at one another. "I

do not know," said Laura. "She has told me only that he was killed in the war."

"But it must be the same man then. He saved a great many English soldiers by flinging his troops into a rearguard action. Why, it was mentioned in all the dispatches. I wish I had known. Perhaps I shall call on Miss Marston."

"She is coming for a visit with us very soon," Clarissa broke in. "You may see her here. Her mother died only a few years ago." She added this as if it explained everything.

"Oh. Ah, how unfortunate," said the earl.

There followed some minutes of commonplace talk; then the earl took his leave. As he went out, Mr. Dunham came in. "Lord Timothy Farnsworth and Sir Robert Barringfors," he announced.

Laura sighed, and Clarissa looked up impatiently as the two slender blond young men strolled into the room. They were dressed with their usual magnificence and immediately began chattering. But it was not until Lord Farnsworth embarked upon a story of a young man who had lost his fortune at the tables that Clarissa looked up and asked, "He lost all his money? What did he do?"

Lord Farnsworth turned to her. "Do? Why, the worst possible thing, of course. Nicholas never had the least particle of sense. Ended by putting a pistol to his head. Foolish, but there you are. He went all to pieces. Even the tradesmen wouldn't give him credit."

Laura's eyes widened. "He shot himself because he had lost his money?"

Sir Robert looked embarrassed. "Here, Tim, not

the thing to talk of in a drawing room. You'll upset the ladies." He kindly turned to Laura. "Didn't manage to kill himself, you know. Botched it. His family has him up in York or some such place. They say he can't speak or…"

"How horrid!" exclaimed Clarissa. "The poor man."

Lord Farnsworth was looking at his friend disgustedly. "And you say I am being loose-tongued. What kind of thing is that to say?" Sir Robert was effectively silenced by this stricture, but Clarissa remained interested.

"But was there no place he could go for money?" she asked.

Lord Farnsworth shook his head. "Family's not at all plump in the pocket. Quite the contrary. They say his sister's gone for a governess or some such thing. Shocking scandal; it's all over the *ton*."

"Could have gone to the Jews," put in Sir Robert helpfully.

His friend's eyes bulged. "The deuce he could. What's wrong with you today?"

"What do you mean, the Jews?" asked Clarissa.

"Nothing at all, Miss Lindley," sputtered Lord Farnsworth, "not a proper subject… Young ladies do not know… That is…" He faltered, staring at Sir Robert balefully.

Clarissa smiled at him. "Are you afraid I too will go to them if you tell me?" she said playfully.

The gentlemen laughed. "Oh that is a corker, Miss Lindley. *You?* Go to a moneylender?" said Lord Farnsworth.

"Well if you are not afraid of that, can't you tell us about them. I am very curious."

Laura looked at her sister narrowly. Could Clarissa somehow have found out about her plight? But Clarissa avoided her eye.

"Well," said Lord Farnsworth slowly. "I suppose there's really no harm. But you mustn't mention that I told you, mind. Bad *ton*."

Clarissa dutifully promised to keep his secret.

"There's not much to it, after all," he went on. "The moneylenders live in the city, roundabout Gold Street and so on. They lend out money to poor chaps foolish enough to ask them, and once they get a hold on a fellow," he shook his head, "well it's the devil to pay. Levy is the chief one, a hard man."

Clarissa considered. "But why? If one pays back the loan, what harm can there be?"

Lord Farnsworth smiled with a superior air. "*If* one pays it back. You simply can't understand such things, Miss Lindley. It is not so easy to repay a loan, especially to the Jews."

"Are the terms unfair?" insisted Clarissa. Then she realized that the other three were looking at her curiously. "I am interested in the question," she finished lamely.

Sir Robert frowned. "Shouldn't be. Not at all the thing. Sorry I mentioned it." He turned to Laura. "My apologies, ma'am. Cork-brained thing to do. Best to say no more about it."

Clarissa was forced to drop the subject, and the talk turned back to the latest *ton* parties and fashion. After a correct quarter of an hour, the gentlemen departed, leaving two thoughtful sisters behind them. Laura was wondering what was wrong with Clarissa and also pondering a plan that had begun to form in her mind. Perhaps she had found the answer to her dilemma. Clarissa stood frowning by the window once more.

"Clarissa, what is wrong?" her sister asked her.

The younger girl turned. "Wrong?"

"Yes, you are abstracted, and you look worried. Has something happened to upset you? You cannot still be angry over our quarrel."

"No, no, of course not," her sister answered impatiently. "There is nothing wrong. I am only rather tired out, I think. I believe I will go upstairs and lie down on my bed for half an hour."

Before Laura could reply, she was gone, and her sister was left to gape after her incredulously. She had never known Clarissa to lie down during the day in the whole course of her life.

Eighteen

LATE THAT AFTERNOON AN OBSERVER ON REGENT Street might have seen Laura Crenshaw come out the front door of her house and descend the steps to the street. Had he been at all familiar with her habits, he might have noted that she was dressed with unusual somberness in a dark gray gown with half cloak and matching bonnet. She also looked rather pale.

Laura, walking quickly to the corner of the street and hailing a hack, was in fact dry-mouthed and quaking inside, though her expression remained fixed. The plan she had pondered all day had gradually begun to seem her only hope, and after tea she had finally resolved to follow it. She was now on her way to the premises of Mr. Levy, chief of the moneylenders, to try to get the two thousand pounds she owed. She knew this was not wise, but she felt if she could just get the money, find her creditors, and pay them quickly, the whole horrid incident might pass without scandal. Perhaps by some miracle no one would tell Eliot she had been at that card party and last night might indeed be a new start for them.

A hack set her down in Gold Street, the driver looking about him dubiously. He did not want to wait for her, but Laura gave him a sovereign, and he agreed to do so. "Be you sartin of this h'address, ma'am?" he asked her, and Laura nodded quickly as she turned to knock on the door. She must not stop to think, else her courage might wholly dissolve.

The door was opened by a neat parlormaid, to Laura's surprise and relief. She had somehow expected a strange and alien welcome. When she asked to see Mr. Levy, the girl curtsied slightly and said she believed Mr. Levy was occupied and would she care to wait. Laura almost cried out with nerves and frustration; how could she sit and wait? But she nodded, and the maid conducted her to a salon off the hall.

She sat down gingerly on the edge of the sofa before the fireplace, stared out the window, and began to rehearse again what she would say to the moneylender. She would ask to borrow the necessary sum and to pay it back in the course of a year. This she could easily manage by curtailing her purchases. She took a piece of paper from her reticule and looked again at the figures she had written there this morning. Yes, she could do it.

Two voices were audible in the next room. One was a woman's, and Laura felt another pang of relief. Mr. Levy must be talking with another client, another woman. For some reason this made her feel much better. She was not the only female to come to him.

She raised her eyes and for the first time looked about her. The salon was not distinguished, though the furnishings and hangings were of good quality and not worn. The only striking thing in the room was a portrait that hung over the mantel. It was of a lovely dark woman with flashing eyes and an aquiline nose. She wore a magnificent gown of amber satin, with diamonds at her neck and wrists and in her hair. Laura gazed at the picture. The woman looked extremely independent and almost fierce, she thought. She did not seem in keeping with this rather drab salon. She certainly never would have been a supplicant here.

The voices from next door grew louder. Was the woman having some trouble? Did Mr. Levy argue with his clients? Lord Farnsworth had given her the impression that one merely asked for the money and was given it. When she thought about this, Laura realized that it was extremely unlikely. She would undoubtedly have to make some guarantee. She put her hand nervously to the pearls at her throat, then rose and moved closer to the opposite wall. There was a connecting door to the room from which the voices came.

Somewhat shamefaced, she put her ear to the door. The man was saying, "But you must tell me your name, miss. You must see that I cannot lend money to unknown persons. What guarantee would I have that they could pay it back?" He sounded as if he were trying to reason with a child. His voice was smooth, but hard, it seemed to Laura.

"But I shall leave the necklace," replied the woman. "Is that not enough?" Laura's brows snapped together. This voice was familiar!

"I fear not," Mr. Levy was saying. "I know something about jewels, and these are not worth the sum you request. I shall need other security. It would be sufficient if I knew your family and their circumstances. You must see what I mean." Though his words were not unkind, their tone was devoid of interest or compassion.

"I cannot tell you," said the woman. "If my family found out I was here…" She trailed off, but Laura was now sure of the speaker's identity. She reached down and tried the door handle; it was not locked. She thrust it open and strode into the next room just as the man was saying, "You can trust my discretion."

"Clarissa!" cried Laura. "What are you doing here?"

Her sister whirled and stared at her, dumbfounded. "Laura! How did you know? How did you find me?"

The sisters stared at each other. "Why are you here?" repeated Laura.

Clarissa sighed, and her shoulders seemed to droop. "It was a stupid scheme, I daresay. I shall have to abandon it."

At this point Mr. Levy intervened. "I take it you are a friend of my client?" he asked smoothly.

Laura turned to him. Mr. Levy was not at all what she had expected. He was a distinguished dark man, with cropped black hair touched with white at the temples and a very smart coat. He fingered a heavy gold watch chain that hung on his waistcoat and watched her speculatively from dark eyes. "I am her sister," answered Laura, raising her chin and hardening her jaw.

"Ah," was the only reply.

"And I shan't let her borrow money. How could

you even consider it, Clarissa?" Clarissa continued to look at the floor.

"I see. You followed her here, I suppose," Mr. Levy said. "Well perhaps it's just as well."

"But you can't have, Laura," put in Clarissa then. "I came from the Rundgates. I was there all afternoon, and I told no one of this plan, not even Nancy. How did you find me?"

Laura felt her cheeks grow hot, but before she could reply, Mr. Levy said, "Perhaps you did not pursue your sister? Perhaps you have come on your own errand?"

Laura flushed even more deeply. "No," she faltered. "That is, I…"

Clarissa suddenly put a hand to her forehead and began to laugh. "You did, Laura, you did. What a hopeless muddle."

Levy smiled blandly. "Perhaps, then, something can still be arranged. You ladies have only to tell me your last names, and we can discuss the matter."

Clarissa sobered instantly. Both sisters cried, "No," at the same moment.

"I have changed my mind in any case," continued Laura positively. "I was foolish to come here."

Mr. Levy spread his hands.

"We both were," added Clarissa. "Come, let us go home."

Laura agreed, and the two girls turned to leave. As they passed the open door of the salon, Laura glanced in; the picture above the mantel was clearly visible behind her, and she felt the woman's fierce gaze was approving.

"Wait," said Mr. Levy sharply.

Laura turned, raising her eyebrows.

"Perhaps I can help you. What is your trouble?" The man's composure seemed broken for some reason.

"It does not matter," said Laura shortly, and signaling to her sister, she went out. They climbed into Laura's waiting hack and started home.

Laura, frowning, turned to her younger sister. "Why did you go there, Clarissa? Are you in debt?"

Clarissa flushed and gazed out the window of the carriage. "No," she replied with some reserve, "I..." She seemed at a loss.

"You what? Why did you need to borrow money? Could you not have come to me?"

"It was a scheme I had," blurted Clarissa. "I could not ask you for the sum I needed. And besides, I knew you would disapprove and stop me."

Laura frowned. "Very likely. What was this scheme?"

Clarissa looked down at her folded hands. "Don't scold, Laura. I hoped to make Mr. Redmon's fortune, you see, so that he might feel free to marry..." She trailed off a bit breathlessly.

Laura's frown had given way to astonishment. "Make Mr. Redmon's fortune by borrowing from a moneylender? Surely this is a foolish start even for you, Clarissa."

Her sister's chin came up. "I needed a large sum," she said. "I was going to bet ten thousand pounds on Devon Lady."

"Devon Lady? What do you mean?"

"It is a horse," Clarissa answered. She saw that Laura was about to speak, so she hurried on. "A sweet goer, Laura. I am sure she will win. We saw her exercising during one of our driving lessons, and Mr. Redmon told me a great deal about her. He knows all the bloodlines, you see. It is quite fantastic. Devon Lady is one of the Duke of Millshire's horses and Mr. Redmon says she is certain to win the big race this week. But she is unknown in racing circles as yet, so the odds are very long."

"Long?" replied Laura dazedly, aghast at this revelation. "Clarissa, you are talking like a groom. Have you gone mad?"

"No, no, you do not understand these things, Laura," said her sister earnestly. "You never cared for horses. This one is a marvel, I promise you. I have seen her, remember. I *know* she will win, and at twenty to one, ten thousand pounds would win two hundred thousand. A fortune, Laura! It would set up Mr. Redmon for anything he chooses."

Laura shook her head as if to clear it. "Let me understand you thoroughly. You planned to borrow this money, bet it on a horse, and then give it to Mr. Redmon?"

Clarissa nodded. "Of course I would have repaid the loan out of the winnings, so the total would not have been quite two hundred thousand."

"How did you expect to persuade Mr. Redmon to accept such a sum from you?"

"Oh he never would have known that it came from me. Do you think me utterly shatterbrained? I should have sent it anonymously."

Laura's eyes bulged a little, and it took her a moment to recover her voice. "An anonymous package containing two hundred thousand pounds," she said to herself wonderingly.

"Only one hundred ninety thousand," put in Clarissa.

Laura shook her head again. "And how did you mean to place such a bet? I suppose you planned to walk boldly into Tattersall's without being noticed?"

Clarissa giggled a little at this impossible picture. "Oh no. Nancy found a way around that. I admit it puzzled me too, at first. But she has a friend who would place the bet for us."

"Or go off with your ten thousand," responded Laura drily.

"No, he is a very close friend. And completely trustworthy, Nancy says."

Laura set aside the question of this unknown man's trustworthiness and that of the unwisdom of confiding such schemes to the servants, and turned to her sister earnestly. "You talk of this so lightly, Clarissa. I am shocked. Have you no notion of how wrong and foolish you have been?"

Clarissa hung her head. "I knew all along it was foolish," she said, "but I could see no other way. You just do not understand, Laura, how vitally important this is. As long as Mr. Redmon is so poor..."

She left it to her sister to finish this thought. "He cannot offer for you. Well I confess I am at a loss. I can only say that I never have heard of such a brazen and harebrained scheme in my life."

"But, Laura," replied her sister almost pleadingly, "if you truly understood how I feel about him. I would do anything..."

"Obviously," interrupted the older girl unsympathetically. "Even go to a moneylender. Oh Clarissa, how could you?"

Her sister looked at her defiantly. "Well you needn't act so self-righteous. It's what you were about to do yourself, isn't it?"

Laura stared at her. She was right, of course, and suddenly it was as if Laura woke from a bad dream. Clarissa had been foolish and unwise, but she herself had been far worse. What had inspired her to be so utterly lost to prudence and propriety? It was entirely her own fault that she was in her current fix, and she blamed herself bitterly.

Clarissa was frightened by her expression. "Laura, what is it?" she cried. "You are in trouble of some kind, are you not? How selfish I have been not to see it. What has happened? Tell me."

Laura looked at her with tragic eyes for a moment. How could she burden her sister with this awful story? But the eager sympathy and love in Clarissa's eyes was too much for her. She stumblingly told her the whole, often pausing to gulp back tears.

❧

By the time Laura had finished, they had reached home. As they climbed down from the hack, Clarissa squeezed Laura's hand. It took only a moment to reach Laura's bedchamber, and there the younger girl hugged her. "Poor darling," she said. "How worried and upset you must have been, and I have not paid any heed. I am a beast."

This brought a smile to Laura's lips. She was thankful and a bit surprised that Clarissa did not seem in the least shocked by her dilemma.

The younger girl plumped herself down on the bed.

"So the thing now is to get money," she said, biting her thumbnail and frowning. "You know, Laura, I daresay our aunts might give it to you."

Laura shook her head miserably. "I could not ask it of them. Two thousand pounds would be a half year's income."

"Would it?" responded Clarissa absently. "But they have the house and things, and I daresay some savings. However you are probably right. We shall have to think of something else." She frowned again, then brightened. "I might go to Eliot," she said. "I could tell him that I had been foolishly lured into a card game and lost the money before I knew it. It is nearly the truth. I daresay he would be angry, but if I swore I had learned my lesson, he would relent and give me the money, I'm sure. And what is two thousand pounds to him? Nothing."

"I could not let you do such a thing, Clarissa. What would Eliot think of you?"

"Well," answered Clarissa practically, "it doesn't matter overmuch what he thinks of me. It is what he thinks of *you* that is important, is it not?"

Laura flushed. "I must go to him and make a clean breast of it," she sighed. "It is the only right thing to do."

"Nonsense," cried her sister. "It is the most foolish of all things to do. Let *me* ask Eliot for the money. It can do no harm."

"No. I have been wickedly imprudent, but I will not compound it by allowing you to bear the blame. That scheme will not do. Besides, a great many people saw me at the card party. Who can say but that one may mention it to Eliot. Then he will immediately suspect the money was for me."

Clarissa frowned. "You are still being silly." But she sounded less certain. "Very well. We shall have to think of something else. But gaming debts must be paid immediately, Laura."

"I know," said her sister miserably.

"Who do you owe?"

"I am not even sure of that. I cannot seem to remember properly."

Clarissa stamped her foot. "Oh it is infamous. They made you tipsy and then fleeced you, just like in those horrid gambling hells. You should not have to pay at all."

Laura put her forehead on her hand and sighed. "Perhaps. But that does not alter the case."

Before Clarissa could reply, there was a knock at the door, and Nancy peeped round it. "Excuse me, ma'am, but a boy has just brought this letter. He said it was important, so I came right up."

Laura put out her hand for it. "All right, Nancy. Thank you." The maid went out again. "I wonder what it can be," said Laura as she tore open the heavy cream-colored envelope. But when she unfolded the sheet inside and read the short note, she turned white and dropped it onto the carpet.

"What is it?" cried Clarissa, picking it up. "My dear Mrs. Crenshaw," she read. "You will be pleased to know that I have possessed myself of all of your vowels from our card party. So much more pleasant, I think, to owe a friend. You may forward the sum to me at your convenience, or failing that, we might come to some other arrangement. There are so many more enjoyable returns than money for the sincere affection that I hold for you. Shall we not meet to discuss the matter? I will await you in the Greek Pavilion at Vauxhall at midnight tomorrow. Do not fail me. I should dislike having to seek you in your husband's house, but I will not hesitate to talk to Eliot if you do not come. Yours in hopes. Jack Allenby." Clarissa threw the letter down with a little sound of disgust. "He is utterly contemptible."

Laura had not moved. She was still very white, and she stared unseeing at the window.

"This is nothing but blackmail," Clarissa went on indignantly. "There is no calling it anything else."

"Yes," said her sister tonelessly. "He will tell Eliot if I do not do as he says, and then I will be ruined." Her face twisted. "But I shall be ruined if I agree also. I am trapped." And she burst into tears.

Clarissa ran to her and put her arms around her. "No, no, do not cry. We shall think of something, you'll see. I shall think of something." But her eyes were bleak as she held her sister close.

Nineteen

LAURA HARDLY SLEPT THAT NIGHT. SHE HAD NOT GONE down to dinner, pleading a headache, because she was afraid to face Eliot, should he be home. She wrestled for hours with various schemes for saving herself. Nothing came to her, and as she fell into an uneasy doze in the early hours of the morning, she had almost resolved to write to her aunts. Perhaps they could lend her the money; she would pay it back. Even after she slept, Laura tossed and groaned. She woke unrested and twisted in her sheets.

Mary brought her breakfast on a tray when Laura rang. She fussed about her, insisting that she stay in bed. Though this was the last thing Laura wanted at this moment, she gave in after one feeble protest. She hadn't the energy to argue over trivialities. There were three envelopes beside the teapot on the tray. Mary was very proud that she had thought to bring the mail with breakfast. But Laura eyed them apprehensively and could hardly choke down a bit of toast with them sitting before her. When Mary left the room, she put the toast back on the plate and stared at the letters.

Was there another note from Mr. Allenby among them? she wondered.

Reluctantly she reached out and took up the first. Turning it over, she saw that it was from Eliot's mother; she knew her hand very well. With a sigh that held both relief and a new worry, she slit it open and unfolded the letter within.

Mrs. Crenshaw was perplexed. "My dear Laura," she wrote, "whatever have the two of you been at? I received the oddest note from Eliot last week, practically ordering me to London to 'take charge of you.' What sort of nonsense is this? I write to tell you that I have refused absolutely to do any such thing. I wrote my lumpish son a rather stiff note, I may say. Take charge, indeed! I shall come up to town only if you also request it, and so I told him." She went on to retail the news of her neighborhood and describe the state of her garden. Laura smiled as she read the affectionate closing. This was like a breath of fresh air.

Her smile lingered as she put down the letter and picked up another. Perhaps she should ask her mother-in-law to come, she thought. Perhaps Mrs. Crenshaw could help her out of the ever increasing tangle she had fallen into. But when she thought of telling Mrs. Crenshaw what she had done, Laura shuddered a little and turned to the next letter. She would never understand.

The second letter was from Marina. Very prettily, she wrote that she had thought over Laura's offer at great length and, much as she appreciated it and was truly grateful, she felt she still must refuse. This made Laura frown a little; she had honestly hoped that

Marina would accept. Laura considered the note again, then put it aside. She would go to speak to Marina later in the day. As she thought this, a wave of color suddenly washed her cheeks. With all the trouble currently threatening her, could she in conscience take Marina into her household? What if she was disgraced? What would become of Marina then? She put her hands to her flaming face and nearly cried in despair.

Shaking her head as if to rid it of such thoughts, she picked up the third envelope and tore it open. The note inside contained only a short message, printed rather than written. "Do nothing hasty about your debt," it said. "Postpone action until tomorrow, and all will be well." Laura stared at this uncomprehendingly for some time. There was no signature. She picked up the envelope. Her name and address was also printed, and there was no identifying mark. She threw back the covers and went over to her writing desk, unlocking it and taking out Mr. Allenby's horrid note of the night before. She compared the two. Though she could not imagine why Mr. Allenby would send a message like this one, he was the only one who knew the whole story. But the notes were not similar. The paper was different, the pens had different tips, and the inks were not at all alike. Still frowning, Laura went back to her bed.

She sat down and considered the two notes further. Mr. Allenby's was clear, frighteningly clear. But the other. Who would send her such a message? Someone who had been at the card party perhaps and seen her losses? She flushed again. It was embarrassing to think that some stranger was taking pity on her. But who else could it be?

Laura sat for a long time, wondering. Then she rose and again went to her desk to write a note. The unknown writer's idea was a good one in any case; she would put off the appointment with Mr. Allenby until tomorrow, gaining time to think of some way out of her predicament. She doubted he would agree to a long delay, but one day should not be a problem. She sealed the note, directed it, and rang for Mary. This made her feel better. At least she was doing *something*.

❧

It was late morning by the time Laura descended the stairs, and the house was quiet. Mary had told her that Eliot was out and Clarissa was changing in her room, so Laura expected to find the drawing room empty when she entered. But a man rose when she walked in, and bowed politely. It was Mr. Redmon, come to fetch Clarissa for her driving lesson.

"Good morning," said Laura. "I am glad to find you here. I have been wanting to speak to you."

Mr. Redmon held up a hand. "There is no need. I believe I know what you would say. You think I should tell the truth. Is that not it?"

"Yes," replied Laura.

He nodded. "As do I. I must tell her, and I am grateful to you for remaining silent so long. I shall make a clean breast of it very soon, I promise you. In fact I was going to seek an opportunity to discuss the matter with you. I want your permission to pay my addresses to Clarissa." His open countenance clouded a little. "I hope you will not think my deception renders me ineligible to be Clarissa's husband?"

Laura repressed a smile. "No. I am very glad that you are going to tell the truth, however. And I wish you success." Privately she thought that there was little doubt of it.

He started to smile, then looked serious again. "There is one thing," he said hesitantly. "I should go up to Millshire first and inform my parents. I should like to do so before all is settled between us." He flushed a little. "You will think this odd, I suppose, but my parents are older and rather, well, sensitive to the proprieties. I…"

Laura did smile this time. "Believe me, I do know what you mean," she said. "By all means, tell them first. But do not delay too long with my sister."

"No, no I won't," he answered, beaming sheepishly. "I have no wish to, I promise. I will leave for Millshire today."

She smiled again, but before she could speak, Clarissa came into the room and the two young people went off together. Laura felt better when they were gone. Things were turning out very well for Clarissa, at any rate.

Laura sat down on the drawing room sofa and picked up a book, but she was too preoccupied to read. She decided to go out and see Marina. It would keep her from brooding on her own problems.

The streets were crowded with carriages, and thus it was nearly noon before Laura reached the shop. The workroom behind the curtain was empty. She sighed impatiently and looked around. There must be someone here.

"Hello," called Laura, but there was no answer.

She walked through the workroom and was about to mount the stairs at the back when she heard the voices of two people coming down. She retreated to the front of the shop again. Thus the curtain hid the speakers from her when they emerged from the stairway. Surprisingly one was a man.

"You can't fool me, Miss Highty-Tighty," he was saying. "I don't know what your game may be, but if it's hopes of getting more money, you've mistaken your man. Jasper Greeley pays what's fair and right and no more."

Laura's frown returned. Could this man be buying a dress?

"Perhaps you've an offer from someone else, hey? One of the dandies you used to know, maybe? No need to look so startled. I've found out about you. I don't strike a bargain without knowing what I'm getting. Maybe you think you're too good for the likes of me, eh? That why you disappeared the other night? Well you may as well leave off these airs, my girl. Do you know what happens to little dressmakers who get above themselves? They end up old and blind in the workhouse is what. There's no pensions for you, my girl, unless you take my offer. I'm a generous man with those as pleases me, as I've told you before now."

"You may be right," said Marina's voice calmly. Her cool cultivated accents were a marked contrast to the man's harsh tones. "But I must take my chances, I fear, and refuse your flattering offer." The irony in her voice was thick. "My upbringing does not allow me to consider an arrangement such as you suggest."

"Ahhh, your upbringing, is it? Your sort makes me

sick, you know that? Because a man makes his pile in trade, you despise him. Never mind that those man-milliners over in St. James are libertines and gamesters, they're the gentlemen, and that's that. Not one of them would treat you as well as I will. Come, these airs and graces are becoming, but you can hardly afford them, now can you?"

His voice had taken on a disagreeable wheedling tone, and there was the sound of a scuffle. Laura started forward and pushed back the curtain. Marina was struggling to throw off the arm of a large beefy looking man in tight yellow pantaloons. Laura lowered her eyelids slightly and, in her coldest and blandest voice, drawled, "Pardon me, but is anyone minding this shop?"

At the sound of her voice, the man started, loosed his hold on Marina, and whirled. In the face of Laura's bored, slightly amused expression, he quailed. Here was no poverty-stricken dressmaker's assistant, he saw at a glance.

Marina had flushed scarlet when she saw Laura, but she recovered herself admirably and said, "Yes indeed, madame, I shall be right with you." She picked up a low-crowned beaver hat from the table and handed it to the man. "Good day, Mr. Greeley," she finished firmly.

He took the hat, started to speak, then jammed it on his head and went out, brushing rudely past Laura in the doorway. The look he threw over his shoulder was angry and threatening.

When he was gone, Marina sank down in one of the chairs beside the table and took several deep breaths. She was shaking. Laura laid a sympathetic hand on her shoulder. "Who was that horrid man?" she asked.

Marina hung her head. "Mr. Greeley," she replied almost inaudibly, "a friend of the owner. He comes here often."

"I daresay," answered Laura grimly. "And how is it you are left alone here to receive him."

Even more softly, Marina said, "Mrs. Smith always sees to it. She, she…" And Marina burst into tears.

Laura's eyes hardened. "I see." She looked around the room. "Have you a hat here or anything else?"

Puzzled, Marina indicated that her gloves and shawl were on a peg at the back of the room. Laura fetched them and came back to take Marina's elbow. "Come along," she said firmly.

Marina stood, still wiping the tears from her cheeks. "Come where?"

Laura put her hands on her hips and regarded the girl. "You are coming home with me," she said with eyes flashing, "And I do not wish to hear any more nonsense. You cannot remain in this place. And you needn't try to argue with me, for I am utterly determined. Marina, why did you not tell me?"

The other girl looked down. "I was ashamed. It was Mr. Greeley who took me to the masquerade. Before that, I had not realized that he…" She paused and swallowed. "I had thought that he meant marriage, you see, and in my position, well, I probably would have accepted him. He is a Cit, but I did not think it likely that I would receive any more eligible offers." She smiled a little at the idea. "Then I found that he has a wife."

"I see," said Laura. "Come along." She put the shawl around Marina's shoulders and urged her toward the door.

"But, oh I cannot," replied Marina. "I cannot allow you to…"

"You have nothing to say about it," snapped Laura. "When I think of that horrid man coming here and you left alone to wait for him, I am so angry I can hardly speak."

"But the shop," protested Marina as Laura hurried her toward the door.

"I do not care if everything is stolen," said Laura. "It would serve her right. In fact I have half a mind to summon some of the street urchins and tell them of the opportunity."

Marina laughed feebly. "Oh you would not. Mrs. Smith would be so angry."

"Mrs. Smith's feelings are no longer of any concern to you. Climb up and let us be off."

Thus urged, Marina got into the barouche, and in a short time they were back at Regent Street, and Laura ushered Marina in. She told Mr. Dunham to have the blue bedchamber prepared and took the girl up to the drawing room. Clarissa was there, returned from her lesson and a little cast down by the news that Mr. Redmon was going out of town. She brightened immediately when she saw Marina and heard that she was coming to stay. "Splendid!" she cried. "I knew Laura would persuade you. How good it will be to have you here."

"Thank you, Miss Lindley. You are very kind."

"Oh you must call me Clarissa," answered the other.

"We will be great friends I know, so we may as well begin at once."

Marina smiled.

"Yes," added Laura, "let us not stand on ceremony."

Their guest's smile wavered, and she sank down in an armchair. "You are too kind to me," she said tremulously. "I do not know what to say."

"Nonsense," said Clarissa. "We are actually being odiously selfish, for we want you here with us. Come, I will show you your room."

Marina made a helpless little gesture, then put herself in Clarissa's hands. Laura smiled a little as the two went out, her sister chattering continuously. She took off her bonnet and set it on the table before the fireplace, then stretched her arms tiredly. She felt as if she hadn't slept properly for days, as in fact she had not. And the moment she was alone, her problems came rushing back to haunt her. Where was she to find two thousand pounds? How could she meet Mr. Allenby alone after his behavior at their last meeting? Who had written the mysterious note telling her to postpone the appointment? Her brain began to spin with all these uncertainties, and she sat down on the sofa and put a hand to her forehead.

"You look utterly done up," said a voice from the doorway.

Laura started violently and jumped up to face her husband.

"I beg your pardon, I didn't mean to startle you. But you do look terribly tired, Laura. You must take better care of yourself. You seemed to have the burdens of the world on your shoulders as you sat there."

It was the first time they had spoken alone since the night of the card party, and Laura was buffeted by conflicting emotions. The concern in his voice and the memory of his tenderness made her want to burst into tears and run to his arms, but guilt and fear kept her frozen where she was. Had he heard anything?

Her frightened expression brought her husband further into the room. He looked at her intently. "Are you tired, Laura? And is that all?"

Again he spoke kindly, but the question raised something like panic in the girl. At all costs Eliot must be kept from knowing of her foolish mistakes.

"Yes," she replied with an attempt at lightness. "Of course. What else?"

He studied her for a moment longer, then made an apparently irrelevant remark. "I received a note from my mother this morning." He smiled wryly. "Or perhaps I should say, I received a scolding. She will not be coming to visit us."

"She wrote me also," said Laura.

"Did she? I am not at all surprised. She found my letter extremely boneheaded, it appears; and after considering the matter in light of her comments, I think she is probably right. I have a damnable temper, Laura, and sometimes it gets the best of me. A visit such as I envisioned would be a mistake, I admit it. I hope you will forgive my hastiness?"

"Oh yes, of course," said Laura breathlessly. She knew he was being very kind to her, and she wanted to respond. But she could think of nothing but Mr. Allenby and the debt, and this made talking to, or even looking directly at, her husband next to impossible.

His eyebrows drew a little together. "My saving grace," he went on, "is that my fits of anger pass as quickly as they come, so that in the rare cases when I cannot control them, they at least dissipate, allowing me to make sincere apologies. I fear I have had to make more of them to you than you deserve. It is my inexperience as a husband, perhaps, that makes me fly out at you on occasion. I shall learn better, I promise." He smiled warmly at her, and Laura tried to return his look. But she clearly did not succeed, for he continued bluntly. "Laura, are you in some sort of trouble?"

"What do you mean?"

"I do not claim to be the most perceptive of men, but even I can see that something is troubling you. I thought all was well with us now."

"Oh there is nothing. I am perfectly all right. Only tired. You needn't worry."

Eliot eyed her questioningly, started to speak, then looked down. There was a pause. When he looked up again, his face was expressionless. "Are you afraid to confide in me?"

At that moment Laura nearly told him the whole. He looked genuinely pained by the idea that she might fear him. But even as she opened her mouth to speak, she thought of how that expression would harden when he knew. She remembered the harsh way he had spoken to her about other more trivial lapses. "Of course not," she said. "Not at all."

"You needn't be." He came and took her hand. "You mustn't be."

"No, no. There is nothing wrong. I am only tired. I think I will go upstairs and lie down a little." She was desperate to get away, for she could not stand being near him and yet feeling so distant.

He drew away a little. "I will see you at dinner then."

She raised her eyes. "Will you be home?"

"If you have no objection," he responded ironically.

"No, no, of course not," said Laura quickly. She gave him an uncertain smile and hurried from the room.

When she was gone, Eliot remained standing beside the sofa for some time. He was frowning and staring at the fireplace grate. Finally he seemed to come to a decision and went over to ring the bell for Mr. Dunham.

Twenty

Dinner that evening was quiet. Laura had not completely recovered from her earlier encounter with her husband, and Marina was somewhat ill at ease. Eliot was thoughtful. Only Clarissa seemed to be able to summon any high spirits; she was delighted with Marina's appearance in one of her gowns, a deep blue crepe. And indeed their visitor's looks were vastly changed by this dress. While in her plain dressmaker's gown she had seemed quite attractive and refined, in the new dress she was striking.

Somewhat to Laura's surprise, Eliot exerted himself to be pleasant. He spoke of Marina's father and the battle of Marengo, revealing a great deal more knowledge than Laura would have credited to him. In the face of his obvious interest and pleasant manner, Marina soon opened up, and by the time the ladies rose to go up to the drawing room, the group was chatting easily.

Eliot did not linger alone in the dining room but followed them upstairs after a quarter of an hour. Once again Laura was surprised. He sat down with the appearance of one who intended to stay and quite as if it was his habit to spend the evenings in the drawing room. No one else appeared to find this unusual, but Laura was first puzzled, then apprehensive. Was he going to question her further? This thought plunged her into silent gloom. She did not notice that Eliot cast several questioning glances in her direction.

This might well be her last such evening in her home, Laura thought with a twinge of self-pity. Tomorrow she must meet Mr. Allenby. She still did not know what she would say to him, but she had no illusions and no hopes of a favorable outcome. Jack Allenby would ruin her; she was sure of it.

Laura was so engrossed in this train of thought that she started when Mr. Dunham announced from the doorway, "The Earl of Stoke-Mannering."

The two younger girls were looking at the door, but Eliot saw Laura's reaction. "What is it?" he asked her.

She shook her head quickly and rose to greet their guest, who had already embarked on a lengthy apology for disturbing them.

"I hope I do not intrude," the earl was saying. "This fashion of calling whenever one pleases, without so much as a note sent round in warning, makes me quite uneasy, I can tell you. But everyone says it is 'all the crack.' I abhor all forms of slang, but there is something striking about that phrase, is there not? I heard another last night—'shot the cat.' It signifies inebriated. Is that not odd? I can't think why."

Eliot was smiling, and Clarissa stifled a giggle, but Laura had lost the thread of his speech in her effort to gather her wits and said only, "Ah."

"Though I cannot, of course, be certain," said Eliot, "I

understand the phrase is of Cockney origin and relates to the possibility of eccentric behavior when in that state."

"Does it indeed?" replied the earl interestedly. At this point he noticed Marina and greeted her effusively. The two sat down with Clarissa on one of the sofas. Eliot and Laura, taking another, watched him launch a discussion of balloons. He seemed very knowledgeable about their workings.

"I do not think your sister has overmuch interest in aeronautics," said Eliot. "Lamentable."

Laura smiled. "He means well."

"I concede that, but I confess the phrase is one that always makes my blood run cold. What horrors are perpetuated in the name of meaning well!"

Laura's smile faded. This hit rather too near the mark. "It is true," she said seriously, looking away.

He watched her closely but went on in the same tone. "Indeed I think the world might be much better off if people meant ill far more often. Then, at least, one would know how to respond; there would be none of this infuriating self-righteousness. Yes, I think bad motives are what is wanted."

Laura shook her head, her expression lightening again. "How absurd you are. My cousin brings out a whole new side of you."

Eliot looked surprised. "Do you find it new?" He frowned. "Perhaps you are right."

Before Laura could reply to this somewhat puzzling remark, Clarissa spoke to them. "Cousin Matthew has invited us to attend a balloon ascension tomorrow, Laura. What say you?" Her expression indicated that she hoped Laura would refuse.

Her sister hesitated. They had no engagement for that afternoon, and Marina looked interested in the outing. "It sounds delightful," she answered, earning a reproachful glance from Clarissa.

"Indeed," added Eliot unexpectedly, "I have just realized that I have never seen a balloon ascension. I believe I will accompany you."

Laura and Clarissa stared at Eliot incredulously, but the earl beamed. "Splendid," he said. "I think everyone will find it most educational. These apparatus are very delicate and extremely interesting, you know."

"So I have heard," said Eliot drily. "When is it?"

"At three," answered their guest. "But one must be on the field rather before the time in order to get a good place. I shall come round at one."

Eliot acknowledged this. "I shall drive my curricle." The earl seemed a bit disappointed that Eliot would not join him in his own vehicle. He turned to tell the ladies about the team he would drive.

"Doubtless you will ride with me?" Eliot murmured to Laura as the earl took his leave a few minutes later.

She nodded, smiling.

Their guest was hardly gone when Clarissa burst out, "What a bore! Balloons! Who cares a fig for balloons? Isn't he a perfect toad, Marina?"

Marina looked down. "I was not really so bored."

Clarissa was astonished. She shook her head, then grinned good-naturedly and shrugged also. "There is no accounting for tastes."

Marina rose. "I am very tired. I believe I will go to bed early, if you will excuse me."

Eliot also rose. "I must go too. I promised to meet March at White's. I shall see you tomorrow at the balloon ascension." He smiled again, bowed slightly, and left the room.

"Well," said Clarissa when he was gone, "whatever has come over him? I have never seen him so pleasant."

Laura shook her head, her eyes still on the door where Eliot had disappeared. Clarissa looked at her face for a moment; then she also rose. "Well I shall go to bed too, I suppose. I must be in good form for this outing tomorrow. It will take all my self-control to be civil, so I had better be well rested."

Laughing, Laura stood. "I will go up with you."

As they started up the stairs, Clarissa said, "Can Marina have meant it when she said that she was not bored by our cousin, do you think? I could hardly believe my ears."

"Perhaps she is interested in balloons. Some people are, after all."

Clarissa shrugged.

They reached the upstairs hall and were about to say good night when Laura's name was called from the head of the stairs. She turned to find Mr. Dunham there, holding an envelope out to her. "This arrived just before dinner, ma'am," he said blandly. "I thought it best not to interrupt your meal."

Laura took it from him slowly. Mr. Dunham's eyes seemed cold and unfeeling to her, and she had come to hate receiving letters. "Thank you, Mr. Dunham," she said. The man bowed and disappeared down the stairs once more.

Both sisters stared at the envelope without moving. "Do you think it is another from *him*?" Clarissa whispered finally, her eyes wide with concern.

Laura took a breath. "I do not know… and will not until I open it." She turned toward her bedroom, and Clarissa followed her in.

Mary was there waiting for her and dropped a small curtsy. But the smile on her face faded at their expressions. "That will be all for tonight, Mary," said Laura. "I shan't need you."

"Yes, ma'am," answered the maid. Her round red face crinkled into a worried frown as she went out.

Laura sank immediately onto the chair in front of her dressing table. She looked at the letter for another moment, then tore it open and read the short note. She fell back when she had finished and cast a despairing glance at her sister. "It is from Mr. Allenby. He says only that he looks forward to seeing me tomorrow evening and that I mustn't put it off again." She put her head in her hands.

Clarissa clenched her fists. "That man is an utter brute. How I wish I could kill him!"

"Clarissa!"

"I do. Why should I not? He does not deserve to live."

"You are overwrought. And killing Mr. Allenby would solve nothing. It would not pay my notes or stop people from talking about my appearance at that awful party. Be sensible."

Clarissa hung her head. "I'm sorry. But it makes me so angry to see you being treated in this way. You do not deserve it, Laura. I am the one who always got into scrapes and counted on you to rescue me. I should be the one in trouble now."

This absurdity drew a laugh from Laura even in her current state. "What a goose you are, Clarissa. How would that mend matters? Do be quiet."

Clarissa looked down again and pounded on the dressing table fiercely. "What can I do?" she cried. "There must be something."

Laura looked at her. "You can stand by me," she said seriously. "I may need it after tomorrow."

Her sister stared at her for a moment, aghast, then burst into tears.

Curiously Clarissa's sobs seemed to harden Laura's resolve. "Please, Clarissa," she said, "this will do us no good. I thank you for your concern, but do not cry, I beg you."

Slowly the younger girl regained control of herself. "I am sorry," she sniffed, "but I cannot bear to see you so."

Laura sighed. "I admit I can see no way out of this tangle. Unless perhaps I can persuade Mr. Allenby to let me pay him gradually."

Clarissa frowned. "I think not. But we are forgetting the other letter you received. Someone is trying to help you; perhaps they will manage something."

Laura's expression did not lighten. "That is no comfort to me. I cannot trust an unsigned note, Clarissa. Most likely it was a cruel prank." She nodded to herself. "Yes, the more I think about it, the more convinced I become that that is what it was."

"No!" exclaimed the younger girl. "I will not believe

that. I refuse. It is too horrid. Someone is trying to help you; I know it!"

Laura shrugged. "As you will."

A silence fell as both girls contemplated Laura's predicament. Their expressions became more and more doleful.

"You are certain," said Clarissa some time later, "that you cannot go to our aunts?"

Her sister shook her head. "I will not."

"And you still refuse to let me go to Eliot?"

"We have talked this over already, Clarissa. I do refuse. But it would not work in any case. Indeed it might make things even worse."

Clarissa sighed. "If only there were someone else…"

"There is not, and I forbid you to speak of this to anyone at all. I will not have you going to anyone to ask for money."

Clarissa's chin came up. "What do you think me? Of course I would not."

Laura nodded. "We may as well go to bed now. There is nothing to be done."

Her sister looked at her stony countenance, started to hold out a hand, then looked down and turned away. "All right," she replied in a muffled voice. "But I shan't sleep. I am going to think of a plan to save you, Laura."

The older girl made a gesture, and Clarissa went out. When the door shut behind her, Laura's head sank and her shoulders drooped. It was a long time before she summoned the energy to undress and fall into bed.

Twenty-one

THE PLEASURE OF HELPING MARINA CHOOSE SOME NEW dresses the next morning nearly drove Laura's problems from her mind once more. The day started with a lively argument at the breakfast table with Marina insisting that she would not accept their generous offer of clothes, and Clarissa insisting that she must. Their disagreement ended with the purchase of several gowns.

They reached home in time for a light luncheon of cold meat and fruit, and then all three ladies went upstairs to change for the balloon ascension.

Laura heard Eliot come in as she dressed; he moved about in his bedchamber talking to someone. As Mary brushed out her black curls and arranged them about her face, she listened to the muffled noises. So he really would come with them. She had not precisely doubted this. He had said he was coming, and he always performed what he promised, but still she was surprised. It was not at all the sort of party he liked.

Mary finished with her hair, and Laura stood to look at herself in the long mirror on the front of the wardrobe. She had chosen a simple dress of pale green muslin. She looked thinner, as well as paler, than when she had come to London, and her eyes seemed large for her face. She picked up a paisley shawl and started downstairs to wait for the others.

Eliot was already in the drawing room when she walked in. He looked at her rather closely, she thought.

Sighing, she compared his unchanged appearance with her own. In his immaculate dark blue coat and buff pantaloons, Eliot looked the same modish Londoner who had been so annoyed when the snow-storm trapped them in the inn. His dark hawk-like face and sharp gray eyes had not changed at all. Her eyes met his, and the unfocused regret she had been feeling was suddenly clear and sharp. Something seemed to catch in her chest, and a sensation that was not exactly pain went through her. Everything seemed horrible at that moment. Eliot had showed he had begun to care for her a little, but her foolhardiness would wreck that small beginning. Lost in these thoughts, she had nearly forgotten her surroundings, but she was suddenly aroused by an exclamation.

"My God, what's wrong? Are you ill?" said Eliot.

"What?"

"Your face… I have never seen such a look." He was frowning at her, puzzled and concerned. "I can hardly describe it. Your eyes seemed to grow enormous all at once, and you looked the picture of despair. Tell me, Laura, what is wrong? What has happened to you?"

She opened her mouth, then shut it. There would be no such concern in his voice if he knew about the two thousand pounds. She looked down at the floor and murmured, "Truly I am quite all right."

His frown did not lift, but Clarissa and Marina came in, just then, and the party set off. Eliot commented on the overcast sky, and Laura agreed that it would be unpleasant should it rain with everyone in open carriages. "Perhaps we will find that the event has been canceled," he added hopefully. "They cannot go up in a storm, of course."

Eliot's tone drew a small smile from Laura. "I do not understand why you said you would accompany us," she answered. "I know you do not care for such things, and we might just as well have gone with my cousin. But it is your own doing, after all, so it is too bad of you to complain."

He bowed his head. "You are quite right, Laura. It is positively mean-spirited of me to repine. Still I hope that it does rain, so that I can show you how well I shall bear it."

Laura laughed, the worries of the morning receding a bit in the face of this absurdity. "Well I do not. The pleasure of observing your fortitude would be greatly dampened by a ruined bonnet."

Her husband chuckled. "Don't you know that puns are the lowest form of wit, my dear? Addison despised them."

Laura shrugged airily. "He was not obliged to work with the subject of balloon ascensions."

"A definite hit. I acknowledge it," he replied. "Had he been forced to do so, or indeed even to attend such an event, I daresay all his wit would have deserted him forthwith."

Laura shook her head, smiling. "My cousin is a marvel in this at least. His mere proximity makes you utterly absurd."

"Is it not strange? I have remarked it myself, but I cannot explain it. Can it be, perhaps, an unconscious effort to leaven his lumpishness by excessive levity? Yes. I think I have hit upon the answer."

"You are right," laughed Laura. "And this also explains why I never see this mood in you otherwise."

❧

They arrived at the site of the balloon ascension in good time. Indeed the earl had gotten them there before almost any other spectators, and they had a wide choice of good viewing spots. In the center of the area, a group of men stood around an expanse of red fabric, evidently discussing the apparatus and the weather, if their gestures and long looks at the sky could be so interpreted.

"Capital!" said the earl, when the curricle pulled up beside his vehicle. "They have not yet started filling the gas bag. We shall see everything." And he launched into an explanation of what the men would do next and why. Since he interspersed this with a repetition of many of his remarks from the previous day's explanation of balloons, his listeners soon allowed their attention to wander. Only Marina seemed to follow the earl's lecture, and her occasional questions constituted the only conversation for nearly a quarter of an hour. Finally Eliot interrupted the earl with, "I believe they have decided to fill the balloon."

Their host looked up. In his enthusiasm he had nearly forgotten the balloon. "They have indeed," he agreed. "Very sharp of you, Mr. Crenshaw."

Eliot raised one eyebrow and smiled. Laura, looking

over the field, did not think the crowd as large as expected. The overcast sky and thickening clouds were perhaps responsible.

"Yes, I think it will rain later," said Eliot when he saw his wife gazing upward. "Let us hope that it will not be until this evening. But it appears to me that it will come on sooner."

"Oh there is Anne Rundgate," exclaimed Clarissa, as if startled, and when the others followed her gaze, she flushed a little.

Laura saw Anne some way down the row of carriages. She was sitting in a high perch phaeton with a young officer, and though Laura could see his scarlet coat, she was not close enough to recognize his features.

"The balloon is full," exclaimed the earl, breaking into her thoughts.

Laura drew in her breath. The thing was much larger than it had appeared when lying on the ground. It towered above them, red with a blue stripe about the middle and oddly beautiful. Men scurried about the bottom, adjusting ropes and checking the apparatus. Two stood well away from it, gazing anxiously into the sky. "It's really rather splendid, isn't it?" said Laura.

Eliot inclined his head.

Another quarter of an hour passed, and still the men bustled about the balloon without showing any signs of raising it. The crowd chatted and flirted unconcernedly. Laura shifted in her seat. "I wonder that they do not begin."

"They are trying to persuade themselves that the weather is good enough to go up," said Eliot. "But it will surely rain." And indeed, even as he said this, the first few drops spattered the dusty ground beside the curricle. "Ah," he added, "this is timely. You see, I was right."

They exchanged a smile, and he tightened his hold on the reins. "We had best try to make our way out before it becomes a rout," he said.

"I have no objection," Laura replied. "Let us just make sure that the earl goes also."

Eliot communicated their intention to their host and was met with loud objections. "A few drops only," scoffed the earl. "It will stop in a moment. These men will not allow a few drops of rain to put an end to their flight. They have filled the bag, after all."

"I cannot agree," answered Eliot. "In fact I believe the chief balloonist is already telling his henchmen that it is impossible." The man who seemed in charge of the event had indeed called the others to him and was telling them something.

"Nonsense. He is undoubtedly explaining the procedures of raising the balloon. It is a quarter past three. You cannot be so poor-spirited as to leave now."

But Eliot merely began to maneuver the curricle out of the press of vehicles around them. The drops were coming faster now, and Laura could feel them striking her through the thin fabric of her shawl. All over the field carriages were beginning to back away and depart.

"Do let us go," said Clarissa, holding up her shawl to shield her bonnet. "Oh now it is truly raining."

Suddenly the drizzle became a downpour. Eliot wasted no more time but quickly turned the curricle and began to thread his way through the maze of vehicles behind them. It was a measure of his skill that they managed to do this with some speed. All around them carriages nearly collided and drivers shouted at one another to get out of the way. Looking back, Laura saw that the earl had not yet been able to turn his unfamiliar team. The landaulet was wheel to wheel with a phaeton, and the earl was having words with the young sprig of fashion who drove it. Clarissa had risen and was trying to take the reins from the earl, who jerked them away indignantly. Just before she lost sight of them, Laura saw a wet bedraggled figure go running up to the earl's carriage and pull at Clarissa's sleeve.

In a surprisingly short time, considering the general confusion, they were on their way home at a spanking pace. The rain had completely soaked Laura's shawl and thin dress and had ruined her bonnet. She could feel droplets running down her neck. In the breeze of their movement, this dampness was unpleasantly cool, and before they reached Mayfair, she was shivering. Eliot saw this in a side glance. "It is not far now," he said encouragingly.

They reached the house soon after. Eliot pulled up at the door and told her to get down. "Change immediately into something dry," he said.

"But what about you?"

"I mean to do the same as soon as I have taken the horses around to the stables."

Laura climbed down and hurried into the house. Mary exclaimed when she saw her. "La, ma'am," she said, "you're soaked through, and your gown is a proper mess." She began to unbutton it in back. "You must change out of these wet things or you'll catch a chill. I'll light the fire as soon as I've helped you out of this."

Laura's teeth were chattering. "Oh do it first," she said. "I can undress, but I am already chilled to the bone, I think. Odd, it is not really cold outside."

"It's the damp as does it, ma'am," said Mary wisely, busying herself at the hearth. "I'll have this going in a trice."

In a short time Laura was wrapped in a dressing gown and seated before the fire, a towel wrapped around her wet hair. Mary had gone down to the kitchen to order her a pot of tea. With a sigh Laura stretched out her legs to the heat. This was much better. She pulled off the towel and began to rub her curls dry. Her black hair fell about her shoulders and face.

She heard the door open. "Oh Mary," she said in a muffled voice, "is the tea here already? How wonderful. It is just what I need. Has Clarissa returned?"

"Not yet," answered a male voice, and Laura threw back her hair to see her husband standing in the doorway. She came to her feet. "I beg your pardon," he added, "I wanted to see if you were all right." He was still in his wet garments, and they dripped a little on the carpet.

Very conscious of her bare feet, tumbled curls, and thin wrapper, Laura said, "I am perfectly all right now." She stole a glance at him from under her lashes. "Mary made a fire," she added, then fell silent, annoyed at the fatuity of this statement.

"Good," he said. He was looking at her with an expression that sent the blood rushing to her cheeks, and for a moment there was silence. Then he moved out of the doorway. "I must change also." And with that he shut the door and was gone.

Laura had had two cups of tea and dressed again before she heard sounds below that indicated the rest of the party had returned. Hurriedly pinning her hair into a knot, she went downstairs, arriving in the hall in time to greet a very wet and annoyed Clarissa. Marina and Anne Rundgate followed her into the house. All of them were soaked. "Where is the earl?" she asked. "He must come in and get dry."

Clarissa tossed her head. "He has gone back to his lodgings," she answered curtly. "What a ham-handed driver!"

Marina was trying not to smile, and Anne looked frightened. Laura looked at Clarissa's smoldering eyes and stubborn mouth and said merely, "You must all go upstairs and change at once. You're drenched."

"Oh yes," agreed Anne softly.

The three of them started up the stairs, but Clarissa turned before she was halfway up. "I may as well tell you that I have quarreled with our cousin, Laura. I doubt we will see him here again. But I do not care because he is an utter toad and the worst judge of horseflesh I have ever seen." Then she turned and disappeared up the stairs.

Twenty-two

AN HOUR LATER THE FOUR LADIES SAT IN THE DRAWING room around the tea tray. The rain had become a driving storm, and a fire and hot cups of tea formed a pleasant contrast to the wind and water outside the windows. Clarissa and Anne Rundgate talked quietly on the sofa before the hearth, contentedly eating buttered muffins, and Laura and Marina sat in armchairs close together at the side.

"I did not yet hear how Anne came to be with you?" Laura said to Marina quietly. She did not want to attract Clarissa's attention.

Marina looked uneasy. "I was wondering whether I should bring up the subject." She frowned and looked at the carpet. "I am your guest, and you have been amazingly kind to me; I do not wish to interfere. But when Miss Rundgate came up to the carriage, she said, 'My mother is here, Clarissa! You must help me. I told her I was with you.' And then, I beg your pardon if I am offending you, then Clarissa said, 'Has she seen you?' and when Miss Rundgate answered no, she told her to get into the carriage." She watched Laura's frowning face closely. "As I said, I am sure it is no more than a misunderstanding, but I do not think that Clarissa, that is…" She trailed off in confusion.

"I am not at all certain you are right," said Laura grimly. "But thank you for telling me. You were very right to do so."

Marina started to speak, then thought better of it.

At this moment Mr. Dunham came into the room and approached Laura. He held out two envelopes. "Pardon me, ma'am, these arrived this morning, but they were carelessly placed beneath a vase, and I just now came across them again. I'm sorry for the delay."

Laura took them reluctantly. She looked up to find Clarissa watching her and put the envelopes in her pocket.

At six the chaise was called for to take Anne Rundgate home, and after seeing her off, Clarissa and Marina went up to dress for dinner. Laura made as if to follow them, then slipped into the library. Eliot was also changing, so the library should be a private retreat.

Once there she shut the door and walked over to the desk. Pulling the two letters from her pocket, she smoothed out the creases and opened the fatter of them. This at least could not be a note from Mr. Allenby; it was by far too large. She pulled the packet out, and then stood frozen, staring at it. It contained all the vowels she had signed on that awful night of the card party. Or at least, she amended to herself, far more than she could remember signing; it must be the lot. Shaking her head, she looked them over, calculating quickly. Yes, these came to just over two thousand pounds. It was all of them.

On the bottom of the pile, she found one of Mr. Allenby's visiting cards. There was no other note, but on the back of the card, he had scrawled, "Touché." She read it aloud softly. What can he mean? she wondered. There was no other explanation for the amazing return of the vowels. She sank down in the desk chair, frowning. Clearly Mr. Allenby had not been suddenly overcome with compassion. He was not that sort of man. Someone had paid them. But who?

Still frowning, Laura slit open the other envelope. Inside was a short note, unsigned. It was in the same hand as the mysterious communication which had urged her to put off her appointment with Mr. Allenby, and it said only, "All is well." Laura read it over repeatedly without discovering the slightest clue to the writer's identity.

She sat at the desk for a long time, staring at the two missives, and trying to think how this thing could have come about, but she was completely at a loss. Someone who had been at the card party might have known of her debts and taken pity on her, a thought which made her flush. But why this secrecy? She would be pleased to pay back her benefactor as soon as she could. Why not come forward? Mr. Allenby must know who it was, and he was not a man to keep a secret.

With this thought, her frown returned. Why had Mr. Allenby not mentioned her benefactor when returning the notes? Surely he would make something of such charity, something scandalous, if possible. This almost assured her that her mysterious patron was not a man. Who then?

Laura clasped her hands tightly together. It frustrated

her almost beyond bearing not to have any idea who had helped her. Her eyes wandered restlessly over the desk top, to be suddenly arrested at the sight of a slim envelope lying near the inkwell. She must have overlooked it twenty times since she had sat down, but now she really noticed it. There was something familiar about the writing. Picking it up, she looked more closely, and as she did so, a whiff of perfume reached her. Yes, it was the same. It was a note from Vera Allenby to her husband. Evidently their relationship was continuing.

Laura looked up, chewing her lip. The letter was opened. It must have been delivered this morning or during the day, as Eliot had already seen it. Could it have any connection with the return of her vowels? It would, of course, be wrong to read Eliot's mail. But when a man openly received billets-doux from his mistress and left them lying about on his desk where his wife or anyone else might pick them up, did he not forfeit some of this consideration? Knowing that in her anger and frustration she was rationalizing, Laura nevertheless pulled the sheet of paper from the envelope.

Vera's note was brief. She merely asked Eliot to visit her that evening, as she had some intriguing news for him. Laura put a hand to the side of her throat when she read this. What news did she mean? Did it involve Laura's debts? As she considered the matter, she realized that this would be a perfect way to use such information if one wished to see her ruined, as she was by now convinced that the Allenbys did, both of them. Perhaps, after all, some compassionate gentleman had taken pity on her. But if Eliot was told that he had paid her debts, would he ever believe that the man was a stranger?

Laura jumped up and looked about her wildly. What could she do? How could she stop this meeting? Now that there was some chance of their marriage succeeding, it was critical that Eliot not believe she had become involved with some other man. Then, suddenly, she remembered that Eliot was going to be home this evening and even had suggested that perhaps they would all see a play. She sat down again, an overwhelming relief filling her. He was not going to Vera; he had chosen to ignore her invitation. Perhaps... something stronger than relief rose in Laura as she thought this, and a hopeful smile lit her features. Might Eliot prefer to be with his wife?

Laura sat in a happy daze for some minutes. When she roused herself and glanced at the clock, she started. It was nearly dinnertime, and she had not even begun to change. She stood and started toward the door, then gasped and returned hurriedly to the desk. She picked up her vowels and the envelopes and was putting Vera Allenby's note back in its original place when the door to the library opened abruptly. Laura whirled, thinking to see Eliot, but Mr. Dunham stood there. He did not look particularly surprised. "Pardon me, ma'am," he said. "I did not realize you were using the library." He made as if to retreat.

"I was just leaving," blurted Laura, and gathering up her papers, she started out.

He held the door for her. As she walked across the hall, he said, "Oh, Mrs. Crenshaw, I nearly forgot."

Laura turned. "Yes?"

"Mr. Crenshaw asked me to inform you that he would not, after all, be home to dinner. Some pressing engagement intervened." Mr. Dunham's expression was bland, but Laura fancied she saw some emotion lurking beneath his ever-correct exterior.

She drew herself up. "I see. Thank you," she replied evenly, and turned back to the stairs.

As she climbed, however, a mist obscured the steps, and she almost tripped more than once. It was wonderful to reach her bedchamber and to find it empty, and she sank down in the armchair and shut her eyes. He was going to Vera; she had been a fool to think otherwise, and she burst into tears.

It was several minutes before Laura could control herself. She was very grateful that no one came in during that time. When she finally stopped crying and wiped her eyes, sniffing, she faced the fact that she had known now for some time.

She was in love with her husband.

She did not know when or precisely how it had happened, but she had come to love Eliot dearly. This was why it was so imperative that he not find out about her debts or think her involved with someone else, and this was why she had felt so elated when she thought he was not going to Vera Allenby. A wave of jealousy and something very like hatred washed over her at the thought of this woman. Laura had never had a chance against her, entrenched as she was even before the marriage, and now, perhaps even at this minute, Mrs. Allenby would tell Eliot everything and Laura would lose him forever.

For a wild moment Laura considered going to the

Allenbys' house to stop this meeting, but she thought better of it almost immediately. Her other like efforts had ended in disaster, and she had no wish to repeat them. No doubt Vera Allenby would be able to keep her out, or even to hand her over to Jack. She would never see Eliot, and he would not even know she was there.

Laura stared into the fire. Her debts had been paid somehow, but she was in no better case than before. For the thing that mattered to her more than money or honor or anything else, her husband's love, was out of her reach. Tears rolled down her cheeks once again, but this time she blinked them back resolutely. Crying was not going to solve anything, and she was expected at dinner in less than ten minutes.

Laura rose. She picked up the packet of vowels and the mysterious note and put them in the fire. She watched until they were completely burned, then went to the washstand and bathed her hot eyes. Mechanically, she ran a comb through her hair. She did not look very well, she thought as she gazed into the dressing table mirror, but what did it matter? Eliot would not be there to see her.

Twenty-three

IT WAS LATE IN THE MORNING WHEN LAURA WENT down to breakfast the next day. She had hoped to find the breakfast room deserted, and indeed Eliot and Clarissa had finished and gone. But Marina still sat at the table, though her plate showed that she had eaten. She was frowning over a sheet of paper and looked up as Laura came in. "Good morning. I have just received this note; it is the strangest thing." For a moment the blood in Laura's veins seemed to freeze; then Marina continued. "The earl wants me to go out driving with him."

Laura sank into a chair opposite her. "Does he? And do you wish to go?"

Marina looked at her uncertainly. "I do not, of course, wish to seem pushing or to be stepping in where I am not wanted."

"Whatever do you mean?" responded Laura, ringing for a fresh pot of tea. "I am sure you could never be either of those things."

The other girl hesitated, then said, "Clarissa happened to mention to me that the earl may have some intention of forming a connection with your family. I do not wish to seem…"

Laura laughed. "I believe our cousin had some such idea when he came to town, but Clarissa would never consent to it, and he must have changed his mind by this time."

"I see," replied Marina, smiling a little. "Well I believe I will go then."

Her hostess looked at her curiously. "You do not find the earl dull?"

"A little… but not so much as you, perhaps. My father used to take an interest in things in much the same way."

"Ah," said Laura. She could not imagine herself enjoying the earl's conversation though her guest evidently did.

"I think I will go upstairs and answer the note then. He says he will come round at one."

Laura nodded. She was not hungry and did not stay at the table. When she had finished her tea, she went in search of Clarissa. After the incidents of yesterday, she felt she must talk to her sister about Anne Rundgate. But as she was going along the corridor to the drawing room, she came upon not Clarissa, but Eliot. He was dressed for riding and obviously on his way out.

Laura stopped, wide-eyed, and waited for him to pass. His face showed nothing; she could not tell whether he had been told of her folly.

"Good morning," he said when he came up with her. "You look tired. I trust you slept well?"

Remembering the hours of waiting to hear him come in, Laura straightened. "No," she said baldly.

He frowned. "You must take better care of yourself. I think the season is too much for you."

Laura shrugged. He *must* know it was not the season that was making her pale and thin, she thought.

"Perhaps we should not go out to Almack's tonight as we planned. I think you should remain at home and go to bed early."

"Oh no, Marina has never been. We cannot disappoint her."

"I am sure she will be happy to go another time when she realizes you are burnt to the socket."

"No, no. I want to go," insisted Laura. An evening at home simply meant more opportunity for Eliot to question her. He did not act as if he had learned anything from Vera Allenby, but who could tell? He was always so correct and controlled.

Eliot turned away. "Very well. I am going riding and then to lunch with March. I shall see you at dinner."

Laura bowed her head, and he went out. After a moment she continued on to the drawing room, finding Clarissa there listlessly flipping over the pages of *Marmion* and looking out the window.

"How abominably dull it is," said the younger girl when Laura came in. "I miss my driving lessons. I wonder when Mr. Redmon will be back. Did he say anything to you?"

Laura shook her head. "I believe he meant to remain a week."

Clarissa nodded resignedly. "Perhaps I will go to visit Anne."

"You see her nearly every day now."

"We are friends," replied Clarissa, a bit defensively.

"Indeed? The poor girl looked quite harried yesterday. What can be the matter, I wonder?" Laura watched her sister closely.

Clarissa's chin came up. "She is miserable. She is afraid she will end up just like her sisters, married to plump rich dullards and wearing out her life gossiping and eating chocolates."

Laura raised her eyebrows.

"Why should she be made so unhappy?" Clarissa moved restlessly about the room. "I cannot bear it. She belongs with Captain Wetmore."

"Clarissa!"

The other girl's eyes flashed. "She loves him. Why will no one believe that?"

"Perhaps because it is less that she loves him than that you have encouraged her to think so and have kept the thing alive with meetings and plotting. Anne strikes me as the sort of girl who does as she is told, and you have told her she loves Captain Wetmore, I imagine."

Clarissa began a hot retort, then stopped. After a moment she said more calmly, "It is true that Anne is not a strong character and I suppose I am." She smiled a little at her sister's expression. "But this thing is not all my doing, as you seem to think. I did not introduce her to Captain Wetmore. She has known him for years, since they were children. It was only timidity that kept her from meeting with him before I arrived. And there is no doubt at all that he loves her. I had nothing to say there. I wish you would meet him, Laura. I know you would like him immensely and approve of my helping them."

"Like him, I might, but I doubt that I would approve. If he is such an estimable young man, why does he not simply go to Mrs. Rundgate and ask for Anne's hand."

"Anne has begged him not to. She is convinced her parents will refuse. And he is so sensitive about his financial inferiority that he agrees, though it rankles, I promise you. He hates the secret meetings."

Laura shrugged. "Not enough to end them, seemingly. And what of you? Do you think Mrs. Rundgate will stand in the way of her daughter's happiness? She does not seem a cruel mother to me."

Clarissa looked doubtful. "No, she does not. I admit that at first I urged them to go to her and reveal the whole, but Anne was terrified. She seems certain that her parents would send her into the country at even a hint of such a relationship. Perhaps it is her father?"

"Highly unlikely," said Laura. "He is a meek little man, Clarissa, and Anne Rundgate is a ninny. How can you be guided by her?"

"Well it is her marriage and her family we are talking about," responded Clarissa reasonably. "I did not wish to force her into a course that clearly frightened her."

Laura sighed. "Well I think you should withdraw from the matter completely, whatever you have done up to now. It is wrong of you to interfere in this, as you well know."

A stubborn look appeared about Clarissa's mouth. "She cannot go on without me. She requires support."

"Exactly."

Clarissa stood. She started to speak, then with one eloquent look at her sister, swept out of the room. Laura was left to make what she could of this response, and she rightly concluded that Clarissa was by no means ready to leave Anne Rundgate to her own devices. Sighing, Laura realized that she would have to try to reason with her sister again.

The rest of the day passed calmly. Marina went out with the earl, and Clarissa went walking in the park with some of her acquaintances. Laura did some sewing and reading. Though tension hung in the air as she wondered who had paid her debts and whether Eliot had been told, she still managed to enjoy the quiet and rest.

❧

The entire party set off for Almack's at nine. Marina looked very well in her new blue gown, and she was understandably excited. Clarissa chatted with her about what she would see and who would be there.

Clarissa saw Mr. Redmon as soon as she entered, and her pleasure in the evening was assured. He came up to them at the same moment as the earl, and the two young ladies were engaged for the first set on the spot and carried off to join it. Clarissa's expression was so joyous that Laura had to smile.

"Yes," said Eliot, "I believe your sister comes close to getting her wish."

Laura looked up at him questioningly.

"To marry a duke," he added. "The thing itself is not possible, as she has very sensibly concluded for herself, but she is doing as well as can be expected."

"She really cares for him," replied Laura. "And she does not know that he is the son of a duke."

"I know it. That makes her luck all the more amazing. Had she set out to do the thing, I would have given her a strong chance. But to do it without even trying, that is what shows that she is favored of the gods." He smiled. "Pray, don't misunderstand me. I mean no criticism. I am pleased to see her get her wish long after she had probably forgotten all about it. Such seems to be the way for Clarissa."

Laura returned his smile. "Yes. She has always gotten what she wants almost without effort."

"And what of you?" asked Eliot more seriously. "Have you gotten what you want?"

Looking into his clear gray eyes, Laura felt herself color. She looked down. Why must he look at her just so? "I don't know what you mean," she said in reply.

He continued to look at her, a crease between his brows. "You were eager to come to London, to have a season. Are you happy now?"

"Yes of course."

"You have made friends who can help you?"

This seemed such an odd question that Laura looked up again. She encountered a set gaze and mouth, and her eyes widened a little. Could Eliot have heard, after all?

Seeing her surprise, he shook his head. "I am not a fool, Laura. I know you have been in trouble. If you cannot or will not come to me, I only hope there is someone to whom you can go."

Laura put a hand to her lips and gave a little gasp.

"Just so," said Eliot coldly, and he turned away from her.

She held out a hand helplessly, utterly overset by this unexpected barb. He had sounded almost hurt. She started to follow him across the floor, but at that moment she was asked to dance, and she realized that this was no place for a serious talk.

One set followed another, and before Laura knew it, it was the interval. She looked around for someone she knew, seeing Mr. Redmon in a curtained alcove on the side of the room. He beckoned when he caught her eye, and she walked over to him, trying not to laugh. "Good evening," she said when she reached the recess. "Whatever are you doing here?"

Mr. Redmon looked harried. "Miss Lindley is surrounded by people who know me."

"I thought you had made up your mind to tell her the truth?"

"Yes, yes. In fact I mean to call tomorrow to do so." He looked down awkwardly, his ruddy face coloring further. "I should also like your permission to pay my addresses, ma'am. I have told my parents all about her, and they are very pleased."

"I hardly think my permission is required. You will have to speak to my aunts. But you may do that later, I think."

"Thank you. And, perhaps all of you will come up to Millshire for a visit later. That is, if she says yes. I don't know whether Mr. Crenshaw will want to... That is..." he stumbled to a halt. "Well I daresay you know what I mean."

Laura smiled. "I think so. And all will be settled tomorrow."

Mr. Redmon heaved a relieved sigh. "Yes. I will take my leave of you now and come tomorrow afternoon. Someone is bound to expose me here."

"Very well."

"Good night."

As Laura turned away, she saw Marina coming toward her. "May I speak with you?" she said.

"Of course."

They sat down, and Marina twisted her fan between her hands. "Something has happened, and I must speak to you."

"What is it?"

Marina looked down for another moment, then blurted, "The earl has offered for me."

"Has he indeed?" answered the older girl. "Well that is very flattering." She was not sure how to reply. Marina looked concerned, and her first impulse, to laugh, seemed wrong.

"Yes," said Marina. She swallowed. "I told him that I would give him an answer tomorrow. I wished to speak with you first. Is it all right?"

"All right?" echoed Laura rather blankly.

"To marry him."

Laura stared at her. "Do you wish to marry him, Marina?"

Marina looked down. "Yes," she answered.

Laura frowned. "Well if you are certain of that, I do not see what I have to do with the matter."

The other girl met her eyes. "You do not mind?"

"Why should I?"

"He is your cousin, and I…" She made a helpless gesture.

"And you are my friend," finished Laura firmly. "I wish you very happy."

Marina smiled shakily. "Thank you."

They stood for a moment, looking at each other. Then, as couples were beginning to drift back into the ballroom, Marina bowed her head slightly and turned toward the doorway that led upstairs to the ladies withdrawing room.

The rest of the evening passed slowly for Laura. Eliot strolled in from the cardroom for a few minutes, but seeing all the ladies of his party dancing, he returned without speaking to them.

Clarissa pouted a little when she discovered that Mr. Redmon had gone, but she was too much in demand to languish long. Before the last set she came up to speak to Laura. "Is it not a fine ball?" she said, her eyes sparkling. "I'm sorry I was so silly today. Forgive me?"

Laura smiled. "Of course. Particularly if you tell me that you have given up interfering."

Clarissa made an airy gesture. "Oh there is nothing to worry about, I promise you. That will all be over now." She smiled.

Laura looked at her suspiciously. "That's splendid. When did this change come about?"

"You'll see. All will be well," laughed Clarissa, and she returned to her friends.

Laura went over and sat down by the wall, puzzling over these remarks. She did not trust her sister to be prudent, and she wondered what new devilry she planned now. She was so engrossed in her thoughts that she did not notice when the set began. Only when someone came and stood directly before her did she look up, and then she started. It was Vera Allenby.

The redhead looked magnificent in pale green satin and emeralds. Her eyes glittered dangerously as she surveyed Laura, making her feel very young and dowdy. "How did you do it?" asked Vera, her lips curling.

"What?" asked Laura, mystified.

"The debts. How did you get them paid? Eliot did not give you the money, that's clear."

Laura stiffened. "I do not see that it is any business of yours."

Mrs. Allenby did not reply but merely eyed her with a combination of speculation and, oddly, amusement. "I admit you are more of an opponent than I first realized. It is quite funny really."

This half contemptuous phrase made Laura's eyes sparkle dangerously. People were beginning to look at them. They must consider it quite a sight, Eliot's wife and his mistress confronting each other at Almack's. She stood. "If you will excuse me."

"But I won't. I don't excuse you anything you have done since you came to London. And there are others who will agree with me, I'm sure," said Vera maliciously. "You are close to the edge, my dear. I am waiting to push you over only because I cannot quite see what has happened and it amuses me to see how you will behave. I can keep my friends silent, you know. So the power is all mine. I can tell Eliot whenever I chose."

Laura looked her enemy straight in the eye. She said

nothing, but her dark eyes bored into the green ones. Neither woman looked away.

"Laura, I believe it is time we were going," said a voice behind them. Both women turned. Eliot was standing there.

"Eliot," said Vera Allenby, "how sweet of you to join us. I was just having a pleasant chat with your lovely wife." Her voice was like a purr.

"Come, Laura," said Eliot, holding out his hand.

"But you cannot mean to go so early," said Vera, smiling sensuously at him.

For a fleeting second Eliot seemed to look at Vera; then he looked away as if he had seen no one standing there. He took Laura's arm, tucked it under his own, and led her away. Murmuring arose in the room around them.

Laura stumbled and would have fallen had not Eliot held her upright. She was stunned. He had given Vera Allenby the cut direct, in front of everyone!

Behind them Mrs. Allenby was the picture of outrage. Her fists were clenched, and her eyes blazed, but even she could not long withstand the many pairs of curious eyes, some amused, some shocked, most greedily interested. She turned on her heel and strode out of the room.

Twenty-four

WHEN LAURA CAME DOWN THE NEXT MORNING, MARY informed her that Clarissa had gone to visit Anne Rundgate, which made Laura frown. Marina had gone upstairs to do some sewing, and Eliot was working in his study with Mr. Dunham. He had asked not to be disturbed. Laura ate quickly, her mind still occupied with the events of the previous evening. Eliot's behavior both puzzled and elated her. Though he had sometimes been angry, he had never treated *her* with the coldness and lack of respect that he had accorded Mrs. Allenby last night. Surely their connection could not be what people thought; Eliot simply could not care for her and treat her that way. This thought made Laura take a quick breath. If he did not love Vera Allenby, perhaps there was a chance that he would someday love her.

Laura's conjectures made her restless; she left the table to go into the drawing room, but she could not settle down there either. Books seemed dull, and her sewing unbearable. She wanted more than anything to speak to her husband and to see how he looked at her this morning. Would he be angry over the scene last night? Or would his eyes show some sympathy for her embarrassment?

At ten o'clock she gave up her efforts to read and walked downstairs. Eliot would surely have finished his business now; he never worked with Mr. Dunham for more than an hour or so. Laura meant just to look into the library and say good morning. She could gauge his mood by that. When she reached the hall, the library door was ajar. She put a hand on the knob and started to push it open, then stopped as she heard Mr. Dunham say, "There is no doubt that she went to Levy's, sir. I have ascertained that myself. In fact everything in Mrs. Allenby's letter appears to be true, insofar as facts are concerned, I mean. Her sarcasm is, of course, exaggerated."

Eliot made some reply that Laura couldn't quite hear; then Mr. Dunham went on in an odiously satisfied voice. "Yes sir, someone paid the debt. Two men visited Allenby in the evening and redeemed the vowels. They were prepared for trouble seemingly, but I have not been able to trace them down." His tone was aggrieved. "They were extraordinarily elusive, I must say. Their employer is still unknown, though I have no doubt I shall unearth him soon."

Again Eliot spoke quietly. His back was to the door, so Laura could not catch his words. But Mr. Dunham faced in her direction, and his replies were cruelly clear. "Oh no, sir, I cannot think that a woman would have dealings with the men I saw. And they seemed very experienced in this sort of transaction."

The chagrin that had transfixed Laura when she first

heard Mr. Dunham speak eased a little, and she backed away from the door. All was lost. Eliot knew the whole story due to the good offices of Vera Allenby and Mr. Dunham. Mr. Dunham *had* been watching her.

With a breath that was almost a sob, Laura turned away and hurried up the stairs again. She must get away from this. She left the door just in time to miss Eliot's final remark. When Mr. Dunham had concluded his story, Eliot turned toward the door with a worried expression and said, "The poor girl. Why did she not come to me?"

"I imagine she feared your reaction, sir," put in Mr. Dunham. "She quite rightly concluded that you would condemn such shameless behavior." The note of satisfaction was strong in his voice again.

Eliot rounded on him, eyes blazing. "If I ever hear you speak so of her again, you are dismissed, Dunham. Your opinion was not requested, and I find it damned impudent."

Mr. Dunham stepped back before the look on his master's face. "Yes sir. Sorry, sir," he said, blinking.

The grim lines about Eliot's mouth did not disappear. "I want this story scotched," he continued. "I don't care what you do. Do you understand me."

"Yes sir, but I do not see…"

"Good. I put the matter in your hands." And with a gesture, he dismissed his rather shaken servitor.

Eliot stood for a few moments beside the fireplace, his hand covering his face as he regained control; then he strode out of the room and up the stairs. He went directly to Laura's bedroom and knocked. When he got no answer, he opened the door. There was no one there. Shrugging, he closed the door again and walked along the corridor. He looked into the drawing room downstairs and, finding it also empty, rang the bell.

"Where is Mrs. Crenshaw?" he asked Mary when she appeared.

Mary looked surprised. "I don't know sir. Has she gone out perhaps? Miss Clarissa is calling on the Rundgates; she may have gone along."

"Ah," he replied, looking down. "Very well. Thank you."

Mary went out, and after a moment Eliot followed her. He walked down to the library once more, but as he reached the doorway, he paused. Sitting on the hall table next to the library door was a book. This was most unusual; no books were kept in the hall. He went over and picked it up, glancing at the title. Then he frowned. This was the book Laura had been reading for several days. Eliot stood quite still for a moment, his frown deepening; then he put the book down and started hastily toward the stairs, but before he reached the rail, there was a sharp knock on the front door behind him.

Mr. Dunham came into the hall, but Eliot was before him. He pulled open the door to disclose Mr. Redmon on the step outside.

"Good morning, Crenshaw," he said. "Fine day." He looked at Mr. Dunham, then said, "I should like to see Miss Lindley."

"She's not in," said Eliot curtly before Mr. Dunham could reply. "Gone out to the Rundgates' I believe." His tone was barely polite; it was clear that he wanted Mr. Redmon away.

The younger man's face fell. "Not in? What damnable luck, just when I have prepared myself for the thing."

This made Eliot smile slightly. "You might go round to the Rundgates'," he suggested. "You could escort Clarissa home."

Mr. Redmon brightened. "That's a capital idea. I'll do it." He turned back toward the door, recollected himself, and took a polite leave of his host. As he was about to pass through the door Mr. Dunham was holding for him, he was arrested by a piercing shriek from upstairs. Both he and Eliot turned in that direction, startled, and the sound came again.

"Good God," said Mr. Redmon. "What is that?"

"I don't know," replied Eliot, "but I mean to find out."

He took the stairs two at a time, Mr. Redmon right behind him.

In the corridor outside the bedrooms, they found Nancy holding a piece of paper in one hand and moaning. The girl's round red face was creased into an expression of anguish, and her eyes were bulging. When she saw the two men, she shrieked once more and waved the paper before them.

Eliot grasped her wrist impatiently. "What is it, my girl? Are you hurt?"

Nancy gasped for breath and finally blurted out, "She's gone, gone away, sir. And she didn't take hardly a gown. Lordy, lordy!"

Eliot's grip on her wrist tightened enough to make the girl wince. "Who is gone?" he demanded. "What are you talking about?"

Nancy fixed her eyes on his face. "Miss Clarissa, sir; she's gone, eloped. I found this note on the dressing table. She's gone." She began moaning again, and Eliot pulled the letter from her fingers with an impatient exclamation.

"What does she say?" he snapped as he unfolded it.

"Oh lawks, Mr. Crenshaw, I never read it. I wouldn't do no such thing. But she's taken her clothes and all, and I thought…"

Eliot cut her off with a gesture as Mr. Redmon crowded forward to read over his shoulder. At first Eliot started to push him away, but a look at the younger man's face stopped him. He held the sheet so that both could see it.

The note was addressed to Laura. It said, "I know you will disapprove of what I am about to do, but it is the only way, Laura. All must be well when true love rules in marriage. I will see you soon again. Love, Clarissa."

Mr. Redmon clenched a fist as he reached the end. "Who is the blackguard? I'll kill him."

Eliot turned. "Don't be ridiculous, Redmon."

The other stared at him fiercely for a moment; then his eyes dropped. "You are right. If she loves the fellow, the best thing for me to do is disappear." He put a hand over his eyes. "Dear God."

Eliot's lips twitched sardonically. "I meant, do not jump to ridiculous conclusions about this note," he said. "I see no positive evidence of an elopement here." He turned to Nancy. "You may go, my girl, but if I hear that you have spread your silly fancies through the house, you will regret it."

Nancy's eyes widened. She dropped a small curtsy and departed.

Eliot took Redmon's arm and led him into his bedroom. Closing the door, he said, "Now then, get hold of yourself, man. I have no doubt that Clarissa has gotten herself into some mad scrape, but that she has eloped, I do not believe. It isn't possible."

Mr. Redmon looked up, hope lighting his eyes. "You think not? But where has she gone then?"

"That I do not know. She said she was going to the Rundgates'." He stopped. "Wait a moment," he added, frowning. There was a pause, and Mr. Redmon watched his face anxiously. "Yes," said Eliot finally, "I think she has hatched some scheme involving the Rundgate girl."

"Anne Rundgate?" replied Redmon.

"Yes. I'm sure that's it. What a tiresome girl Clarissa can be. I suppose someone must rescue her from this tangle, but I haven't the time. You must go after her."

"I?" echoed the younger man stupidly.

"You," said Eliot impatiently. "I am not wrong in assuming that you want to marry the girl, I suppose."

"No. That is, yes, I do want to marry her... but I have not... that is, she has not..."

"Just so. And if your mother gets wind of the devilry Clarissa is up to today, neither of you ever will. So it is up to you to save her from the consequences of her own folly. I should set off at once if I were you."

The younger man stared at him. "But what should I... Where do I begin? We do not know how she travels or even *if* she travels."

"I daresay she is in a post chaise going north. You

may easily catch up with her on the north road. The pike keepers will be able to help you there, I fancy. I advise you to take your team of grays; they'll outrun any job horses in existence."

"But, but…"

"There's no time to waste, man." And he hustled Mr. Redmon down the stairs and out the door almost before the young man could snatch his hat from Mr. Dunham. "Bring her back here," said Eliot as he saw him out. "I put my faith in you." And he shut the door.

There was a slight smile on his face as he turned back, but it faded as he again sighted the book on the hall table. He strode into the library and sent for Nancy.

"Miss Lindley's note was on her dressing table, you said?" he asked the nervous maid when she entered.

"Yes sir," replied Nancy, curtsying slightly.

"Had it been disturbed?"

"Sir?"

"Did it appear that anyone else had seen it?" asked Eliot impatiently.

"Oh. No, sir. I was the first in there this morning."

"My wife did not go to look for her sister, perhaps?"

Nancy frowned. "No sir, I don't believe so. Unless she went in before she went out shopping."

"Ah, she is shopping this morning?" Eliot's tone was carefully casual.

"Yes sir. Mrs. Crenshaw went out before eleven. I met her in the hall. Properly put out she seemed, too. Said the dressmaker hadn't delivered something she promised, and she had to go and get it. I offered to go myself, but she didn't want that. I've never seen her so put out, I haven't."

"I see. Thank you. That will be all."

When the maid was gone, Eliot went directly upstairs to his room. When he emerged, he was wearing top boots and a riding coat and carrying a crop. As he started down the stairs again, someone called his name, and he turned to find Marina standing in the corridor. "What is wrong?" she asked rather breathlessly. "I heard the screams, but I was trying on a new pattern and I, that is, I could not come out. Is someone hurt. Can I help you?"

"Thank you, no," answered Eliot. "One of the maids was upset, but all is well now."

"I see," said Marina.

"If you will excuse me, I am in a hurry."

"Of course."

And Eliot turned once more and went quickly down the stairs, leaving Marina staring after him, a frown of puzzlement on her face.

Twenty-five

LAURA HAD BEEN WALKING THE STREETS OF MAYFAIR for nearly an hour before she looked about to see where she was. She had rushed upstairs, pulled out her old brown cloak, and thrown it on without looking in the mirror. Hurrying out the back door, she had simply walked, paying no attention to where she went and trying to think what to do. It had no doubt been foolish to run away, but she could not face Eliot now that he knew everything. She had wanted so much to make him respect her, and just when some hopes had begun to grow, all was lost. He would never forgive her for going directly against his orders and disgracing his name.

She came out into a wider thoroughfare and turned aimlessly to the left. Here, the shops were larger, and she looked blankly at the goods displayed as she went. Gradually her pace slowed, and she paused before a fishmonger's to make a plan. Perhaps she could return to her aunts, she thought. They would be very angry and disappointed when she told them the story, but they would not refuse to take her in. Then she would not have to see Eliot. Perhaps he would even prefer that sort of solution; it was discreet. They could put out some tale to explain her absence, and slowly people would forget all about her.

Tears came into Laura's eyes at this picture, but she shook her head angrily. Self-pity was entirely out of place in this situation. Self-blame was more logical; she had gotten herself into this tangle, and it was up to her to get out.

"Can I 'elp you, ma'am?" asked an unctuous voice.

Laura looked up, startled, to find a small man in a white apron before her. "What?" she said.

"We have some particular nice whitings today," he continued, "or perhaps you'd fancy a lobster? All prime fresh, ma'am."

"No, no thank you," stammered Laura, and she turned away hastily, but as she walked on, a smile curved her lips. How ridiculous to be asked to buy fish at such a moment.

The incident somehow cheered her, perhaps by its absurdity, and she looked about once more to get her bearings. Home was this way, and she had best walk no farther away from it until she was certain what she would do.

Walking more rapidly, Laura soon came into Green Street, which was filled with a press of vehicles headed for the north road. She gazed at the traffic idly as she continued to think, but suddenly something caught her attention and she stopped. Someone in that chaise was familiar. She leaned forward. Yes. It was Clarissa. Laura turned and followed the carriage along the street. It could not be, but it was—Clarissa sitting in a post chaise with every appearance of starting out on a long journey. There were trunks tied on the back. Walking, faster, she caught a glimpse of the other occupants of the chaise, and her heart sank. On the rear seat, side by side, sat Anne Rundgate and a young man in regimentals.

Laura thought of crying out, but at that moment the line of vehicles speeded up, and the chaise moved ahead at a pace she could not match. She watched helplessly as it passed along the street and disappeared around the corner. Clarissa was aiding an elopement; she had no doubt of it. How could she be so foolish, Laura wondered. It would create a terrible scandal, and the Rundgates would never forgive her. Nor would their aunts, nor Eliot. And neither will I, finished Laura bitterly. She did not understand how her sister could do such a thing at this of all times.

I must stop her, resolved Laura. She looked up and down the street. There was no hack in sight, and in any case, a cab could not keep pace with a post chaise. She scanned the passing vehicles eagerly. If only someone she knew happened by... but there was no one.

Grimly Laura started to walk, confident that she would find transportation sooner or later. She pushed her way through the crowd on the pavement as quickly as she could, and her rapid passage was attracting undue attention. When she suddenly spied a familiar carriage, she waved frantically and, after a bad moment when several gentlemen in the street seemed about to respond, caught the attention of the driver. He maneuvered the curricle over to her, not without great difficulty and much abuse from various other drivers and pedestrians, and looked down bemusedly. "Hello, Mrs. Crenshaw," said Lord Farnsworth then. "Fine morning, what?" He looked about curiously for her companion.

"Lord Farnsworth," said Laura firmly. "You must help me."

He goggled at her. "Happy to," he replied finally.

Laura was already climbing up into the curricle, having motioned Lord Farnsworth's groom out of the way. "Thank you," she said as she sat down. "Drive that way, toward the north road."

His rather prominent eyes seemed about to start from his head. "Er, just so. But, ah, where are we going?"

Laura had been formulating an explanation ever since she first glimpsed his carriage, so she was ready for this question. "My sister went out visiting this morning, to a rather out-of-the-way place, the home of our old governess. It is just on the outskirts of London, but for some reason the coachman misunderstood and left her there. She has no way to get home, and I must fetch her."

"Ah," said Lord Farnsworth wisely. He started his horses once again, but as they drove, something occurred to him. "But, I say, why not just send your coachman back there? Serve the fellow right for coming away as he did."

"Alas," answered Laura glibly, "Eliot took out the town coach, not realizing that Clarissa would need it."

"Ah," said the man again, and nodded.

Laura was too engrossed, and Lord Farnsworth too oblivious, to notice the odd behavior of two pedestrians during their interchange and departure. The first, a rough-looking individual in a frieze overcoat, had seemed both surprised and displeased when he saw Laura get into the curricle. He had immediately summoned a hack and, after following them for a space, had ordered the jarvey to turn down a side street and proceed double quick to an address nearby. The other man, a neat, dark person dressed unobtrusively in dark gray, had watched Laura's actions dispassionately. But when he saw the man in the overcoat, he reacted visibly and quickly summoned a hack of his own and drove rapidly off.

At the north road Lord Farnsworth balked. "No, now, come now," he said when Laura indicated that he should take this route. "Your old governess doesn't live in York, I hope. How far is it? I have an engagement to dine at White's with Sir Robert and a few friends. We're to play whist; he'll be mad as fire if I don't show."

Laura looked at her reluctant escort measuringly, then sighed. If only she had come upon someone else in the street. She turned all her powers of persuasion to convincing him to go on. "I am sorry, Lord Farnsworth," she said, looking at him with large eyes. "I did not tell you the truth before; I was trying to spare you. But the thing is, my sister is in trouble, and I must go to her. Surely you will not refuse to take me?"

Lord Farnsworth seemed unimpressed. "What sort of trouble? And why not take your own carriage? Why doesn't your husband escort you, hey?"

"Eliot must not know," said Laura melodramatically, bringing a look of frozen terror to her

companion's face. "I could not order my carriage for
fear of alerting him. He is very angry at Clarissa, and I
do not want them to quarrel again."

Lord Farnsworth looked hunted. "Why is he angry?"

"It doesn't matter. It has nothing to do with this,"
snapped Laura, very impatient with the unfortunate
baron. "If you will not take me, at least lend me your
curricle. I will do my best to drive it. I have no more
time to waste."

"Can't go about the countryside alone in a curricle,"
he said, shocked. "Not the proper thing for a female.
Won't do at all."

"Then come with me."

"But I…"

Her patience exhausted, Laura tried to take the reins
from Lord Farnsworth's hands. He resisted feebly, then
finally said, "All right, all right, I will drive you. But
I dare swear I am making the biggest mistake of my
life." And they set off along the north road at as good
a pace as Laura could urge him to.

Twenty-six

THE STREAM OF TRAFFIC ON THE NORTH ROAD WAS NOT great, and thus it was noticeable when, not half an hour after Laura and Lord Farnsworth had crossed the town borders, another curricle drove smartly by. The fashionably dressed gentleman driver was slight and brown-haired, and his bright hazel eyes were intent.

Soon after, a light traveling carriage came along at spanking pace. The grays pulling it were perfectly matched and highly bred, but the broad ruddy face of the gentleman within showed no pleasure in this when he peered out at the road. He looked, in fact, both anxious and harried. But he contented himself with urging his tall coachman to further speed, then retreated into the carriage again.

A little later in the day, near noontime, an obviously new high-perch phaeton came bowling by, drawn by two horses whose paces and lines made it clear that they came from some London livery rather than the stables of a gentleman. A man and a lady rode in it, and the latter was speaking earnestly to her companion. He looked extremely doubtful, but resolute, and used his whip.

No further traffic of interest passed during the noon hour. Several carts trundled by, and a clergyman in a gig crossed into a side street. But about one o'clock a closed carriage shot along the road at a dangerous speed. A slight dark man drove it, expertly but with some nervous glances at the buildings streaming past; the occupants could not be seen.

Laura and Lord Timothy made good progress, in spite of his complaints and repinings. But she was soon exhausted, less with the jolting of the curricle than with the constant effort to keep her companion going. Lord Farnsworth was eager to stop at the least excuse and made a great work of asking the keepers at the tollgates whether Clarissa had passed. Laura finally began to inquire herself, her annoyance overcoming any embarrassment or hesitation she might have felt in other circumstances.

It was soon clear that they were on her sister's trail. Most of the keepers quickly recognized Clarissa from her description, and at each gate they seemed a little closer. As the afternoon drew on, they were first more than an hour behind the others, then three quarters, a half, and finally at five o'clock only a quarter of an hour. Laura was exultant. Surely she would come up with the post chaise very soon; and though she would not be able to return the trio to London the same day, she could at least take them back tomorrow, acting as chaperone in the meantime. She had even concocted a story to explain their journey. They had gone for a drive in the country and had had an accident, she thought, picturing herself saying this to Mrs. Rundgate. Though they tried every means possible to have their carriage repaired, it was impossible, and they had been forced to stay the night at an inn nearby. She nodded to herself.

In her preoccupation Laura had not been paying any heed to Lord Farnsworth, and this gentleman, after stealing a covert glance at her, had been unobtrusively slowing the curricle. The team they had picked up at a posting house along the route was not at all averse to this. A walk, in fact, was their preferred gait, and they sank gratefully into it.

Some minutes later Laura looked up. "What are you doing?" she cried. "Why have you slowed down? We were nearly up with them."

Lord Farnsworth started, but recovered himself quickly. "Well now, don't fly up into the boughs... but I have been thinking."

Laura stifled a scornful reply and merely looked at him.

"Yes. Well I was wondering, you know, what we are to do when we catch up to your sister. I am not one of your needle-witted fellows, but this looks very like an elopement to me. And if it is so, then the gentleman in question may not take our interference kindly, if you see what I mean. And if you're thinking of persuading me to call him out or anything of that sort, well you're fair and far out, that's all I can say, for I won't do it." He tried to look Laura resolutely in the eye but succeeded only in staring like a pigeon fascinated by a snake.

Laura almost laughed. "Of course I do not expect you to call anyone out," she replied soothingly. "Indeed there will be no need for anything of that

kind. I promise you that Clarissa is not eloping."
Looking at Lord Farnsworth's woebegone posture, she
excused herself for this half-lie by resolving that she
would let him go home as soon as she found Clarissa.

"Ah, hm, well then," muttered her companion, "I
suppose it's all right."

"It is. So, please, will you go faster?"

With a grimace Lord Farnsworth whipped up the
horses. "How much longer must we go on?" he asked
her after a few minutes.

For the first time Laura looked a little worried. "I
am not sure. Would they not stop at an inn soon? It is
coming on six o'clock."

"Well that depends upon where they're headed.
If it was Gretna Green, which it ain't, of course,"
he added hastily with a side glance at Laura, "but if
it was, then I wager they'd stop fairly soon. That's a
three-day trip no matter how hard you travel, so one
may as well not kill the horses. But if they are making
for someplace closer, then they might go on for hours
yet. It won't be full dark until close on eight."

"Ah," was Laura's only reply, but she began to
watch the sides of the road more closely, searching for
likely inns.

⌘

It was past six before she came on one, and the
innkeeper there had seen no sign of their quarry. But
about five miles further they came upon The Pony,
a small rundown hostelry set back from the road in a
grove of trees. A post chaise stood outside in the yard,
and there was a trunk strapped to it that seemed to

Laura the one she had seen earlier. She ordered Lord Farnsworth to stop.

Eying the post chaise, he reluctantly did so. And as soon as they reached the inn, Laura jumped down. A very fat, rosy woman bustled out, wiping her hands on a rag. "Mercy!" she exclaimed. "Two carriages all in one night. I've never seen the like. What am I to give you for supper? For room I cannot give you, ma'am, the other party has engaged all I have."

"That's quite all right," answered Laura. "We are here to meet some friends and do not require rooms. In fact I hope it may be our party that has arrived. Two ladies, one blond, one dark, and a military gentleman?"

"Why that's them indeed, ma'am. They're in my parlor this minute. I'll take you to them."

"That won't be necessary," said a voice from the doorway, and Laura swung sharply round to face her irate sister. Conscious of the landlady, Clarissa said nothing further but turned her back on Laura and went into the inn. Laura followed her into a small but neat private parlor, where Anne Rundgate sat with a fresh-faced young man in uniform. The sisters faced each other.

"Clarissa, how could you be so foolish?" asked Laura. "You will create a terrible scandal, and you will be blamed for the whole. It is ruinous."

Clarissa's eyes flashed. "No one would have known anything about it if you had not come charging after me in this idiotic way. And riding with Lord Farnsworth! However did you come to do so?"

Laura made an impatient gesture. "Not have known?" she cried. "How not? Surely you left Anne's house with her, and her mother will know very well who to thank, I think, when she hears what has happened."

Clarissa had the grace to hang her head a bit, but surprisingly before she could answer, Anne Rundgate spoke up behind them. "It is not her fault. I wished it. I would do *anything* to marry Robert."

Laura looked at her, astonished, and saw the young man squeeze her hand. Anne was trembling and pale, but she faced Laura resolutely. Exasperated, Laura snapped, "Even ruin my sister with yourself, it appears."

Anne whitened further and began to stammer a reply, but Clarissa went to her and put a hand on her shoulder. "How can you be so cruel, Laura?" she said. "Of course she did not want me to come. I insisted. I thought if they had a chaperone, the elopement might not seem so bad. You see…"

Laura's anger threatened for a moment to overcome her. She clenched her fists, took a breath, then put a hand to her head and started to laugh helplessly. "A chaperone," she echoed, "on an elopement. And such a chaperone." Her laughter was a little hysterical. "I would not allow you to chaperone our aunts, Clarissa," she added.

The three young people did not share her amusement. Clarissa continued to glare at her sister indignantly, while Anne Rundgate watched Laura wide-eyed, as if she feared for her mental stability, and young Captain Wetmore frowned. He rose and started to speak, but Lord Farnsworth chose this moment to join them in the parlor.

All of them turned when he entered, and he bowed apologetically. "Beg pardon," he said, holding his hat clutched to his chest. "Dashed drafty in the corridor. Hate to intrude, but I'm convinced I shall catch a chill if I remain there much longer. Can't go to the kitchen; landlady won't allow it, and besides, it ain't good *ton*. Perhaps you won't be wanting me any longer?" This was hopefully addressed to Laura.

Laura's laughter bubbled up again. "Certainly go back, Lord Timothy. I can return to town in my sister's chaise."

"No you can't," exclaimed Clarissa. "We are going to Gretna Green."

Something like satisfaction passed across Lord Farnsworth's face, but as he surveyed the room's occupants, it was once more replaced by puzzlement. He nodded nervously to Anne Rundgate and eyed the captain with ill-concealed astonishment. "Just, just so," he said vaguely.

"Nonsense," said Laura. "Lord Farnsworth, you had best start immediately; it will be dark in less than two hours."

He started. "Yes, yes indeed. I'll just…"

But Captain Wetmore interrupted. "I beg your pardon," he said in a cultivated sensible voice, "but I greatly regret that I cannot allow it. I was against this mad scheme from the start, but having begun, I say we should push on. So if you will excuse us, Mrs. Crenshaw. I think our best course would be to drive on tonight."

"And if I will not?" asked Laura.

"Then we drive on in any case. Miss Lindley need not accompany us. I was very grateful for her support of Anne, but I am well able to care for my future wife myself."

Anne Rundgate made a small sound and clung to his arm.

"Of course I will come with you," put in Clarissa. "I am not so poor-spirited as to desert you now." She began to gather her bonnet and pelisse from the sofa, urging Anne to do the same.

The captain strode over and rang the bell as Laura watched helplessly. "You can't," she murmured, "it is lunacy."

No one bothered to reply, though Lord Farnsworth nodded vigorously, and in the silence the sound of a carriage approaching could be clearly heard. Captain Wetmore sighed. "Who now?" he wondered aloud. "This is a remarkably public elopement."

"It will go by," Clarissa assured him. "No one else can have found out." This raised a question in her mind, and she turned to her sister. "Unless Laura told someone. Just how did you discover our plan, Laura? I made sure my note was vague."

"I happened to see you drive by," replied Laura absently, "and I followed."

Clarissa glanced at Lord Farnsworth and summoned a small smile. "With Lord Farnsworth."

Laura looked up. "What? Yes." She was listening to the approaching vehicle. Could this be help in some form? She had no idea how she could keep them from leaving on her own.

The sound of wheels neared, and to Clarissa's manifest surprise, stopped outside the inn. The landlady, who bustled in at that moment, was astonished. Her mouth gaping at this unaccustomed business, she ran out again, forgetting to ask what they wanted.

There was some noise outside, and then in the corridor. Finally the door burst open and Mr. Redmon came hurrying in. "Clarissa," he cried when he saw her, "you cannot, you must not do this thing. I beg you." His eyes lit on Captain Wetmore and his expression hardened "Ah," he said and strode over to the other man, "You are the blackguard responsible." He gripped the captain's cravat in one hand and shook him. "I should call you out and put a bullet through your worthless heart," he finished.

Anne Rundgate screamed, as did the landlady, who had followed Mr. Redmon into the room. Lord Farnsworth muttered, "Here, no, I say," and retreated to the far corner of the room, holding a scented handkerchief to his lips. Laura said, "Wait a moment," but Mr. Redmon did not appear to hear her. It was not until Clarissa reached him and began to tug at his arm that he recalled himself.

The captain pushed his hand away and straightened his cravat. "I don't know what right you think you have to speak to me in this way," he said hotly, "but be assured that I will meet you when and where you like."

Anne screamed again and ran to him, but Mr. Redmon did not seem to hear. His eyes were painfully fixed on Clarissa's face. "How could you?" he began, then added quickly, "that is, I have no right to censure your actions, of course, but I thought we were…" He broke off and bent his head.

Clarissa shook his arm again. "Mr. Redmon, I am not eloping. It is Anne."

He looked up as if dazed. "You are not? But your maid said…"

"Nancy?" Clarissa frowned. "What has she to do with it? I told her nothing."

Mr. Redmon continued to stare at her. "She had a letter. She said that you had run away. Mr. Crenshaw sent me after you."

"Oh he did?" said Clarissa indignantly.

"Eliot knows of this?" put in Laura.

Mr. Redmon merely nodded.

Laura went to an armchair and sank into it with an exhausted sigh.

Clarissa frowned, but before she could speak again, Mr. Redmon said, "Miss Lindley, Clarissa, when I thought you had eloped, I was in despair. It is not the right moment, but I cannot wait any longer to ask you to be my wife."

The girl blinked at him, then smiled. "Of course I will, Geoffrey. I have been waiting weeks for you to ask me."

A small gasp from Anne Rundgate was the only sound, then both Mr. Redmon and Laura began to laugh. Laura fell back in her chair and put a hand over her face.

Clarissa eyed them balefully. "Yes, but that does not solve our present problem, does it?" she said. "Anne and Captain Wetmore must get to Gretna Green, and I shall go with them. None of you can stop me."

Mr. Redmon stopped laughing "What?" he said. "That is preposterous."

Clarissa swung on him. "Don't you begin now. I have had this from Laura, and I will not listen to any more. We are going." She looked toward the captain, who nodded.

"But why?" exclaimed Mr. Redmon. He seemed to really see Anne and her companion for the first time. "Surely, Miss Rundgate, you cannot wish to marry in such a way."

Anne looked frightened, but said, "My parents will not permit it in any other."

Mr. Redmon looked thoughtful. "Ah, they have refused consent."

Captain Wetmore seemed uncomfortable, and Laura put in, "They have refused then? I did not realize you had finally consulted them."

"Ah, well we did not precisely..." began the captain.

"They would not allow it, I know," blurted Anne. "My sister wished to marry Mr. Browne, and they talked and talked for days until she gave it up. They would do the same to me."

"But if you refuse to allow them to persuade you," replied Laura in as reasonable a voice as she could muster, "they would no doubt come around in time."

"I have tried to tell her that, Mrs. Crenshaw," said the captain, "but Anne finds the thought very upsetting."

"So should you," cried Anne wildly. "They will give me no peace. I cannot stand up to them; I do not know how. You cannot ask it of me." Her voice was rising, and the captain quickly put an arm around her and assured her that they would not.

"Of course we shall not," added Clarissa. She looked reproachfully at Laura. "How can you be so unfeeling?"

Laura started to make a sharp reply, but at that moment Mr. Redmon said, "But why not a special license?"

They all looked at him. "Special license?" said Clarissa.

"Just the thing," agreed Lord Farnsworth. He had

come out of the corner when it was clear that there
would be no violence, and now the group swung
round to face him. "Just the thing," he repeated a
bit nervously under five pairs of eyes. "Should have
thought of it myself. No need to elope. Very bad *ton*,
you know. Get a special license. My great uncle could
do it all right and tight."

"Your great uncle," murmured Clarissa weakly.

To everyone's surprise Lord Farnsworth blushed.
"Yes, er, well you see, m'great uncle Charles is a bishop."

Mr. Redmon smiled. "That's perfect then. We shall
all return to town and procure a special license from
Lord Farnsworth's great uncle. A splendid scheme."

Lord Farnsworth bowed. "Thank you, Lord
Redmon. Nothing at all, assure you. The old man
will be glad of a visit, I daresay."

But a wail from Anne Rundgate halted their mutual
congratulation. "Return?" she cried. "But my mother
will find it all out. How will I explain where I have
been? She will know something is wrong; I should
have been home these two hours, dressing for an
evening party."

The captain tried to soothe her, looking to Clarissa
for help, but Laura's sister seemed absorbed in her
own thoughts. During the pause that followed,
Clarissa looked up and said, "*Lord* Redmon?" in a
bewildered voice.

Lord Geoffrey Redmon looked uncomfortable.

"Lord Redmon will explain later, Clarissa," Laura
put in crisply. "But now I think we should follow his
plan. Anne, if I engage to explain your absence to your
mother, will you return to town now?"

After several minutes of discussion, Anne conceded that she would. Clarissa did not join in this argument but merely stared at Redmon in a way that made that gentleman very uneasy.

At last it was settled that Laura would drive back to London with Anne and the captain. Lord Farnsworth would depart immediately, but they would call on him to fulfill his promise the following day. Privately Laura vowed that she would make an opportunity to talk with Mrs. Rundgate before that time, to sound her out on the subject of Captain Wetmore. At first Clarissa was to join the party in the post chaise, but Lord Redmon urgently requested that she ride in his curricle, and she consented. Since it was an open carriage, Laura made no objection.

"Well then," she said, when all the arrangements had been agreed upon, "let us go as soon as may be. We will be sadly late reaching London as it is."

The captain started toward the bell to ring it yet again, but before he reached it, a man's voice spoke from the doorway. "I think not yet," he said. "There is one modification I must make to your admirable plans."

They all turned. Laura paled, and Clarissa looked at her, wide-eyed. Jack Allenby stood in the doorway, holding a pistol trained on the group. In the excitement of their discussion, they had not heard his carriage arrive.

"Here," said Lord Redmon immediately, "what is the meaning of this? What are you doing with that pistol, Allenby? Is this some sort of joke?"

"Alas, I fear not," responded Mr. Allenby, "though I promise you I mean no one here the least harm. I must ask only Mrs. Crenshaw to come with me, and all will be well."

"Never!" exclaimed Clarissa.

The others eyed Mr. Allenby with astonishment.

"All what?" asked Laura after a short pause.

Mr. Allenby smiled slightly. "More than you can well imagine, I believe. Somehow you have inconvenienced me greatly out of proportion to your importance. Certain forces that have been set in motion can be stopped only by your influence. I require it urgently."

"Do you think I would help you in any way?" asked Laura contemptuously.

He smiled more broadly. "Of course not. I am not so stupid or so vain. That is why I hold a pistol and why I require that you come with me now. I shall hold you, unharmed naturally, until matters are adjusted to my satisfaction. A regrettable necessity. I apologize. Had I known the stakes when I began this game, I doubt not I would have passed."

"Game?" repeated Laura. "For you it has been a game and nothing more."

Mr. Allenby's smile was almost frightening. "But of course. What else is life, after all?"

Laura turned away from him abruptly. It was nearly more than she could bear that he called the ruin of her life a game. Mr. Allenby shrugged. "Come, let us go. The sooner you see the sense of my request, the sooner your friends will be released."

At the same moment Captain Wetmore and Lord Redmon moved. The captain dived for the bell rope and gave it a vigorous pull, and Lord Redmon started toward Mr. Allenby. A shot rang out. The marquess grasped his arm and almost fell. With a cry Clarissa ran to support him. His smile gone, Mr. Allenby put down his smoking pistol and drew its mate from the pocket of his greatcoat. "It is a pair you see," he said. "I would not advise any more foolish tricks. And I regret to tell you, sir," he added, turning to the captain, "that the inhabitants of the inn are in the care of my associate." Mr. Allenby was obviously not entirely clear on who the captain was, but just as obviously, he did not care a whit.

The door of the parlor opened, and a burly individual in a frieze coat looked in. "Everything all right?" he asked. "I heard a shot."

"Yes indeed, Dikes," replied Mr. Allenby. "We will be going shortly."

The man nodded and disappeared.

"Now, Mrs. Crenshaw, come along."

Laura looked about the room for some means of escape.

"Perhaps you would prefer that I demonstrate my seriousness by shooting another of your friends? Or perhaps your sister? The longer you linger, the more time that passes before young Redmon sees a doctor."

Laura moved forward, and Mr. Allenby nodded approvingly. Clarissa turned from her work on Lord Redmon's arm to exclaim, "No, Laura, do not go. We shall manage somehow."

Lord Redmon seconded this sentiment weakly. Blood was spreading across his coat sleeve.

Laura looked at them sadly, shook her head, and turned away. Mr. Allenby gripped her arm above the elbow and started to back out of the room, his pistol still aimed at its occupants.

Twenty-seven

THE CORRIDOR WAS DARK AFTER THE CROWDED parlor, and Mr. Allenby's grip on Laura's arm was tight. His burly friend joined them, and all three started down the corridor together after the latter turned a key in the parlor door. "Jem's got the 'orses in hand," he added. "We can be off directly."

Mr. Allenby made no answer but merely continued to guide Laura down the hall. They reached the door all too quickly and stepped out into the innyard. It was extremely crowded with carriages, far more than it had been constructed to hold, and Mr. Allenby paused warily to find a clear route through them. It occurred to Laura that some of the drivers would help her if they knew her plight, and she started to call out. But her captor sensed her intention and covered her mouth with a hand. "Must you make this more distasteful than it is already?" he said impatiently, and the girl's eyes widened.

They began to move again, but the sound of a carriage approaching stopped Mr. Allenby. He listened. When the vehicle slowed, as if to come into the yard, he retreated quickly to the shelter of the doorway again. "Who now?" he muttered. "All of London will be here next."

A phaeton pulled up as close to the inn as it could get, and a man hopped down. Laura struggled a bit, but this served only to make Mr. Allenby tighten his grip and swear.

"Here, ostler," called the new arrival. "Ostler."

A woman jumped down from the chaise. "He must be busy, with all these carriages. Tie them, and let us go directly in. This must be the place. Oh I hope nothing dreadful has occurred."

Laura recognized the voice immediately. It was Marina, and when the man spoke again, she knew it must be the earl. How they had come here, she had no idea. Surely they could not be eloping also? This thought would have made her smile had she not been so intent upon using this new turn of events to get away from Mr. Allenby.

The earl and Marina approached the door, and Mr. Allenby backed away a little. He swore under his breath again but did not loosen his grip on Laura. The couple entered the dim corridor. Mr. Allenby backed up further and said, "Please do not come any closer. I have a pistol and will not hesitate to use it, as your friend will testify." He released Laura's mouth, there being no need to silence her now.

Laura saw the earl start violently and Marina swing around. Before anyone could think further, Marina leaped toward Mr. Allenby. Laura immediately twisted away from him, and as Marina hit him as hard as she could in the side, Laura lashed out with her heels and managed to pull out of his arm. The earl watched these movements in consternation as the pistol wavered from his heart to his head, saying, "Look out there. Watch the gun. Look out!"

Mr. Allenby aimed a backhanded blow at Marina, who dodged out of the way and turned to pursue Laura. As he did, Marina grabbed his gun hand and hung on. "Help me," she shouted to the earl.

This gentleman, jumping from the line of fire, started toward her, but at that moment Mr. Allenby's accomplice spoke from the shadows at the end of the corridor. "All right now, that's enough fun and games. I 'ave a shotgun on you all."

Marina froze at the sound of his voice, and Mr. Allenby jerked away from her and walked down the hall to fetch Laura, who had almost reached the front door. The burly man held the gun on them as Mr. Allenby unlocked the parlor door again and shoved Marina in. "Here, you hellion," he said. "Gods!"

The earl objected to this mode of address. "That is no way to address a lady," he said. "I insist that you apologize."

Allenby shook his head helplessly and apologized, "Pure farce," he murmured, "the story of my life." Then he shoved the earl after Marina and shut the door again.

Laura leaned against the wall of the corridor with her eyes closed. The shotgun was trained on her unwaveringly, and she dared not move. Allenby turned to her once again. "I am heartily sorry I must start down this corridor again myself."

"Why must you then?" snapped Laura immediately. "Why not simply return home and leave this idiocy?"

Mr. Allenby rubbed his temples wearily. "I wish I could; you have no idea how much. But I doubt you will call off your dogs without some strong urging, and Vera will not forgive me if I lose all now." He laughed without humor. "She may not forgive me in any case, though the whole thing was her scheme."

Laura did not follow all of this, but she grasped one point. "I do not know what you mean by dogs," she answered. "I have not asked anyone to harm you. It has nothing to do with me, whatever it is."

Mr. Allenby looked at her quizzically. "I believe you are serious, Laura. Well it is no matter. Someone is hounding me because of you, and if he is not called off, I shall be ruined in a fortnight. I must stop it, you can see that." His tone was almost appealing, and some of Laura's anger dissolved.

"I have no quarrel with you, now that my debt is paid," she said. "I will write a letter or talk with the man, whatever you like. There is no need to go through with this foolish scheme."

Allenby considered; he looked tempted... but then he shook his head. "No, it will not do. Neither of us knows who it is, you see... if you are telling me the truth, that is. How can you write to a phantom? Unfortunate, but it won't work."

Laura started to speak again, but he waved her to silence, and they started out. "Did you bring the chaise up?" Mr. Allenby asked the other man.

"Aye."

They went quickly through the passage and into the yard once more. A post chaise now stood just before the door. Laura was pushed into it, and the door slammed behind her. She found when she tried the handles that both doors were secured and could not be opened from the inside. The windows were muffled with cloth. There was some quiet talk outside the door; then footsteps retreated. Silence fell, and Laura waited tensely for the carriage to start off.

But before it could do so, there was a repeated pounding noise, then a tremendous shattering of glass. Shouts broke out, seemingly all around her. Laura cried, "Help, help me," several times, but she doubted she could be heard in the confusion. Two shots rang out almost simultaneously, and there was more shouting. Then all was quiet for so long a time that Laura was nearly frantic. She jerked the door handles ineffectually and pounded on the windows. Nothing gave way. She was just about to take off her shoe and try what the heel could do against the glass when the door handle shook and began to open. She retreated to the other side of the chaise and watched the door fixedly. It opened.

"My dear," said Eliot, "allow me to hand you down."

Twenty-eight

A QUARTER OF AN HOUR LATER, A LARGE GROUP OF people once again stood about in the small parlor of the inn. A baize curtain had been hung over the west window, which had been pushed completely out of its frame, and the bright fire was welcome as the now chilly night air made its way around this obstacle. Lord Farnsworth was gone, having departed hastily for London some ten minutes previous, but Anne Rundgate and the captain remained, sitting side by side on the sofa, and the earl and Marina had joined them. Clarissa sat beside Lord Redmon, who was stretched out on the opposite settee, his arm now tightly bandaged. Laura was again in the armchair in the corner. Mr. Allenby was not in sight.

Two latecomers stood in the center of the room. Eliot Crenshaw was splendid in his modish riding dress, but it was his unusual companion who was the center of attention now, as he related his story. Mr. Levy, the moneylender, was telling the group how he had come to find out Jack Allenby's plot and to rescue

Laura from him. Dressed in a black coat and panta-loons, with his dark face and aquiline nose highlighted by the radiance from an oil lamp, Mr. Levy held his audience spellbound.

"It was through my friend Rothschild that I was able to act," he was saying. "Without the help of his organization, I could not have accomplished all I did."

"Rothschild," repeated the earl meditatively, "that's the fellow who made all the war loans, ain't it? They say he had carrier pigeons at Waterloo."

Mr. Levy bowed his head. "He did indeed. He has one of the most efficient information services in England. He saved the Exchange in '15, and he has now helped me punish a scoundrel. Mr. John Allenby will not run a gaming house in London again."

"Saved the Change," murmured the earl, "Splendid. Rothschild, Rothschild, must remember the name."

"The Baron Nathan de Rothschild," put in Mr. Levy with something very like pride.

The earl looked up. "Ah, baron?"

Levy nodded. "An Austrian title."

"Oh well." The earl shrugged. "Still it's better than nothing."

"He does not use it."

The other man gaped. "Not use it! Why, the man…"

Laura could not keep still any longer. "But why?" she cried. "Why did you help me in this way? I don't understand."

Marina took the earl's hand gently and patted it; he subsided.

Mr. Levy turned to Laura and bowed slightly. "It must indeed seem strange to you, madame, and my explanation may appear even more illogical. I helped you because of my sister."

Laura looked at him. "Your sister?"

"Yes. My sister, Adrienne Levy, took her own life four years ago after having lost her fortune at the gaming tables. She didn't come to me; I had lectured her about gambling more than once. She was alone and afraid, and no one aided her, least of all the scoundrels who had taken her money, men like Allenby." Mr. Levy gazed at the floor for a moment. There was a sympathetic silence in the room. He cleared his throat. "It was when you came out of the parlor to speak to your sister," he continued. "Up to that time I had thought only of negotiating the loan, but when I got a glimpse of Adrienne's portrait…"

"The dark woman above the fireplace!" exclaimed Laura.

He nodded. "Yes. That was Adrienne in happier days. I saw her, and then my eyes fell to the two of you." He looked from Laura to Clarissa. "The resemblance is of the slightest, nonexistent save in my mind, I suppose, but I was suddenly struck. And I made up my mind to help you then and there. After that it was a simple matter to set men to find out why you needed money."

Laura looked at him wonderingly. "You sent the notes, paid the debts?"

Mr. Levy bowed his head once again. "And when I found what had been done to you, I went further." His dark eyes burned for a moment. "The Allenbys shan't lure any more young men or women into losing more than they can pay, you may be sure of that. I now hold the mortgage on the house and certain other bills. I should imagine that he, at least, will soon find this country too hot for him."

"Where is he?" asked Laura, looking around.

"Safely locked away for now, though I fear we cannot hold him."

Something like regret passed across Laura's face. Eliot watched her narrowly. She wished Jack Allenby no harm now that she was free of him. But then she thought of the others he might pull into his everlasting games, and her expression hardened. It was no doubt best that Mr. Levy carry through his plan. She looked up to find both Mr. Levy and Eliot considering her. She stood and held out a hand. "I do not know how to thank you, Mr. Levy. You have saved me in truth. I shall always be grateful."

The moneylender took her hand and bowed over it. "A pleasure, I assure you, madame. And more; it allowed me to feel that I have somewhat atoned for my sister's death."

Laura smiled uncertainly.

"And now I will take my leave," continued Mr. Levy. "I wish to reach London before morning, so I had best be on my way." He bid the group good-bye, and all returned his farewell cordially as he went out.

"Whew!" exclaimed Clarissa when he was gone. "What do you think of that? If I hadn't heard him tell it, I should never have believed the story."

"Strange indeed," said Eliot, speaking for the first time since they had entered the parlor. "When he came to the house to fetch me, I could scarcely credit it myself."

"He came for you?" asked Clarissa, rendering her sister eternally grateful.

"Yes. As soon as his man reported that he had seen Allenby follow Laura out of town. Both Allenby and Levy had someone stationed to observe her movements."

Clarissa took a breath. "Amazing."

Eliot smiled. "Indeed. But now I think we should all follow our friend's example. It is growing late and has been a strenuous evening. We should return to town. Levy has taken Allenby, as we agreed, and I shall use his carriage. The rest of you have vehicles, it appears. The yard is certainly crowded with them."

"Yes," replied Clarissa rising, "we must get Geoffrey to a proper doctor as soon as may be."

Lord Redmon grinned. "You didn't think of that until the story was finished, I note. A man might have bled to death."

"I knew perfectly well that you were bandaged," retorted Clarissa.

"Yes, but would it have mattered? That's what worries me."

Clarissa put her hands on her hips. "You put little trust in me, *my lord*."

At this form of address, Lord Redmon subsided, his cheeks reddening.

"Exactly," put in Eliot. "We all have much to discuss. We had best get under way." The earl and Marina rose also, but there was a strangled sound from the sofa behind them.

Anne Rundgate had begun to cry. "What am I to

do?" she stammered between sobs. "My mother will never forgive me."

"Ah yes, Miss Rundgate," said Eliot blandly, his face showing no interest in the girl's tears. "I took the liberty of sending a note to your mother before I left London."

Anne jumped to her feet. "You told her! Oh no!" The captain stood to comfort her, for she seemed about to fall into hysterics.

Eliot's eyebrows went up. "I did. And before I could depart, she had sent my man back telling me not to be such a lackwit. Evidently she had been expecting for some weeks to receive Captain Wetmore's proposal for your hand."

Both Anne and the captain gaped at him.

"You have been indulging yourself shockingly, young woman," finished Eliot severely. "I suggest you go home to your mother immediately and ask her pardon."

Anne continued to stare, but the captain took her arm in a firm grip and started to lead her out of the room. "You may be sure we shall, sir," he said as they passed through the door.

The earl and Marina followed them as Clarissa helped Lord Redmon to his feet. "Well done," said the latter. "That girl has needed someone to speak to her sharply for years, I'd say."

"I think it was horrid," began Clarissa, but Lord Redmon guided her firmly toward the door. Eliot and Laura were left alone.

Laura gazed steadfastly at the floor. For some minutes her thoughts had been occupied with this scene. What would Eliot say to her? Was he very angry?

He came closer, still saying nothing. When the silence grew too long, she looked up and met his eyes. He was watching her steadily. "Laura," he said, his voice full of feeling, "will you forgive me?"

Her eyes widened. "I?" she stammered, "forgive *you*?"

"Yes. I have been an arrogant fool. If recent events had not been enough to show it to me, my talk with Levy during the drive today would have done so. You could not come to me, could you?"

"I… I…" Laura could not find the words.

Eliot nodded sadly. "I was harsh, unyielding. I did not listen. But you see, I had never before encountered a woman like you. I did not know how to go on, particularly when my own feelings became so strong."

"You are not fair to yourself. You have always been kind and just."

He groaned a little.

"The only thing I really minded…" Laura broke off, embarrassed.

"Yes?"

She looked down. She could not seem to say that the only thing she had minded was his mistress. "We never should have married," she replied miserably.

The lines beside his mouth deepened. "Is that how you truly feel now?"

Laura stared at the floor. "I have made a mull of everything. There will be a great scandal, and you will hate that so. It is all so awful; I can't bear it."

Eliot reached down and put one finger under her chin, raising her face to his. The movement caused her tears to spill over her cheeks. "I would not see you unhappy for the world," he told her. "Everything will be just as you wish. The marriage can be dissolved, if that is what you want."

Laura's tears fell faster. "I know that would be best," she gulped. "Your name would not be disgraced. I will do it, of course. I'm sorry."

"My *name* has nothing to do with the matter," he answered so harshly that Laura blinked. "Only *you*, your feelings, are important."

"I? But how can you care, after what I have done? I am not at all the sort of proper wife you wanted."

He laughed bitterly. "Not the sort I wanted? But my darling, I was the greatest fool in nature until I met you."

Laura stared at him, her tears abating. "Do you mean…"

"I love you, Laura. I never thought to hear myself saying those words, but they are true. I will do whatever you wish."

Laura blinked again, hardly able to believe what she heard. "But I have been in love with you almost from the beginning," she said.

There was a moment of stillness during which they stared at each other; then she was in his arms being passionately kissed. She returned his embrace wholeheartedly, and it was several minutes before they separated and laughed shakily. Keeping one arm around her, he led her to the sofa.

"What fools we have been," he said.

Laura nodded.

"Tell me now. What was the one thing you minded," he added.

She looked down again. "Well, Eliot, I did mind your mistress." She smiled slightly. "I shan't allow that sort of thing now, you know. How I should have liked to slap her!"

Eliot frowned. "My mistress? But dear heart…"

"Yes. I did not realize I could dislike anyone as I do Vera Allenby."

"But my darling Laura, Vera and I have not had any connection since you and I were snowbound."

"But she… Lady Quale said…"

Eliot's smile died. "Ah. I didn't count on the gossips. Nevertheless it is true that I severed all connection with Vera when we married. Could you think I would do anything less?"

"I should have known better, for you are first of all a man of honor, are you not, Eliot?"

He looked at her sharply, caught the laugh in her eyes, and smiled. "I am. Are you disappointed in that?"

"Not at all. Quite the contrary."

Their eyes held for a moment more; then she was in his arms again.

Don't miss this brand-new Regency romance from
beloved bestseller Jane Ashford

Once Again a Bride

Available now from Sourcebooks Casablanca

CHARLOTTE RUTHERFORD WYLDE CLOSED HER EYES
and enjoyed the sensation of the brush moving rhyth-
mically through her long hair. Lucy had been her maid
since she was eleven years old and was well aware that
her mistress's lacerated feelings needed soothing. The
whole household was aware, no doubt, but only Lucy
cared. The rest of the servants had a hundred subtle,
unprovable ways of intensifying the laceration. It had
become a kind of sport for them, Charlotte believed,
growing more daring as the months passed without
reprimand, denied with a practiced blankness that
made her doubly a fool.

Lucy stopped brushing and began to braid Charlotte's
hair for the night. Charlotte opened her eyes and faced
up to the dressing table mirror. Candlelight gleamed
on the creamy lace of her nightdress, just visible under
the heavy dressing gown that protected her from drafts.
Her bedchamber was cold despite the fire on this bitter
March night. Every room in this tall, narrow London
house was cold. Cold in so many different ways.

She ought to be changed utterly by these months,

Charlotte thought. But the mirror showed her hair of the same coppery gold, eyes the same hazel—though without any hint of the sparkle that had once been called alluring. Her familiar oval face, straight nose, and full lips had been judged pretty a scant year, and a lifetime, ago. She was perhaps too thin, now that each meal was an ordeal. There were dark smudges under her eyes, and they looked hopelessly back at her like those of a trapped animal. She remembered suddenly a squirrel she had found one long-ago winter—frozen during a terrible cold snap that had turned the countryside hard and bitter. It had lain on its side in the snow, its legs poised as if running from icy death.

"There you are, Miss Charlotte." Lucy put a comforting hand on her shoulder. When they were alone, she always used the old familiar form of address. It was a futile but comforting pretense. "Can I get you anything…?"

"No, thank you, Lucy." Charlotte tried to put a world of gratitude into her tone as she repeated, "Thank you."

"You should get into bed. I warmed the sheets."

"I will. In a moment. You go on to bed yourself."

"Are you sure I can't…?"

"I'm all right."

Neither of them believed it. Lucy pressed her lips together on some reply, then sketched a curtsy and turned to go. Slender, yet solid as a rock, her familiar figure was such a comfort that Charlotte almost called her back. But Lucy deserved her sleep. She shouldn't be deprived just because Charlotte expected none.

The door opened and closed. The candles guttered

and steadied. Charlotte sat on, rehearsing thoughts and plans she had already gone over a hundred times. There must be something she could do, some approach she could discover to make things—if not right, at least better. Not hopeless, not unendurable.

Her father—her dear, scattered, and now departed father—had done his best. She had to believe that. Tears came as she thought of him; when he died six months ago, he'd no longer remembered who she was. The brutal erosion of his mind, his most prized possession, had been complete.

It had happened so quickly. Yes, he'd always been distracted, so deep in his scholarly work that practicalities escaped him. But in his library, reading and writing, corresponding with other historians, he'd never lost or mistaken the smallest detail. Until two years ago, when the insidious slide began—unnoticed, dismissed, denied until undeniable. Then he had set all his fading faculties on getting her "safely" married. That one idea had obsessed and sustained him as all else slipped away. Perforce, he'd looked among his own few friends and acquaintances for a groom. Why, why had he chosen Henry Wylde?

In her grief and fear, Charlotte had put up no protest. She'd even been excited by the thought of moving from her isolated country home to the city, with all its diversions and amusements. And so, at age eighteen, she'd been married to a man almost thirty years older. Had she imagined it would be some sort of eccentric fairy tale? How silly and ignorant had she been? She couldn't remember now.

It wasn't all stupidity; unequal matches need not

be disastrous. She had observed a few older husbands who treated their young wives with every appearance of delight and appreciation. Not quite so much older, perhaps. But... from the day after the wedding, Henry had treated her like a troublesome pupil foisted upon his household for the express purpose of irritating him. He criticized everything she did. Just this morning, at breakfast, he had accused her of forgetting his precise instructions on how to brew his tea. She had *not* forgotten, not one single fussy step; she had carefully counted out the minutes in her head—easily done because Henry allowed no conversation at breakfast. He always brought a book. She was sure she had timed it exactly right, and still he railed at her for ten minutes, in front of the housemaid. She had ended up with the knot in her stomach and lump in her throat that were her constant companions now. The food lost all appeal.

If her husband did talk to her, it was most often about Tiberius or Hadrian or some other ancient. He spent his money—quite a lot of money, she suspected, and most of it hers—and all his affection on his collections. The lower floor of the house was like a museum, filled with cases of Roman coins and artifacts, shelves of books about Rome. For Henry, these things were important, and she, emphatically, was not.

After nearly a year of marriage, Charlotte still felt like a schoolgirl. It might have been different if there were a chance of children, but her husband seemed wholly uninterested in the process of getting them. And by this time, the thought of any physical contact with him repelled Charlotte so completely that she didn't know what she would do if he suddenly changed his mind.

She stared into the mirror, watching the golden candle flames dance, feeling the drafts caress the back of her neck, seeing her life stretch out for decades in this intolerable way. It had become quite clear that it would drive her mad. And so, she had made her plan. Henry avoided her during the day, and she could not speak to him at meals, with the prying eyes of servants all around them. After dinner, he went to his club and stayed until she had gone to bed. So she would not go to bed. She would stay up and confront him, no matter how late. She would insist on changes.

She had tried waiting warm under the bedclothes but had failed to stay awake for two nights. Last night, she'd fallen asleep in the armchair and missed her opportunity. Tonight, she would sit up straight on the dressing table stool with no possibility of slumber. She rose and set the door ajar, ignoring the increased draft this created. She could see the head of the stairs from here; he could not get by her. She would thrash it out tonight, no matter what insults he flung at her. The memory of that cold, dispassionate voice reciting her seemingly endless list of faults made her shiver, but she would not give up.

The candles fluttered and burned down faster. Charlotte waited, jerking upright whenever she started to nod off. Once, she nearly fell off the backless stool. But she endured, hour after hour, into the deeps of the night. She replaced the stubs of the candles. She added coals to the fire, piled on another heavy shawl against the chill. She rubbed her hands together to warm them, gritted her teeth, and held on until light showed in the crevices of the draperies and birds began to twitter outside. Another day had dawned, and Henry Wylde had not come home. Her husband had spent the night elsewhere.

Pulling her shawls closer, Charlotte contemplated this stupefying fact. The man she saw as made of ice had a secret life? He kept a mistress? He drank himself into insensibility and collapsed at his club? He haunted the gaming hells with feverish wagers? Impossible to picture any of these things. But she had never waited up so long before. She had no idea what he did with his nights.

Chilled to the bone, she rose, shut the bedroom door, and crawled into her cold bed. She needed to get warm; she needed to decide if she could use this new information to change the bitter circumstances of her life. Perhaps Henry was not completely without feelings, as she had thought. Her eyelids drooped. Perhaps there was hope.

❦

Lucy Bowman tested the temperature of a flatiron she'd set heating on the hearth. It hissed obligingly. Satisfied, she carried it to a small cloth-draped table in the corner of the kitchen and applied it to the frill of a cambric gown. She was good at fine ironing, and she liked being good at things. She also liked—these days—doing her work in the hours when most of the staff was elsewhere. This early, the cook and scullery maid had just begun to prepare breakfast. Barely out of bed, and sullen with it, they didn't speak. Not that there ever was much conversation in this house—and none of it the easy back-and-forth of the servants' hall in Hampshire.

The Rutherford manor had been a very heaven compared to this place. Everyone below stairs got along; they'd gone together to church fetes and dances and formed up a kind of family. For certain, the old housekeeper had been a second mother to her. When Lucy'd arrived, sent into service at twelve to save her parents a mouth to feed, Mrs. Beckham had welcomed her and looked after her. She'd been the first person ever to tell Lucy that she was smart and capable and had a chance to make something of herself. Thinking of her, and of that household, comforted and hurt at the same time.

Lucy eased the iron around an embroidered placket, enjoying the crisp scent of starched cloth rising in the steam. She'd made a place for herself in Hampshire, starting in the laundry and working her way up, learning all she could as fast as she could, with kindly training. She'd been so proud to be chosen as Miss Charlotte's lady's maid eight years ago. Mrs. Beckham had told her straight out, in front of the others, how well she'd done, called her an example for the younger staff. It had warmed her right down to her toes to see them smiling at her, glad for her advancement.

And now it was all gone. The house sold, the people she'd known retired or scattered to other positions, and none of them much for letters. Well, she wasn't either, as far as that went. But she couldn't even pretend she'd be back in that house, in the country, one day.

Not that she'd ever leave Miss Charlotte alone

in this terrible place. Lucy put her head down and maneuvered the iron around a double frill.

Mr. Hines tromped in, heavy-eyed and growling for tea. A head on him, no doubt, from swilling his way through another evening. Cook's husband, who called himself the butler, was really just a man of all work. Lucy had seen a proper butler, and that he was not. What he was was a raw-boned, tight-mouthed package of sheer meanness. Lucy stayed well out of his way. It was no wonder Cook was short-tempered, shackled to a bear like him. As for the young women on the staff who might have been her friends, both the scullery maid and the housemaid were slow-witted and spiritless. If you tried to talk to them—which she didn't, not anymore—they mostly stared like they didn't understand plain English. And if that wasn't enough, the valet Holcombe took every chance to put a sneaky hand where it didn't belong. Him, she outright despised. Every word he said to her was obviously supposed to mean something different. The ones she understood were disgusting. She'd spent some of her own wages on a bolt for her bedroom door because of him. Couldn't ask Miss Charlotte for the money because she didn't need another worry, did she?

The iron had cooled. She exchanged it for another that had been heating near the coals and deftly pressed the scalloped sleeve of a morning dress. The rising warmth on her face was welcome, though the kitchen was the most tolerable room in this cold house. She had to pile on blankets until she felt like a clothes press to sleep warm.

The scullery maid brushed past her on the way to

the pantry. "Mort o' trouble for a gown no one'll see," she said.

Lucy ignored her. Any remark the staff made to her was carping, about her work or her mistress, though they'd eased up on that when they saw they weren't going to cause any trouble. But they baited and humiliated Miss Charlotte something terrible. It still shocked Lucy after all this time. She couldn't quite give up expecting *him*—she refused to name the master of this house—to step in and stop them. But he was a pure devil; he seemed to enjoy it. Lucy liked to understand a problem and find a solution for it if she any way could, but there was nothing to be done about this pure disaster of a marriage.

Holcombe surged into the kitchen. He'd be after early morning tea for *him,* and nothing in the world more important, in his book. Lucy turned her back and concentrated on her ironing. "Have you seen Mr. Henry?" he asked. "Hines?"

"Why would I?" was the sullen reply from the man sitting at the kitchen table.

Holcombe stood frowning for a moment, then hurried out—without any tea. Which was strange, and interesting. Lucy eyed the others. They showed no signs of curiosity. As far as she'd been able to tell over the months, they didn't have any.

The scent of porridge wafted from the hearth, and Lucy's stomach growled. Mrs. Hines could make a decent porridge, at least. She wasn't good at much else. On the other hand, *he* ordered such bland dishes that it was hardly worth any bother.

Holcombe popped back in. "Hines, come with

me," he said. The cook's husband grumbled but pushed up from his chair and obeyed. This was one of the things that showed Hines wasn't a real butler. He snapped to when the valet spoke in that particular tone and did as he was told. The two men left the kitchen, and they didn't come back.

Something was up, Lucy thought. *He* next to worshipped his routines, threw a fit if any little detail was altered. Despite months of grinding frustration, she felt a shred of hope. Any difference had to be for the better, didn't it? She took her finished ironing and headed upstairs to see what she could see before waking her mistress.

A classic Regency romance from Jane Ashford, soon
to be released by Sourcebooks Casablanca

The Three Graces

Available October 2013

THE THREE MISSES HARTINGTON SAT BEFORE THE
schoolroom fire, sewing sheets. Though their
surroundings were decidedly shabby, the dull brown
carpet worn and the furniture discarded from more
elegant apartments and earlier times, they presented a
charming picture. Their close relationship was evident
in their appearance; all had hair of the shade commonly
called auburn, a deep russet red, and the pale clear
ivory skin that sometimes goes with such a color.
The eldest sister, who was but nineteen, had eyes of
celestial blue, while those of the two younger girls,
aged eighteen and seventeen, were dazzling green.
An observer would have been hard put to pick the
prettiest of them. All were slender, with neat ankles,
elegant wrists, and an air of unconscious distinction
that did much to outweigh their dowdy gowns and
unfashionable braids. He might perhaps venture that
Miss Hartington's nose was a trifle straighter than her
sisters' and her mouth a more perfect bow. But the
second girl's eyebrows formed a finer arch, and the
youngest one's expression held the greater promise of

liveliness. Altogether, there was little to choose among this delightful trio.

Silence had reigned for some time in the room as they plied their needles with varying degrees of diligence. Having lived together for all of their lives and served during that short period as each other's only companions and confidantes, they knew one another's moods too well to chatter. The afternoon was passing; soon it would be teatime, and the girls would put up their sewing and join their aunt in the drawing room.

A sound at the door across the room attracted their attention. It was followed by the entrance of first a very large yellow tomcat, then a smaller gray tabby, and finally three kittens of varying hues, bounding forward awkwardly and falling over one another in their eagerness to keep up with their elders. Miss Hartington smiled. "Hannibal's family has found us already," she said, "I told you it would not be long."

The youngest girl wrinkled her nose. "I cannot understand his behavior in the least. They are not even his kittens."

Her middle sister smiled. "But he has adopted them, you see, so they are all the more precious to him."

"I don't see why you say that," sniffed the other. "Our aunt adopted us, but we are certainly not dear to her."

"Euphie!" Miss Hartington looked shocked. "Mind your tongue. How can you say such a thing?"

"Well, it is true. If she cared a button for us, she would let us go about more and visit and… and do all the things other young girls are allowed to do. Indeed, she would bring you out this season, Aggie, as she should have done last year."

"Hush," replied her sister repressively. "Aunt has done everything for us, and you must not speak so of her. If she had not given us a home when Father died, we should be in desperate straits, and you know it."

The youngest girl sighed, shaking her head. "Yes, I know it. Not but what Father showed a decided lack of sympathy, too. Only think of our ridiculous names. He can't have considered what it would be like to go through life being called Euphrosyne."

Miss Hartington frowned at her, but the third sister laughed. "It was not he, Euphie. It was our mother. Aunt Elvira has told me that she was inspired by a passage the vicar read aloud to her just before Aggie was born. From Homer. How did it go? Something about the three Graces." She concentrated a moment, then quoted in Greek, translating for the others: "Most beauteous goddesses and to mortals most kind."

Euphrosyne Hartington wrinkled her nose once more. "Well, I never knew her, since she died when I was born, but though I do not wish to be disrespectful, I think she showed a shocking lack of sensibility. It is very well for you two to tease me. Your names are not nearly so queer."

Her middle sister smiled again. "I suppose you would prefer Thalia? I must say it seems just as burdensome to me."

Miss Hartington rallied at this. "Well, neither of you was persecuted by Johnny Dudley as I was. He could never pronounce 'Aglaia' properly, and he used to dance around me singing 'Uglea, Uglea,' until I thought I should scream. He thought it excessively witty."

Exasperated, Euphrosyne jumped up and faced her sisters. "How can you sit there calmly chattering about nothing?" she exclaimed. "What are we to do?"

Thalia only looked amused, but Miss Hartington said, "Do about what, Euphie? Please try to control yourself; you mustn't fly into a pelter every second minute, you know."

Euphrosyne put her hands on her hips. "Someone must," she retorted. "I am tired of hearing about propriety and what I must do and must not. Sitting meekly in our rooms sewing will do us no good at all. We must make a plan, Aggie. We must *do* something!"

Thalia smiled at her ironically. "What do you suggest?"

"Oh, if I only knew what to suggest," Euphie cried. "You are the scholar. Surely you can tell how we are to escape this dreadful situation."

Aglaia looked bewildered. "What situation? I declare, Euphie, you get no conduct as you grow older. What are you talking about?"

"Can you ask? We are trapped in this house. We never go out; we meet no young people, only Aunt's crusty old friends and the cats!" She directed a venomous look at Hannibal where he reclined luxuriously in the window seat. Ignoring her, he yawned hugely and began to lick one of the kittens. "What is to become of us? How are we ever to marry, for example?"

Thalia laughed. "Take care that Aunt Elvira does not hear you, Euphie. She would give you a thundering scold for presuming to think of marriage."

Euphrosyne whirled to face her. "Oh, sometimes I think I hate Aunt Elvira." This drew a shocked gasp from her eldest sister, and she hastened to add, "I do not, of course. She has been wonderfully kind to us. But I get so angry. She never cared to marry. I understand that. But she cannot expect that we will feel as she did at every point in life. It is selfish of her to keep us hemmed up here."

Thalia sputtered, "Never cared to marry? You are a master of understatement, Euphie."

But Miss Hartington looked disapproving. "You are exaggerating all out of reason. And you should not encourage her, Thalia. We often go out; we are certainly not prisoners in my aunt's house. And she does what she believes is best for us and gives us all we ask. Did she not engage special teachers for you, Euphie, when you wished to continue your music beyond what Miss Lewes could teach? And did she not allow Thalia to study Greek and Latin and anything else she wished, again with special, and very expensive, teachers?

Euphrosyne pushed out a rebellious lip, but before she could speak again they were all frozen by a bloodcurdling shriek coming from the direction of the drawing room. Thalia stood, and Euphrosyne started toward the door. There was a patter of footsteps in the hall outside; then the door was thrown open by an hysterical maid. "Oh, miss, miss," she gasped, "it's your aunt!"

As one, the sisters hurried down the stairs to the drawing room. In the doorway they paused, for there was clearly something very wrong. They could see the top of their aunt's head, as usual, above her tall chair before the fireplace, but most unusually, they did not see any other creature.

"Where are the cats?" asked Euphie, voicing their puzzlement. They had never seen their aunt's drawing room without at least five, and more commonly ten or twelve, cats. And now there were none at all.

Aggie hurried around the chair, stopped, and put a hand to her mouth. At this moment, the maid caught up with them, and seeing Miss Hartington's expression, she screeched again. "That's just how I found her, miss, when I come in to ask about the tea. Gave me the nastiest turn of my life, it did. She's gone, ain't she?"

Aggie, rather pale, nodded. "I think she is. But you had best send for the doctor."

Aglaia's sisters had joined her by this time, and the three girls looked down wide-eyed at the spare figure in the armchair. Elvira Hartington was, or had been, a harsh-featured woman, with deep lines beside her mouth and a hawk nose. In death, her face had not relaxed, but held its customary expression of doubting disapproval. Her hand was clutched to her chest, and her pale gray eyes stared sightlessly at her nieces.

Aggie shuddered and turned away. "Poor Aunt Elvira," she murmured.

Thalia took the old woman's wrist. "Cold," she said. "She is indeed dead, and has been for some time, I think."

Aggie shuddered again, but Euphie merely stared at the corpse curiously. "She does not look peaceful," said the youngest girl. "I thought dead people were supposed to be peaceful. Aunt looks just as she did before giving me a scold."

"Euphie, please!" said Miss Hartington.

The other looked abashed. "I didn't mean anything. I wonder what happened? She seemed fine this morning. Remember, she was going to write a letter to the *Times* about Wellington?"

"We are at least spared that," murmured Thalia.

"I don't know," replied Aggie. "She seems to have been taken suddenly. The doctor will tell us."

"Well, I am only sorry for St. Peter," added Euphie, looking sidelong at her middle sister. "She will probably tell him he is not at all what she expected and is used to."

Thalia choked back a laugh and turned away as the maid came hurrying back into the room. "Dr. Perkins will be here directly," she said. "Should I send for anyone else, Miss Hartington?" She spoke to Aggie with a new respect, as her new mistress.

Aggie put a hand to her forehead. "No, I don't think quite yet... Oh, you might send word to Miss Hitchins. She will want to know immediately."

"Yes, miss." And the girl was gone again.

The next few hours passed in a kind of muddle. The realities of death soon depressed even Euphie's spirits, and by the time the doctor had come and gone and all the details were settled, the three sisters were weary and silent. They went up to bed much subdued, for all of them had been attached to their aunt, whatever they might sometimes say.

The next morning, two early visitors arrived almost together—Miss Hitchins and their aunt's solicitor.

The former, a forbidding woman of fifty-odd, had been Elvira Hartington's closest friend for many years, ever since they had met at a meeting of the Feline Protectionist Society and discovered like feelings on this important subject. Miss Hitchins often gave her friend's nieces the impression that she disapproved of them, though she remained unfailingly polite, and they greeted her with some nervousness on this solemn occasion. She pressed each of their hands in turn. "So sudden," she murmured. "Poor dear Elvira. None can count himself secure in this world."

Miss Hitchins looked even more somber than usual this morning. She habitually wore black, but today, she had added a black bonnet and veil to her customary dark gown. All of the girls were relieved when the solicitor, Mr. Gaines, came in behind her.

But even the usually jovial Gaines seemed oppressed today. "Tch, tch," he said as he returned the sisters' greeting. "This is an uncomfortable situation. More than uncomfortable. Outrageous, I call it. But she never would listen."

Euphie exchanged a puzzled glance with Thalia.

"Each of us must face death," replied Miss Hitchins reprovingly. "And we must all endeavor to do so with Christian resignation, as I am certain Elvira did."

"Oh, death," said Mr. Gaines, dismissing the question with an impatient wave of his hand. "I daresay, I was speaking of the will, you know."

Miss Hitchins's eyes sharpened. "The will?"

The solicitor scanned four pairs of unblinking eyes. "None of you knows? No, of course you don't. She left that to me. Just like her, too. I've been urging her for years to change the blasted thing, and she always said she meant to. But she didn't. And so, here we are, aren't we? Outrageous."

"I don't understand, Mr. Gaines," said Aggie. "Is there some problem with my aunt's will?"

"There is, and there isn't. And I shan't say another word until the reading this afternoon. If you'll excuse me, I'll go to the library now. I want to go over Miss Hartington's papers as soon as may be."

"Of course. I'll…"

"That's all right. I know my way." Mr. Gaines started out of the drawing room, but in the doorway he paused. "You'll want to come for the reading, Miss Hitchins," he added gruffly. Then he was gone.

Miss Hitchins looked highly gratified.

"Whatever can be wrong with Mr. Gaines?" wondered Euphie. "He is not at all like himself. I have never seen him so abrupt."

Aggie shook her head. Thalia stared at the doorway where he had gone out, a worried frown on her face.

"Oh, I daresay he ate something that disagreed with him at breakfast," said Miss Hitchins brightly. "Men are sensitive to such things, I believe. Women are really much the stronger sex, in spite of what they say."

Euphie made a slight choking sound, and Aggie said quickly, "Would you care for a cup of tea, Miss Hitchins?"

The older woman straightened and indicated that tea would be welcome. Euphie made a face at Thalia, who shook her head slightly, though she too smiled.

The following half hour was very uncomfortable, and the girls were painfully wondering if Miss

Hitchins meant to stay to luncheon when she got up at last and took her leave. "I shall return in the afternoon," she told them, "as Mr. Gaines has asked me to. I shouldn't have dreamed of doing so otherwise, of course." She pressed each girl's hand once again. "If there is anything I can do, you need only call on me," she finished, and the maid showed her out.

"Whew!" said Euphie when she was gone. "I thought she was settled for the day. What a dreary woman!" The girl fell back on the sofa dramatically.

"Euphie!" Miss Hartington glared at her.

"Well, it is the truth, and I do not see why I should not tell the truth, even if it is impolite."

Her sister opened her mouth to reply, then shut it again. The question seemed too large to grapple with at this moment.

"I wonder what is wrong with the will?" said Thalia, who had been sitting in a corner, very quiet, for some time.

"What do you mean?" asked her younger sister.

"There is something wrong with it. Mr. Gaines said as much. But what?"

"He said, 'There is, and there isn't,'" responded Aggie.

Thalia nodded. "Yes, but that means there is. Why bring it up otherwise? Oh, I wish he had told us. I shall worry about it all day."

A classic Regency romance from Jane Ashford, soon
to be released by Sourcebooks Casablanca

The Marriage Wager

Available November 2013

COLIN WAREHAM, FIFTH BARON ST. MAWR, STOOD AT
the ship's rail watching the foam and heave of the
English Channel. Even though it was late June, the
day was damp and cool, with a sky of streaming black
clouds and a sharp wind from the north. Yet Wareham
made no effort to restrain the flapping of his long cloak
or to avoid the slap of spray as the ship beat through
the waves. He was bone-tired. He could no longer
remember, in fact, when he hadn't been tired.

"Nearly home, my lord," said his valet, Reddings,
who stood solicitously beside him. He pointed to the
smudge of gray at the horizon that was England.

"Home." Colin examined the word as if he couldn't
quite remember its meaning. For eight years, his
home had been a military encampment. In the duke
of Wellington's army, he had fought his way up the
Iberian Peninsula—Coruña, Talavera, Salamanca—he
had fought his way through France, and then done it
again after Napoleon escaped Saint Helena and rallied
the country behind him once more. He had lived with
blood and death and filth until all the joy had gone out

of him. And now he was going home, back to a family that lived for the amusements of fashionable London, to the responsibilities of an eldest son.

Reddings watched his master with surreptitious anxiety. The baron was a big man, broad-shouldered and rangy. But just now, he was thin from the privations of war and silent with its memories. Reddings didn't like the brooding quiet that had come to dominate St. Mawr, which the recent victory at Waterloo had done nothing to lift. He would even have preferred flares of temper, complaints, bitter railing against the fate that had decreed that his lordship's youth be spent at war. Most of all, he would have rejoiced to see some sign of the laughing, gallant young lad who had first taken him into his service.

That had been a day, Reddings thought, glad to retreat into memories of happier times. His lordship had returned from his last year at Eton six inches taller than when he left in the fall, with a wardrobe that had by no means kept up with his growth. The old baron, his father, had taken one look at Master Colin and let off one of his great barks of laughter, declaring that the boy must have a valet before he went up to Cambridge or the family reputation would fall into tatters along with his coat. Colin had grinned and replied that he would never live up to his father's sartorial splendor. They had a bond, those two, Reddings thought.

He'd been a footman, then, and had actually been on duty in the front hall of the house when this exchange took place in the study. He had heard it all, including the heart-stopping words that concluded the conversation. The old baron had said, "Fetch young

Sam Reddings. He follows my man about like a starving hound and is always full of questions. I daresay he'll make you a tolerable valet," And so Readings had been granted his dearest wish and never had a moment's regret, despite going off to war and all the rest of it. It was a terrible pity the old baron had died so soon after that day, he thought. He'd be the man to make a difference in his lordship now.

The ship's prow crashed into a mountainous gray wave, throwing cold spray in great gleaming arcs to either side. The wind sang in the rigging and cut through layers of clothing like the slash of a cavalry-man's saber. It had been a rough crossing. Most of the passengers were ill below, fervently wishing for an end to the journey or, if that were not possible, to their miserable lives.

The pitch and heave of the deck left Colin Wareham unscathed. What an adventure he had imag-ined war would be, he was thinking. What a young idiot he had been, dreaming of exotic places and wild escapades, fancying himself a hero. Colin's lip curled with contempt for his youthful self. That naïveté had been wrung out of him by years of hard campaigning. The realities of war made all his medals and commen-dations seem a dark joke. And what was left to him now? The numbing boredom of the London Season; hunting parties and the changeless tasks of a noble landholder; his widowed mother's nagging to marry and produce an heir; the tiresome attentions of insipid debutantes and their rapacious parents. In short, nothing but duty. Wareham's mouth tightened. He knew about duty, and he would do it.

The pale cliffs of Dover were definitely visible now as the ship beat against the wind to reach, shore. The mate was shouting orders, and the sailors were swarming over the ropes. A few hardy gulls added their plaintive cries to the uproar as the ship tacked toward the harbor entrance.

A movement on the opposite side of the deck caught Colin's eye. Two other passengers had left the refuge of their cabins and dared the elements to watch the landing. The first was most unusual—a giant of a man with swarthy skin, dark flashing eyes, and huge hands. Though he wore European dress, he was obviously from some eastern country, an Arab or a Turk, Colin thought, and wondered what he could be doing so far from home. He didn't look very happy with his first view of the English coastline.

The fellow moved, and Colin got a clear look at the woman who stood next to him. A gust of wind molded her clothing against her slender form and caught the hood of her gray cloak and threw it back, revealing hair of the very palest gold; even on this dim day, it glowed like burnished metal. She had a delicately etched profile like an antique cameo, a small straight nose, and high unyielding cheekbones, but Colin also noticed the promise of passion in her full lips and soft curve of jaw. She was exquisite—a woman like a blade of moonlight—tall and square-shouldered, perhaps five and twenty, her pale skin flushed from the bitter wind. His interest caught, Colin noticed that her gaze at the shore was steady and serious. She looked as if she were facing a potential enemy instead of a friendly harbor.

As he watched, she turned, letting her eyes run along

the coast to the south, her gaze glancing across his. Her expression was so full of longing and loss that he felt a spark of curiosity. Who was she? What had taken her across the Channel, and what brought her back? She turned to speak to the dark giant—undoubtedly her servant, he thought—and he wondered if she had been in the East, a most unlikely destination for a lady. She smiled slightly, sadly, and he felt a sudden tug of attraction. For a moment, he was tempted to cross the deck and speak to her, taking advantage of the freedom among ship passengers to scrape an introduction. Surely that pensive face held fascinating secrets. He took one step before rationality intervened, reminding him that most of the truly tedious women he had known in his life had been quite pretty. It would be unbearable to discover that only silly chatter and wearisome affectation lay behind that beautiful facade.

❧

"There it is, Ferik," she said after a while. "Home." Her tone was quietly sarcastic.

The huge man viewed the buildings of Dover without enthusiasm. A gull floated by at the level of his head, and he looked at it as if measuring it for the roasting spit.

"When I left here seven years ago," said the woman, "I had a husband, a fortune, six servants, and trunks of fashionable gowns. I return with little but my wits."

"And me, mistress," answered the giant in a deep sonorous voice with a heavy accent to his English.

"And you," she replied warmly. "I still don't think you will like England, Ferik."

"It must be better than where I came from, mistress," was the reply.

Remembering the horrors she had rescued him from, Emma Tarrant had to agree.

"Except for maybe the rain," he added, a bit plaintively.

Emma laughed. "I warned you about that, and the cold, too."

"Yes, mistress," agreed her huge servitor, sounding aggrieved nonetheless.

Emma surveyed the shore, drinking in the peaked roofs of English houses, the greenery, the very English carriage and pair with a crest on the door, waiting for some passenger. Seven years, she thought, seven years she'd been gone, and it felt like a lifetime. Probably it was a mistake to come back. She only wanted to live among familiar surroundings again, to speak her own language, to feel other than an alien on foreign soil.

The sailors were throwing lines to be secured and readying the gangplank. Men bustled on the docks. "Come, Ferik," said Emma. "We'd best see to our boxes."

On the steep, ladderlike stair leading below deck, they had to squeeze past a tall gentleman and his valet who were coming up. Even their few pieces of worn, battered luggage jammed the opening, so that for a moment, Emma was caught and held against the ship's timbers on one side and the departing passenger on the other. Looking up to protest, she encountered eyes of a startling, unusual blue, almost violet, and undeniable magnetism. From a distance of less than five inches they examined her, seeming to look beneath the surface and search for something important. Emma couldn't look away. She felt a deep internal pulse answer that search, as if it was a quest she too had been pursuing for a long time. Her lips parted in surprise; her heartbeat accelerated.

Colin Wareham found himself seized by an over-whelming desire to kiss this stranger to whom he had never spoken a word. Her nearness roused him; the startled intelligence of her expression intrigued him. It would be so very easy to bend his head and take her lips for his own. The mere thought of their yielding softness made him rigid with longing.

Then the giant moved, backing out of the passage and hauling one of the offending pieces of luggage with him. The woman was freed. "Are you all right, mistress?" the huge servant asked when she did not move at once.

She started, and slipped quickly down the stair to the lower deck. "Yes," she said. "Thank you, Ferik."

"Beg pardon," murmured Reddings, and hurried up.

Colin hesitated, about to speak. One part of him declared that he would always regret it if he let this woman slip away, while another insisted that this was madness. Reddings leaned over the open hatch above him. "Can I help, my lord?" he asked. The outsized man started down the stair again, effectively filling the opening. It *was* madness, Colin concluded, and pushed past the giant into the open air.

About the Author

Bestselling author Jane Ashford discovered Georgette Heyer in junior high school and was captivated by the glittering world and witty language of Regency England. That delight led her to study English literature and travel widely in Britain and Europe. Her historical and contemporary romances have been published in Sweden, Italy, England, Denmark, France, Russia, Latvia, and Spain, as well as the United States. Jane has been nominated for a Career Achievement Award by *RT Book Reviews*. Born in Ohio, Jane currently lives in Boston.